'A grippingly atmospheric ya____ ____ ____ ____anger mounts,
the landscape, weather and people of the former Danish
colony are piercingly observed. Chilling.'
Sunday Times Crime Club

'While there are similarities to Stieg Larsson's
Millennium series, Nordbo's writing is far more poetic.
Though dazzled by the icecap's beauty, he's not
blinded to the darkness of man.'
SA Weekend

'This intricate crime novel mixes a grisly plot with
interesting insights into Greenland's history and culture.'
Canberra Weekly

'A very satisfying thriller. Packed to the brim
with grisly murders, corrupt officials, and sinister
secrets, all set against the bleak, yet oddly
beautiful, Greenlandic landscape.'
AU Review

'Offer[s] intriguing glimpses of Greenland, its relentless
summer light and oppressive winter darkness...Fans of
Nordic crime fiction have a new author to follow.'
Kirkus Reviews

'A complex atmospheric and menacing read...the story
is enmeshed in the culture and politics of Greenland.'
NB

MADS PEDER NORDBO is a Danish writer who lives in Greenland and works at the town hall in Nuuk. He holds degrees in literature, communications and philosophy from the University of Southern Denmark and the University of Stockholm. He is the author of seven novels and has been published in eighteen languages. *Cold Fear* is the second of his books to be translated into English.

CHARLOTTE BARSLUND is a Scandinavian translator. Recent novels translated include *The Girl Without Skin* by Mads Peder Nordbo, *Resin* by Ane Riel (shortlisted for the 2019 Petrona Award), and *Will and Testament* and *A House in Norway* by Vigdis Hjorth (longlisted for the 2019 International DUBLIN Literary Award). She has worked with writers such as Samuel Bjork, Jo Nesbo, Karin Fossum, Per Petterson, Thomas Enger, Jonas T. Bengtsson, Steffen Jacobsen, Carsten Jensen and Lene Kaaberbøl. She lives in the UK.

COLD FEAR

MADS PEDER NORDBO

Translated from the Danish by Charlotte Barslund

TEXT PUBLISHING MELBOURNE AUSTRALIA

textpublishing.com.au
textpublishing.co.uk

The Text Publishing Company
Swann House, 22 William Street, Melbourne Victoria 3000, Australia

The Text Publishing Company (UK) Ltd
130 Wood Street, London EC2V 6DL, United Kingdom

Originally published in Denmark under the title *Kold Angst* by Politikens Forlag, Copenhagen, 2018

First published in English by The Text Publishing Company, 2019

Cover design by Text
Cover image from iStock
Page design by Jessica Horrocks
Typeset by J&M Typesetting

Printed and bound in Australia by Griffin Press, part of Ovato, an accredited ISO/NZS 14001:2004 Environmental Management System printer

ISBN: 9781911231301 (paperback)
ISBN: 9781925774849 (ebook)

A catalogue record for this book is available from the National Library of Australia

COLD FEAR

THE
HUNTER

1

Tupaarnaq looked down the cliff to the outskirts of the town. Scattered clusters of red, green, blue and yellow wooden houses glowed orange in the afternoon sunshine. The sea between the small town of Tasiilaq and the mountains on the far side of the fjord was filled with floating growlers of glacier ice. Some had foundered on the shore; others moved slowly with the tide. Long tongues of snow had settled down the mountainsides, several reaching as far as the sea. Soon everything would be buried in white.

She sat there every day, close to a game track flattened over several decades by animals and hunters. From this spot she could see practically every single house in Tasiilaq, a place she hated more than anywhere else on earth. She could see where the cars went when they left the heliport and, through the telescopic sight on her rifle, she could watch the people going in and out of the houses.

Two Greenlandic men were standing not far away. A few minutes earlier they had left the track and deliberately walked around her. She saw one of them point at her while the other one nodded.

Both men had rifles slung over their shoulders but were otherwise empty-handed. No prey hung from their belts and their backpacks flapped limply. Even so, she knew that they weren't discussing an unsuccessful hunting trip. They were talking about her. No one liked a woman with a rifle. Especially not one who just sat by the game track, day in, day out.

Tupaarnaq was sure that most people in Tasiilaq knew who she was, but no one greeted her and no one spoke to her.

She closed her eyes and ran her hand across her naked scalp. The skin felt cold. Smooth. If she could feel the cold, she'd probably have been freezing by now—she'd been sitting still for a long time without moving, and the temperature had plummeted. It might already be below zero. She inhaled deep into her lungs. The air felt cleansing.

In Tasiilaq people turned a blind eye to everything, although everyone knew what was going on.

She tensed her muscles under her black clothes: first her arms, then her chest, stomach and legs. She clenched her jaw, gritting her teeth.

The wind blew icily across her scalp. She exhaled and opened her eyes. The two men were still there. 'What are you looking at?' she whispered to herself. Her breath condensed in the air in front of her lips as she reached for her rifle. The cold wood and steel felt smooth. Clean. She held the weapon in front of her and loaded a cartridge into the breech. Very calmly she positioned the butt up against her shoulder and aimed the rifle at the two men.

One of them quickly grabbed his own rifle, but he didn't have time to aim before she had fired hers. The men jumped as the echo from the gunshot rolled up the steep mountain behind them.

'What the hell do you think you're doing, you crazy bitch?' one of them shouted as he threw up his hands in exasperation. 'Go back to where you came from!'

She lowered the rifle. The other man was shouting something at her too, but she wasn't listening. Her gaze rested on a crippled dwarf willow not far from them.

'Hey!'

She looked up and into the men's eyes as she started walking towards them. She had slung her rifle over her shoulder.

'We don't want you here,' one of them said. 'Piss off home.'

'I've never had a home,' she said.

'No, that's what happens when you kill your own family,' he went on. His voice was trembling now.

Tupaarnaq stopped about five metres away from them. The man who had spoken was still holding his rifle, his fingers tight around the stock.

'I only killed one of them,' Tupaarnaq said. The muscles quivered under her skin. 'And he wasn't a human being.'

The man raised his rifle, ready to fire. 'You fucking whore—'

'Stop,' the other man said, putting a hand on his friend's shoulder. 'You can't just shoot her.'

'Why not? No one gives a damn about that murderer,' the man behind the rifle sneered. He glared at her along the barrel, around the telescopic sight.

'She's not worth it,' the other man went on.

Tupaarnaq snorted and sized up the angry man. 'You're just as rotten as your brother.'

'He was your father,' the man said angrily.

'He was a pig,' Tupaarnaq said. 'I never had a father.'

The man let out a roar and aimed his rifle at a rock not far from Tupaarnaq. He emptied the magazine, the shots reverberating in the air. Tupaarnaq's ears were ringing. Small clouds of dust and powdered snow rose in the air where the projectiles landed.

She shook her head. 'You're just like your brother.'

The other man grabbed hold of the shooter's jacket, glaring at Tupaarnaq over his friend's shoulder. 'You shouldn't be here,' he said quietly. 'You make people feel unsafe and angry.'

'I'll go back to Nuuk when I'm done,' she said and resumed

walking towards them. She bent down and pulled a dead hare out of the low Arctic scrub. Blood stained its white winter fur. She held the hare up to her face and tilted her head, examining it. Then she shrugged, tossed the dead animal at the feet of the two men, stepped around them and made her way down towards the town.

She had been waiting for almost two months now. One day he would turn up, she was sure of it. One day he would come walking up that track, and she would stop him as she had stopped her father twelve years ago, when she had come home and found him sitting near the dead bodies of her mother and little sisters. His rifle in his hand. His screams as she had cut open his stomach and slashed his throat. Blood. Her father was dead and had rotted away long ago; now it was Abelsen's turn.

THE
EXPERIMENT

2

Darkness enveloped the figures of the five silent men sitting in the snow. The last reading they had carried out showed minus thirteen degrees Celsius, and the wind, which swept the top layers off the snow and whirled it around them, worsened the biting chill.

Tom looked down at his body. Snow had gathered in several places in the folds of his white cotton underwear. At the beginning his body heat had melted the snow, but now the skin under the thin cotton was so cold that the snow stayed put. The fabric felt stiff, frozen to his skin. He looked at the others—his three friends from the base and Sakkak, a young Greenlander from the nearby village of Moriusaq. They all wore only their army-issued undergarments, the thin white trousers and long-sleeved shirts covering their bodies down to the blue trainers on their feet. The snow had stuck to their eyebrows and crew cuts like beads of ice on fur. Their skin was pale, the blood having retreated from the outer blood vessels.

Sakkak was panting and shaking all over, his hands clenching and unclenching every second. Pumping.

They had decided to include Sakkak halfway through the trial as a control element, and today was his first day outside with them.

They needed to have someone present whose body reacted normally.

Tom closed his eyes. He could feel his heartbeat and the blood flowing under his skin. His heart was beating slowly. Idly. His pulse was low. His body still hurt, but not as much as during the early weeks of the experiment.

He felt like he was dying. His brain instinctively fought the cold. Every time they went to sit outside in the snow, he felt his body go through the stages that would prevent it from dying. His muscles would start to shiver. His pulse rose. His lungs demanded more oxygen. His skin grew pale.

Until the men achieved full control of the blood circulation in their cooled-down bodies, the Inuit was their insurance against death. When Sakkak started shaking severely and his fingers and earlobes turned blue, their limit had been reached and it was time to go inside. None of the others had mentioned that they were freezing yet, but the critical point must be close for all of them.

A hard gust of wind came down between the barracks, shaking them in their foundations. Tom turned his gaze towards the sky. It was dense with cloud, grey and black, with no light to be seen anywhere. There was only the prickling snow. He touched his fingertips. They felt alien, as if he wasn't touching his own body. He reached a hand backwards and knocked on the external wall of the wooden building. His joints tightened as he moved.

They were called in one by one. Sakkak. Briggs. Bradley. Reese. Then Tom. They weren't allowed to wait inside the building—the monitoring equipment had to be attached to them the moment they went from the cold into the warmth.

Tom inhaled deep into his lungs as he stepped inside. The heat felt intense and his skin started to tingle and sting immediately.

The others were sitting on a long bench, their bodies covered with small rubber patches, through which thin electrodes were connected to a series of measuring devices set up behind them.

Tom exhaled heavily as he pulled off his top and long johns, leaving only his boxer shorts. He found a space next to the young Inuit and felt the small rubber patches being pressed onto his skin.

Sakkak looked at Tom. 'Are you Danish?'

'No, but I speak Danish.'

'The others don't speak Danish,' Sakkak went on. 'Or Greenlandic.'

'They're from the base,' Tom said. 'They're American like me.'

'I'm Sakkak,' the young Inuit introduced himself with a smile. 'My Danish isn't that good either.' He rubbed his thighs and cleared his throat. 'It is your first time as well?'

'No.' Tom inhaled heavily through his nose. 'We've been doing this for just under two months.'

'Wow,' Sakkak said, his eyes widening. 'That's a long time.' He continued to rub his thighs with the palms of his hands.

'We need to keep still while they carry out the readings.' Tom looked at Sakkak. 'My name is Tom.'

'I live with my girlfriend in Moriusaq,' Sakkak said.

Tom nodded. He already knew that.

'I'm a hunter.'

Tom looked at the body of the young Inuit. His skin was red and speckled with white dots. He was still shaking.

Sakkak gazed out the dark windows. 'My girlfriend's name is Najârak. She's twenty-two and we've been together for almost three years.' A tremor went through his body. He chuckled to himself. 'She's from Savissivik. We met in Moriusaq one year when my village was chosen as the summer meeting point for everyone from the other villages. I had just killed my first polar bear, and Najârak was butchering it. She was pretty hopeless at it and asked me for help, but I didn't know what to do either, so we both ended up covered in blood. We caught sight of one another and we started to laugh.' Sakkak looked back at Tom. 'She bore me a son this year. His name is Nukannguaq. I'm so happy that we have him.'

'That's great,' Tom said. 'I also have a son, but he's in Denmark with his mother. He's three years old.'

'Denmark?' Sakkak said. 'You need to go see him soon. A son needs his father to teach him, that much I know. No one cares for orphans…Nukannguaq has me.'

'We just need to finish all of this,' Tom said, nodding in the direction of the equipment and the scientists taking readings.

Sakkak smiled. Then he frowned. 'I don't understand why I get so cold when none of you lot do?'

'Sergeant Cave?'

Tom turned his head and looked over his shoulder.

'What's the Eskimo saying?' the voice behind them continued in English.

'He's just talking about his girlfriend and their son,' Tom replied.

'Make him shut up, will you?'

Tom looked back at Sakkak. 'We need to be quiet.' He nodded down at the rubber patches on his arm. 'It interferes with the readings.'

Sakkak studied his feet. 'Perhaps the pills are more effective on you white people.'

Tom closed his eyes and withdrew inside himself. His skin was still tingling. The blood was running freely again. They had sat outside for more than an hour this time and he hadn't felt cold at any point. His body had been stiff and it had ached when he stood up, but the sensation of being cold had been completely absent.

3

'How's the aggression?'

Tom looked at his colleague. 'I'm not sure, but I think it's changing.'

The three biochemists, Christine, Lee and Tom, were the only ones left in the room. Sakkak, Briggs, Bradley and Reese had gone once they had been disconnected from the monitors.

'Actually, there's a definite change,' Tom corrected himself. He checked his notes. 'In the last month there has been a marked change in my mood and social skills.'

'Negatively?'

'Yes, negatively.'

'Our data also shows increased activity in the amygdala,' Christine said. 'And yesterday's scans showed a clear deterioration in the pathway between the amygdala and the frontal lobes.'

'Which supports the theory that we're becoming increasingly aggressive?' Tom said.

'Absolutely,' Christine said. 'Such symptoms have also been observed in many people with convictions for violence. The diminished pathway between the amygdala and the frontal lobes and the sudden outbursts of rage, I mean.'

'Is it worse than expected?' Tom wanted to know.

Christine nodded. 'After only six weeks on the drug? Yes.'

'But at the same time, we've also concluded that your ability to tolerate very low temperatures has risen significantly,' Lee said. 'Our data is unequivocal as far as that's concerned, so we're on the right track. It became even more obvious once we doubled the dose.'

'Sadly that also increased the side effects,' Christine added.

'Yes,' Lee said. 'However, the positives outweigh the negatives, as far as I'm concerned.'

Tom shrugged. 'I find it hard to give an accurate assessment of the others, but it's clear that everyone keeps more and more to themselves, avoiding contact and conversation.'

'Including you?'

'Yes. I'm not feeling very motivated these days, and in the mornings I can lose my temper over nothing, but I'm still in control.'

'I would really like to double your dose again,' Lee said.

Tom looked at his notes. 'Okay.'

'It's too soon,' Christine objected. 'We need to see if the side effects stabilise first.'

Lee nodded. 'And what about Sakkak? Do we keep giving him the placebo or do we start giving him the real thing?'

'Placebo,' Christine interjected quickly. 'We're not having civilians taking those pills yet.'

Tom rubbed his forehead. 'We could also look at the formulation.'

'I don't think we should tinker with it at this stage,' Lee said. 'We'll increase the dose in two weeks and see what the readings tell us. Anything else would confuse the results.'

'I agree,' Christine said. 'We daren't do otherwise. If the deterioration between the amygdala and the frontal lobes continues, we could end up with blackouts and psychosis.' She caught Tom's eye. 'After all, you're taking the same dose.'

'I know.' Tom pressed both hands against the bridge of his nose, then rubbed his eyelids. 'But I think we should increase the dose now.'

4

Tom reached out his hand and moved his Spy right up close to one of Briggs's red Stratego pieces. He looked up for a reaction.

'Boom,' Briggs said.

Tom nodded contentedly. 'I thought so.'

Briggs pushed one of his pieces alongside the bomb.

'Three star?' Tom wanted to know.

'I'm not going to tell you that.'

'You can't blame a guy for trying,' Tom said and pushed a Miner in behind the four star he had sitting close to Briggs's bombs.

Briggs's legs twitched. 'I can't focus on this bloody game.'

'That's why we're playing it,' Tom said.

Briggs looked at the pieces as if they were poisonous snakes.

'Just make your move,' Tom said. 'You know I'm going to beat you—I always do.'

'Screw this game,' Briggs exploded. He kicked the table with his foot, upsetting a couple of pieces.

Tom looked up from the board. 'Easy now.'

'I can't do this any longer,' Briggs said. His breathing was agitated, his chest heaving and sinking under his grey sweatshirt. 'They're trying to break us.'

Tom got up and went over to the only window in the room. It was pitch black outside, although it was the middle of the afternoon. The snow reached all the way up to the bottom of the window. He pushed it up. It was minus fifteen degrees Celsius outside at least. The clean air enveloped him. He could feel it entering deep into his lungs, but he didn't feel cold, although he could see from his arms that his skin reacted the moment it came into contact with the frosty air. He stuffed both hands deep into the snow below the window and rested his chin on the wooden frame.

'What the hell are you doing?' Briggs said.

'I can't feel a thing,' Tom said. 'I'm not cold at all…Crazy, isn't it?'

'Who gives a toss about that if you fry your brain in the process?' Briggs said. 'Look at my God damn hands!'

Tom extracted himself from the snow and turned to Briggs, who was standing with both hands outstretched.

'I can't think straight when they shake like this,' Briggs said. 'And my head is completely messed up…I shouldn't have to be a part of this experiment, it's not right.'

Tom slowly slid his hands over his face. They felt wet, but not cold. 'Do you want me to get you a sedative?'

'What? A sedative…No. I've had enough of playing chemistry games. I want out. All out.'

'It's not that easy,' Tom said.

'I don't give a crap,' Briggs said. 'This stuff will mess us up for good…and for what? So that we can stomp around the Arctic without getting cold?' He threw up his hands. 'Nothing ever happens here. What the hell are we even doing up here in this shithole country?'

'It's not about Greenland,' Tom said. 'There's enormous potential in the ability to tolerate low temperatures. Neanderthals were more cold-resistant than we are, and if we can recreate that gene, then—'

'Neanderthals?' Briggs cut him off. 'Fucking hell, Tom. If it was that important surely they wouldn't have died out?'

'The climate changes all the time.'

'Yes, and it's getting warmer…Thanks a million for messing up my brain with this experiment, but at least I won't be freezing my balls off while the ice cap melts around us.'

'The climate will change again,' Tom said patiently. 'And it might do so abruptly. But that's irrelevant anyway, because this experiment is about the here and now. If we can use drugs to increase our resistance to very low temperatures, all of NATO's Arctic units will be stronger. It might even pave the way for new settlements so that people from overpopulated and drought-stricken regions around the equator can begin a new life in the colder, sparsely populated Arctic.'

'No one in their right mind would want to live here,' Briggs shouted, punching the wall behind the sofa so hard that the skin on his knuckles split. He stared at his hand. 'I don't know what's happening to me. I can't sleep. I flare up and I can't control my temper. It can't go on. I want out.'

'Do you also want out of Tupilak?'

'There's no way out of Tupilak,' Briggs said abruptly. 'Tupilak goes on, and the rest of you will have to handle the cold as best you can.'

Tom stared at his own hands. They were shaking. He closed his eyes. Rubbed them carefully. A sense of fatigue gnawed deep inside his body. 'We'll need to scale down your dose,' he said. 'Reduce you to half a dose for one week, then phase you out completely. It's the only safe way to do it.'

Briggs sat down on the sofa and buried his face in his hands. 'Can't you see what it's doing to us?'

'We knew that from the start.'

'Bullshit,' Briggs said. 'You and I can decide how many pills we take. It must be enough just to run the trial on Bradley and Reese.'

'No. That's above our pay grade and you know it.'

'Just as long as we don't end up in the loony bin,' Briggs said angrily.

'It's a question of adjustment,' Tom said. 'The rage will pass.'

Briggs shook his head. 'How are Annelise and Matthew?'

'What do you mean?'

'How are they doing in Denmark?'

'They're good,' Tom said. 'They live in a village in the country-side. It's called Tommerup.'

'Don't you miss them?'

'Yes.'

'Then quit this madness and join them before it's too late. You must be owed a lot of leave.'

Tom closed the window again. 'You said it yourself: there's no way out of Tupilak.'

Briggs looked down at a small white scar just above his left wrist.

'That was a long time ago,' Tom said with a smile.

'You always were a nut job,' Briggs said. 'Make it a deep cut, you said. That way we'll be blood brothers.' He looked up. 'That was another time you damn well nearly got us killed.'

Tom glanced at the scar on his own wrist. 'Listen...if anything happens to me, will you keep an eye on Matthew?'

'If anything happens?'

'If I disappear or die, I mean.'

'Don't. I can't stand kids.'

'I'm being serious!'

Briggs inhaled the air deep into his lungs before exhaling. 'There's no way I can look after a kid.'

'I'm not asking you to adopt him.' Tom grabbed his left wrist and rubbed the scar lightly with his thumb. 'I just want you to follow him...from a distance. And be there if he gets himself mixed up in something bad. If you ever have any kids, I'll do the same for them.'

'Okay,' Briggs said. 'I'll watch him. From a distance!'

'Is that a promise?'

'Yes, I just said so. But try not to die, will you? I'm crap with kids.' Briggs shook his head and got up again. 'I'm going to the gym to pump some iron. Wanna join me?'

'Not today.'

Tom walked Briggs to the door of his room, then went to the ensuite bathroom where he opened a small mirrored door in the cabinet above the sink. He took out a jar with no label, shook out two uneven pills and popped them into his mouth.

He stared at himself in the mirror. His face was narrow. Pale. His eyes stared back at him. One of them had two pupils. Matthew had inherited this pigmentation error; the black dot that made it look as if he had two pupils in the same eye. Tom closed his eyes and saw his little blond boy smile at him. On the day Annelise and Matthew had boarded the plane in Thule to travel to Denmark, the little boy had also smiled and waved. He was too young to understand how much time would pass before he saw his father again. But given how the experiment had been progressing, Tom couldn't keep them on the base. He simply didn't dare.

The pills kicked in. His muscles tensed. Tom let himself fall forwards onto the linoleum, starting his press-ups the moment he hit the floor; he carried on for longer than he could be bothered to count.

A knocking on the door to his quarters brought his attention back to the present. He got up from the floor and quickly rinsed his face.

The sweat trickled down him along with the water.

The knocking resumed.

'Hang on. I'm coming.'

He opened the door and saw one of the short Inuit women from the mess on the other side. His arms and chest were tightening and throbbing.

She smiled at him. 'Sergeant Cave. You have a phone call…from Denmark.'

TIME'S
SHADOWS

5

The body of Jørgen Emil Lyberth, former speaker of the Inatsisartut, was found in a flat in Nuuk on Wednesday afternoon. Nuuk Police have released very few details, but sources say that Lyberth suffered a violent death, during which he was nailed to the floor and gutted. Police say they have little evidence to go on, but are working on the theory that the murder was motivated by Lyberth's outspoken support for Greenland's independence from Denmark. The police are now looking for Kjeld Abelsen, a senior civil servant with the Greenlandic government, and a young woman from Tasiilaq who was recently released after serving a prison sentence in Denmark. Both are regarded as persons of interest, according to lead investiagtor Michael Ottesen.

Matthew pushed aside the article he had printed out from *Sermitsiaq*'s website almost two months ago. The paper was grubby and crinkled from having lain too long in his bag. His colleague, Leiff, had written the article shortly after Lyberth's mutilated body had been found in Tupaarnaq's flat in a run-down apartment block on the very edge of the headland. Matthew had kept a low profile following the murder, at least until Abelsen had been caught a few days later and Matthew had been forced to kill a police officer in self-defence.

The first time Matthew had met the young police officer, Ulrik had been a cheerful and ambitious man about to follow in the political footsteps of his foster father, Jørgen Emil Lyberth. That was before Ulrik's life violently imploded, when he learned that he was Abelsen's biological son, a result of rape, and that his sister, Tupaarnaq, who had recently been released from prison after serving twelve years for killing their biological family, was back in Greenland. While Tupaarnaq blamed their father and Abelsen for the death of their mother and two young sisters, Ulrik had blamed Tupaarnaq for everything. At the age of fifteen she had been found next to the gutted body of their father, covered in the blood of all the victims, and had subsequently been convicted of all four killings. When Ulrik had discovered that Abelsen was his biological father, he had tried to kill both Abelsen and Tupaarnaq, and Matthew had had no choice but to kill Ulrik. Ulrik and Tupaarnaq had grown up together in Tasiilaq, but the killing of their parents and two younger sisters, Tupaarnaq's many years in prison and Ulrik's bottomless hatred of his older sister had kept the two apart, until she turned up unexpectedly in Nuuk and found herself in the middle of another murder case.

The rising sun bathed most of Matthew's living room in a sharp golden light. The sofa was cluttered because he had upended his bag looking for a USB stick and the cushions were covered with detritus. Papers. Pictures. Everything. He rubbed his eyes with the palms of his hands. Everything was one big mess. His eyes itched in the dry Arctic air. The long nights without sleep didn't help either. Four months ago he had moved to Nuuk from Denmark to find peace and serenity, but when he'd met Tupaarnaq and the two of them had begun to investigate a cold case about revenge killings and the sexual assault of children, everything had spiralled out of control. Before he knew it, he had found himself on the first floor of Jakob's house, watching Ulrik plunge a knife into Tupaarnaq, while Abelsen sat tied to a chair in the living room below them.

In the days that followed, Matthew had mostly stayed with Tupaarnaq at the hospital, but as she regained consciousness he began to have flashbacks to the violent events in Jakob's house. Tupaarnaq bleeding from the side, where Ulrik had stabbed her. The feeling in his hands as he hurled Jakob's old harpoon at Ulrik's back. The sound of the curved blade of the ulo as it sliced into Ulrik's throat. Blood had spurted from the diagonal cut onto his chest. His body had slumped forwards and crashed onto the floor, with the harpoon still sticking out of his back.

The bile rose in Matthew's throat. He swallowed a few times, suppressing the nausea and saliva. He looked over towards the big living room windows and the balcony door. The autumn wind swept across Nuuk clear and clean. It was only a few degrees above zero; a couple of days earlier a violent storm, full of lashing icy rain, had squeezed the last signs of life out of the late summer. The mountains had wept as never before and the water cascading down them had created wild waterfalls everywhere.

Matthew found a cigarette and lit it. He studied his hands. The smoke felt good. He closed his eyes and took a deep drag, letting the cigarette dangle between his lips.

Questions had been asked after Ulrik's death, but the police and Ottesen in particularly had been good at shielding him. The post mortem concluded that it wasn't the harpoon to his back but the slashing of his throat that had caused Ulrik's death, and thus there would be no court case, no trial. Matthew had killed Ulrik in self-defence, only that wasn't how he remembered it. Ulrik had been straddling Tupaarnaq on the bed. She had been naked, and when Ulrik had stabbed her, Matthew had hurled the harpoon into his back so forcefully that it had come out the other side.

Matthew had covered Tupaarnaq's naked body and pressed his hand against her wound. The blood had run out between her tattooed leaves and his fingers and onto the mattress.

Then followed days at the hospital. Scattered interviews. Tupaarnaq regained consciousness and left Nuuk without even having been discharged from the hospital. She had held his hand and then she was gone. Ottesen had discovered that she had bought a one-way ticket to Tasiilaq, and that was all the information Matthew had. She didn't reply when he texted her; she didn't answer her phone. She hadn't been well enough to travel, but she was gone—and silent. He had tried writing all sorts of text messages in the hope that something would make her react, but nothing did.

Matthew let the cigarette butt fall into a cup on the coffee table, where it hissed briefly. He looked at the pictures on the sofa. Pictures of Tine. Tine's belly. The picture had been taken only a few weeks before the car crash in which both Tine and Emily, the baby in Tine's belly, had been killed. His fingers brushed the wedding ring in his jeans pocket. He still wasn't ready to put it away, unable to let go of the security the ring had represented. Sometimes he would put it in a drawer for a day or two, but it always left him feeling lonely and naked. Tine had been buried wearing her wedding ring. It had all happened so quickly. The accident. Death. Tine's eyes as she died. His fingers on the curve of her stomach. The life that disappeared before it was born.

Most of Matthew's photographs were dog-eared by now. Some of them were as old as he was. Those of his father were the oldest. They were from the Thule base, taken before Matthew and his mother had left; his father had never followed. Matthew turned over the postcard his father had sent from Nuuk in August 1990. *I'm not able to come to Denmark as soon as planned. Sorry, love you both.* Apart from the pictures from the Thule base, where his parents were mostly photographed together, the postcard was all he had left of his father. The last proof of life.

In the middle of the mess on the sofa was the black notebook where he had started to write down his thoughts. He wrote them down for Emily. He needed to tell her about life and the world, although she had never been, and never would be, a part of it.

The air tasted of smoke as he inhaled it. The sun sat high above the low buildings that reached down towards the Moravian Brethren cemetery. He opened the thread of unanswered text messages he had sent to Tupaarnaq and stared at them. Then he reached for his cigarettes, lit a fresh one and got to his feet. The dust danced in the air around him. The apartment stank.

'Let's get some fresh air in here,' he said to himself.

The balcony door opened easily and stayed open when he let go of it. There had been days when it was so windy that he could barely control it.

He took a deep breath, mixing the clean Arctic air with the smoke from his cigarette. Tupaarnaq was right. He really ought to quit. Except that right after the car crash it was all he had been able to do: light cigarettes and stare into space.

Thoughts were buzzing around his head. It was less than two months since the deaths of Lyberth and Ulrik, and now he had to write about three violent suicides that had occurred a few days earlier in Ittoqqortoormiit, on Greenland's east coast. Last night his editor had sent him some pictures and the initial witness statements. There was only one proper police officer in Ittoqqortoormiit. His two assistants were untrained and employed on a casual basis, and it was one of them who had supplied his editor with the information about the deaths. There was nothing legitimate about that arrangement, and Matthew had immediately passed the material on to Ottesen. Not because he wanted to grass on his editor's sources, but because they would run into problems if they used the material. There were several close-ups of the dead bodies. Two of the men had been shot in the chest and one through the mouth. The room in which they were lying looked like a trashed cannabis den, but was apparently the home of one of the young men. Ittoqqortoormiit was a small town in decline, although a dozen of its remaining four hundred inhabitants did their best to keep it alive. It was the smallest town in Greenland, close to becoming just a village. It was also Greenland's most remote town. Perhaps even the most remote town in the whole world, with eight hundred and fifty kilometres of mountains and ice separating it from its nearest neighbour, Tasiilaq.

There had been four people in the room, four young men from Ittoqqortoormiit, but only three of them had died. The fourth man had also shot himself, but he had survived. It was the picture of him that had caused Matthew to pass everything on to Ottesen. The picture was a close-up of his head. Half of the young man's face had been blown off. His lips hung limply and his cheek had burst open so that you could see the teeth on his jawbone. A few teeth were shattered, lying like white splinters across his gutted cheek. His face was smeared with blood, as was his throat. In the middle of it all, one eye stared at the photographer. Just the one. The other eye was covered in blood.

Matthew let the cigarette drop into a glass bowl full of water and other cigarette butts on the balcony and looked across to Mount Ukkusissat, which towered against the blue sky behind Nuuk's outer residential area, Qinngorput. Behind Mount Ukkusissat there was another ridge of mountain peaks, after which the ice cap began. If you stood at the top of Mount Ukkusissat and looked in the direction of Ittoqqortoormiit, one thousand five hundred kilometres of ice separated the two locations. There was nothing else in between. No life. Just a kilometre-thick carpet of ice larger than France.

The man who had shot himself in the face and survived was called Nukannguaq, and going on the notes Matthew had been sent, the men all appeared to have been high at the time. Nukannguaq even claimed that a demon had killed the others, then forced him to shoot himself. He had been found immediately after the shooting and flown to Reykjavik, where doctors had spent hours fighting to save his life and his face.

When Nukannguaq had been interviewed by Icelandic police officers, he told them that the men had found a bag of homemade pills that had made them go berserk. To begin with they had only taken two each, but the pills had made them feel so amazing that they had all swallowed some more. Perhaps another six or seven. The pills had made them high pretty much instantly, but afterwards they had all crashed. It was like hurtling into hell and being ripped apart by evil spirits. Everything dark and black inside them was torn to pieces, and they all started screaming and shouting. Nukannguaq didn't know what had happened. When he came around, he was sitting in a chair and the others were lying near him, soaked in blood. He hadn't realised that there had been any shooting. He thought the noises were coming from inside his own head. He had shot himself soon afterwards, when the demon had broken through the living room window. Death had seemed the only escape from the screams of the demon and the blood-soaked bodies.

However, according to Matthew's editor's source, there was absolutely no trace of pills in the house. Or demons. Only a lot of empty bottles and some cannabis, which added up to a bad trip that had driven three young Greenlanders to take their own lives. Sadly that was all too common.

Matthew picked up a ballpoint pen from the pile on the sofa and wrote *Suicide? Who shot whom? What pills?* on the back of the photos he had printed out of the dead bodies from Ittoqqortoormiit. Four young men shooting themselves pretty much at the same time, in the same room, with the same rifle, was brutal. Even by east Greenlandic standards.

Matthew looked at the photo of the living room and tried to imagine the stench of cannabis and gunpowder residue. The old tiled coffee table in the middle of the room was covered with empty beer bottles and two plates overflowing with what appeared to be the ash and butts of joints as well as cigarettes. Several bottles had been knocked over. One of them had been full and the yellow liquid had run across the green tiles and onto the stained carpet below. On the sofa behind the coffee table lay two young men whose names were listed as Salik and Miki. They had both been shot at close range. Salik just sat there, slumped, while the shot had pushed Miki off the sofa so that he was half-lying across Salik's thighs. Salik's sweatshirt and trackpants were soaked with their blood. His eyes were open and vacant. A third young man was lying on the floor. Konrad. He had fallen forwards and his face was pressed against the carpet. The back of his head had been blown off. Clumps of dried blood hung from his hair, along with pieces of pink brain.

6

It was just past two o'clock in the afternoon when Matthew sat down at the small table in Else's kitchen. Else was the mother of his half-sister. They lived in one of the low, rundown apartment blocks at the top of Radiofjeldet, not far from his own flat. He often thought about visiting them, but nothing had ever come of it because of the chaos of the past few months. Discovering that he had a sister after being an only child all his life had affected him more profoundly than he had expected.

Matthew forced a smile and turned his attention to the table. The envelope was a standard white one, with no sender. It was addressed to Matthew, but it had Else's address on it.

'Would you like some coffee?'

'No, thank you.' Matthew studied the handwriting on the envelope. Sweat spread on his forehead as he opened it.

'Is it a letter?' Else said.

He nodded and pulled out a note. 'I think it's from Tom,' he said in a hoarse voice and put the note on the table so that she could see it too.

I read your articles in Sermitsiaq. *Come to Ittoqqortoormiit. House number 87. I want to tell you about Tupilak.* That was all it said.

'So after twenty-four years he suddenly wants to tell me about some tupilak?' Matthew mumbled to himself. He felt a knot of unease in the pit of his stomach. He got up and left the kitchen, stepping outside into the fresh air. The sun was still shining, but it hung low now, turning everything orange. Matthew stared up at the sky. He had been missing his father for so long that his yearning had turned into a strange emotion, which more than anything resembled the kind of residual hatred you feel for people even though you've forgotten why you hated them in the first place.

'Are you okay?' Else asked Matthew when he returned to the kitchen a few minutes later.

Matthew nodded and rubbed his eyelids.

'Do you think your father lives there now?' she went on. 'In Ittoqqortoormiit?'

'I've no idea,' Matthew said, sitting down again on the chair by the small kitchen table. 'But it's his handwriting. I have a postcard from 1990 that he sent to my mother and me, and it's the same style. I've stared at that postcard thousands of times so there's no doubt in my mind. My father wrote this note.'

'I recognise his handwriting too,' Else said. 'And hiding in a place like that would be just like him. He was always on the run somehow or other, so the more remote the better.'

Matthew looked at the photograph of his half-sister on the fridge behind Else. 'How does Arnaq feel about Tom?'

'We never really talked about him, but once she got used to the idea that she had a brother, she started asking lots of questions. In fact, I think she would like to see her father now. Only so much time has passed. After all, Arnaq was only two years old when he disappeared.'

Matthew looked down at the note. 'Is Arnaq around?'

'No, three friends from her school in Denmark have come to visit, and the four of them have gone camping in Færingehavn.'

He looked up. 'They're spending the night there?'

'Yes, I think they'll have a great time. Her friends have never been to Greenland before so it's a new experience for them, and it's not as if anyone lives there.'

Matthew nodded. 'How long are they away for?'

'At least until after the weekend,' Else said with a smile. 'They packed tents, plenty of warm clothing and good sleeping bags, and if they change their minds they can always sleep in one of the abandoned houses.'

'Definitely…As long as they stay away from the old quay.'

'Is that where you found the dead girl last summer?'

'Yes, but the point I was making is that the quay is completely unsafe.'

'She had been dead a long time, hadn't she?'

'Yes, since 1973, so there's nothing to worry about.'

Else smiled and took a sip of her coffee. 'Oh, I'm not worried or I wouldn't have said that they could go camping there. Besides, my friend Lars, who took them there in his boat and will be bringing them back, has promised to stop by every day to check that they're okay.'

'Just as well…There's no mobile phone coverage down there.'

'No, I know. There never has been.' She tilted her head slightly. 'Lars teaches at the local sixth-form college so he knows just how people the same age as Arnaq think and act.'

'Is she enjoying sixth form?'

'Yes, I think so. She certainly seems to and there are lots of new things to do.'

'And now on top of everything our father has turned up.'

Else nodded and her gaze grew distant.

'I'll talk to Arnaq about it when she comes back,' Matthew said. 'Thank you.'

Matthew looked at the brief message again. He frowned. 'It's twenty-four years since I last heard from him.'

'He's good at disappearing,' Else said. She picked at the handle of her cup. 'Do you remember me telling you about a man Tom was scared of?'

Matthew looked at her. 'Not really. The last few months have been a bit of a blur.'

'He was around back when Tom disappeared,' she went on.

'Ah…A fellow soldier, was he?'

'Yes, and Tom was scared of him, this stranger.'

'Could that be why he left Nuuk?'

'I don't know. He simply disappeared from one day to the next and I never heard from him again. But, yes, Tom was so scared of this stranger that he refused to leave the house, and then one day he was just gone.'

'Do you know his name? The stranger?'

'I found him,' Else said with a distant expression in her eyes. 'The first time Tom spotted him, the man was heading into a government building. Tom went white as a sheet and insisted that we go home immediately. He called the man Briggs. Tom went straight to the bathroom when we got home and stayed there for hours.'

'But you just said you found him? The man? Briggs?'

'I was frightened of what might have happened to Tom when he disappeared, so I went to that government building and asked for Briggs. He was there all right, but he said that he had no idea who Tom was. Only I didn't believe him. One of my cousins worked in the same building and she told me that as far as she was aware, Briggs was a former US officer from the Thule base and was now head of HR for the Greenlandic government. She also said that he spoke only a few words of Danish when he first arrived, but that he had picked it up really quickly.'

'But you never found out why my father was scared of him?'

'No…And I guess after several months I stopped believing that

Tom would come back. There was no record of him anywhere, so there was nothing the police could do. I don't think they could be bothered, either.'

'Do you think that Briggs guy is still there?'

'I've no idea.' Else looked towards the window at the end of the narrow kitchen. The view was entirely of the next dilapidated apartment block.

Matthew picked up the envelope and looked at Else. 'Do you have a picture of Tom and Arnaq together?'

Else squeezed her eyes shut and nodded slowly. 'Tom didn't like pictures, but I think I have one or two. They're from my niece's confirmation.' She pushed her chair backwards and stood up. 'You stay here—I'll go check.'

7

A cold fog had settled across Nuuk when Matthew left Else's flat. The chilly, dissolving droplets in the air pricked his skin, and the scent of the icy Arctic sea mixed with the moisture between the tired, grey apartment blocks on Radiofjeldet.

He turned into Lyngby-Tårbæksvej and took the long wooden steps down across the rocks between Kiassaateqarfik and the blue community hall at the corner of the TelePost building.

His mobile buzzed in his pocket. It was his editor wanting an update on the article on the Ittoqqortoormiit suicides from three days ago. *It's on its way*, he quickly replied. Then he texted Tupaarnaq. *I've heard from my father*, he wrote. *My sister is in Færingehavn with some friends. They've gone camping there for the weekend.*

He automatically found his cigarettes and lit one while he continued towards the grey wooden building.

His mobile buzzed in his hand. The Tupaarnaq thread lit up on his screen. *Your father? I'm on my way.*

He stared at the small white text box. She was coming to Nuuk? Was that what she meant? A flush of heat surged in his chest. Everyone began to move in slow motion. The smoke filled his lungs. He exhaled and watched as the smoke mingled with the cold fog. A half-full yellow Nuup Busii bus passed him at a leisurely pace. Cars. Faces. He placed the cigarette between his lips and narrowed his eyes as he replied to her: *Good. Text me when you'll be landing in Nuuk and I'll pick you up.* He stared at the screen for a few minutes, then threw away the cigarette and slipped his mobile back in his pocket. He knew there wouldn't be any more from her for some time.

He had folded Tom's letter and stuffed it into his back pocket along with two photographs that Else had found for him. Once he got home he would find out how to get to Ittoqqortoormiit. As far as he was aware, he would have to fly to Reykjavik and then backtrack to Ittoqqortoormiit by helicopter.

He entered the white building that housed the Greenlandic government's administrative offices and made a beeline for a narrow counter where a Greenlandic woman was staring at a screen.

She turned to him with a smile. Her skin and black hair shone in the bright beam of the lights above the reception. 'Hello?'

'Hello,' Matthew said. 'This might sound weird, but is there a man working here called Briggs?'

The woman nodded. 'Yes, do you have an appointment?'

Matthew shook his head. 'No, it's a private matter. Family business.'

'Ah,' she said, looking back at the screen and typing quickly. 'It says he's around, so why don't you just go in.'

'Okay…Thank you.' Matthew looked around the reception area. Several doors and corridors led further into the building.

The woman smiled again and pointed to a corridor on the far side of the lobby. 'It's the fourth office on your right.'

Matthew nodded and headed for the corridor she had pointed to. It was narrow and had the feel of an old wooden barracks. Just like the other doors in the corridor, the fourth door on the right was open. As he passed, he could see into each office, where one or more people were working at low desks.

On the fourth door there was a sign with only one name: Robert Briggs.

Matthew's heart started pounding and he took a few deep breaths while he gently caressed the ring in his jeans pocket. Then he stepped into the doorway.

In the middle of the room was a man who looked about fifty years old. He seemed tall, although he was sitting down.

Matthew cleared his throat.

The man looked up. 'Are you looking for someone?'

'Yes,' Matthew said. 'I think I'm looking for you. Are you Briggs?'

'Yes. How can I help you? Have you been fired?'

'No...No, I'm a reporter from *Sermitsiaq*.' Matthew took a step into the room. 'But I'm here on a private matter. My name is Matthew Cave.'

'Cave?'

'Yes. I think you served with my father...At the Thule base.'

Briggs straightened up in his office chair and looked at Matthew for a few seconds. 'It's true that I served at the Thule base, but that was a long time ago now.'

'I think my father was there twenty-four years ago,' Matthew said. 'His name is Tom.'

Briggs continued to look closely at Matthew. Then he shook his head slowly. 'I don't remember anyone called Tom from those days... unfortunately. He's your father, you say?'

'Yes, Tom Roger Cave,' Matthew said, rubbing his empty ring finger. 'I'm guessing you must be about the same age.'

'There was no one called Cave when I was there,' Briggs said. He pressed his lips together and shrugged.

'He lived at the base until 1990,' Matthew went on. 'I lived there myself with my mother when I was a boy.'

'I'm sorry,' Briggs said. 'I don't remember him.'

'Okay.' Matthew looked at his feet. He felt as if the floor was dragging him down, as if he had suddenly turned to lead. 'I knew it was a long shot.'

'So you haven't heard from your father since 1990?'

Matthew looked up again. 'No…Not a word. My mother and I travelled to Denmark just before I turned four and he was meant to follow on, but he never did.'

'I'm sorry to hear that,' Briggs said. 'If there have been no signs of life from him for twenty-four years, he could be dead.'

'He lived here in Nuuk for a while. After 1990.'

'But you just said—'

'I only found out two months ago,' Matthew interrupted him.

'So you think he's still alive?' Briggs said, making a whistling sound out of the corner of his mouth.

'Yes.' Matthew frowned and looked quizzically at Briggs. 'He lived here in Nuuk with a woman throughout the 1990s…They had a child, so I have a half-sister, as it turns out, but I still have no idea where my father might be.'

Briggs raked his hand through his short, blond hair and drummed his fingers on the table.

'I've been told that he fled when you came to Nuuk,' Matthew went on. 'My sister was two years old at the time, and she never heard from him again either.'

'I can't help you, Matthew. Unfortunately.'

'Okay,' Matthew said, looking down glumly once more. 'I'm sorry for wasting your time.'

'That's quite all right,' Briggs said with a smile. He hesitated, then looked gravely at Matthew. 'What made you turn up here, today of all days?'

'I've had a letter from my father, and then…Well, I ended up here because my half-sister's mother mentioned you.'

Briggs moved right to the edge of his seat and looked at Matthew with an expression that was simultaneously surprised and insistent.

'You've heard from him?'

'Yes, but not until today…And there's no sender on the letter. I just recognised his handwriting.'

'Did you bring the letter?'

Matthew shook his head.

Briggs kept trying to make eye contact with Matthew. 'What did his letter say?'

'Not a lot…Just that he wanted to tell me about some tupilak.'

'A tupilak?' Briggs frowned, closed his eyes for a moment and exhaled heavily through his nose. Then he looked up again. 'Is that all you've heard from him for twenty-four years?'

'Yes.' Matthew was starting to sweat. He slipped his fingers into his back pocket and pulled out the two photographs of Tom and Arnaq. 'That's my father and my sister.'

Briggs reached out and took the pictures. He looked at them and his upper body slumped a little. 'Okay,' he then said, and got up. He was just under a head taller than Matthew and looked like a man who spent a lot of time working out. He stepped around Matthew and closed the door to the corridor. 'In my world, Tom died in 1990.' He shook his head. 'But you're his son, I can tell from your eye, and there's no doubt that it's him in these pictures.'

'What are you talking about?' Matthew exclaimed. 'Now you suddenly know him?'

Briggs heaved a sigh. 'Why don't you take a seat?'

'Did you know my father or didn't you?'

Briggs nodded wearily and pointed to the chair. 'Sit down.'

Matthew sat down on the chair opposite the desk.

'I didn't know that Tom also had a daughter,' Briggs went on. 'But I remember very clearly the day he died…or rather, the day I thought he died.'

'I don't understand?' Matthew said. 'Why would he be dead? When?'

'March 1990.'

'But why would you think he had died then?'

Briggs slumped even more in his chair. 'I knew him quite well, your father. Before things went wrong. He could be a bit crazy, but he was otherwise an okay guy. We grew up together in Portland, Oregon.' He stuck out his left arm and pushed up his sleeve. 'I got this scar when Tom and I decided to become blood brothers. Make it a deep cut, he said. Crazy bastard. It cost me four stitches and a thrashing at home for trying to kill myself.'

'So now you suddenly grew up together?'

'There's nothing suddenly about it,' Briggs said. 'I just had to process some information. But, yes, we lived two streets away from each other and we stayed friends all the way to college, then we went our separate ways for a few years. When Tom told me one day that he was going to join the Marines, I thought why not. I hadn't made a lot of myself back then, while Tom had spent four years studying biochemistry at the University of Oregon.' He drummed his fingers on the table. 'I can tell you a lot about Tom, but I'm guessing it ought to be out of the office, don't you think?'

'Yes.' Matthew cleared his throat and exhaled hard between his lips. 'But why do you think he's dead?'

Briggs looked up. 'I saw his coffin…I saw all three coffins when they were flown home to the US.'

Matthew looked out of the window. Across the road to the rusty brown TelePost building. 'There were other fatalities?'

'Put your mobile on my desk so that I can see the screen,' Briggs said. 'It's nothing personal, but you said you're a reporter, and this is purely private, okay?'

'Okay.' Matthew took out his mobile and placed it on the desk between them. Screen facing upwards.

A moment of silence followed.

'We were taking part in an experiment,' Briggs then said. 'A medical experiment. We were testing a new drug. There was me, Tom and three others. The aim of the drug was to increase our ability to withstand very low temperatures. It worked, and your father was pretty excited about it all. He would sit there, week in week out, in minus ten to minus twelve degrees Celsius, practically naked. It was crazy. And as the experiment progressed, we could feel the cold less and less.' He paused. 'Except other things happened…Things we couldn't control.'

'You're saying the others froze to death?'

'No, they didn't. The ultimate aim was to program the human body not to die of hypothermia. No, it was our minds that couldn't handle it. We lost our self-control.' He took a deep breath. Ran his hand through his short hair. 'I quit, but the others carried on. It was insane. And I told Tom, but he refused to stop. He was obsessed with the progress we were making.'

'And then something went wrong?'

'Yes…' Briggs hesitated. 'The side effects were severe, and the scientists kept forcing us to increase our doses.'

Outside the windows a big yellow truck drove past, its bed laden with newly hewn blocks of granite the size of a man.

'Two of the others, Bradley and Reese, were found dead in Tom's quarters,' Briggs said. 'Shot through the head with Tom's pistol. And Tom had shot himself.'

Matthew could feel the blood throb in his temples. 'But he went on to live in Nuuk?'

'What I was told back then,' Briggs said, 'was that your father killed two of my friends before turning his gun on himself.'

'Did you see them? Their bodies?'

'I saw the coffins being sent home and there was a ceremony at the base. At the time no one…no one at all could understand why Tom would do a thing like that, but the whole incident was suppressed and put down to a case of deep depression. It's dark twenty-four seven up there in the winter.'

'And then my father turned up here in Nuuk.'

'I haven't seen him since shortly before the murders.' Briggs looked at Matthew across the computer screen. 'If you hear anything else from him, I would like to know.'

Matthew pressed his eyes shut and tried to process the news. 'If my father had been a killer, I would have heard about it.'

'There's a lot about Thule that people don't know,' Briggs said. 'Matthew, if the two of us happen to meet again and there are others present, then I'll deny everything I've just told you. This was a one off, a personal favour. I owe it to your father, despite what happened. After all, I remember you when you were a little boy. At the base. I also remember your mother.'

Briggs pushed his chair back and got up.

'So what do I do now?' Matthew wondered out loud.

'Nothing,' was all Briggs said. 'Or do what your father couldn't do—leave this place.'

'No,' Matthew said, and hesitated for a moment. 'Why did you lie about not knowing my father? Why didn't you just tell me the truth from the start?'

'Fair point...But let me remind you that Tom is a killer. I'm sorry, but there's no easy way to say it. It's not a story I'm desperate to share with anyone else, especially not his son, but now you know and...' He heaved another sigh. 'Matthew, your father's a murderer. Whichever way we look it...I'm so very sorry. He was my friend once. If it's really true that he isn't dead and he turns up again, then contact me immediately, okay? This isn't something you should tackle on your own.'

8

The red Dash-8 roared across the low buildings that sat on the mountain plateau between the Nuuk neighbourhoods of Nuussuaq and Qinngorput. Matthew watched the aircraft as its wheels bumped down on the short landing strip and it braked with a sound as if the plane's propellers had suddenly feathered.

The sky was a clear and frosty blue. Behind the fjord, which reached around the headland that carried Nuuk on its back, he could see the ridge and sharp peak of Mount Sermitsiaq.

He dropped his cigarette into a metal bucket and entered the small arrivals hall in Nuuk Airport. The doors were battered and the tiles on the floor well worn. He positioned himself near a table by a kiosk and looked across to the aircraft, which had moved away from the runway and was now slowly taxiing to its disembarkation point.

Another Dash-8 was parked there, as was a Bell Huey helicopter. Otherwise there were no other aircraft about.

The pilot turned off the engines and the noise of the propellers faded away. The door at the front of the red steel body opened and the passengers began to disembark. The last person to leave was Tupaarnaq.

Matthew placed his hand on his chest and breathed deeply and slowly a couple of times. It was more than a month since he had last seen her, but she looked exactly like the first time they had met. The same shaved head, dressed entirely in black. Her expression was as grim as always. He was convinced that she loathed flying simply because it forced her into close proximity with other human beings in a confined space.

She disappeared out of Matthew's field of vision, only to reappear in front of him. Her black combat trousers hugged her legs tightly and ended in a pair of scuffed army boots. She wore a dark hoodie and had a black coat draped over one arm.

'You still smell of smoke,' she said, giving him a quick hug.

'Yes…I'm…Hi.'

'That's why you're so skinny and pale…Hi. I thought you decided to quit smoking?'

'Well, I…' Matthew hesitated. 'You disappeared.'

She nodded. 'I went hunting.'

'For all that time?'

She shrugged. 'There was nothing to shoot.'

Matthew looked towards the door to the luggage hall.

'Did you bring a suitcase?'

'No. Just my rifle.' She turned and went to the counter where oversize luggage was checked in and collected.

His eyes followed her back. She had rarely left his thoughts. Her many tattoos, the leaves covering every inch of her body except her head, hands and feet. The leaves weren't delicate or pretty, but rather lush and concealing. There was no other design except in the soft crooks of her elbows where a sharp set of teeth grew from the darkness of the foliage. Bared teeth the size of fingers. A frozen glimpse of snarling skulls. He had seen her arms and shoulders many times, her whole body only twice. The first time when she was taking a shower—she had spotted him and stormed out in anger. The second time was when Ulrik had tried to kill her. The expression in the insane police officer's eyes that day had burned itself deep into Matthew's memories. Ulrik hadn't cared that Tupaarnaq was his sister; in his madness all he could see was the woman who had destroyed his family, although the truth was that their own father had killed their mother and two younger sisters. The only person Tupaarnaq had killed was their father, but his murder had been so brutal that she had ended up being blamed for all four deaths.

'There was no need for you to come out here,' Tupaarnaq said, turning to Matthew again. She carried her rifle in a long bag, which she swung over her shoulder.

'I borrowed Malik's car,' Matthew said, shaking his head to rid himself of the intrusive thoughts. 'I thought it would be a good idea.'

She nodded. 'Why has your sister gone to Færingehavn?'

'She decided to go camping for the weekend with some friends from her old school in Denmark.'

'Good…Let's go see them and you can tell me all about your father on the way.'

'Now? Someone visits them every day, a guy called Lars, so Else tells me.'

'Yes, yes, I'm sure they're fine, but I'd like to have a look for myself, okay?'

'Sure…We've got a boat at work now, which we can use, so we don't have to steal boats anymore.'

'Cool, what kind is it?'

'I've no idea.'

She shook her head. 'It doesn't matter as long as it's seaworthy.'

'It's a great boat, but…'

Tupaarnaq pushed open the door and left the airport building. 'But what?'

'Paneeraq is throwing a kaffemik party for Jakob today. It's his eighty-third birthday.'

'So you want to go there first?'

'Yes, I was hoping to.' Matthew looked down. He wanted to stare at her all the time, but he also knew that it quickly got too much for both of them. 'Malik will be there too,' he added. 'So I can return the car to him at the same time.'

'Fine. I'm coming with you.'

'The others keep asking about you, but I didn't know what to say.'

'No.'

Matthew looked at her across the roof of the car. 'Are you really okay about going to Jakob's old house again?'

She threw the case with her rifle onto the back seat. 'How do you feel about it?'

'I've been there a few times since they moved back a month ago. But I haven't been upstairs.'

'It's just a place like any other,' she said.

'I guess so.' Matthew looked back at the airport as Tupaarnaq got into the car and slammed the door shut. Jakob's house was where Ulrik had tried to rape and murder Tupaarnaq. Abelsen had taken over Jakob's old house as everyone had believed that Jakob and his stepdaughter, Paneeraq, had died back in 1973. Years later they had returned to Nuuk. No one had any idea of Jakob's true identity until the old man had revealed himself to Matthew. He had fled Nuuk in the winter of 1973 in order to protect Paneeraq, who had been eleven years old at the time, along with Lisbeth, the woman he loved. He was a police officer; Lisbeth was a murderer. Paneeraq and Jakob hadn't emerged from their hiding place until Lisbeth had died of old age.

9

Matthew sat down at a dining table laden with many different types of cakes. He was very close to the window, squashed against a dark red velvet curtain with broad lilac stripes.

Paneeraq had pulled Tupaarnaq aside the moment they arrived. Matthew knew that Paneeraq and Jakob had been worried when Tupaarnaq had disappeared shortly after Ulrik's attempt to kill her. Matthew glanced cautiously up at the wall above the rosewood sideboard where the old wooden harpoon with which he had killed Ulrik had previously been displayed.

Ottesen took a seat next to Matthew. He ran a hand through his short, dark hair and grinned from ear to ear at the sight of the cakes. 'I think I'd better add thirty minutes to my run tonight.' His eyes lit up. 'How about you, Matt? Isn't it time you came running with me? The air will do you good.'

'I never go running,' Matthew said. 'I don't even own a pair of running shoes.'

'We have those and suitable clothing down at the police station,' Ottesen continued with a grin so broad it made the skin on his face even more lined. 'We're fit to fight, let me tell you.'

'I think I'd better stick to writing,' Matthew said. 'There's a lot going on right now.'

Jakob and two young police officers were sitting opposite them, while Malik was at the end of the table with a woman Matthew didn't know. Of everyone here he knew Malik the best; Malik was a photographer at *Sermitsiaq* and the two of them had quickly hit it off.

'Did you manage to finish your story?' Ottesen said.

'The one about the dead men from Ittoqqortoormiit?'

'Yes.'

'I've written about the survivor and his bizarre claims of a demon being outside the window and the pills…I've yet to make head or tail of the rest of it.'

'Less talking, more eating,' Jakob interrupted them. His blue eyes sparkled in his wrinkled face.

Matthew nodded and reached for a plate. 'There's no way we can ever eat all these cakes.'

'Exactly,' said the young officer who was sitting next to Jakob. 'That's the whole point.'

'What is?' Matthew looked at her. He recognised her; she had been on guard outside Block 17 two months ago, when they had found Lyberth murdered in Tupaarnaq's flat.

'Rakel is right,' said Paneeraq as she passed a jug of red cordial across the table. 'Not running out of cakes is the sign of a good kaffemik party. And pay no attention to Jakob, he always complains whenever there are more than three people in his house.'

'All right, all right,' Jakob said, looking at Ottesen. 'Any news about Kjeld Abelsen?'

Ottesen brushed a few crumbs off his trousers. 'No…He's still at large, I'm afraid.'

Rakel looked at Matthew, who quickly looked down at his plate.

'We've looked everywhere.' Ottesen picked at his upper lip. 'I wonder if he managed to leave Greenland after all.'

'What about the people who helped him escape?' Matthew wanted to know.

'We couldn't prove anything,' Rakel said.

'That man belongs in prison,' Jakob declared, reaching for a buttered roll.

'We'll get him eventually,' Ottesen said. 'He's bound to turn up some day.'

'He's a master of spin and opportunism,' Jakob said, munching his roll. 'The only way you'll get him is if he makes a mistake...'

'Everyone makes mistakes,' Rakel said, turning her plate.

Matthew looked down again, putting his cake fork down quietly. His temples had started to throb. 'Does anyone here know anything about two murders and a suicide at the Thule base in 1990?'

'Have you sniffed out another cold case?' Ottesen said.

'Possibly...I'm not sure. There were three soldiers, I believe. One of them is thought to have killed the other two before taking his own life.'

'Nineteen ninety,' Jakob said. 'At that time I was living in Qeqertarsuatsiaat, but someone came—'

Tupaarnaq placed her hand on Matthew's shoulder. 'So how about that boat?' she said.

'Ah, yes.'

'I've just been talking to Else in the kitchen and I've promised her that we'll sail to Færingehavn to check up on your sister and her friends.'

'Now?'

'Is that a problem?'

Matthew looked across to Jakob and Rakel. 'No, not at all. I just wanted to—'

'Come on, then.'

●

As he put on his jacket in the hall, Matthew watched Else and Tupaarnaq. Else had convinced Tupaarnaq to take some cake to Færingehavn and Paneeraq had immediately started filling Tupperware containers.

'Where are you off to, Matt?'

Matthew looked at Malik, who had appeared in the doorway to the living room. 'The marina behind the tunnel.'

'I'll give you a lift,' Malik said, patting his stomach. 'I'll die if I eat any more cake.'

'Thank you,' Matthew said with a grin.

Jakob grabbed Matthew by the elbow. 'When you come back, I need to talk to you about the time we lived in Qeqertarsuatsiaat… Only not today.' Jakob yawned. 'My old head has had enough already.'

'No wonder,' Matthew said, patting Jakob lightly on the shoulder. 'Happy birthday and many happy returns.'

Tupaarnaq handed Matthew a bag. 'Are you ready?'

Matthew nodded.

Next to him Malik let out a loud burp as he pulled on a boot. 'Oh, God, why are my feet so far away?'

'Let's just get out of here,' Tupaarnaq said. 'Having to be social gives me a rash…Especially in a room full of cops.'

10

Malik parked halfway down the potholed gravel road, just after the tunnel through the rock that separated the industrial estate and Nuussuaq marina. The tide was high, lifting up the pontoon bridge.

Matthew took the bag with the cakes and gave Tupaarnaq the key to the boat.

'Which one is it?'

'The third from the end,' he said. 'White and light brown.'

'Excellent.' Tupaarnaq swung her rifle bag over her shoulder. 'I was afraid it might be one of the slow ones.' She started walking towards the pontoon bridge. 'If we didn't already have a key, I would have taken a boat like that.'

'Just text me if you want picking up later,' Malik called out from the car. 'I'm only going to spend the rest of the day gaming, so it's no trouble.'

Matthew nodded and followed Tupaarnaq. She was boarding the boat via the steel pulpit at the prow.

'I've checked the battery,' she said as soon as Matthew was on board. 'How about fuel?'

'The deal is that you always return it with a full tank,' Matthew said. 'But we'd better check.'

'Do you know how to do that?'

He shook his head as he closed the door of the wheelhouse behind him. The wheelhouse seated six people. Two seats faced forwards, with two double seats behind them, a pair on each side.

'You really need to learn how to sail,' Tupaarnaq said. 'Turn on the ignition, would you?'

Matthew turned the key. The engine started immediately and Tupaarnaq let the lid to the battery compartment fall back into place.

'I met a man today,' Matthew said, making himself comfortable on the seat to the left. 'He said that my father died in 1990.'

'But your sister was born in 1998,' Tupaarnaq objected.

'Exactly. So now I'm thinking that my father might have killed two men at the Thule base, then hid out in Nuuk until he was discovered and had to go on the run a second time.'

Tupaarnaq turned her gaze towards Matthew. 'Well, that would explain why you never saw him again.'

'Yes.' Matthew looked away. 'Only I never imagined him being a killer.'

'Had you ever imagined yourself as a killer?'

The hairs stood up on Matthew's back. The saliva thickened in his mouth.

'I'm sorry,' she said quietly. 'But you see my point. How do you think I feel, having done twelve years in a crappy prison for killing a man who was far worse than Ulrik in every possible respect?'

The boat jolted as she pushed the throttle and they pulled away from the pontoon bridge.

'Can you load the rifle?' she said, nodding towards the bag by her rifle. 'There's a clip of cartridges in the small side pocket.'

'I didn't know you were allowed to keep your gun and your ammunition in the same place.'

'There are no rules up here.'

Matthew picked up the rifle and took out the magazine. Once

it was filled and back in place, he lifted the rifle and looked back towards the marina through the telescopic sight. Nuuk was disappearing slowly but steadily as the fjord widened and the mountains grew more desolate.

'We're not hunting seals today, are we?'

'You never know what you might meet.'

Matthew grimaced. He could still remember the taste of the raw seal liver she had forced him to eat when she had taken him hunting two months ago, the blood smeared across the bottom of the boat, the pink intestines spilling out of the steaming animal when she gutted its belly, the greasy skin that Tupaarnaq had peeled off the seal's body with her hands and a small ulo. He shook off his thoughts. 'Can't we shoot something other than seals?'

'Relax,' she said. 'I only shoot when I have to, and I don't intend to do so today unless we happen to come across the very animal I'm looking for.'

'And that is?'

'A pig.'

'A pig? You mean a man?'

'When we get a bit further south and are sheltered by the mountains,' Tupaarnaq said, 'then you can have a go at steering if you like.'

The waves bounced against the hull of the boat. Matthew could see that they were travelling at around thirty knots. 'I'd like to try. But I'll be slower than you.'

'You'll soon get the hang of it,' Tupaarnaq said. 'This boat is easy to drive. It's the rocks you need to watch out for.'

Matthew nodded and looked out at the mountains, which rose steeply and suddenly out of the sea as far as the eye could see. There were no towns or villages between Nuuk and Færingehavn. Only the endless range of bleak mountains and the icy sea below them. 'How do you know where the rocks are?'

'I can tell from the sea…from the colours and the waves.'

He studied the sea. They had reached a shaded area and the water looked pitch black to him.

'I'm messing with you,' she said. 'The small monitor over here tells me. It even shows up large shoals of fish, if that's what you're looking for.' She pulled the throttle back and the boat settled on the sea. The engine idled.

'What are you doing?' Matthew asked. 'Are you worried we might be getting close to some rocks?'

She pointed to one of the steep rock faces close to the surface of the water. Carefully she pushed the throttle again and let the boat cruise slowly towards the grey and brown mountain. Snow had started to collect in its cracks and on any ledges over a hundred metres above the sea. Within the next month the white carpet would reach all the way down to the water's edge.

Matthew peered into the deep below them.

'Go to the bow,' she said. 'And take your mobile if you want photos...I saw a whale.'

'A whale? This close to the mountains?'

'Yes, it surfaced just now. It'll be back. Just wait.' She let go of the throttle and looked at him. 'You can drop the anchor...But don't forget to check that the other end of the rope is attached first.'

Matthew smiled and shook his head.

The boat glided across the water. The whale came up twice to turn over at the surface. It was a humpback, with a black-and-white speckled tailfin.

'It's feeding,' Tupaarnaq said. 'I thought so.'

'This close to the shore?'

'There are often big shoals of small fish near the rocks and a young humpback whale like that one will swim anywhere.' She turned off the engine. 'Drop the anchor or we'll start to drift towards the rocks.'

Matthew let the anchor plop into the sea and watched as several metres of rope were sucked from the boat. 'Bloody hell, it's deep!'

'Yes, the mountains drop really steeply here.'

He zipped his jacket right up to his chin and cricked his neck a couple of times.

When the whale surfaced, they could hear it breathing in long, hoarse gasps. Water sprayed in misty clouds over its blowhole. It turned over, lazily slapping the surface of the water.

Tupaarnaq had joined Matthew at the bow and together they watched the enormous animal rolling around and diving right under the surface. She had brought her rifle.

'Is it dangerous?' Matthew asked.

'Not in the least.'

'What were you hunting in Tasiilaq?' Matthew said, glancing at the rifle.

There was silence for a moment. 'Men.'

'Men?'

She nodded absentmindedly. 'Abelsen.'

'Do you really think he would hide out over there?'

'I don't know, but I know that it wouldn't be the first time...And there are many men like him in that shithole.'

Matthew looked at her black clothes. The thin jacket and her combat trousers. 'How do you hunt a man?'

She shrugged. 'I just sit there and I wait. At a spot above the town where I can see almost everything.'

'What happens if he turns up?'

'Then he dies.' She raised the rifle and aimed it at the mountains.

'But if you shoot him, won't you go down for another twelve years...like you did with your father?'

'Just how stupid are you?' She turned her head and glared at Matthew. 'You've read my case file, haven't you? I only did twelve years because I was also convicted of killing my mother and sisters... If I kill Abelsen, I'll get five to eight years at most.'

'Setting aside the minor point that it would be your second murder conviction,' Matthew said. 'You have a law degree, so you do the maths…How about moving on and making a new life for yourself?'

'A new life?' she echoed scornfully. 'How? When you're raped as a child, you can never grow up. Your ability to grow up like other people has gone. Raped from you.' Her hands clenched the rifle; her knuckles glowed white. The whale had surfaced again and its hoarse breathing lingered in the air. 'When that pig plunges his dick into you, when you scream because it hurts, when you're beaten so that you'll keep your mouth shut, when he rapes you again while the blood is still running out of you…Then you lose the ability to have a life like other people. When you feel his disgusting body press you into the mattress. His sweat. The stench of his rotting teeth. The noises coming from that bastard's throat.'

Matthew sat down heavily on the moulded plastic seat behind them. 'I'm sorry…I didn't know.'

'Sorry is the most useless word ever invented.' Tupaarnaq pressed the stock of the rifle against her cheek. Her hands tightened around the grip. Her gaze was focused.

The whale wheezed and turned over heavily in the sea. Its body glistened like wet rubber as it exhaled in a long, rusty hiss that filled the air above it with moisture.

Tupaarnaq aimed her rifle at the mountain behind the whale and fired it three times.

Matthew jumped and pressed his eyes shut in response to the echo between the rocks.

'That's why the suicide rate up here is so high,' Tupaarnaq went on, firing again. 'Damaged young women and men. They take their own lives because they're incapable of growing up. Everything in their mind has been raped. Nothing can ever feel good…And a child who has been raped attracts new rapists…like vultures circling a dying animal.' She fired towards the mountains again before letting the rifle slip along her leg. 'Abelsen raped my mother and it's his fault that my father went berserk and killed my sisters…He has to die. Just like my father.'

11

It had started to snow as they sailed into the fjord that led to Færingehavn. Matthew had steered the boat along the coast, but Tupaarnaq had taken over so they wouldn't be too long in getting there.

Matthew had gone outside and was sitting at the stern, looking towards the shore. He had Tupaarnaq's rifle lying across his thighs; every now and then he would pick it up to study the shoreline through the telescopic sight.

They sailed past the long wooden quay with its row of large, dilapidated warehouses, some square, others curved. Two months ago, inside one of the arched metal buildings, they had found the remains of an eleven-year-old girl who had been starved and tortured to death in a converted shipping container over forty years earlier. Images of the terrified little girl in the container gnawed furiously at Matthew's thoughts.

'We can't dock here,' Tupaarnaq called from the wheelhouse as she turned the boat right and let it drift towards the grey building at the far end of the quay where they had dropped anchor the last time. 'Drop the anchor and untie the dinghy,' she added.

Matthew nodded and threw the anchor overboard. The sea wasn't nearly as deep here.

He undid the knots holding the rubber dinghy in place and pulled the rope. A thin layer of snow had already settled on the black bottom of the dinghy, but it fell out the moment he flipped it over.

'You are holding on to the rope, aren't you?'

'Yes, of course I am,' he said, handing her the rifle. 'Are you taking this?'

'What do you think?'

She grabbed the weapon and stepped around him and down into the black rubber dinghy.

'It's bloody freezing,' he said, looking ashore. The place hadn't changed since their last visit. The medium-sized wooden houses with broken windows and peeling paintwork all looked the same. Only the roofs seemed different now that they had been given a dusting of virgin snow, but under the snow was the same old rusty corrugated sheet metal or faded roofing felt. Although the houses were badly damaged from having been abandoned over thirty years earlier, the colours were still clear on the many red, green and grey wooden walls. Most of the buildings were one storey, but some had two. All were trashed and battered by an endless series of storms and Arctic winters.

'Are you coming?'

'Yes, sorry.' Matthew shook his head and grabbed the bag with the cakes that Else had given him.

'What did I tell you about that word?' Tupaarnaq took the oars and a few minutes later they were close enough that she and Matthew could jump ashore. They pulled the dinghy higher up than the last time, right up past the furthest building, which had light grey walls. Alongside it, out of the wind, were piles of dark, rusting oil barrels.

Matthew looked around. He could see thirty or so large buildings. Many seemed to be houses of some sort or another, though the ones that lay along the harbourfront were all warehouses.

'I wonder where they can be,' he said.

'They should have heard the boat,' Tupaarnaq said with a shrug.

'Let's take a look around. Perhaps they're down by that big grey house.'

Matthew looked up at the first row of houses and then across the open plain, which had a large, grey house at the end of it.

Tupaarnaq swung her rifle over her shoulder.

The grass on the plain was brown and withered, and the cold wind was bringing with it snow that had started to settle in the many hollows. Matthew remembered from his last visit the importance of stepping on the mounds, as there were often puddles of water in the dark, muddy holes and cracks between them.

Above them the sky was gathering in heavy grey clouds and the snow began to fall faster.

They walked the last stretch to the grey house along a wooden walkway. This house was just as damaged as the others, but its corrugated sheet-metal roof was still intact. It was stained and rusty, but it had no holes. The house consisted of a wide main building and two short wings; a damaged door hung diagonally at the front of the left wing. Every window was smashed, either by the weather or by people.

'Hello?' a voice called out from the house.

Matthew and Tupaarnaq both stopped and looked towards the house. The owner of the voice was a slim young man who had called out to them from the first floor.

'Someone's coming,' he called out over his shoulder. 'They have a gun.'

Three other people quickly appeared in the wide window.

Matthew waved to them and saw his sister wave back.

'They seem fine to me,' Tupaarnaq said.

The young people disappeared from the window and came running down the walkway towards Matthew and Tupaarnaq soon afterwards.

'What's up?' Arnaq said. 'Did my mum send you out here?'

Matthew nodded and handed her the bag. 'Sort of...We bring cake. Leftovers from Jakob's kaffemik party.'

'Thanks,' Arnaq said. 'But we're fine and we don't need any more babysitters...Lars is plenty.' She turned and introduced her friends. 'Meet Lasse, Alma and Andreas.'

'Hi,' Matthew said, looking at the three young people. It was Lasse who had called out from the window; he was the tallest of them and had blond, shoulder-length hair. Andreas was shorter with reddish hair, while Alma was blonde like Lasse, but with the addition of freckles.

'It's seriously cool out here,' Andreas said. 'A-ma-zing.'

'And so cold,' Alma said.

'Didn't you bring any other clothes than what you're wearing?' Tupaarnaq asked.

'Oh, sure,' Arnaq said. 'They're inside...We're camping out up on the first floor. The rooms are full of old stuff.'

'A-ma-zing,' Andreas said again.

'She looks like you,' Tupaarnaq said. 'Arnaq.'

Matthew smiled. 'Does she?'

'Yes, something about her cheeks and nose.'

'Is this your brother?' Lasse wanted to know.

Arnaq nodded. 'Yes, this is Matthew.' She turned her gaze to Matthew. 'We've only met a couple of times.'

Lasse looked at Tupaarnaq. 'And do you hunt?'

'Yes.'

'Father says that women and guns are like women and cars,' he grinned.

Alma elbowed him. 'Is your dad from the Stone Age?'

'So what?' Lasse exclaimed, flinging out his arms. 'That's how they talk at Father's hunting lodge.'

Tupaarnaq pulled the rifle from her shoulder and held it in her right hand while she picked up a rusty can with the other. She walked up to Lasse and placed the can on his head.

'What do you think you're doing?' he said.

'Shut up and don't move,' Tupaarnaq said angrily.

He removed the can from his head without looking at her.

Tupaarnaq grabbed his arm forcefully and prised the can from his hands. She jabbed a finger hard against his forehead. 'Didn't I just tell you to shut up?' She looked him right in the eye until he stood very still. Then she replaced the can on his head. 'If you move, I'll blow your ear off, understand?'

Lasse said nothing. His hair had grown wet in the snow and was sticking to his head and cheeks.

'Let him go,' Matthew said, catching Tupaarnaq's eye. 'I think he's got the point.'

'No.' Tupaarnaq winked at Matthew, who wasn't sure how far she was going with this. She walked to the end of the walkway, a distance of about ten metres, and turned around, raising the rifle. Her shaved skull was wet from melted snow. Her black eyes shone in the grey twilight. 'Don't move,' she shouted. 'And stop shaking. You're going to drop the can.'

'Don't shoot,' Lasse said. His voice was trembling now. 'I'm sorry.'

Andreas and Alma looked back and forth between Matthew and Tupaarnaq. Both had instinctively retreated from their friend.

Matthew shook his head as he stepped up to Lasse and knocked the can off him.

The pale boy twitched and ducked.

'She can hit a seal in the head at a distance of over a hundred metres,' Matthew said. 'So don't even think about crossing her.'

Tupaarnaq lowered the rifle and walked over to them.

'Is it loaded?' Arnaq asked.

Tupaarnaq turned around and aimed the rifle at an old Esso oil can some distance away. The shot flung the jerry can several metres backwards, the snow whirling around it.

'You're hardcore,' Arnaq grinned and looked at Matthew. 'Is she your girlfriend or something?'

Matthew stared at the ground without looking at Tupaarnaq. 'No, no…We just help each other out from time to time.'

'That's all there is to it,' Tupaarnaq said. 'Let's go inside. You kids are shivering.'

'Come upstairs and see where we sleep,' Arnaq said. She nudged Lasse. 'Relax. You're still alive, aren't you?'

He shook his head. Then he started to smile again. 'What an awesome woman.'

Together they walked inside the house and up the damaged staircase, which took them to the first floor of the right wing. The ceilings sagged with heavy, damp stains, brown spots that seemed to have taken over everything that was once white. Bit of plaster and wallpaper lay scattered along the narrow corridor. The huge wooden floor planks were rough, and the varnish had been worn off in most places. The few lights left in the ceiling were broken and dangling from thin cables.

Matthew pointed to two bullet holes in the wall above the doorway to the room where he and Tupaarnaq had once hidden. 'Look, you missed.'

'It was dark,' Tupaarnaq said.

'He was a pretty big guy,' Matthew teased her.

Tupaarnaq stopped and inspected the wall. 'I can't imagine how I could have missed him.'

'What are you talking about?' Arnaq wanted to know.

'Tupaarnaq and I were out here in August,' Matthew said. He hesitated and looked at Arnaq. 'We were attacked in the night, right here, and Tupaarnaq shot at them.'

'Seriously? Then what the hell are we doing here?' Lasse said.

'What happened to us had nothing to do with this place,' Matthew said. 'Some people decided to follow us because I had something that one of them was willing to kill for.'

Arnaq frowned and looked at Tupaarnaq. 'Is that true?'

Tupaarnaq nodded. 'It was a close call, but it's in the past; they're gone now and one of them is dead.'

'We had to swim back to our boat while they were shooting at us,' Matthew said. 'I nearly drowned; the water is seriously cold up here.'

'The shooter is dead now,' Tupaarnaq added.

'Actually, two men came out here yesterday,' Arnaq said, looking back and forth between Tupaarnaq and Matthew.

'One of them was called Símin. He was a little younger than you,' Alma said. She had fetched a towel and was dabbing her hair dry. She smiled.

Arnaq nodded. 'Símin had just turned twenty-three, the older one said.'

'Why would they tell you how old they were?' Matthew wondered out loud.

'I don't know,' Arnaq went on. 'The older guy just said that the younger guy was his son, and that it was his birthday.'

'That Símin guy was crazy pale,' Alma added. 'His hair was almost completely white.'

'He looked a bit like an albino,' Andreas said. 'It was quite spooky, come to think of it...He kept looking at us as if he'd never seen people before.'

'And he totally fancied Arnaq,' Lasse cut in. 'What a freak.'

Arnaq smiled and looked at the floor.

'What about the other one?' Matthew wanted to know. 'The man?'

'He was tall and fat,' Alma said. 'He was sixty, at least.'

Arnaq nodded. 'He had a red beard and small eyes.'

'He looked like Andreas,' Lasse said with a grin. 'Except that he was twice as big.'

'Get lost,' Andreas exclaimed, elbowing Lasse.

'Did they head off again?' Matthew asked.

'Yes,' Arnaq said. 'But before they did, the old man asked all sorts of questions.'

'That was a bit creepy as well,' Andreas added.

'Nah,' Alma said. 'He was just curious.'

'What did he want to know?' Tupaarnaq said.

'All sorts of things,' Arnaq said. 'If I was from Nuuk, who my parents were.'

'Yes,' Lasse said. 'And he was only interested in Arnaq. He didn't give a toss about the rest of us. It was like "Hi, my name is Lasse and I'm completely invisible."'

The others nodded.

'I told him that I had no idea who my father was, except that he was American,' Arnaq went on. 'I didn't really know what to say.'

'I think he was just trying to make conversation—' Alma protested.

'Then what happened to them?' Tupaarnaq interrupted her. Her fingers had started to tighten around the rifle.

'They disappeared into one of the houses down by the water,' Arnaq said. 'And soon afterwards they drove off in their boat.'

'I don't know who they could be,' Matthew said, looking at Tupaarnaq.

She shook her head.

'I guess they were tourists,' Alma said. 'They spoke Danish with a bit of an accent, but they didn't speak Greenlandic.'

'They're everywhere these days,' Arnaq said in a surly voice.

'But we're tourists as well,' Alma said with a smile.

'That's different,' Arnaq said. She turned her attention to Matthew. 'I think the old guy might have lived here once.'

Matthew nodded slowly. 'They could be Faroese.'

'They were certainly weird,' Lasse said. 'That Símin mumbled to himself as they left. It sounded as if he said *demon, demon* or something like that.'

'No, he didn't say demon,' Alma said. 'I certainly didn't hear anything.'

Lasse flung out his hands and pulled a face of resignation.

'You're just saying that because he fancied Arnaq,' Alma added.

Lasse stared at the floor. 'But you have to agree he was mega spooky with that pale face and those clammy, sunken eyes.'

'I thought he looked nice,' Alma said. 'He seemed a little shy, but apart from that, I think he was all right.'

'Has Lars been here today?' Matthew interjected.

Arnaq nodded. 'Yes, he stops by in the morning so that we can get back to Nuuk before it gets dark, if we need to.'

'Did he know anything about the two men who came here?'

'No, he just laughed and said that we were exaggerating... Especially Lasse.'

'That's true, he does,' Alma said.

'Screw you,' Lasse said. 'So what sort of cake did you bring?'

THE MASK
DANCER

12

The light bulbs hummed in the lamps. Tom peered up at their yellow glow, then looked away. His eyes itched; they were dry and irritated from lack of sleep. Bradley and Reese were sitting to one side of him on the bench, with Sakkak on the other. None of them wore anything except long underwear. Behind them the two scientists, Lee and Christine, were busy noting down the results of the day's experiment. A third person was present, too; an old doctor whom Tom knew only vaguely.

Bradley and Reese were both staring vacantly into space. Their bodies seemed locked and rigid. Their skin had resumed its normal colour after just under half an hour in the warm room. Numerous small rubber patches on their bodies sent data back to the monitoring equipment.

Tom pressed his lips together and nodded gently to himself. His temples were throbbing and he felt a shooting sensation down the nerves in his neck. When he was on his own, both outside in the frost and back in the warmth, he found it hard not to think of Annelise and Matthew. He clenched and unclenched his fists. His elbows creaked, though not so loudly that he could hear them. It was more a sensation in his joints; they felt tight and stiff.

Sakkak shuddered. His skin was more speckled than the others and still covered in red patches from the frost. They had discussed Sakkak yesterday because Christine was worried that they might end up killing the Inuit, but there was little data to indicate that it was heading that way. Sakkak's body temperature would plummet, but he was incredibly resistant to the cold. Even on the placebo drug.

Sakkak looked at Tom. A smile formed around the corners of his mouth and in his black eyes as he met Tom's gaze.

'I don't think this stuff has any effect on me,' Sakkak said, looking at the others in turn.

Neither Bradley nor Reese reacted to his voice.

'I'm still bloody freezing,' he went on.

Tom shrugged. 'Perhaps it's all in your genes.'

Sakkak nodded dubiously, then his eyes lit up again. 'Yesterday I went hunting with Minik, my best friend. We shot three seals with our rifles. As we were dragging them home, Minik slipped and fell headfirst into one of the seals.'

Tom stared out into the air. His throat tightened. It felt dry and cracked. 'One you'd gutted already?'

Sakkak laughed out loud. 'Yes!'

From the back Lee hushed them.

Sakkak ducked but carried on, grinning. 'It was so funny,' he whispered. 'Minik's head pretty much ended up inside the seal... splat. He whined about it and kicked the seal and the lump of ice he had tripped over...he had blood all over his face...he looked just like a mask dancer.' Sakkak gazed up at the ceiling and shook his head. 'Imaneq, my father-in-law, is a mask dancer.' He hesitated for a moment before he turned to Tom, who was staring right ahead. 'I know how to do it as well...mask dancing and drumming.'

Tom nodded slowly without turning his head.

'Would you like me to show you?' Sakkak's eyes were shining.

'That major, the one you all call JJ, asked me if I would dance for you one day. I could bring my gear next week? All I have to do is paint my face and bring my drum.'

Tom nodded mechanically. 'Sure, why not?' He was struggling to follow Sakkak's train of thought. Images of Annelise and Matthew kept slipping in front of everything else. The boy was smiling, he could remember that, but the other images in his mind were sad. As though they were crying. He looked down at his forearms. They were tense and the veins stood out proudly. It felt as if the blood under his skin flowed more slowly than normal. Coagulating. He closed his eyes. He could feel throbbing and pressure.

He jumped when Lee placed a hand on his shoulder. 'Time's up.'

Tom exhaled slowly, glanced over his shoulder and nodded. 'Thank you.'

The four of them started peeling off the rubber patches and handing them to Christine and Lee.

'Don't forget we have a visitor today, Tom,' Lee said.

'Oh yes, that's right. The guy from the Greenlandic government, yeah?'

'Yes, he'll be here in a moment, along with Briggs.'

'I thought Briggs had dropped out?'

'It made more sense to let Briggs show him around, so we don't have to involve more people than necessary.'

Tom pulled a T-shirt over his head.

'Nice talking to you, my friend.' Sakkak patted Tom on the shoulder.

Tom smiled. 'Get home safely, Sakkak.'

Sakkak looked at the other two men. 'You look so miserable.'

'Bradley and Reese are men of few words,' Tom said.

Sakkak clapped a short, monotonous rhythm with his hands on his thighs. 'I think I better do some drumming for you when I come back…See you next week?'

'Yes, see you next week,' Tom said.

'What you lot need is some drum dancing,' Sakkak said. 'It's a rhythm you need to feel inside; it's like being at one with nature. It's called Pulse...we'll dance it next week, okay?'

Tom rubbed his eyelids. 'I'll talk to JJ about it. We could meet in my quarters next time, if you like...after the test.'

Sakkak nodded and made a half-turn to leave. He patted Reese on the shoulder while Tom explained Sakkak's idea to the others.

Before they reached the main door, it was opened from the outside and a tongue of icy air licked the room.

Briggs entered and nodded politely to everyone.

Sakkak, Bradley and Reese left.

'This is our guest from the Greenlandic government,' Briggs said.

Tom looked at the thin man with the dark hair. He had piercing eyes and a narrow face with high cheekbones.

The man dusted a little snow off his coat and walked towards Lee and Christine with his hand extended. 'Hello,' he said. 'My name is Kjeld Abelsen. I'm a senior civil servant...I'm responsible for research, among other things.'

Lee introduced himself and shook Abelsen's hand. 'I'm a biochemist and a member of the research team.'

'Likewise,' Christine said, greeting Abelsen. 'I'm Christine.' She turned her attention to Briggs. 'Aren't we getting a week ahead of ourselves?'

'What do you mean?' Briggs said.

'It's too soon to try it out on civilians.'

Abelsen cleared his throat. The others looked at him. 'Pardon me for butting in, but we're ready to try out the drug on people in Qaanaaq.'

'Who will take responsibility?' Christine wanted to know.

'I will,' Abelsen said quickly with a stiff nod. 'My department, I mean. We're ready.'

'We need to be ready too,' Lee said. 'And we're not quite there yet.'

'We had a deal,' Abelsen insisted. A couple of fine lines emerged around his eyes. 'There's a lot of money at stake for us so this thing needs to get off the ground.' He patted Tom on the shoulder. 'Let's check your data again. After all, you've been experimenting for months now, haven't you? At this point you must know if it's working?'

Tom shrugged. 'We need to analyse today's data, then combine it with previous readings and review all the results with the medical team.'

'The medical team?' Abelsen echoed scornfully. 'That's not the reason I flew all the way up here, is it?' He looked at Briggs. 'We're ready, my friend. People are waiting for the wonder drug that will help them fight the cold. So let's get going. Given that your people have been taking it for ages, it can't be that dangerous, can it?'

'I've been taking the same dose as the others the whole time,' Tom said. 'The issue here is increasing or decreasing the dosage; if we do it too quickly, we risk brain damage.'

'Brain damage,' Abelsen grinned. 'They're already braindead in Qaanaaq. Bunch of inbreeds. That's why we're using them as guinea pigs.' He threw up his hands in exasperation while looking around at the others. 'Let's just get on with it. I'll take responsibility, don't you worry about a thing.'

'What exactly did you tell them in Qaanaaq?' Tom wanted to know.

Abelsen looked up at the ceiling. 'They're really excited about it and they've all signed up.'

Lee shook his head. 'We're not ready yet and the buck stops with you, if you haven't got your trial group in place.'

'We're ready,' Abelsen said icily. 'I just told you.'

'This stuff can kill people in minutes,' Christine said. 'It's not a game.'

'Do I look like a man who plays games?' Abelsen said, fixing his gaze on her. His voice had grown sharp. 'We made a deal, my friends. This won't do.'

'It is what it is,' Tom said. 'If you can't wait, go back to Nuuk, but then you're no longer a part of this.'

Abelsen pressed his lips together so hard they glowed like two white lines. He breathed heavily and with control a couple of times. 'At least give me some pills to try for myself. I need to have something to work with here.'

Tom shook his head.

'We'll know more in a week,' Lee said. 'You won't get anything before that.'

'A week?' Abelsen sighed. 'Why the long wait?'

'We'll stop upping the dose next week,' Christine said. 'We can't keep increasing it for much longer...not if we want to be responsible.'

'We've upped the dose for all the test subjects today,' Lee said. 'It's the last round, so now we wait and see what happens.'

Tom looked at Abelsen. 'You need to understand that this is dangerous stuff. If we cut corners, you'll end up with a village full of dead people. We've seen a steady increase in aggressive behaviour and if we can't find a way of managing that, then it's too dangerous to start testing it on civilians.'

'But it works as it was supposed to, doesn't it?' Abelsen raised both eyebrows in quizzical grimace.

'Yes, there's no doubt that we've successfully enhanced the human body's ability to withstand very low temperatures,' Christine said. 'The problem is the aggression.'

Briggs placed a hand on Abelsen's shoulder. 'Let's look at it in a week. And if you choose to wait for the news here on the base, we'll make sure you're looked after.'

13

Sakkak moved rhythmically on the spot while monotonously beating a home-made leather drum, which he held in his left hand, with a square drumstick. Before he started dancing and singing, he had told them that the drum was made by his great-grandfather a very long time ago.

Tom looked at Bradley and Reese, who were sitting on the sofa. One of Reese's cheekbones was swollen and red. The two of them had got into a fight a couple of hours after that day's readings had been taken. Tom didn't know what had triggered it, but suddenly Bradley and Reese were on the floor trying to strangle one another. Sakkak had asked if they should cancel the drum dancing, but JJ thought it would take their minds off the experiment and had insisted that it go ahead as planned. Tom was struggling with his thoughts as well. The experiment had gone much further than he had imagined when they had started taking the pills, and it was no longer enough for him to get out of the experiment; he needed to stop the whole project.

Sakkak's chanting disturbed Tom's thoughts. Normally the drumming and the dancing wouldn't be performed by the same person, but Sakkak had chosen to do both. His face was painted red and black in a demonic expression. The incomprehensible words and the monotonous sound of the stick hitting the wooden edge of the drum felt numbing and terrifying at once. Tom had had to snap out of a sense of unreality several times.

'Heyi, eyi, eyi, eyiieyi,' Sakkak's voice chanted in low, hoarse utterances. 'Raa, raaa…'

Before he started drumming and singing, Sakkak had explained what he would be singing about. It was a story so old that no one could remember where it had first come from. It was about a raven that falls in love with a goose one summer. The raven lived permanently on his island, while the goose was merely passing through. They spent the summer together, but when it started to get cold, the goose decided to head on south with her flock. The raven didn't want to be without her, so the geese agreed that every night they would land on the sea and rest close together so that he could sit on them. 'Make me an island,' the raven said, and the geese promised that they would. But they broke their promise the very first night and scattered across the sea. Slowly the raven sank into the water and drowned.

Sakkak's hair stuck out stiffly in all directions. His gaze moved in wild and anxious jumps around the room, and his artificially inflated cheeks made his song lisping and hissing.

Tom fought the rhythm. He could feel how it had got a hold in him. As if Sakkak was trying to force his heart to follow the rhythm of the drum and the song. Waves of warmth and icy shivers alternated through Tom's body.

The sounds coming from Sakkak grew more agitated and panicky.

Suddenly a violent roar yanked Tom out of his trance.

Bradley had jumped onto Reese and was now straddling him with his hands locked around Reese's neck.

Tom got up and grabbed Bradley, who lashed out in anger, flooring Tom with a hard punch to the side of his head.

Tom felt a crunching sensation in his head and blacked out for a moment.

Reese shouted something, but Tom couldn't hear what it was. He rolled over on the floor and saw Sakkak fleeing out of the door. Behind the table, Bradley had grabbed a pair of scissors and was lunging at Reese.

Tom got up onto his knees and opened the drawer of a low dresser. He grabbed his pistol and loaded it. He called out. Then he was knocked to the floor again.

14

Abelsen drummed his fingers angrily on the desk. 'So what you're telling me is that I've waited here a whole week for nothing?'

Lee shook his head. 'I can't help you as long as we're not ready, and it's only a few hours since we took the last readings.'

'I think we upped the dose too much,' Christine said.

'But you haven't analysed the data yet,' Abelsen said, looking towards the door. 'And yet last week everything was just fine. I need something I can take away with me now!'

'I don't actually care how busy you are,' Christine said. 'And I'm not taking about the data; it's the behaviour. What happened today was bad.'

'But it's just one day,' Abelsen exclaimed. 'Seriously...You really have to...I've been waiting for those pills for a week.' He nudged a pile of papers on the desk between them. 'Where the hell is Briggs? I've got all the paperwork in place. All I need is the pills, and then we can all move on.'

'Given how things look like right now, we can't start the second phase of the experiment,' Lee said with a shrug.

Abelsen leaned across the desk. 'I have all the signatures here, for fuck's sake. How hard can it be? I don't care about your tests...I just want the pills I was promised.'

Christine got up and went over to a desk with two computers, while Lee pushed himself backwards in his chair. 'You'll have to wait...As will everyone else.'

'I've been waiting long enough,' Abelsen said. 'I'll speak to the Minister of Defence...in Denmark.'

'He holds no sway here.'

Abelsen's chin slumped to his chest. 'Very well. Name your price.'

'What do you mean?'

'Money,' Abelsen said calmly. 'Cars, foreign holidays, jewellery, watches...art. What do you want so that we can do this now?'

'You can forget about that for a start!' Christine's voice from the back cut in between the other two.

At the same moment the front door to the low wooden barracks was pushed open and two soldiers entered.

'Bradley and Reese have been shot,' one of them announced in a firm voice. 'In Tom's quarters.'

'What?' Lee said, jumping up. He looked at Christine, who leaned on the desk for support. Her gaze flitted nervously back and forth between him and the soldiers. 'Are they dead?'

'Yes,' the other soldier said. There was still snow on his cheeks, but it melted quickly in the warm room.

'They were found about an hour ago,' said the soldier who had spoken first. 'You need to stay in here until you're told otherwise. Everyone is being interviewed.'

'What about Tom?' Lee wanted to know.

'Suicide, or so it looks. Same room and same weapon.'

'Tom shot them?' Lee said, clasping his mouth in horror.

'Lieutenant Briggs will brief you later.'

'I'm shutting this thing down right now,' a new voice interjected.

Everyone turned to face the door. Briggs and a gruff looking major were standing right inside the doorway.

'At last! There you are,' Abelsen exclaimed, rushing up to Briggs. 'We can't be sure this has anything to do with the experiment, can we?'

'There'll be no more of this,' the major said, nodding in the direction of the lab equipment. He was as big and broad as Briggs, but just under a decade older.

'But I have a signed agreement,' Abelsen shrieked. His pale face had acquired a reddish glow. 'I want my pills.'

'Shut up,' the major snarled. 'One more word from you and I'll have you detained.'

Abelsen stared at Briggs, who merely shrugged.

'JJ is right,' Briggs said. 'You're on American territory.'

'I claim diplomatic immunity,' Abelsen exclaimed angrily, grabbing the papers on the desk.

'You mind your own business,' Briggs said, fixing his eyes on Abelsen's. 'And I'll mind mine.' He turned his attention to the two soldiers. 'Escort Mr Abelsen to his quarters. Our discussions from now on are of no concern to him.'

•

A few minutes later Abelsen was back in his room in one of the long accommodation barracks. He slammed the door behind him, turning the lock angrily before slumping to the floor and beginning to slowly hit his forehead against it.

'Shit,' he whispered into the shiny linoleum surface. The floor breathed hot, moist air back at him.

He stood up and took a few deep breaths as he walked over to the two tall wardrobes that lined one of the walls. His fingers rested briefly on the handle of one of them, and then he opened the door. Two shining eyes were waiting inside the darkness. They squinted apathetically at the light.

Abelsen looked down at the man curled up in the bottom of the wardrobe. 'You'll be charged with manslaughter,' he said. 'They want this incident suppressed and the experiment shut down immediately.' He knelt down so that his face was level with that of the other man. 'They'll blame you for the killings, Tom...and the experiment will be kept out of public knowledge.'

Tom stared passively into the air. His face, arms and shirt were soaked in blood.

'Now, pull yourself together,' Abelsen said, extending his hand to Tom. 'We need to get you showered and find you some clean clothes.'

Tom grabbed Abelsen's hand and got up slowly and reluctantly. He touched his head. One temple was swollen and red. 'I can't remember what happened,' he whispered, his face contorting in agony.

'We'll find out in due course,' Abelsen said. 'But first we need to agree on a few things.'

Tom narrowed his eyes and touched his head again.

'I believe you studied chemistry before you joined the army?' Abelsen went on.

'Yes, I joined up to finance my PhD,' Tom said, shaking his head. 'And the experiment was another...Not that it matters now...' Tears welled in his eyes. 'Did they stab one another? Bradley and Reese? Did someone fire a gun? Shit...They went berserk...But they didn't have their handguns, did they?' He shook his head, but then had to shut his eyes from the pain. 'I should have stopped the experiment weeks ago...Now they're dead.' Tom looked at Abelsen. 'You were there! You were there as well, weren't you?' His gaze scanned the room. 'The mask dancer? Where is he? Is Sakkak dead as well?'

'Stop it!' Abelsen grabbed Tom's arm. 'You're losing it...Yes, they're dead, and you will be court-martialled for their killings. You'll be locked up for good...and who knows? Perhaps you really did kill them.'

Tom tore himself free of Abelsen's hold. 'I didn't…I know I didn't.'

'Your fingerprints are all over everything, you're covered in their blood…and your pistol is missing.'

Tom buried his face in his hands and slumped to the floor. 'That's a lie. I know it is.' He looked at the blood on his hands. 'There were three empty cartridges, weren't there? On the floor next to me…But what happened to my pistol?'

'I can get you out,' Abelsen cut him off calmly. 'Far away from here. It's not a problem. If I ask to be picked up by a government helicopter and use my connections here at the base, we can travel to Qaanaaq and from there on to Nuuk. I know of an abandoned place a few hours south of Nuuk where we can hide you underground.'

Tom sighed and shook his head. 'No. I won't run away.'

'You don't have a choice,' Abelsen said. 'And once you're there, you can recreate the experiment in your own time. I can get you everything you need.'

'You must be out of your mind,' Tom said, looking up. He stared into the thin man's black eyes. 'Two men, three possibly, died today because of that experiment. I'll turn myself in.'

Abelsen heaved a sigh. 'That's not going to happen, Tom. Listen, how's your son doing in Denmark? It must be such a comfort to know that he's living in such a safe place…and in the countryside, too. Tommerup is a quiet little village, isn't it? And so small. I'm tempted to visit it myself…Play a bit with Matthew perhaps. That's his name, isn't it? Your son? Matthew? It didn't take my friends long to find him in Tommerup.'

Tom stared at Abelsen in disbelief. 'You stay away from Matthew,' he said hoarsely.

Abelsen squatted down on his haunches. He took a piece of paper from his pocket and unfolded it. 'Look,' he said. 'One of my friends took this picture a few days ago. Do you recognise this little chap?'

84

Tom bashed the paper from Abelsen's hand. 'Touch him and you're dead.'

'We'll see,' Abelsen said. 'Now stand up. We need to get you cleaned up so that I can get you out of here.'

15

Tom turned over on the mattress, which wasn't much more than a flimsy sheet of foam. The grey woollen blanket was too small to cover his upper body and legs at the same time. Dust irritated his throat and eyes.

The cell was windowless, the iron door old and studded. It had once been grey, but now it was covered with patches of rust and most of the paint had peeled off. Everything inside the room was concrete; dark grey, rough concrete.

Tom had already paced up and down the cell more times than he could count, his hand trailing along the wall. Only the door broke the concrete surface. He felt restless and scared.

Several naked lightbulbs hung suspended from the ceiling, but only one of them appeared to be working. The ceiling was as concrete as the walls. And the floor.

At the bottom of the door was a hatch, and nearby were a bucket and a plastic bottle of water. In the just under twenty-four hours in which Tom had been locked in the cell, he had been given no food. Only water.

He lay down on the thin mattress. The room had a dry smell.

Like old mortar that had become damp and then dried out again for decades.

His knuckles were smeared with dried blood and he could see bloodstains on the wall where he had slammed his fists into the concrete.

He hadn't slept for days. There was no way he could have killed them. It was unthinkable. But then again, he could only remember odd glimpses. Bradley and Reese fighting like crazed animals. Sakkak with his mask fleeing the room. The darkness when he was knocked out. Then blood everywhere. On his hands and clothes. The cut to his temple. The empty cartridges on the floor next to him. Abelsen, who blackmailed him into fleeing, demanding that Tom recreate the experiment so that he could make millions out of the formula, which would increase the ability of humans and animals to survive the cold. There were huge sums to be made from improving the cold resistance in farm animals such as cows and pigs, to make them better suited for life in the Arctic.

Tom turned over. He could hear noises in the corridor behind the door. First footsteps, then a metallic grating from the lock in the door.

'Hello, Tom. Making any progress?'

'With what?' Tom said, sitting up on the mattress.

'Finding out how the two of us will be working together.'

'You're out of your mind.'

'No,' Abelsen said. 'I want what I was promised.'

'You weren't promised shit,' Tom said, sinking back onto the mattress.

'You seem tired,' Abelsen said. 'I wonder if you could do with something to eat? Or your pills, perhaps? I'm guessing your body is crying out for them.'

'Get lost.'

'All right, all right,' Abelsen said, taking out some prints from his pocket. He tossed them onto the floor by the mattress. 'Tom, foot soldiers like you, you're proper tough guys, aren't you? But you have just as many weaknesses as everybody else.' He nudged the papers with his foot. 'Look at them…And take as long as you like.'

Tom reached for the papers. They were all pictures of Matthew in Denmark. Three of them had been taken from a distance, but there was also one where Matthew smiled happily to the camera. His eyes were shining. It looked like he was at some sort of nursery school because there were lots of other children in the background. Tom scrunched up the papers. 'He's not even mine.'

Abelsen grinned. 'Oh, you can do better than that, Tom.'

'You stay away from him,' Tom snarled.

'That's entirely up to you,' Abelsen said. 'As you can see, we're making great friends with your boy, so it won't be difficult to persuade him to come along with us for a little trip.'

Tom glowered up at Abelsen. 'Just get the hell out of here.'

'As you wish, my friend.'

Abelsen disappeared out of the door and soon afterwards the light in the cell went out. The darkness was total. Tom couldn't even see his own hands when he held them up in front of his face. Slowly he crawled in the direction of the door, feeling his way. First he bumped into the bucket, then the bottle. He untwisted the cap and drained the bottle of water. Hunger gnawed at his stomach, although he didn't feel any real appetite. He rolled onto his back. His thoughts were spinning. His stomach rumbled.

Tom didn't know for how long he lay on the floor. He was broken out of his trance by a flash near the ceiling. It was a glimpse of light and it startled him. He stared around the darkness. Had someone been in here? Had he seen something in the brief moment when the cell was lit up?

Another flash of light shot through the room. His heart started pumping so quickly that his fingers and temples began to throb. He closed his eyes. He forced himself to breathe slowly and calmly. It was just the lightbulb going on and off. That was all.

He banged the back of his head softly against the iron door. 'You're an amateur, Abelsen,' he cried out into the darkness.

A shrill voice cut through the cell as the intercom system was switched on. 'Oops,' Abelsen's voice crackled. 'Then you've played all of your aces and shown your hand to an amateur, Tom. That's bad news for you.'

The intercom buzzed and went quiet.

'Let me out!' Tom shouted at the ceiling.

The intercom came on again with another howl that turned into a buzzing noise. 'I'll let you out when we have a deal.' White noise took over for a moment. 'Otherwise you'll never get out of here, and you won't ever know if I let Matthew live—'

'You bastard!' Tom yelled.

'That's enough!' The intercom buzzed. 'I can also have the boy strangled right now and that will end our partnership. Goodbye, Tom.'

'No…No…I'm sorry.'

'That's better. Enjoy the show.'

Tom's brow furrowed in confusion.

The buzzing noise disappeared and the darkness grew silent. Tom started fumbling his way back to the mattress, but stopped when the light came on again. He looked up. The light wasn't as bright as earlier, instead it was veiled and it was coming from one of the walls. It was a flickering square. Like the light from a projector. The film being screened on the wall looked like old 8mm footage.

The light flickered while the image on the wall zoomed in and grew sharper. Tom stared up at the glowing square. The footage had been recorded in a small room whose walls were covered with a shiny material that looked like thick tinfoil. From the ceiling hung a lightbulb, which kept coming on and going off. The light was naked and sharp. At times it would be dark for only a few seconds. At other times for longer. It switched constantly between light and dark in an unstable rhythm. A small, dark-haired girl sat in the middle of the room. She disappeared from the wall and returned with the light. She wasn't wearing any shoes, but she was wearing tights. Her upper body was covered by a green coat that was wrapped tightly around her. She was clutching a dark knitted woollen hat, pressing it against her face as if it were a teddy bear. She was nibbling at the hat. Her eyes were closed.

'What's this?' Tom shouted. His voice broke. 'Why the hell are you showing me this?'

Tom saw how the girl's body jerked whenever the light came on. When it went off everything grew dark around him, as it did with her.

'For God's sake,' Tom said in a hoarse voice. 'Stop it!'

The film carried on monotonously.

Tom slammed both hands onto the floor. 'Stop it now!'

The film and the light went out, and the darkness settled closely around him once more. He gasped for air and turned around quickly. The light began to spread from the wall again. Grainy and flickering. It was the same room as before. The shiny metal walls. The glowing lightbulb that segmented everything into moments of light and darkness. The girl was curled up in the corner with her hat pressed against her mouth. Her hair was more matted than in the first clip. Her tights were stained. Tom got up and took a few steps towards the wall with the flickering film.

At that same moment the camera making the recording started moving towards the curled-up girl. The light continued to blink erratically. Disappearing. Returning. Disappearing. The girl flinched. She was shaking. The camera moved very close to her and a hand reached out and snatched the hat from her.

Tom roared in anger and slammed his right hand into the wall just below the film.

The girl's mouth opened and it looked as if she was screaming. She hid her face. Her hands were trembling. Her lips nibbled the skin on one of her hands.

Tom ran towards to door and banged on the iron surface, but nothing happened. 'What sort of person are you?' he shouted. 'Let her go, for pity's sake...Let her go...I promise to help you...But please just let her go.'

The shrill noises of the intercom interrupted him. 'Can I get you some popcorn?'

'Stop the damn film,' Tom shouted.

The buzzing sound of the intercom disappeared. The film carried on playing. The little girl was still curled up and pressing herself against the wall. She was shivering. More time had passed. Her hair was even messier and more matted, and her tights were gone. Her legs were naked and filthy.

Tom's heart was pounding and his whole body was shaking too. He was breathing in short gasps. He made himself watch. He could see a little of the girl's face. She couldn't be more than ten years old. Inuit. She was sucking her hand and there were traces of dried tears down her cheeks.

Tom ran to the door, where he picked up the bucket and hurled it up against the ceiling. It hit the concrete with a hollow metallic sound, and his own urine rained down onto the floor. He picked up the bucket and flung it at the ceiling again. This time the bucket hit the lightbulb, which scattered in a shower of tiny shards.

'So do you want her to die?' The intercom crackled. 'Do you want the girl to die, Tom?'

Tom picked up the bucket again and scanned the cell in order to spot the intercom in the dusty glow of light from the film.

The film stopped and all light disappeared. He let the bucket sink to the floor.

'That's right, Tom,' the voice went on. 'You decide if little Najak here lives or dies…Just as you decide if Matthew dies. Put down the bucket so we can get started.'

Tom let go of the bucket and stared around at the darkness. He was no longer sure that the voice belonged to Abelsen.

Once again a bright, dust-filled beam of light illuminated the room. The square on the wall flickered. The girl was still sitting in the erratic light. Her hair was messy. Filthy. More tangled. She wasn't wearing any underwear now. Her whole body was shaking. Neither the light nor the darkness seemed to affect her closed eyelids. Her hands were pressed against her mouth and nose. Her face was grimy from tears.

'I'm going to kill you,' Tom hissed angrily into the air. His fists were clenched, his veins bulging under his skin.

The room fell dark again and the intercom crackled above him. 'We'll talk about it tomorrow.'

The film looped back to the start. Najak was dressed, with clean hair.

16

The light from the movie didn't come back. Tom didn't know how much time had passed. He estimated that the short film clips went for about an hour before they restarted. The same clips were shown again and again.

Tom had tried and failed to keep track of how long the film had been playing. It might have been a day, maybe two.

He pulled the blanket over his head. It was dark now. Deep, black darkness. For the first time in hours, days possibly, his eyes could rest. He couldn't remember the last time he'd had something to drink. His lips felt cracked and his neck and throat hurt when he moved his tongue.

He tried to sit up but he couldn't. His arms were limp, his body weary and sore. The back of his head and neck were pounding. His body was starting to stink.

He screamed when the light in the room came on again. Another lightbulb. He screamed again and raised a hand to his face. His arm hurt as he moved it.

He turned over onto his side and looked along the floor. The upended bucket lay close to the door, and thin, curved shards of glass from the smashed lightbulb were scattered in the middle of the cell. His eyes began to close. They stung behind the eyelids, but he couldn't sleep; he hadn't slept since before the killings.

The howl of the intercom returned. 'So, Tom, how are you doing?'

Tom rolled onto his back. He couldn't speak. He tried to organise his thoughts.

'Isn't it about time we moved on?' the voice continued.

It sounded like Abelsen. Tom nodded.

'I can't hear you?'

Tom slowly raised one arm. 'Yes.'

The intercom buzzed for a few minutes before falling silent. Soon afterwards the door opened.

'Jesus,' Abelsen exclaimed. 'Did you piss all over the place?'

Tom shook his head. He didn't have the energy to respond.

Abelsen looked down at Tom. 'Are you able to stand up?'

'Yes,' Tom croaked. 'Water...'

'Water?' Abelsen echoed, looking down at the full half-litre bottle by the door. He picked it up and placed it in Tom's hand. 'Drink some and then come with me. This place stinks.'

'Okay...' With difficulty Tom managed to push himself up so that he could rest on his elbow. He emptied the bottle before collapsing back onto the floor. His empty stomach churned and he nearly blacked out. He felt the urge to throw up, but fought it. He swallowed the saliva that welled up in his mouth and forced the nausea back down his throat.

'I'm going...I'm going to throw up...if I stand up...' Tom panted in short, wheezing gasps.

Abelsen picked up the bucket and placed it upside down so that he could sit on it. 'Tom, we need to move on, don't we?'

Tom nodded. Inside his turmoil of nausea and exhaustion he had tried to find a way out of this nightmare, but there was none.

'We'll carry on,' Tom said in a resigned voice, and took a few breaths. 'I'll do whatever you say.' He fixed his gaze on Abelsen. 'And you stay away from Matthew…and you let the little girl go. What kind of a sick person are you?'

'Don't you worry about that,' Abelsen said.

'Who is the girl?' Tom continued. 'You can't do that to a child. Shit…If I…' He clutched his stomach and grimaced.

'Relax, Tom,' Abelsen said. 'You haven't got the strength to get worked up. If you keep your end of the deal, I'll keep mine; it's as simple as that. But if you even think of double-crossing me…' He paused and his eyes swept around the room. 'Then you'll be back here.'

'I won't fail you,' Tom panted. 'Just leave the children alone.'

Abelsen slapped his thighs energetically as he nodded. 'Right, time to shop. I'll get you some paper and a pencil so you can make a list of everything you need…And I mean everything; we'll be starting from scratch here, but I can get you anything you want.'

'I'll make a list,' Tom said.

'You must be hungry,' Abelsen said, taking out a small bag. 'I brought you some rye bread.'

Tom reached for the bag.

Abelsen shook his head and broke a chunk off the bread. He tossed it to Tom, who stuffed it into his mouth.

'But first I need to tell you a bit about this place,' Abelsen said, tossing another chunk of bread to Tom. 'Because you're not alone out here.'

Tom wolfed down the second piece of bread and looked at Abelsen. 'You mean you live here?'

'No, I only make the occasional visit,' Abelsen said. 'I was referring to Bárdur, who lives here with his family.'

'What's a guy from the Faroe Islands doing here?' Tom said. 'Just give me that damn bread.'

Abelsen broke off another chunk and chucked it at Tom. 'Yes, Bárdur is the last Faroese left in this place—except that he doesn't live above ground in the abandoned town, but down here in the corridors in his own little world.' Abelsen let out a short laugh. 'He has built it all himself...I mean, the bunker was already here, but everything else is down to him. He dragged furniture down here and made himself comfortable...He has done a really good job.'

'Can I have some more water?'

'Yes, in a moment, Tom.' Abelsen cleared his throat. 'I've been looking after Bárdur since he was a boy. His father was killed in Nuuk in 1973, and when people started to leave Færingehavn, I took care of the boy.'

Tom looked at Abelsen's narrow face. The thin, pale lips and the black eyes.

Abelsen tossed the rest of the rye bread onto the floor. 'By the mid-eighties only Bárdur was living here, and it was about that time he set up his underworld. After all, the people who moved away left all their belongings behind, and it's easy for a big guy like Bárdur to lug stuff down here...And when he fancied getting himself a girlfriend one day, I found him one and brought her out here.'

Tom looked up. He was still chewing the last mouthful of bread. 'Someone actually chose to live here?'

'You don't know much about life in Greenland, do you?' Abelsen said with a wry smile. 'Bárdur grew up in a tiny, remote community of deeply religious Faroese immigrants. It was another time, not like today. Corporal punishment and Bible school were par for the course. Apart from that, the lad hasn't had much education, but he has seen his world slowly collapse as he grew up. The fishing died out and the money disappeared with it...and then his father was killed. Bárdur is a very simple man, but good to those he trusts.'

'Like you?'

'Yes,' Abelsen said with a light shrug. 'I'm probably the only one.'

Tom managed to shift himself into a sitting position. He briefly closed his eyes and pulled a face. 'Why are you telling me all this?'

'For two reasons,' Abelsen said with a cold smile. 'Number one. I intend to use Bárdur and his family as guinea pigs, and I won't be taking any pills which they haven't taken first. Number two. You need to understand that no one gets out of here alive without my say so. It's impossible to escape without a boat. You would die from hunger and exposure before you came even close to help. Besides, you won't be the only one to suffer if you don't honour our deal, will you?'

17

FÆRINGEHAVN, WEST GREENLAND, 27 MARCH 1990

Abelsen had left the bunker a few hours earlier, but unlike on the other days the door to Tom's room was no longer locked.

The room where he was staying now was smaller than the cell where he had first been kept, but it was less austere. Everything was still grey concrete, but there were carpets, furniture and a sink. He pushed himself up from the orange-brown couch and went over to the sink. There was only one tap, which let out a faint stream of icy water. He bent over the sink and filled his hands with water. It felt good to splash his face. Above the sink a round mirror was glued to a piece of chipboard that had been painted orange. His cheeks looked grey and sunken in the mirror. His blond hair was too short to become matted. His fingers traced the stubble on his cheek.

The door to the corridor was ajar, but no light or sound came through. Tom pulled on his boots and laced them up. They were the only footwear he had brought with him from the base. He could feel the air in the corridor even before he opened the door fully. Only his room was heated, while the corridor was dark and cold. He fumbled for a light switch, but couldn't find one. His best option was to walk slowly down the corridor trailing one hand along the wall.

The corridor was short and formed a T-junction where it met another corridor. He turned right, but stopped when he heard what sounded like a knife being sharpened. Tom stood very still and listened. The grinding sound was followed by a couple of dull thuds. He moved slowly down the corridor towards the sound.

He jumped when a light suddenly came on above him. Looking around, he spotted a sensor in this section of the corridor, which was now lit up as far back as the eye could see.

Not far from him a door was ajar. The sound had stopped the moment the light came on, but now it resumed.

Tom pushed open the door and peeked inside. The room looked like a mixture of a slaughterhouse and an old infirmary. A couple of shapeless cadavers were lying on the steel table in the middle of the room; behind them stood a tall, broad man with his back to Tom, working on yet another bloody cadaver.

Tom cleared his throat. 'Hello, my name's Tom. Are you Bárdur?'

Without rushing, the man wiggled a haunch of meat back and forth, then bashed the joint with a cleaver before glancing over his shoulder and nodding briefly; then he turned his attention back to the meat.

'Is that reindeer?' Tom asked, stepping inside the room. The sight of blood made him feel faint.

'It's meat,' Bárdur said, taking a step to the right and blocking Tom's view. His voice was heavy and calm.

Tom nodded. 'Are you the person to talk to if I want something to eat?'

Bárdur shrugged. 'There'll be meat later.'

'Meat…Good, okay.' Tom looked at the man's broad back. Bárdur was wearing an old lumberjack shirt, jeans and black wooden clog boots. His hands continued to handle the meat, and every time Tom moved, Bárdur moved too, that so he blocked Tom's view.

'I'm going to go back,' Tom said. He paused and then added: 'Do you know anything about the little girl who is being held in a room with tinfoil on the walls? I think her name might be Najak?'

The big man looked briefly at Tom before shaking his head. 'It wasn't me.'

'No, but do you have a room with tinfoil on the walls?'

Bárdur frowned and shook his head. 'Go back to your room,' he said before turning back to the meat and picking up his cleaver.

The place smelled of death. Tom looked around at the tables and the walls. The room was clean, lined with steel and tiles, with a few kitchen implements scattered around. All knives. From the ceiling hung several chains with big hooks at the ends. All empty and clean. An icy shiver went down Tom's spine. The only door out was the one through which he had entered.

Back in the corridor, the light was still shining brightly. To his right were a couple of closed wooden doors, while the corridor leading back to the side passage where his room was located seemed endless. It dissolved in darkness thirty metres away at least.

The wooden doors to his right looked like the one to his own room. Tom grabbed the first door handle and slowly pushed it down. The room behind it was pitch black. The air inside felt dry and warm, but he couldn't see anything, so he tried the next door. It opened just like the first one and here there was light on the other side. He carefully released the handle and peered through the gap.

Behind the door a living room had been furnished with items from various decades. Bookcases, chairs, tables and carpets. Bárdur had even dragged down a few paintings and a big crucifix that looked like something he must have taken from a church or chapel. Right below the crucifix was a table with two tall candlesticks. It looked like an altar.

Tom gave the door another push.

A woman was sitting in an armchair in the middle of the room. Her features were Nordic. She was knitting and her fingers moved monotonously, while the knitting needles clicked softly.

On a woven rug next to her sat two little girls. They both had red hair like Bárdur. A couple of dolls lay between them. They had stopped playing and were watching Tom attentively.

The woman looked up. Her face was ashen and her eyes devoid of expression. For a moment Tom thought he sensed something in her gaze, but then it disappeared and she became introverted once more.

Tom looked back and forth between the woman and the girls. All three of them wore long dresses and had their hair up.

The girls continued to stare at him. They didn't say a word, nor did they move. One of the woman's ankles was encircled by an iron ring, which was attached to a chain. He couldn't see where the chain ended; only that it continued into another room.

'Hello,' he said tentatively and straightened up.

One girl let out a scream at the sound of his voice, and both of them sought refuge by their mother's legs immediately.

There was a noise behind Tom and before he could say another word, Bárdur had grabbed him with a roar and pulled him close.

Bárdur stared into Tom's eyes. His lips quivered inside the dense, red beard. 'If you ever come in here again, I swear I'll kill you.'

THE FACE OF
THE DEMON

18

The fire crackled between the four young people gathered around the campfire, wrapped up warmly in their unzipped sleeping bags. It had been Lasse's idea to light a fire outside. At first they had wandered around trying to get a mobile signal, but only Alma had briefly got a single bar out of four close to the old dam a short walk from the town.

It hadn't taken them long to find wood for the fire from the trashed houses, and they built their fire on a broad concrete platform near the long wooden quay.

Arnaq nudged a tray of sausages with her foot. They had barbecued them on sticks over the fire and toasted some rolls, but they hadn't been able to eat all of them.

It had stopped snowing a couple of hours after Matthew and Tupaarnaq had left, but even so a lot of snow remained. It was one of the things Arnaq had missed the most while she had been at school in Denmark: the clear, frosty air and the snow. She closed her eyes and leaned back. It was growing dark, but the snow would retain the light between the old houses in the abandoned town.

'Want any more, mate?' Lasse held up his vodka bottle and looked at Andreas.

Andreas drained his plastic cup. 'Yes…half and half.'

Lasse took the cup and started pouring. 'Thank fuck our baby-sitters don't come out here in the evening as well.'

Andreas grinned. 'How many bottles did you manage to smuggle in?'

'Two.'

'Nice.' Andreas looked at Arnaq. 'This is a seriously awesome place.'

'Yeah, it's cool, isn't it?'

He nodded. 'Where have they gone, the people who used to live here?'

'I think they moved away in the eighties or something. I'm not sure, but I think they left when the fish ran out.'

'Were they all from the Faroe Islands?' Alma asked.

'I believe so,' Arnaq said.

'It's insane to think that they just left all their stuff behind,' Lasse said.

'It would have cost more to ship than to buy new,' Arnaq said. 'There are heaps of abandoned towns along Greenland's west coast.'

'Cool!' Andreas exclaimed.

'It's a bit of a bummer that there's no 3G here, though,' Lasse added quickly. 'I'm experiencing digital withdrawal.'

'It'll do you good,' Alma said.

'Screw that, you want to be online as well,' Lasse retorted.

'Right now all I want is to be warm,' Alma said. She had pulled her thick hat so far down around her ears that only a little of her long, blonde hair could be seen at the back.

'I'll chuck some more wood on the fire,' Andreas said, getting up.

'Please can we just go inside?' Alma pleaded. 'It's so dark.'

'Man up,' Lasse said. 'There's plenty of light here…Isn't there, Arnaq?'

Arnaq looked at the fire and nodded. 'It's fine, but if Alma is cold—'

'I'll walk you up to the house,' Andreas said, dumping an armful of old planks on the fire. 'Who knows, there might be some mobile coverage now.' Embers and sparks flew out to all sides before the heat and the smoke whirled them upwards.

'Easy does it,' Arnaq said, finding a packet of cigarettes in her coat pocket.

Alma looked up at Andreas. His reddish-blond hair glistened in the glow from the fire. Behind him the sky was dark and grey.

He looked back at her with a bashful smile. 'Sitting out here getting cold is silly.'

'I think it's warmer out here than inside the house,' Arnaq said, looking at the two of them.

'Well, we're going back inside anyway,' Andreas decided, and held out his hand to Alma.

She nodded and got to her feet. 'I certainly wouldn't mind going back inside for a while.'

Lasse shrugged. 'Whatever floats your boat,' he said with a smile and took a big gulp of his vodka and orange. 'Any more for you?' he went on, now addressing Arnaq.

She exhaled the smoke and watched her friends, who were heading back up towards the big, grey house. They were almost the same height, the two of them. She shook her head with a smile. Andreas really was a short-arse.

'Any more for you?' Lasse said again.

'Eh?' she said, taking a drag. The tip lit up.

'More vodka, I mean?'

Arnaq shook her head. 'Not now.' She studied Lasse. 'Do you think they're having sex?'

He gave a light shrug. 'We can go up and check if they're shagging in a sec.'

Arnaq flicked her cigarette butt at him.

'What's your problem?' he exclaimed, jumping up to brush the smouldering cigarette butt off his sleeping bag.

'You talk so much crap,' Arnaq said, getting up. 'Come on, let's go for a walk along the quay…It's great when it's dark.'

'That old pile of crap?' he said, looking at her. 'Couldn't we fall through it?'

'Yes. That's the whole point.'

Lasse surveyed the long wooden quay. The tall warehouses loomed even larger now the darkness had settled around them, while the snow lit up the ground and the quay.

'Are you being a wuss again?' Arnaq goaded him.

He drained his plastic cup and shook his head. 'Hell no.'

Arnaq reached out her hand to him, but quickly snatched it back when they heard a violent scream in the darkness. She stared at Lasse. The hairs on her arms and the back of her neck stood up.

Lasse's jaw dropped and his eyes shone with fear. 'What the—?' he croaked, looking up at the house.

They heard another scream across the dark plain.

'It's Alma,' he said.

'Yes,' Arnaq said. 'What the hell is going on?'

Lasse shook his head. His breath was rapid and sent clouds of steam into the air. 'Do you think Andreas is being a dick?'

Arnaq shook her head. 'We're going up there now.'

'I have a torch,' he said, rummaging around the bag with the vodka bottles and the orange juice. He found the torch and switched it on. Pointed it at Arnaq.

'Stop it,' she said, holding up her hand.

Alma's shrill voice could be heard in the night again.

'She's calling for help,' Arnaq shouted. 'Get a bloody move on!' She started running towards the house. 'One of them must have stepped through the floor or something.'

Lasse, too, started running and quickly caught up with her. The light from his torch danced around the uneven white terrain in front of them. Their feet sank into the muddy holes between the mounds. The grip of the frost was only superficial—for now.

'Why the hell is Alma the only one screaming?' Lasse panted. He was nearly out of breath. His gaze jumped around between the mounds, Arnaq and the black windows in the house, which was getting closer and closer.

19

The darkness inside the house was solid. Arnaq and Lasse called out to their friends, but there was no reply. They hadn't heard any more screaming as they ran the last stretch across the plain, and the silence when they stopped on the ground floor to listen out for the others was even more ominous.

'What the hell do we do if something bad has happened?' Lasse said, gripping Arnaq's upper arm as they approached the steps leading to the first floor.

Arnaq stopped and looked at him.

He pointed the torch at the dusty old floorboards underneath them.

'We can do sod-all here,' he went on. 'We need to call for help.'

'You've been staring at your dead mobile all day,' Arnaq snapped, looking up the steps. 'We can't contact anyone! Shit, I hope they're having us on, the morons. Lars won't be back until sometime tomorrow.'

Lasse craned his neck and looked up. A scraping sound reached them.

'There. Upstairs,' Arnaq exclaimed. 'Point the light at the steps!'

The wood creaked under their feet as they headed upstairs. The banister was crumbling and some sections had broken off and fallen to the ground floor. They heard the scratching sound again and Arnaq took the last few steps in one long leap. She looked around the dilapidated first floor. Lasse pointed the torch down the two corridors which spread out from the landing they had reached. His breathing was quick and heavy.

'Shine the light into that first room there,' she said, pointing diagonally to her right.

Lasse stepped around her and through the black doorway. 'Oh, no...' He slumped to his knees and clutched his head with the hand holding the torch; the light swept across the ceiling above them.

'What?' Arnaq called out. 'What's happening?' She grabbed the torch from Lasse in order to light up the room. Andreas was lying on his stomach in the middle of the room. His skull had been bashed in, pushing out parts of his brain. His upper body lay in a pool of blood. 'Andreas, Jesus Christ,' Arnaq shrieked. She pulled at Lasse. His face was wet from snot and tears.

'What the hell do we do?' he sobbed.

Arnaq entered the room and shone the torch around it. 'Alma! Alma, for God's...' The words stuck in her throat. She threw herself onto the floor next to her friend.

Alma stared vacantly at her without moving her head.

'What happened, Alma?' Arnaq said, putting the torch on the floor.

Alma said nothing. Her eyes were closed, her breathing shallow. She, too, had received a blow to the head, but not as severe as the one that had killed Andreas. Her hair was covered with blood, but there were no open fractures to her skull.

'Alma, shit,' Arnaq whispered, putting her head close to Alma's forehead. 'We'll help you.'

Alma jerked. She gasped for air, opened her eyes and looked at Arnaq. Then she shook her head very slightly. Her eyes closed again.

Behind them the stairs started to creak. Arnaq looked towards the door. Lasse stared at her. There was a panicky expression in his eyes and he was shaking all over.

'Come over here,' Arnaq whispered.

Lasse hurried towards her and knelt down beside her. He switched off the torch.

Outside the house the wind was rising and the cold air swept through the broken window and into the room. The door had come off its hinges long ago.

There was more creaking from the stairs.

Arnaq had grabbed Alma's hand. She could hear Lasse hyperventilating. The tears were flowing down her cheeks and she was finding it hard to breathe.

Then she heard footsteps from the corridor. The crunching sound of shoes or boots stepping on the filthy floor. There was no light other than what penetrated from the outside.

The sound stopped for a moment, only to return as a big, dark silhouette that loomed in the doorway. The silhouette grunted and took a step into the room.

Arnaq switched on the torch and pointed it straight at the man. He shook his head in irritation and raised a hand in front of his face so all she could see was his short hair.

Lasse screamed and jumped up to strike the man, but he was instantly floored by a hammer blow so powerful that it split open his skull.

The torch slipped from Arnaq's hand as she looked down at herself. Her face and coat were spattered with blood. The circle of light on the wall reflected back into the room where Lasse lay completely limp next to Andreas.

Arnaq looked at her hands. So much blood. She hadn't realised that she was screaming, but stopped in order to get her breath back and was overcome with nausea. She vomited all over herself before she managed to lean forwards.

Alma stared emptily at her.

Out of the corner of her eye Arnaq saw the big man pick up Lasse's body and toss it on top of Andreas.

'We need the girl,' the man mumbled to himself, while softly swinging the heavy copper hammer he was holding in his hand.

TUPILAK

20

The sun hung low over the mountains behind the broad mouth of the fjord west of Nuuk. In less than half an hour it would be gone completely. Its dying rays cast an orange glow so strong that nothing in this last, short hour of the day could retain its own colour; even the snow on the growlers lit up in warm hues.

Matthew sat between two beached growlers, enjoying the clean, pure air from the cold sea. Jakob's many notes about the age, colour and breath of the ice had taught him to love it deeply. These days he could not walk past one of the big, stranded lumps of glacier ice without breathing at its icy skin and feeling it breathe back.

He would often pop a small lump of ice into his mouth and feel how the cold drops were resurrected as they came into contact with his tongue after being trapped as ice for over a hundred thousand years.

Jakob called the lumps of ice time machines, because the water which constituted them had last been liquid in so remote a past that *Homo sapiens* had been but one of many species of humans on the Earth.

Matthew picked up a stone and placed it on top of the notebook that was resting on his thigh. It was the book he was writing for Emily. He hadn't got very far with it yet; he wrote solely to feel that she had lived. She would have been about one year old, if he and Tine hadn't been in that car crash. One year old. Perhaps she would have started to walk by now, even learned to say a few words.

A chunk of ice broke off a growler close to him and the sound made him look up. He moved the stone and closed the notebook. He had left his mobile at home so he could think without distraction. His editor was nagging him for another story about the dead men in Ittoqqortoormiit, but Matthew had written himself into a dead end and needed to talk to Ottesen in order to find a way out. There was something about Nukannguaq's insistence that demons and pills were mixed up with everything that could be the key to unlocking it all.

He found his cigarettes and lit one. The smoke wrapped itself around his face. As soon as Arnaq came back, he would ask her if she would like to go with him to Ittoqqortoormiit to look for their father. Even if he turned out to be the crazed killer that Briggs had warned him against tracking down, he would like to see him with his own eyes before passing the information about him on to anyone else.

Matthew threw aside his cigarette and rubbed his eyes. His fingers gave off an acrid smell of smoke. He looked down at the stones, then picked up the discarded cigarette and returned it to the packet so as not to litter. He got up and started walking back over the dry mounds and pieces of rock which led away from the shore. He had arranged to meet Tupaarnaq at the Katuaq Art Centre, where he could also pick up some takeaway food. He didn't know what she had been doing all day, but neither did he care; she was back in Nuuk and that was all that mattered.

•

It took Matthew twenty-five minutes to walk from Ørneøen to Katuaq, but he had only got as far as the corner of the dilapidated Block 1 when he spotted Tupaarnaq waving to him outside the Nuuk Centre. He waved back and smiled, but soon realised that she wasn't waving because she was pleased to see him.

'Where have you been?' she declared in a loud voice when he was still some distance away from her.

He checked his watch. 'We're not due to meet for another fifteen minutes?'

'I know,' she said, nodding in the direction of the city centre. 'But we've got to head over to Else's right away.'

'Why? What about our food?'

'That'll have to wait,' Tupaarnaq said. 'Lars couldn't find them when he went to pick them up...your sister and her friends.'

'In Færingehavn?'

'Yes.'

'So they're not back yet?'

'No, they're not, but...' She hesitated and looked away. 'We'll talk about it once we get to Else's...You and I can head out there tomorrow at first light.'

'What aren't you telling me?' he demanded. His fingers had instantly started rubbing the missing wedding ring. 'What do you know?'

She looked him firmly in the eye. 'There's blood out there...A lot of blood.'

Matthew's heart plummeted. He knew he should have brought Arnaq back when he and Tupaarnaq went to see them. They should have brought all four of them back to Nuuk.

'We're also the last people to see them,' Tupaarnaq continued. 'So the police want to talk to us as soon as possible.'

Matthew shook his head. 'That'll have to wait.' He looked at Tupaarnaq. 'Could we go now? This evening?'

The corners of her mouth moved downwards as she scanned the sky. There was little light left and within the hour it would be completely dark. 'Only if we drive slowly,' she said. 'But we could do it.'

'Right then, if you fetch your rifle, I'll run home to get my mobile and the keys for the boat, okay?'

Tupaarnaq nodded slowly. 'What about Else? She's scared and waiting for us.'

'Shit...Yes...We'll meet at her flat before we go. Then she'll know we've gone.'

21

Matthew and Tupaarnaq walked together to the steps behind the blue community hall. Tupaarnaq turned right up towards Radiofjeldet and the low housing blocks where Else lived, while Matthew made a beeline for the grey and yellow apartment block that housed his flat.

He glanced up at the sky, where a few stars were already twinkling although it was only early evening.

The glass door to his stairwell was ajar, as it often was. The man who lived on the first floor had a small black cat, and although he wasn't supposed to, he would often wedge open the front door so the cat could run in and out.

It took Matthew only a few minutes to fetch the keys to the boat and his mobile from his flat, then lock his door so that he could make his way to Else's. He couldn't be bothered to wait for the lift, so he ran down the two flights of stairs and continued swiftly out of the glass door.

'Hello?'

Matthew turned towards the voice. It was coming from the blue terraced houses across the narrow road from his apartment block. He couldn't see anyone over there. The building had been condemned because of mould and there was no light under the slanted half roof which spanned the whole building and the eleven front doors that led to the empty houses.

'Hello?' the voice called out again. 'Matthew?'

Matthew took a step backwards and narrowed his eyes. Was there someone across the road?

'Are you Matthew Cave?'

'Yes,' Matthew said. The voice from the darkness was deep. A powerful male voice. 'I'm afraid I haven't got time to talk right now,' Matthew said. 'Why do you want to know?'

'Come over here,' the man said.

'No, now is not a good time,' Matthew said apologetically. 'I really have to go...Family emergency.'

'Yes,' the man said quickly. 'It's about your sister.'

'My sister?' Matthew took a step forward. 'What do you know about my sister? Come out so I can see you.'

'No,' the man said. 'You come over here or I'll drive off.'

Matthew exhaled slowly. 'I'm not sure I feel like doing that.'

'All right, then, I'm off.'

'Wait!' Matthew walked alongside the ditch next to the road and jumped across it. He kept looking at the figure in the darkness under the half roof. All he could see was the man's legs.

'Who are you?' Matthew said when he was only a short distance from the gallery that ran along the building.

'I'm Olí.'

Matthew stopped and tried looking under the half roof. 'What do you know about Arnaq?'

'Arnaq?' the voice echoed.

'My sister,' Matthew said, starting to lose patience. He took a step in the direction of the voice.

At that moment the figure threw a handful of sand in Matthew's face, blinding him.

Startled, Matthew stumbled backwards. The big man grabbed

Matthew's wrist and twisted his arm behind his back, while another big hand clamped itself across his mouth. Matthew could taste salty skin and tried fighting back with his free arm. He screamed behind the hand as his other arm was pressed so hard into his back that he thought it would dislocate. Saliva from his mouth was smeared against the rough hand now gripping him so violently that his cheeks were squashed against his teeth.

'We need him alive,' the man mumbled to himself as he brusquely pushed Matthew towards a car. 'Alive...I get it.'

The man continued to mumble as he forced Matthew to lie down on the gravel in front of the car. He removed his hand from Matthew's mouth and shoved a gag so hard down Matthew's throat that he nearly threw up. Then he pulled Matthew back up to standing and slipped a sack over his head. Matthew could feel the sack being tied tightly around his neck, and the next moment he was bundled onto the back seat of the car.

The man had got into the driver's seat and started the car immediately. Matthew tried to breathe through his nose, but it was filled with snot and the gag blocked his mouth. He snorted and felt snot pouring down his face as he dragged air into his lungs.

The car rounded a corner and Matthew fell onto his side. He tried to brace his fall, but he couldn't get hold of anything and had practically ended up at the bottom of the car when he received a strong blow to his ribs.

'Sit still,' the man ordered him from the front.

He hit him again, but merely brushed him this time. The man couldn't reach very far back and Matthew had managed to get himself back onto the seat and to push himself against the door furthest away from the driver. Air hissed in and out through his half-blocked nostrils. The window felt cold against the sack. He tried digging around his mouth with his fingers to get a hold of the fabric, but the sack was too tight for him to grip anything.

He could hear the big man grunt in the front. At times he could make out words; other times it was mostly sounds. The word 'alive' was repeated. As was the word 'kill'.

Matthew squashed his face up against the window in the hope that someone might see him. He also pressed the palms of his hands against the cold glass. He forced snot out of his nostrils a second time, trying to breathe. The snot mixed with the sweat running down his face.

The engine stopped and Matthew heard the man get out of the car and slam the door shut behind him. He shook his head and tried to hear what was going on. Soon afterwards his own door was opened so brusquely that Matthew nearly tumbled out. Big hands grabbed his arms and yanked him out of the seat. His arms and shoulders hurt and he tried to scream, but not a single sound made it past the cloth. He buckled in a coughing fit and fell onto the ground. He couldn't breathe and was aware that he was close to blacking out. Sweat was pouring down his back and chest. He flailed his arms about him and tore at the hood. He shook his head. He snorted again, but could no longer unblock his nostrils.

Pain shot through his arm as a heavy foot trod on it. 'Lie still,' the man sneered angrily.

Matthew was aware of the string being loosened, the hood pulled off his head and the fabric gag yanked out of his mouth. He rolled onto his side and coughed violently into the gravel. Gasped for air and then spluttered again. His clothes stuck to his body and he could taste his own mucus.

Matthew looked up at the man. He was about two metres tall, but his face was concealed behind a tight-fitting black balaclava. Only his eyes were visible, and they were difficult to make out in the darkness. The man started walking towards the sea.

'Where's my sister?' Matthew shouted, trying to get to his feet. His arm was twitching with pain.

The man turned and looked at Matthew. 'You're coming with me.'

'What? Where?'

The man merely heaved a sigh and carried on walking.

Matthew's fingers clawed at the gravel and he got hold of a broad, sharp stone. The moment the man came back and bent down over him in order to pull him up, he smashed the stone into the man's face as hard as he could. He only managed to hit the back of his head, but it was enough.

The man roared as he took a step backwards and clutched his head. 'Alive,' he snarled. 'Alive.'

Matthew got up, reaching the car in a few strides and jumping into the driver's side. He quickly locked the car, then fumbled for the key. There it was. The man had run up to the car as well and was pulling at the door so forcefully that the chassis wobbled. Matthew screamed, put the car in reverse and hit the accelerator. He couldn't see much behind him, but he knew that the gravel road which led up to the main road was straight and wide.

The big man chased the car. Matthew looked at him through the windscreen. He seemed clumsy and slow.

Matthew eased his foot off the accelerator and reversed onto the main road. The big man had just about caught up with the car by the time Matthew slammed the car into gear and accelerated past the man towards the town.

Just before the Nuussuaq roundabout he pulled over on the wide road and took out his mobile.

Where are you now? he texted Ottesen, before picking up the thread from Tupaarnaq: *I was attacked. Need to talk to Ottesen. I'll meet you later at Else's.*

22

'The car belongs to Apollo,' Ottesen said. 'Only he wasn't your driver because Apollo isn't that tall, and I'm pretty sure he doesn't drive around attacking people or their sisters.'

'So the car was stolen?'

'Definitely…I'll call Apollo so that he can get it back.' Ottesen paused. 'Lots of people leave their keys in the ignition round here. After all, there are no roads leading out of Nuuk, so if a car gets nicked it usually turns up pretty quickly.'

'Shit,' Matthew said and turned to Ottesen, who looked like he was starting to get cold in his tight-fitting, pale green running clothes. Matthew's gaze continued to the low, dark brown wooden building which housed Nuuk's police station. 'Will you carry out forensic tests and all that?'

'Yes, of course. Apollo won't get his car back until we've been through it.'

'I thought I was going to die,' Matthew said, more quietly now. 'He was so strong…incredibly strong.'

'And you didn't catch a glimpse of his face?'

'No, but like I said, he was two metres tall and very strong, and he wore clog boots and spoke with an accent…He can't be that hard to find.' Matthew looked at Ottesen. 'He said his name was Olí—there can't be many of those about.'

'I've lived here for almost forty years,' Ottesen said. 'And I don't remember ever meeting a single person called Olí, but then again, I'm willing to bet you a lot of money that his real name isn't Olí or that he lives in Nuuk...There was probably a reason he wanted to put you on a boat.'

'I think he's Faroese,' Matthew said.

Ottesen nodded. 'He might well be...The only Faroese that tall that I know of is the guy who lives out by the old Polaroil bunker point across the fjord from Færingehavn, but his name is Bárdur.'

'We need to talk to him,' Matthew said. 'Is it close to Færingehavn?'

'Yes, by boat, but not by land. The fjord is deep and it would take you several days to walk from Polaroil to Færingehavn across the mountains.' Ottesen shook his head. 'Bárdur tends to keep to himself, but we need to have a chat to him about all of this...I'm sure he knows which boats go in and out of there.' Ottesen patted the roof of the car. 'We've already had officers out there, Matt, and they didn't find anything on his side of the fjord.'

'But it's true that you found blood in the big grey house in Færingehavn?'

'We don't know if it's human blood yet.'

Matthew covered his eyes with his hand, then let it slide in front of his mouth. 'I was out there...I could have brought them home.'

At that moment one of Nuuk Police's dark blue SUVs pulled up and stopped alongside the stolen car.

'Nothing,' Rakel said the moment she opened the door of the SUV.

'Did you check the houses across from my flat and the area behind the public swimming pool?'

Rakel raised her eyebrows apologetically as she nodded. 'There was nothing...Sorry.'

'It's all right.' Ottesen bent down and greeted the other officer in the SUV. 'Hello, Frederik.' Then he straightened up again. 'Can you please go and see Apollo and ask him what he has been doing today, seeing as he hasn't noticed that his car is missing?'

Rakel nodded and pulled the door shut.

Ottesen placed his hand on Matthew's shoulder. 'We have two other patrol cars out looking for a two-metre-tall Faroese man.'

'I know…Shit. I've got a really bad feeling about my sister and her friends.' Matthew hesitated for a moment. 'That night Tupaarnaq and I were attacked in Færingehavn it was also by some giant, but I saw even less then than I did just now because it was so bloody dark. But we were attacked in the same house. Arrgghh…I should have brought them home.'

'Apart from that one day when the two of you headed out there, nothing ever happens in Færingehavn,' Ottesen said. He shook his head. 'It makes no sense for someone to sail out there in order to…'

Matthew looked at Ottesen. 'How much blood was there?'

Ottesen shrugged. 'A little blood always goes a long way, Matt.'

'I really want to meet that Bárdur guy,' Matthew said, looking down. 'Preferably now.'

'That's a job for the police, my friend.'

'But she's my sister! She could be dead…' His voice ebbed out. His fingers fumbled for the pocket with the wedding ring. He felt its roundness through the fabric and pressed his fingers against it.

'Matt…' Ottesen hesitated. 'There's another matter I need to ask you about. We've been contacted by an American officer.'

'And?'

'He says that the US military is thinking about resuming its search for a marine who deserted and vanished without a trace in 1990. It was the name of the marine that made me think of you. Tom Roger Cave. Do you know him? After all, you told me your father was American.'

'That's my father,' Matthew said. The thoughts jumped around his head. Briggs must have had the case reopened.

'Are you in contact with him?' Ottesen said.

Matthew shook his head. 'I haven't seen him since I was barely four years old, but in the meantime he had Arnaq, so he must have lived in Nuuk once.'

'Exactly,' Ottesen said. 'Except he never registered here officially. He lived off the grid, as they say. And that was pretty much all we could tell the Americans.'

Matthew looked up at the black night sky. The air was cold, the temperature just below zero.

'Did you know that he shot two men before he went AWOL?' Ottesen said. 'Your father, I mean.'

'Yes,' Matthew said.

'So when you asked about the case in Jakob's house, you already knew that it was about your own father?'

'I had only just found out.'

Ottesen squatted down on his haunches and rocked back and forth to stretch his muscles. 'It was pretty violent, the way it was told to me...that business in Thule. The American officer warned us to approach your father with caution—should we find him, that is.'

'The case is similar to the one with the dead men in Ittoqqortoormiit,' Matthew said. His gaze ranged over the Katuaq Art Centre on the far side of the square between the police station and the government building. 'In my opinion it's hard to tell who shot who.'

'Oh, the American officer seemed pretty clear,' Ottesen said. 'Your father shot the other men...Besides, they were shot with your father's pistol, and both that pistol and your father have been missing since the killings.'

'Maybe,' Matthew said, throwing up his hands. 'I don't know, okay...'

'No, no…Of course not.' Ottesen stood up again. 'It's fine…I've had the survivor from Ittoqqortoormiit arrested.'

'Nukannguaq?'

'Yes, that's him…We've put an officer by his bed while we wait for the technical evidence.'

Matthew's mobile started buzzing in his pocket; seconds later Ottesen's mobile rang inside his waist pack.

Matthew pulled out his mobile. It was Tupaarnaq. She was calling from Else's flat.

Ottesen had already rung off.

'Jakob has been killed!' Matthew said, looking blankly at Ottesen.

'Come with me,' Ottesen said. 'I'm driving over there right now.'

23

The light in Jakob's living room stood in stark contrast to the darkness and the cold outside.

Matthew followed Ottesen inside, but stopped when Ottesen stuck out his arm behind him.

'Probably best if you stay here, Matt,' he said. 'Me stomping about in here in my running clothes is bad enough.'

'Hi, Matt.'

Matthew was surprised to find Rakel here. She held out a pair of blue plastic shoe covers to him.

She smiled slightly, but her eyes were sad. 'We hadn't even reached Apollo when—'

'What happened?' Matthew said.

Rakel withdrew her hand with the plastic shoe covers, as Matthew didn't seem to notice them. 'You'd better stay out in the hall.'

She walked around Matthew and joined Ottesen. Three other officers were present. All in uniform.

Jakob was sitting in the middle of the room in his old armchair. He was wearing his threadbare brown cords and a blue shirt. He was leaning to one side and it looked as if he had tried to get up to defend himself. The top button of his shirt had been torn loose and his shirt was pulled up on one side. His head lolled against his chest.

'Why don't you come outside?'

Matthew hadn't realised that Rakel had come back to him. She looked just as rattled as he felt.

'It will do you good,' she added.

His gaze jumped back to Jakob. His shirt had been slashed by a knife, which had been plunged into his lower abdomen and then pulled upwards, as if the killer had attempted to gut Jakob from his groin to his chest. He looked like Lyberth on Tupaarnaq's floor two months ago, and the dead men from the 1973 case. Except here the knife had only cut a hole in Jakob's abdomen rather than opened him all the way up. Matthew could see a little of Jakob's intestines in the wound; on the floor by the side of the armchair was a puddle of something that very much resembled vomit.

Rakel grabbed Matthew's arm. 'Come on, Matt, it's time we left.'

The air outside felt simultaneously damp and cold. Police cars, ambulances and fire engines were parked along the road. They had a habit of all turning up regardless of the nature of the emergency because their pay was based purely on the number of callouts. The blue lights disturbed the darkness. There were many voices.

'Why don't you come for a walk with me?' Rakel said. 'Let's get away from all the noise here.'

Matthew nodded and they started walking down the street. Around them lay lots of wooden houses, which in daylight added colour to the area of Myggedalen.

They turned down Stephen Møllerip Aqqutaa and Matthew looked across to the small pond which had been dug back in colonial times.

'Do you think Abelsen did it?' Rakel said. 'I mean…with the knife?'

'No,' Matthew said quietly, but then he shook his head. 'Was that vomit on the floor?'

'Yes, somebody threw up right next to...the deceased.'

'Could it have been Jakob himself?' Matthew's voice failed him. 'Because of the pain?'

'I don't think so...it's in the wrong place, if it was him.'

'So you think it's the killer's?'

'What kind of killer throws up right in front of his victim?'

'Well, not Abelsen.'

'No, that's my point.'

Matthew found a cigarette in his pocket. His hands were shaking so badly he couldn't operate the lighter.

'Breathe in.' Rakel took it from him and held the flame close to the cigarette. 'You really ought to quit that, Matt.'

He nodded and exhaled. 'Yes...But not today.'

'No, probably not.' She put the lighter back in his pocket.

The glow of the cigarette lit up the darkness. Matthew looked at Rakel. 'Who the hell would do something like that?'

She gave a light shrug. 'You would know that better than me, wouldn't you?'

Matthew looked down. 'Have you ever killed anyone?'

'No.' She shook her head and her ponytail bounced from side to side. 'Were you thinking about your father and the dead men in Thule?'

'I was thinking about me,' Matthew said, blowing the smoke out hard. 'After all, I killed Ulrik.'

'Ulrik was my friend,' Rakel said quietly. 'And a bloody good one...I don't want to talk about it. But you didn't have a choice, did you? So it's not the same thing.'

Matthew took another drag on his cigarette. 'What if Arnaq is dead? I didn't bring her back when I could have. I could have saved her life...And what about my wife and the little girl in her belly? I was driving when they died.'

'It's still not the same as killing, Matthew,' Rakel said. She had stopped walking; her voice had softened to a whisper. 'I didn't know that you used to be married. I'm so sorry to hear…I don't know what to say. But being involved in an accident isn't the same as killing someone.'

'But if I hadn't been driving the car that day…If I hadn't left Arnaq and her friends behind in Færingehavn.'

Rakel placed her hand on Matthew's arm. 'That has nothing to do with killing and it's completely wrong to think like that, Matt. Whereas your father; he shot two men in the head. Now that's a totally different matter.'

'Ottesen says that you have planes searching the area around Færingehavn.'

'Yes. We'll keep looking until we find them.'

'Dead or alive…'

'I'm sure your sister is alive.' Rakel's voice grew quiet again as she spoke about Arnaq.

'Why?' Matthew tried to catch her eye, but she avoided him.

Rakel let go of his arm and looked across the pond towards the emergency vehicles outside Jakob's house. 'We should be getting back.'

'Are you just saying that about Arnaq? Or did you see something out there?'

Rakel sighed and ran her hand over her face. 'I don't know… Given how it looked…I don't know. To me it looked like two killings and two kidnappings, and I have a hunch that the boys are dead.'

'What makes you say that?'

Rakel looked away.

'You're thinking that girls can be raped?'

'Yes.'

'I have to go there now.'

'You need to talk to Ottesen first and nothing can happen until tomorrow morning.'

The blue flashing lights grew brighter as Matthew and Rakel

returned to the house.

'If you don't want to be alone tonight,' Rakel ventured cautiously, 'then you're welcome to stay at my place…You must be really upset by everything that's happening right now. We can carry on talking in an hour when I get off duty.'

'Thank you,' Matthew said. 'Right now my brain is mush…I think I'll be staring at the ceiling all night.'

'We can talk all night, if you like,' Rakel said. 'I usually go to the gym after work, but it's too late today, and I just want to go home. You can sleep on the sofa, if you're able to sleep. The kids are with their father.'

'You have children?'

'Yes, two of them.' She smiled. Her upper front teeth were set back slightly from the rest. Her black eyes started shining again. 'Minik and Paarnuuna.'

'Lovely.' He looked briefly at her face. 'You must have had them young?'

'I was twenty-one when I had Paarnuuna. They're the greatest kids in the world.'

'I would like to meet them one day.'

'We should go for ice cream some time,' Rakel said. 'A day the kids are home, I mean.'

'Yes, let's do that,' Matthew said. 'Right now all I want to do is lie in the darkness on my own.' He looked up. Ottesen was standing outside Jakob's house, holding his mobile.

'What are you two up to?'

'Shooting the breeze,' Rakel said quickly.

'Probably a good idea,' Ottesen said, nodding towards the house. 'We found plenty of DNA evidence in there which will help our investigation, including vomit and some hairs from under Jakob's nails.'

'Black hair?' Matthew wanted to know.

'No.' Ottesen shook his head. 'Just as blond as yours.'

24

The water swayed softly underneath him. It was calming and alien at the same time. It felt cold. As though he was floating in the sea. The waves caressed his skin in long, gentle strokes. They felt like hands. Two hands massaging him firmly but softly, making his skin tingle.

The fingertips dug softly into his skin in calm, languid movements. The hands grabbed him and turned him over so that he was facing down. Rakel was lying right underneath him. She was naked and her eyes smiled inscrutably. Her mouth was open in a broad smile so he could see her teeth; the two front ones, which were set back a little from the others, drew his gaze. Freckles spread out around her smile. Her eyes were black, alive. They looked into him. They seemed expectant.

She nudged his chest and swam downwards. Through the water. For a moment he flailed his arms before realising that he was floating. Below him he could see all of her naked body. Her hips. Her small breasts. Her strong shoulders. Her hair was so dark brown that it seemed black as it flowed out into the sea in slow, undulating movements.

She beckoned him and he dived down towards her. Her smile broadened and fine lines appeared in the skin around her eyes.

He stared at her naked body. She moved her arms and legs in a sensuous, dancing motion. She swayed from side to side, pivoting at her waist.

Her lips whispered to him, but he couldn't understand her. His chest was starting to feel tight. He needed air. He turned his head and looked up towards the surface. It was meant to be very near, but now it was nothing but a flickering light somewhere far above him. He started to panic.

He could feel her hands again. Exploring his body. She pressed herself close against his skin. Her face was in front of his. There was no fear in her eyes. No death. They shone right into him while her lips covered his mouth. Her legs locked themselves around his hips. Her hands cradled his head and she caressed his ears with her fingers. He gave into the kiss. Letting in her tongue. Letting in the air. He breathed through her kiss.

.

Matthew sat up in bed with a jolt. The flat was completely dark. There was no light in the night. Slowly he began to calm down.

'What the hell,' he whispered to himself, and got out of bed. He had a strong erection, but ignored it.

He found his cigarettes and pushed open the door to the balcony.

He tried to fight the lust the dream had left him with. It was a long time since he had touched a woman. Eighteen months, almost. After the accident he had been sure that it would never happen again, but now he had doubts. The smoke was blowing into the living room and he dropped the cigarette into the big bowl of water and cigarette ends. He found his mobile and looked up Rakel on Facebook. She was pretty. More than pretty. But she wasn't the one who distracted his thoughts; it might have been her for a brief moment, but not deep down within him. Not deep inside, where Tupaarnaq's eyes, freckles and lips had latched onto him.

He put on a jumper and sat down on the sofa. He shouldn't have dozed off. There was far too much going on. The images of the injuries to Jakob's stomach chased each other around his thoughts. At times he imagined Arnaq cut up in the same way, in the same chair. Then Tine in the wrecked car. Ulrik with blood foaming from his mouth.

Matthew grabbed the notebook that he wrote to Emily in and opened it. At first he couldn't concentrate, but after closing his eyes and taking a few deep breaths the letters and the words began to appear.

25

The autumn snow had melted, apart from the odd patch, but it was only a matter of days or weeks before winter would strike the small, abandoned town again.

Matthew looked at Tupaarnaq's back. Her stride was strong and long. Her rifle hung over her shoulder and her dark jacket.

They had agreed with Ottesen that they wouldn't enter any area cordoned off by the police, but it wasn't a promise that they would be able to keep. The whole house was cordoned off, and they hadn't sailed all this way for nothing.

'Shall I go first?' Tupaarnaq had stopped at the cordon. The flimsy plastic police tape flapped in the wind. 'That way you're prepared.'

'Rakel and Ottesen said too much yesterday, so I'm ready.' He looked up at the windows. 'After all, she's my sister and I just want to find her.'

'You're never ready for blood,' Tupaarnaq said through gritted teeth as she lifted up the plastic tape so that they could slip under it. 'You think you're ready, but no...'

Matthew looked into Tupaarnaq's eyes for a moment. When the

sun didn't reflect in them, they were as black as the darkest night.

'Remember,' Tupaarnaq went on. 'Don't pick anything up in there…It's useless as evidence, if we touch it.'

'I won't touch anything.'

'I'm talking to your subconscious,' she said, releasing the tape, which sprang back into place between two rusty iron spears. 'It won't react rationally to blood.'

'There's no need for you to freak me out completely before we've even set foot inside,' Matthew snapped, and walked up the few steps to the external landing, which ran like a gallery along the front of the main building of the dilapidated house.

'Yes, there is.' She took her rifle from her shoulder, held it in front of her and pulled back the bolt to slip a cartridge into the chamber. 'And watch your step.'

The wind howled through the empty first floor above them. Not a single window was intact in any of the three wings, and the doors at the end of each corridor were missing. The wallpaper was coming off the walls and plaster was falling from the ceilings. You could see exposed wood in several places, and over the years a palette of tired colours had formed in big patches. There were crumbling books and magazines on the first landing, mixed with plaster and dirt. In several places empty bakelite fittings hung from the stained ceilings.

'It's the first room to your right,' Tupaarnaq said.

Matthew looked at her. 'We'll check all the rooms.'

'Of course, but you should always start with the one you fear the most, otherwise your fear will dull your senses while you look at the other rooms.' She looked at him. 'In you go.'

The floor of the small room was covered by a thick layer of dirt, small pieces of plaster, and wooden splinters from the wall. A rusty single bed frame with no mattress was pushed up against one wall. The biggest bloodstain was in the middle of the room. It had run in several directions and was the width of the bed. In front of the bed was a smaller puddle. Much of the larger stain had been smeared. Most of the blood had seeped through the floor.

Matthew slumped to the floor with his back against the wall near the window. He stared impotently at the sloping wall, which reached across the bed and was stained with damp patches.

Tupaarnaq squatted down on her haunches and studied the stains in the middle of the floor. She held her rifle in one hand so the butt rested on the floor as she looked back and forth between the two bloodstains.

'Two people died in here,' she said.

Matthew looked at the bloodstains in front of her. He had to make an effort to speak. 'Two?'

'There's blood from two people here.' She pointed to a small piece of wood lying at the edge of the dried blood pool. 'When you've slaughtered a lot of animals, you learn how blood moves, and right here two people lost their lives.'

'You're sure that they're dead?' Matthew's voice was quivering.

She nodded. 'There's a lot of blood here. I've seen men as well as animals die from losing less blood than there is here. The two who lay here were dead before they were moved.'

'What about the last stain?' Matthew said. 'Over by the bed...Is that also from one of those two people?'

Tupaarnaq shook her head. 'I don't think so. It doesn't seem logical.'

A shiver went down Matthew's spine.

'What did Rakel say to you yesterday?' Tupaarnaq wanted to know.

'She thinks that the boys are dead and that someone took the girls.'

'Why?'

'Because...girls are raped.'

'Let's see,' Tupaarnaq said quietly. 'I can tell from the dirt that someone sat here. The girls possibly.'

Matthew nodded slowly. The same thought had crossed his mind when he examined the floor at the end of the bed. He wished more than anything in the world that his sister was alive, even if it meant that the others were most likely dead. The thought that he wanted the others to be dead hurt, but he did. Rather them than Arnaq.

Tupaarnaq looked at the spot, then trained her gaze on the corridor. 'Either there was more than one killer or he was incredibly strong. There are no drag marks here or in the corridor. No blood traces apart from in this room.' She turned her head. 'I agree, I think the girls are alive.'

Matthew pushed himself up off the floor. 'Let's keep looking. There must be traces of them somewhere.' He surveyed the arm of the fjord through the broken window. 'And we need to have a word with that Faroese guy from the bunker point when we're done here,' he added. He followed Tupaarnaq out into the corridor. 'The guy who attacked me was also very big, and perhaps he killed Jakob just before...or just after attacking me.' He shook his head.

'The one we met when we were out here with Abelsen was also big,' Tupaarnaq said. 'A giant...Are there other men as tall as him in Nuuk?'

Matthew shrugged. 'I've only met one, a former US officer now working for the Greenlandic government. But there might be more.'

'It's possible,' Tupaarnaq said. 'But it's not as common to be two metres tall up here as it is in Denmark.'

They became aware of the sound of a helicopter. Matthew and Tupaarnaq rushed down the stairs and outside. The sound grew louder and soon a red AS 350 helicopter flew across the ground and began to circle. It went so low that they could see the pilot as well as the two officers inside it.

Matthew didn't recognise the pilot, but one of the officers was Rakel. He waved to her just as the helicopter veered to the right and continued along the outskirts of the abandoned town, after which it flew across the quay at low speed while it searched the area.

'I think they're searching from the air only,' Matthew said, repressing the thought of him and Rakel in the sea.

26

Tupaarnaq looked up at the sky, which was heavy with charcoal clouds. 'I've spent far too many winters in a Danish prison.'

Matthew looked at her. He was busy securing the rubber dinghy.

'The days are shorter up here in the winter,' she continued. 'In a month we'll have just a couple of hours of daylight around noon at most. I've missed that.'

'You've missed the darkness?'

'Call it what you like,' she said. 'To me it's not just darkness; it's also light.' She looked at him. 'You haven't experienced a Greenlandic winter yet, have you?'

'No, I only arrived this spring,' Matthew said, taking in the many abandoned houses.

'I'd like to show you the light in the darkness,' she went on. 'Except that's not how it works; you have to find your own light. Or it won't shine.'

It had taken Matthew and Tupaarnaq a couple of hours to search every building. They examined the ones around the plain as well as the warehouses. They had been inside most of them before. Two months earlier they had been looking for a little girl who had gone missing in 1973. Some old 8mm films had led them to search

Færingehavn. The footage showed how Najak had been slowly broken down until she died.

The Air Greenland helicopter had circled the area for almost two hours before it had flown off.

Shortly afterwards Matthew and Tupaarnaq had rowed the dinghy back to the boat and climbed on board so that they could reach the Polaroil bunker point before it got too dark. The light had already started to fade.

Snow started to fall on and around the boat. Matthew went inside the wheelhouse to join Tupaarnaq, who had started the engine.

'Right,' she said. 'You can drive us over there.'

'Me? You want me to take the wheel?'

'Yes, there are few places where the water is as calm as here, so why not?'

Matthew nodded and smiled.

'It's not hard,' she went on. 'And you did okay last time.'

'And the rocks?'

'You can see those on the monitor, but I can watch it for you as long as you drive slowly.'

Matthew pushed the shiny throttle upwards and felt how the bow of the boat rose immediately as it carved its way through the water.

Outside the wheelhouse, the snow was falling more densely. Tupaarnaq flicked a small switch, which got the windscreen wipers going.

'Will the sea freeze over here?' Matthew asked, accelerating with caution.

'No, I'm guessing it's like Tasiilaq,' Tupaarnaq said. 'The tides are too strong for the ice to set.'

The boat shot across the sea. On the small screen next to the wheel Matthew could see that they were cruising at between twelve and fourteen knots. He knew that Tupaarnaq could easily get the boat to go thirty knots, and more in calm weather.

'I would like to hear more about Tasiilaq,' Matthew said. He pushed the throttle a little more so they reached twenty knots, but then pulled it back again. The sea bashing against the hull of the boat felt powerful, even at that speed.

'I've already said plenty,' Tupaarnaq said, and pulled the wheel slightly. Matthew's hands followed and the boat made a soft curve across the sea.

'I was thinking about the landscape and so on.'

'The landscape? Yes, it's beautiful, but my life…Well, there was a lot of hunting and blood even before…' She pointed ashore. 'We can dock over there. The bunker point is built for big ships.'

Matthew followed her finger with his eyes. He had seen the Polaroil bunker point from a distance before, but this would be the first time he would be going ashore there.

It looked like any big installation in a small Danish coastal town. The big grey oil silos and the many pipes which connected the tanks and the plant by the quay belonged to an era when both big freighters and trawlers would call at Færingehavn to unload and refuel. White painted steps led up the rocks behind the bunker point, and although the place felt abandoned, it was also evident that someone was looking after it. The woodwork was freshly painted and the residential buildings that could be seen from the sea were all intact. As far as Matthew knew, the bunker point was still active and was maintained by just one man, Bárdur, who spent most of the year out here alone on this lump of rock.

'I would go crazy if I had to live here on my own,' Matthew said.

'Maybe he has.'

At the water's edge the bunker point was divided into several smaller sections. A tall bunker for very big ships, and then a lower section for smaller boats like theirs. In addition, a couple of pontoons stretched out into the sea, where small boats could tie up.

'Move over.' Tupaarnaq took over the wheel and the throttle

from Matthew and straightened up the boat so that it glided calmly towards and then bumped into the pontoon.

Tupaarnaq pushed open the door and stepped out into the snow.

Matthew crawled after her up onto the wide wooden pontoon. The fuel hoses were so long that they crisscrossed each other over most of the pontoon. She twisted one free and wrenched the nozzle from the stand.

'See if you can find the guy who lives here,' she said, dragging the hose towards the boat.

Matthew nodded and straightened up. He looked towards the first house. It was low and red, made from wood, with a grey roof and white window frames. Not far behind it lay another building of more than three storeys, but otherwise identical; a little further behind that was a tall, square building, which looked like an office block or small production factory.

On the quay itself was a cabin constructed from corrugated fibro-cement sheets. The door at one end was ajar and near it was a sign listing the opening hours. There was also a lifebuoy, a ladder and warning signs that read 'No Open Flame'.

Matthew leapt up a few steps and walked towards the cabin.

'Hello?' he called out. All the signs were in Danish. 'Is anyone here?' He had reached the open doorway and could see inside the dark room behind the iron door. 'We're refuelling. Where can we pay?' Matthew popped his head around the door. 'Hello?'

'Is anyone there?' said Tupaarnaq, who had come up to him from behind.

'Doesn't look like it.'

'Let's take a closer look.' She peered up towards the houses. 'This place gives me the creeps.'

They followed the steps up to the first house, and then onto the next as the first one was locked. The rooms inside it looked like offices, but it was hard to imagine them being in use now, although they looked like they had only just been abandoned.

The second building seemed more promising. There was furniture. A living room with a television and a stereo. Everything looked dated, but there was stuff on the tables and everything looked to be in use.

Matthew knocked on the front door. There was no postbox, but a small nameplate next to the door knocker said 'Bárdur Hjaltalín'.

Tupaarnaq continued round to the back of the house. Matthew knocked again. Harder this time. Then he tried the handle, but the door was locked. He knocked a third time and called out along the wall.

It was so quiet that he could hear it snow when he closed his eyes. A crackling, scattering sound.

'It's locked all the way around.'

Matthew looked at Tupaarnaq, who had walked around the whole house.

'I'm tempted to break in,' Matthew said. 'I really want to see that man.'

'Not now,' Tupaarnaq said. 'It's like the abandoned houses across the fjord…If there's evidence and we mess with it, then it's worthless.'

27

The boat jolted when Matthew tried reversing it away from the pontoon.

'What do you think you're doing?' Tupaarnaq exclaimed.

'Reversing the boat,' Matthew said. 'Like you told me to.'

She heaved a sigh and pushed him out of the way. 'Move…I said watch the screen. That was what I said.'

She hauled Matthew off the seat and grabbed the throttle. It made a strange noise and the boat barely moved.

'Shit,' she said, and looked at him. 'You've damaged the propeller.'

She tried accelerating again, but nothing much happened—there was merely a vague sense of the boat swinging its stern.

'Drop the anchor,' she said, turning off the engine. 'I'll dive down and check out the propeller before it gets dark.'

'Eh? Do you know how cold it is? You'll die.'

She shook her head. 'I won't be long.'

'I'll do it,' Matthew said. 'It was my mistake.'

She rewarded him with a weary smile. 'A: This water will kill you. B: You've got no idea what you're looking for.'

Matthew looked down.

'Now, go outside and drop the anchor before we run into the

rocks,' she told him. 'I'll go get ready.'

'And what if you don't make it back up?'

'I always make it back up. My father would throw me into the sea at least once a week all year round when I was a kid to get my body used to the shock. You'll thank me one day, he used to say. Who knows? Perhaps today is the day he's proved right. I haven't had anything to thank him for yet, but I guess there's a first time for everything.' She pulled her jumper over her head, briefly exposing her stomach, and he could see the many dark plants and leaves on her skin. 'Now, go and drop that bloody anchor!'

Matthew hurried to the back of the boat and dropped the anchor over the side. The bottom of the sea was only a few metres below where they were.

Tupaarnaq was standing in the doorway wearing black knickers and a black spaghetti-strap vest. Her tattoos curled like living creatures around her arms and legs.

'Stop staring, you moron,' she snapped, shoving him hard in the chest.

She stepped past him and down onto a small ledge near the water, right next to the rubber dinghy. Her arms and legs were thin, but sharply delineated by muscles and the dark colours of her tattoos. Matthew forced himself to look away and dusted some snow off the bottom of the rubber dinghy with one hand. The water could only be about one degree Celsius.

'I can manage two trips,' she said. 'One minute each time.'

She disappeared under the surface immediately. He moved to the gunwale and peered into the water. This seabed seemed dark, although it wasn't very far away. He checked his watch. A minute was a long time. She couldn't manage a minute. Not in this water. He started hyperventilating, gulped a couple of times, then checked his watch again. He didn't know where the hands had been when she dived in. She should have come back up by now. The snow started to fall more heavily. He could feel it melting on the skin at the back of his neck. When the snowflakes hit the sea, they dissolved instantly.

She broke through the surface and looked up at him. 'We can't... fix it...moment...'

The water closed over her head.

'Tupaarnaq!' Matthew said and reached over the gunwale to grab her. She had said two trips, but she had been almost incoherent from cold after the first one. The skin on her head had been speckled, red and white. Had she dived back in? Or had she succumbed to cramps? Was she drowning?

Matthew tore off his jacket and threw his watch on top of it. He was about to pull off a boot when she resurfaced. She had a heavy, floppy white object in one hand. It looked like an animal skin. She threw the hide up on the ledge and followed suit.

'Give me your hand,' she said, sounding exhausted.

He reached out his hand to her and felt her grip it and pull herself up onto the deck.

'I need to get inside,' she said. Her voice was trembling.

Her skin was icy and Matthew could feel the cold spread from her hand to his.

She was shaking and was barely able to turn the ignition key.

'Hang on,' Matthew said and knelt down to open one of the small storage cupboards in between the seats. He remembered having seen blankets in there previously. He passed a blanket backwards to her and found another two. Tupaarnaq dropped the blanket instantly. He picked it up and wrapped all three blankets around her.

'Thank you,' she stuttered, and looked at the steering wheel while she sat down on one of the two double seats at the back of the wheelhouse. 'I couldn't turn on the heating.'

Matthew turned the heating up to the maximum and found another blanket, which he wrapped around her feet.

'Why did you dive the second time?'

'I saw something at the bottom.' She breathed in and out a couple of times. 'I was scared that it might be a human being...But it was just a seal.'

Matthew nodded grimly. 'Are we safe to go?'

She shook her head. 'I don't want to risk going along the coast in the dark with all those rocks, given the state the propeller is in.'

'Do you want me to radio for help?'

She shook her head again. 'I'm not sure its range reaches as far as Nuuk.'

Matthew frowned. 'Surely that's not very far...for a ship's radio?'

'No one would sail down here at this hour anyway.' She tightened the blankets around her body. The only visible part of her was her face from the nose up.

'They could send a helicopter.'

'Matthew.'

He looked up at her.

'I just want to sit here, okay?'

Matthew was about to say something, but stopped himself. It was because of him. He could see it in her eyes. She wanted to be alone with him.

'Okay, that way we can also see if anything happens during the night,' he said in a hoarse voice, looking feverishly out of the window, while at the same time trying not to catch her eye.

'That was what I was thinking too,' she said abruptly, and tightened the blankets even more.

He nodded and stared across the sea. Very soon they would be surrounded by total darkness, and the dense snow made it hard to see anything at all. Except light. Any light would stand out clearly in the all-consuming darkness.

28

The snow continued falling for several hours, and except for the faint glow coming from the boat's dashboard, there was no light anywhere.

Arnaq and her friends had now been missing for two nights.

Matthew had only known Arnaq for a couple of months and now she was gone. Perhaps she had been abducted, perhaps she was already dead, and there was nothing Matthew could do apart from search and wait.

They had turned off the engine. The boat had an oil heater which ran independently of the boat's engine. There was a faint hum from the heater but apart from that, everything was quiet. The snow lay thick across the windscreen of the boat but had slid off the side windows. There was a cold draught coming from the sliding door to the deck at the back of the boat. It was flimsy and didn't close fully.

'Are you still cold?' Matthew looked at Tupaarnaq, who was resting her head against the window.

She shook her head slowly. Her breath made a circle on the glass. 'If you relax completely, you can send heat around your body.'

'Seriously?'

She nodded. 'I don't know if it works for everyone.' She extended her foot from under the blanket. 'Feel.'

Matthew gently touched her warm foot. He looked up. 'Wow.'

Tupaarnaq withdrew her foot, leaned her head against the glass again and resumed staring out into the darkness. 'Do you think the kids are out there?'

'I don't know.' Matthew's voice had grown faint. 'It's so messed up. I have to hope that someone abducted them, because they wouldn't survive another night outdoors in this weather.'

'As long as you keep moving, you're alive,' Tupaarnaq said. 'At this time of year, at least...in a couple of months it'll be hard to survive several hours in the snow.' She looked back at Matthew. She had loosened her grip on the blankets, baring one arm. 'Let's talk about something else.'

Matthew's eyes traced her tattoos from her shoulder and down to her hand. It wasn't often that he got a proper look at the dark tattoos, although he always wanted to. 'What's it like to be in prison for that long?'

Tupaarnaq raised her eyebrows, the only hairs on her body. 'Gee thanks...Let's talk about something other than that.'

Matthew smiled and looked down. 'I've been wondering about your tattoos...They must have taken a long time. Did you have them done in prison?'

'Ah...okay.' She straightened up. 'Many years ago I started going out on accompanied day release, and I had several years of unaccompanied weekend release as well. My outings were always a trip straight to the tattooist. Her name is Lis.'

'I didn't know you were allowed that much leave when you're in prison.'

'Most Danish prisoners start accompanied leave about a third into their sentence, and unaccompanied leave often starts when you're halfway through. That doesn't apply to everyone, but it does apply to most people. If you're in for terrorist offences, they rarely let you go out a whole lot, though…No open prison or unaccompanied releases for you.'

'But you were allowed them early?'

She nodded. 'Yes, I was only a big kid when I was first locked up, and I stuck with my education the whole way through. Year Twelve. The law degree. It was easy for me to get leave. I was part killer, part Greenlandic girl fighting to rebuild her life.'

The boat rocked. Not much, but more than it had done so far. It had stopped snowing and it looked as if the wind was trying to blow a hole in the clouds.

Matthew thought about the evening he had seen Tupaarnaq under the steaming hot water in his shower. Every tiny part of her body was covered by tattoos and she scraped her skin clean with a razor, so that no hair broke the soft surface of the leaves. He winced as he remembered her rage when she noticed him watching her, and said, 'I'll go outside for a moment, so that you can get dressed again.'

'Okay.' She looked across to the other seat row where she had left her clothes and jacket.

Matthew got up and slid open the door. The air outside was icy and his face tightened immediately. He found his cigarettes and shut the door. Lighting a cigarette, he closed his eyes and sniffed the night. The sea smelled fresh, cold and salty. The smoke from his cigarette wafted around his face as he exhaled. The gaps in the clouds had grown and in several places the starlight reached the sea. The moon was a thin crescent, barely visible. He looked towards the shore. The buildings stood out like dark silhouettes against the luminous white snowscape.

He flicked away the cigarette butt. The sea seemed calm, though the boat was swaying gently.

Tupaarnaq shook her head at him when he came inside. 'You're an idiot.'

'Am I? Why?' Matthew closed the door behind him.

'Give me your cigarettes…'

'Ah…'

'Give them to me!' She extended her hand. She was fully dressed again. Black army trousers, the high army boots and the dark hoodie.

'Why?' He found his cigarette packet and handed it to her.

She quickly slid open the door and threw them into the sea. 'I've had enough of that crap.'

'Hey…I only brought one packet!'

'Well, thank God for that. I hate the smell of them. You reek of man…of Tasiilaq.'

'If you'd like to talk about…all of it…Tasiilaq. Then I'm here.'

'Talk about it?' she echoed scornfully. 'What's there to talk about? Two thousand people live in that hellhole, of which nine hundred are children, and out of those nine hundred children, five hundred are on social services' at-risk register. And those are just the statistics—real life is far worse. No one gives a toss about those children. Rape. Abuse. Violence…What the hell is there to talk about? I want to take out all the men over there one by one…bastards.' She buried her face in her hands and breathed heavily a couple of times. Then she shook her head. 'I'm sorry. So many wounds are being ripped open right now…with your sister and everything. Let's talk about something else.' She smiled wistfully. 'I know, why don't you read something to me? From that book you're writing? Like you did at the hospital.' She looked down at his backpack. 'If you brought it, that is?'

'You heard me? When I read to you?'

'Yes.'

Matthew smiled tentatively. 'I did bring it. Are you serious?'

'Yes, as long as you sit as far away from me as possible…You still stink.'

Matthew got up, but Tupaarnaq pushed him with her foot so that he fell back onto the seat. 'I'm just kidding.'

'What do you want me to read about?' he said, picking up his backpack. 'The rocks? The universe? Or perhaps something about being a father...although I never really tried that.'

'The last bit.'

'Okay...' Matthew flicked through his notebook. 'Right, I've got something.' He began to smile. 'I'm calling it *Thoughts about Being the Father of a Girl.*'

Tupaarnaq wrapped herself in one of the blankets again and rested her head against the glass as before. Her gaze disappeared out into the darkness. 'I would like to hear that.'

29

Matthew was woken by the sound of a helicopter flying low over the boat. He cricked his neck; his back felt stiff and sore. He couldn't remember falling asleep, but discovered that he was now lying curled up on one of the seat rows with his head on his jacket.

The oil heater had gone out and the cold had slowly crept into the cabin, leaving ice crystals on the inside of the windows.

Tupaarnaq was awake. She was looking out of the window. 'I think it's the police again.'

'Good.' Matthew rubbed his eyelids and pushed a couple of blankets aside. He could see his own breath in the air as he exhaled. 'Will they be able to land around here?'

'I'm guessing they can land that thing most places.' She went over to the dashboard and started the engine. 'Raise the anchor so that we can dock.'

From the back of the boat Matthew watched the helicopter search between the houses, but soon the sound of the rotors disappeared, one chop at a time. He knocked on the windowpane and indicated with a thumbs-up that the anchor had been raised.

'Throw the fenders over the side,' Tupaarnaq shouted from the cabin. 'Steering is tricky and the current has got hold of us.'

Matthew looked about him. 'You mean those blue cushions?'

'Yes, throw them over the side…now!'

Matthew had only just thrown the last of the blue fenders over the side of the hull when they hit the pontoon bridge. The boat bounced back so hard that Matthew had to grip the rubber dinghy in order not to be thrown overboard. The cold bit into his hand.

'Didn't I tell you,' Tupaarnaq said from the cabin. 'It's impossible to control the boat in its current state…Just as well we didn't try sailing to Nuuk.'

Matthew nodded and waved to Ottesen, who had appeared around the corner of the first red building. 'Let's get off this boat,' he said to Tupaarnaq, rubbing his fingers. 'I'm bloody freezing.'

'I'll wait here,' Tupaarnaq said with a glance at the police officer.

'Okay.' Matthew jumped up on the staging by the bunker point and continued towards the grey cabin with the opening hours sign and fire risk warnings.

'Am I glad to see you,' Ottesen called out to him. 'Did you spend the night out here?'

'Yes, the boat broke down. We reversed into some rocks…or rather, I did.'

'Have you seen anything?'

'No, nothing at all…Only darkness and snow.'

Ottesen smiled. 'I'm glad to find you here. We've been looking for you along the coast all the way down from Nuuk. We were afraid you might have sunk. Why didn't you call us on the boat's radio?'

'I don't know.' Matthew hesitated. 'I'm not sure if it's working…'

Ottesen waved to another police officer and a couple of people in civilian clothes. 'Never mind, as long as you're all right.' He turned to Matthew again. 'Malik is on his way here by boat…He was pretty worried about you. But that means he can tow you back to Nuuk, doesn't it?'

Matthew nodded and looked towards the boat. The only foot-prints in the snow were his. Virgin snow glistened in the sunrays that penetrated the scattered clouds. 'Any news?'

'No,' Ottesen said. 'Not yet, but we'll keep looking.'

'It's not good if they're out here on their own in this weather.'

'I don't think they're out here on their own,' Ottesen said. 'If they had been sheltering somewhere and heard the helicopter, Arnaq would have recognised it and made herself known, don't you think? We circled the houses on the other side a few more times before landing here, and there's absolutely no sign of life in the snow.'

'What about over here?' Matthew said. 'I wanted to talk to Bárdur, but he seems to have vanished into thin air.'

'Yes, Rakel brought him back on their return flight. His answers were so cryptic that she decided to interview him at the station.'

'So he's in Nuuk now?'

'Yes, for the time being.'

'Did he know anything?'

'He doesn't have even a hint of an alibi for anything,' Ottesen said. 'But neither do we have the tiniest piece of evidence implicating him, so we're going to search his house thoroughly—yet again—and then we'll have to see. Otherwise we'll have to let him go.'

30

It had been snowing in Nuuk as well. Matthew made sure no one was lingering by the blue terraced houses across the street before he took out his keys.

It had taken them more than five hours to get back. Malik had towed them with his boat, and once they docked, Tupaarnaq had made her way to Else's, who was going out of her mind with worry.

Matthew needed to stop by the newspaper office, but he wanted to pick up a few things from his flat first.

'Hello.'

The hairs on Matthew's arm stood up. He looked towards a black Humvee in the car park not far from him, heaving a sigh of relief when he saw Briggs get out of the car with a broad smile.

'Are you okay?' Briggs said, sticking out his hand to Matthew.

'Yes, we both are.' Matthew shook Briggs's hand. 'Thank you.'

'I'm so glad to hear it,' Briggs said. 'I heard you got stranded further south, and I just wanted to make sure that you were both back safe and sound.'

'We're good,' Matthew said. 'I just need to pop by my office, and then I'm going to visit my sister's mother.'

'Yes, what a terrible thing to have happened,' Briggs said, making a short, whistling sound out of the corner of his mouth. 'The reason I'm here is that I've been thinking about this business with your father…Did you know that we were only six years old when we started to go out on our bikes together back home?' His face lit up and he produced a folded sheet of paper from his jacket pocket. 'I got my sister to scan a couple of pictures of us when we were kids. They're from the late sixties; we were only seven or eight in them.'

Matthew took the sheet and unfolded it. They contained several photographs featuring two skinny, blond boys. 'That's you?'

'Yep.' Briggs leaned forwards and pointed to a picture. 'That's Tom with the yellow bicycle. He loved those dropped handlebars.'

There was silence for a moment.

'Tom was an only child,' Briggs then said. 'But I think that his mother—I mean, your grandmother—is still alive.'

'Okay.'

'Nice lady.' Briggs whistled again out of the corner of his mouth. 'I'm sure she would be pleased to see you.'

Matthew smiled feebly.

'Just let me know if one day you would like to see the place Tom was from and I'll help you.'

'Thank you,' Matthew said, closing his eyes for a moment. 'I just need to…it doesn't matter right now. I just need to process all of this.'

'Yes, sure.' Briggs smiled. His face was open. 'It's just me reminiscing about the old days.' He chuckled to himself. 'Those shards of glass that we used to cut ourselves to become blood brothers when we were kids…damned well nearly killed us…He was proper crazy, your father.'

'You keep saying *was*,' Matthew said.

Briggs's gaze grew serious. 'Yes, you're right. It's just that for many years I thought he was dead. It's a real mess. He's a dangerous man, Matthew. Don't get me wrong, I understand why you want to meet him, but I don't feel entirely comfortable with it. He has taken enough lives, don't you think?'

'All I've heard from him for the last twenty-four years is that letter from Ittoqqortoormiit.'

'Ittoqqortoormiit?' Briggs exclaimed. 'He wrote to you from Ittoqqortoormiit? What on earth would he be doing there? It's pretty much the remotest town in the Arctic.'

Matthew shrugged and looked across the road that led up to the low buildings that housed *Sermitsiaq*'s offices and the Video-Leif shop. 'I can't even be sure that it really was from him. Maybe it was just meant to look like it.'

'I know his handwriting,' Briggs said. 'Give the letter to me and we'll soon know.'

'The police told me that you had been in touch with them,' Matthew said, looking back at the tall man. 'I would like to meet my father before you lock him up for good.'

'Yes, I was,' Briggs said, then he paused. 'Their current investigation relates to the old case at the Thule base, and as far as the US military is concerned, those cases never die—there's no statute of limitations. So once I read about the killings in Ittoqqortoormiit, especially the pills, I decided to have a word with Ottesen. We would very much like to know more about those pills.' He cleared his throat.

'We being the Greenlandic government or—?'

Briggs pressed his lips together. 'We want those pills.'

'But it's only the survivor, Nukannguaq, who claims there were some,' Matthew said. 'And he was high as a kite...The police said there were no pills at the crime scene.'

'Oh, the pills were there, I'm sure of it,' Briggs said. 'And those two cases...Listen...if you hear from Tom again, you will let me know, won't you?'

Matthew nodded slowly. 'Right now I'm more concerned with finding my sister...And the rest of you should be too.'

'Yes, that's true.' Briggs paused again. 'I'll look into it. Would you like a lift?'

Matthew shook his head. 'I'm only going across the road.'

THOSE WHO LIVE
UNDERGROUND

31

The air in the room was dense. Tom trailed his hand over the glass flask simmering over a low Bunsen burner. The glass felt warm. The fumes smelt of vinegar and bicarbonate of soda.

They had set up a lab in the old doctor's surgery a few doors down from Tom's room. It was distinguished from the other rooms that Tom had seen by having a window in the ceiling. As far as he could work out, it wasn't one he could escape through, but still it was a window, and although the sun was never visible at any time, it let in some light.

Tom had dragged a couple of tables inside the room on which he could set up his equipment, but he was still missing many items and it would take time before Abelsen could source the right measuring devices for the experiment.

He removed his hand from the flask and walked across to an old mahogany desk that had once belonged to a doctor. As far as Tom knew, the bunker under Færingehavn had never been used, but people must have been down there, because the doctor's surgery was well-equipped. He had found several types of medication and instruments, but also quaint items such as wooden pill moulds and pill rollers.

Tom pressed his finger into one of the little hollows of a pill mould. Then he put his finger into his mouth. The taste was sharp. Chemical. Mainly amphetamine and ketobemidone chloride.

Abelsen had left the room a few minutes ago and would undoubtedly soon return. Tom had pointed out—yet again—the difficulties of performing an experiment on resistance to low temperatures now that summer was on its way; although the Nuuk summer wasn't all that warm, it was still unrealistic to expect frost in the daytime before October. Abelsen had demanded that Tom hurry up and get the work done before the frost disappeared, but Tom had insisted that they didn't have the necessary equipment for him to analyse the experiment.

In the meantime, Tom had produced some pills to shut Abelsen up. His tormentor didn't know the first thing about chemistry and now he would suffer the consequences of his own ignorance.

The pills were drying under the green reading lamp on the desk. Tom had put them in a small metal box and lowered the green glass shade as close to them as possible. When he bent over the lamp, he could smell chemicals.

The rest was just smoke and mirrors. Nothing in the flasks had anything to do with the experiment or pill-making. It was window-dressing meant to confuse and slow Abelsen down.

Behind the desk was an old leather armchair with dark wooden armrests. Tom sat down, picked up a pill and dabbed it against the tip of his tongue. Then he put it back and ran his fingers up and down his thigh. He was wearing dark brown cords. A pair of trousers that Abelsen had left in his room along with some other clothes. The shirt was beige with orange and lilac stripes. His jumper the colour of urine. He looked like an idiot from the seventies.

Tom turned to the door the moment he heard Abelsen's footsteps in the corridor. The skinny man's movements were always quick and decisive.

'Tom!' Abelsen said in a loud voice as he pushed open the door. 'I've got the answer.'

'To what?'

'To the cold, obviously—what else?' Abelsen shook his head and flapped one hand dismissively in the air. 'Listen to this: we'll use the old pool down here. It's filled with seawater and it's never more than two degrees Celsius. It's perfect. They'll freeze their backsides off in that water.'

'The bunker has a pool?' Tom said in disbelief.

'Yes, there's an old swimming pool at the end of this corridor,' Abelsen said. 'But I don't want you going down there unless I'm with you.'

Tom scrunched up his nose. 'It's not sub-zero, but we could try it.'

'Great!' Abelsen exclaimed with a broad smile. 'So we're in business.'

'But…'

'Yes?'

'You'll have a hard time selling a product whose test result you can't document.'

'What's your point?'

'It makes no sense to get someone to take these pills and then chuck them into an icy swimming pool when we don't have the equipment to measure and analyse the results. You'll end up with a product you can't sell…Unless you're happy to be just another small-time pusher.'

'Pusher? What on earth are you talking about?'

'If you want to sell this stuff to big pharma, your test results must be in order and cover a long period.'

'Tom, I thought our deal was clear? You make my product, and I let Matthew live.'

'And the girl.'

'Yes, yes, whatever…Stop harping on about that girl. I want my goods, okay?' He pointed at the wall. 'Your old room is just over there and you could be back there sooner than you think.'

Tom heaved a sigh and straightened up in the chair. 'I get it. I'm not an idiot. But there are two things you need to understand or the whole effort is wasted. One: if we don't analyse and document the experiment properly, then it's worthless…completely! The only money you'll make is by selling it on the street. Now, listen to me…I'm telling you this because it's not in my interest, sadly, that you screw up.'

The corners of Abelsen's lips turned downwards and he nodded slowly.

'Two,' Tom went on. 'I've made a demo version of the pills with the ingredients we do have. You're welcome to try them right now. And if you decide to jump into a freezing cold swimming pool afterwards, well, knock yourself out.'

'What?' Abelsen walked up to the desk. 'You've made some pills already? Like the ones in Thule?'

'Pretty much,' Tom said, nudging the box towards Abelsen.

'Why didn't you say so?'

'I'm telling you now…They needed time to dry.'

Abelsen folded his hands and looked at Tom. 'So if I wanted to, I could try them myself?'

'Be my guest,' Tom said. 'They're yours.' He got up and rested the palms of his hands on the desk. 'Why do you want to try them?'

'Do you think I don't know why you took them?'

'I know that you saw what happened when we did.'

'I saw what you became able to withstand,' Abelsen said. He struggled to hide his smile, but he tried. 'Just remember what I told you, I'll be testing them on Bárdur's family as well—and you have met his girls, haven't you? I think they'll be having some of these.'

'Take one, go on,' Tom said. 'Take two, damn it.'

'You first,' Abelsen said with a scornful look.

Tom shrugged, popped a pill in his mouth and swallowed it.

•

Abelsen looked at him for a few seconds, then reached for the pillbox and picked two pills at random. He smiled disdainfully, stuffed them into his mouth and swallowed them. 'It'll be fun to see if we both drop dead now.'

'They need a few minutes to take effect,' Tom went on, ignoring Abelsen's sarcasm. 'And it takes a long time to develop resistance to very low temperatures, but you'll feel something in a moment.'

Abelsen nodded and walked over to the tables with Tom's equipment. 'Why is it so complicated to make the pills? I mean, we have all the ingredients.'

'Yes,' Tom said. 'The challenge isn't making something that works, it's making something that works without killing people at the same time.'

Abelsen tapped his forefinger on a box on the table. 'A man like you must know thousands of ways to kill people.'

'Yes, but most of them can be detected.'

'Most of them?'

'Let's talk about it some other day,' Tom said wearily. 'Feel anything yet?'

'A buzzing,' Abelsen said. He looked down at his arms. He clenched his fists and relaxed them. Then he clenched them again. 'I can feel it under my skin.' He looked up. Smiled broadly and turned his gaze to the ceiling. 'Wow...This is wonderful.'

Tom leaned back in his seat and studied the gaunt man's face. The colour was rising in his pale grey skin. His eyes were glowing.

Abelsen inhaled hard through his nose. 'This is amazing, Tom...

bloody amazing.' He spun on his own axis once and waved his hands in the air as if conducting an orchestra. 'Can you feel it? *Dies irae...* The angels are singing...Crescendo and crescendo.' He looked down at Tom. 'Let's go hunting.'

'Hunting?' Tom furrowed his brow without taking his eyes off Abelsen's enlarged pupils.

'I feel like shooting something,' Abelsen went on, moistening his lower lip with his tongue. He looked at the pills and reached out for the box. 'And these are coming with me.'

'I made them just for you,' Tom said, still keeping his gaze trained on Abelsen's face.

'People like you don't get Verdi,' Abelsen announced, marching towards the door. 'I'll arrange for you to have everything you need so we can do this properly.'

Abelsen closed the door behind him and Tom collapsed in the chair. A shiver ran through him. When Abelsen had started talking about shooting, a flashback of Reese and Bradley had appeared in Tom's mind. With dark, bleeding bullet holes to their faces. Shot at close range. Tom didn't know where the images had come from. He was sure that he hadn't shot them, that he hadn't seen them, yet doubt was eating away at him. It had to be Abelsen who was behind it all. It couldn't have been anybody else. Bradley and Reese. Matthew and the little girl. Even the simpleminded giant and his wife, chained to a chair. All of them dancing at the end of the strings Abelsen pulled.

Tom got up and tore off his jumper. And his shirt. He lay down flat on the floor and started doing push-ups. He carried on until his arms were shaking and the sweat was dripping from his forehead and onto the grey floor. He gave in and collapsed from exhaustion, his upper body sticking to the floor.

32

Tom was haunted by the image of the chained woman. He knew that it was up to him and him alone if she and her children were to be freed from their nightmare.

Once Abelsen had left, Tom spent the rest of the day exploring the corridors, except the area where Bárdur and his family lived. He needed to familiarise himself with the layout so that he could find his way around in the dark as well as the light.

Many of the doors in the old bunker were locked and he was tempted to force them, but he quickly dropped the idea. It was too risky if Abelsen was still around.

The last door at the end of his own corridor was broken. It looked as if someone had come at it with an axe. The wood was splintered and cracked, and the handle had been almost knocked off.

Tom walked right up to the door and opened it carefully. The room behind it smelled mouldy and rotten. He breathed slowly and with control. The room was as dark as the cell he had lain in first while Abelsen had subjected him to light torture. He fumbled around the wall by the door for a light switch, but found nothing but concrete.

The room was quiet and cold. Tom took a few steps inside it but could see nothing, and so he stopped. He needed to find a source of light so he could explore, but the smell intrigued him and made him reluctant to leave. He closed his eyes and listened. There was something more to the smell. There was salt. The sea.

Slowly he fumbled his way in the darkness with his hands and feet. He slid his feet across the floor as quietly as possible while stretching out his arms. It wasn't a big room. After only four or five metres he reached a new door. A set of doors. Made from glass with big, curved handles. The smell of the sea came through the gap between the two doors. When he moved his head very close to the gap, he could feel the sea breathe coolly against his skin.

It was just as dark on the other side of the doors. The smell of rot accompanied the smell of the sea.

He let his hand glide down the smooth surface; the glass was filthy on the inside. He could feel traces of something that had dried on its surface. He moistened his fingertips and rubbed them against the dried trails. Sniffed his fingers. He could smell iron.

The floor in this room was covered with linoleum, and his fingers told him that there was also some dried material on the floor.

The smell of decay grew stronger—not by much, but enough for him to detect differences in his nose and mouth.

Everything inside him wanted to leave, but he continued to move forward in the darkness. He felt his way across sections of linoleum. He crawled on his knees, his hands exploring the floor. He could hear water moving. Not like the sea outside, but loud enough for him to hear it. Or perhaps mostly sense it.

He crawled a bit further until his fingers bumped into a low raised section. Then he touched water. This had to be Abelsen's swimming pool, and it was indeed filled with seawater. It certainly smelled of salt. Tom tasted the water and spat it out immediately. It was salty, but tasted fresh, although the room itself smelt putrid.

Tom shuffled along the edge of the pool until he bumped into the wall. The same happened on the opposite side. There was no way around the swimming pool. If he wanted to find a channel that might lead to the sea, he would have to enter the water, and it was very cold.

He got up and slowly made his way back to the double doors. No matter what the swimming pool concealed, the chained woman was his first priority.

•

The abattoir at the opposite end of the bunker near Bárdur's quarters was empty, but the light was on. There were dark lumps of meat on a table, along with a couple of long, skinned haunches, but that was all.

He looked around the room. The tiles were gleaming. The sink had been scoured clean of blood. The meat hooks under the ceiling glistened in the glow from the lamp, as did the steel tables. If there had been some kitchen appliances, it would have looked like any other commercial kitchen. But this room was used exclusively for butchering and carving up dead animals.

Tom returned to the corridor and went to the door to the living room where he had last seen the chained woman. He cautiously pressed his ear against the door and listened. He could hear voices from the other side, Bárdur shouting something unintelligible. Tom quickly sought refuge in the dark room next to the living room. It had been locked the last time, but it wasn't now.

He could clearly hear Bárdur in the other room, his deep voice switching between Danish and Faroese.

'Come on,' Bárdur said. 'It's bedtime now.'

The door from the living room to the corridor was opened. Tom retreated even further into the pitch-black room. He grabbed something which felt like a garment rail with coats on it and hid behind it. Pressed himself up against the wall to the living room.

Shortly afterwards the door to the room where he was hiding was opened and light from the corridor poured in. Sweat broke out on his forehead. He held his breath and pressed his eyes shut. He felt like an idiot who had accidentally descended into hell without remembering to die first.

Tom was startled when the light in the room was switched on. Then he looked at the coats in front of him. With a bit of luck, he was completely concealed. There was a slight gap between two of the coats, but it was too late to do anything about it. He caught glimpses of Bárdur on the other side. He saw the two little girls the big man was carrying, one on each arm.

'Go to sleep now, Solva,' Bárdur said. 'Good night, Kristina.'

One of the girls protested briefly, but was stopped by a grunt. 'Dada is tired.'

Tom heard how each girl got a kiss before Bárdur went back to the door. He turned off the light. 'God's peace,' he whispered to them before closing the door.

Dense darkness descended upon the room. Tom could hear the two little girls breathing. The younger one was chatting to her doll.

'Be quiet, Solva,' her big sister hushed her.

Back in the living room Bárdur started shouting at the woman. She didn't reply and so he shouted at her again.

Tom heard Solva titter. 'The whore,' she whispered. 'The whore.'

It was the same word they could hear coming from the living room.

Bárdur shouted it again and both girls giggled in the darkness.

'I want to hit the mummy beast as well,' Solva said.

Kristina hushed her again. 'Not now…We have to go to sleep.'

Another outburst from Bárdur silenced them both.

'No, no, I don't want to.' The woman's voice was raw and desperate. 'Please don't…I can't take any more.'

'Shut your mouth, Mona,' Bárdur roared.

It sounded as if he hit her. Several times. Then there was silence.

Tom could hear her chain rattle. Rhythmically. Bárdur's moaning grew louder and louder.

Mona began to whimper.

Solva mimicked the noises her father was making. Only much more quietly.

33

The girls had fallen quiet. Their tittering and grunting had stopped. As had Bárdur's strained moaning and panting.

Tom was still hiding behind the garment rail. He had closed his eyes and was leaning against the wall.

Bárdur stirred in the living room. The chain rattled and Mona started whimpering again. Her whimpers turned into sobs, and there was a noise as if Bárdur had tossed her aside. The chain rattled metallically and grated against some item of furniture.

Mona's weeping was drowned out by Bárdur's voice as he started chanting a prayer. 'Thyatira, Thyatira…Do not tolerate the woman Jezebel who claims to be a prophetess…She teaches you to commit fornication and eat the sacrificial meat.'

There was silence for a moment. Mona sniffled. The chain clattered faintly.

'I've given her time to convert,' Bárdur went on. It sounded as if he was reading aloud. 'But she will not turn away from her sin. Now I will throw her on the sickbed, and also those who lie with her, I will throw into great turmoil them unless they turn away from her deeds, and I will kill her children. All believers will know that I am the one who examines their kidneys and hearts, and I will give to each according to his deeds.'

Tom reached out an arm and let his hand glide slowly along the many coats.

The girls were still quiet. His fingers clutched a sleeve. Both girls must have been conceived through rape, and Mona had probably given birth to them alone down here in the bunker. No midwife, no stitches, no opportunity to heal after the birth.

'Now kill every boy and every woman. Kill every boy and girl who has lain with a man. However, all the girls who have not lain with a man, you shall let live among you.'

You're a sick and twisted creature, Tom thought, shuffling his feet. The two little girls continued to lie still and Tom hoped that they had fallen asleep. Perhaps they were used to falling asleep to the sound of rape.

He followed the coats carefully one by one until he reached the end of the garment rail, then he slowly disentangled himself and stepped out into the room.

When his foot hit the crossbar, it was already too late to turn back. The noise sounded like thunder in the dark room.

'Daddy?' Kristina called out.

'Shhh...' Tom said softly. 'I'm here to help you, I—'

'Demon,' Solva screamed. 'Demon, demon, demon.'

Tom threw himself in the direction of the door, but hit the wall. He took a step to the right and felt wood. He grabbed the handle and tore open the door.

Inside the living room Bárdur yelled something and it sounded as if an item of furniture had been knocked over. Bárdur shouted again, more loudly this time, and Tom started running down the corridor. He ran until he started seeing black spots in front of his eyes. He turned the corner leading to his own corridor and carried on past his room. The door to his room was too flimsy. The big man could break it down with just a few blows.

He ran right to the end of the corridor, but the first two doors he tried were locked, so he continued onwards to the swimming pool. It was too late to turn around. He could hear Bárdur shouting not far from him.

The room with the swimming pool was just as dark as earlier, but he didn't have time to look for other escape routes. Instead he lowered himself carefully into the cold water in the pool. The water was just as black as the room itself and it closed tightly around his body. He could feel his skin shrink and his muscles contract, but it was nothing compared to the experiments in Thule. This was what he had trained for—what his pills could do.

He breathed slowly and inhaled air deep into his lungs. Then he let himself sink towards the bottom with his back against the side.

A gentle current flowed through the pool. It wasn't powerful, but it was enough to confirm his hunch that a couple of underground channels from the sea fed the swimming pool.

The water flickered above him. Light from a torch pierced the darkness and the room grew brighter. The surface of the water hadn't settled yet, but Tom was counting on it never being entirely flat.

The torch light searched the water and the bottom of the pool. Tom noticed several silhouettes on the bottom. He couldn't see what they were. Some were short, curled up and white. Others long and dark.

He slowly reached out to touch the white objects close to him, only for his fingertips to realise almost immediately that they were bones.

He looked around the pool. The torch flickered and the light glistened in the water, but everything was blurry and unclear to him.

The beam of light disappeared from the pool.

Tom fought his pulse. He had to keep it low for a little while longer so that he wouldn't be forced up and out of the water while Bárdur could still hear him break through the surface.

PRISONER OF
THE DEMONS

34

FÆRINGEHAVN, WEST GREENLAND, 22 OCTOBER 2014

Arnaq counted the seconds between light and darkness. Sometimes there would be only a few before the light went out. Most times a little more. The first hour she had lain sobbing on the floor. She had also screamed and shouted to be let out, but no one had come.

To begin with the light had caused her severe stress. Every flash was unexpected. It wasn't until she started counting that she regained some control over herself. She counted the light. She counted it for as long as it lasted. Not the intervals between the flashes or the darkness. Just the light. At times it was just one second. Often five or six. The record was thirteen. Thirteen seconds of light. Thirteen seconds to study the cell in which she lay.

She had lost track of how long she had been there, but it was a long time and she was exhausted. She was frequently on the verge of falling asleep, but the alternating, aggressive light kept her awake. If she dozed off, it was for only a few seconds. Perhaps a day had passed, twenty-four hours. Maybe more.

There hadn't been anyone but her in the cell since she was thrown onto the thin foam mattress. Not a sound. Only the light, the darkness and the silence.

There was a metal bucket near the iron door. The bucket was old and dented. She had peed in it three times. The four water bottles were empty. She had drunk them quickly. She couldn't remember when she had emptied the last bottle, but her throat was dry and raw. Her body felt limp. She merely counted the light and stared at nothing. Sometimes she counted with her eyes closed. The light cut red and sharp through her eyelids.

She counted the light. Three. Six. Two. One. Seven. Three. Five. Eleven. Two. Three. Three. Six. One. Three. Nine. At some point it must exceed thirteen. It was all she was waiting for.

As she had been dragged down the corridor by the big man, she had caught a glimpse of Lasse and Andreas lying on a steel table in a room that looked like a kitchen. They just lay there. With their smashed skulls. She had had nothing more to throw up and she had stopped screaming. Every time she had screamed, the giant would hit her. His face contorted, he would narrow his eyes and strike her with the back of his hand. His knuckles were big and dug into her skin with each blow.

It was him, the giant, and his albino son, Símin, who were keeping her prisoner and who had killed her friends. Símin would hide behind his father while his eyes crept around everywhere. He was disgusting. His gaze was sticky. They had told them nothing but lies when they came over to chat to them in the abandoned town. They weren't on a trip. They lived below Færingehavn.

Alma was gone. Arnaq hadn't seen her since she was injured in the room where Andreas had lain bludgeoned on the floor and Lasse had been killed.

Her stomach churned. It hurt too much. She couldn't. Seven. Three. Three. Four. Eight. Twelve. Five. Three. Eight. Five. Twelve was close. Twelve was almost thirteen. Almost fourteen.

Four. Six. Two. Four. Eight, nine, ten, eleven, twelve, thirteen, fourteen, fifteen, sixteen, seventeen, eighteen, nineteen, twenty,

twenty-one, twenty-two, twenty-three, twenty-four, twenty-five, twenty-six, twenty-seven, twenty-eight, twenty-nine, thirty.

Arnaq pushed herself to a sitting position without taking her eyes off the naked lightbulb under the ceiling and without pausing her counting. She was getting close to a minute.

After two minutes and seventeen seconds a grating sound from the outside forced its way in. A moment later the door was pushed open.

The giant appeared. He was carrying a tray, and Símin crept in behind him. He wasn't as big as his father, but he wasn't small either. Perhaps he was almost as tall as him, only skinny and pale. Very pale.

The giant set down the tray. There were four new bottles of water and a plate of fried ribs. The meat looked like seal, except that Arnaq thought that the bones were too big and the meat too pale.

'It's seal,' the giant said. He followed her gaze. 'Meat.' He picked up a water bottle and handed it to her.

She unscrewed the cap and drained the bottle so quickly that some of the water trickled down her chin and throat.

The pressure from the water on her stomach made her retch. She looked at the ribs and vomited water all over the floor. She bent double and threw up again. Her throat was stinging.

Bárdur kicked another bottle towards her. 'Drink slowly,' he ordered her.

Símin stared at Arnaq. He chewed his lower lip and grinned in short bursts at his father. He was clasping his penis through his trousers with one hand.

Bárdur spotted the hand and whacked Símin hard across the head. The next blow swiped Símin's hand away.

'Say your prayers,' Bárdur sneered. 'She's unclean.'

'Honour your father,' Símin chanted, still hunched up. 'He who curses his father shall suffer death...'

'Where's my friend?' Arnaq managed to say. She got herself into a squatting position. Her voice was trembling from fear and exhaustion. 'Where is she? Tell me now!'

'It's not appropriate for a woman to speak in the church,' Símin said, still not daring to stand upright. He glanced sideways at Arnaq. Then he clutched his groin again. 'It was Eve who was deceived and who disobeyed God's command. It was Eve, wasn't it, Dad?'

'Eve is always a whore,' Bárdur said, knocking Símin's hand away again.

'The two of you are fucking crazy,' Arnaq said. The tears were flowing down her cheeks. 'Sick bastards, the pair of you...Lunatics.'

'She will not turn away from sin,' Símin mumbled, squeezing his penis hard. 'Those who lie with her, I will throw into great turmoil unless they turn away from her deeds, and I will kill her children.'

Arnaq collapsed onto the mattress from exhaustion.

Bárdur patted Símin on the head and pushed the plate of ribs closer to Arnaq with his foot. 'You need to eat if you want to live.'

'No.' Arnaq shook her head. 'I won't touch your food until I see my friends.' She didn't look at them. She kept her eyes firmly on the rough concrete floor.

Símin reached down a hand to pick up a rib. 'It's tasty.'

'Eat!' Bárdur commanded her. He grabbed Símin and dragged him out of the door.

'I want to see my friend,' Arnaq screamed with her last strength. She heard the door glide shut and the bolt being slid across.

The light went out. Then it came back on. It went out. Came back on.

35

Arnaq's number sequence was disrupted when the door opened again. She hadn't even noticed that the light had stayed on. Her eyes stung and hurt. She had dried-up sleep gunk in the corners of her eyes, and she could smell her own body. Her breath was dry and reeked of disease. The cell stank of urine. Her urine. She could no longer remember if she peed in the bucket or just let it trickle out where she lay. They brought her water every day and she drank it. Then she peed it out again. Many days must have passed. She had no idea how long it would take her to starve to death. She had expected to be dead by now, but the pains in her stomach came and went without really sapping the life out of her. Perhaps the light was keeping her alive. The by now endless sequence of numbers. The highest was fifteen. Except when something was being put into the room. Like now.

It usually happened quickly. A new bucket. More water. Meat she didn't touch. And then they took it away. She didn't have the energy to look at him. She had counted him. It took about eighty-five seconds from the door opening until it was shut again.

Arnaq frowned when she went past one hundred and twenty. At

one hundred and forty she turned her head and looked towards to door.

She blinked. Símin was standing just inside the door. She couldn't see the giant. She closed her eyes again and tried to organise her thoughts. The numbers kept going around her head. She could still feel the light coming and going, although it was now permanently on.

When she opened her eyes again, Símin had moved closer to her. She was exhausted right to the marrow in her bones, but she managed to straighten herself up so that she was sitting almost upright.

The pale young man handed her a piece of bread.

She snatched it and stuffed the whole chunk into her mouth at once. She chewed and swallowed it so quickly that it almost came up again. She started to sweat and fought her nausea. She closed her eyes and breathed in short, controlled breaths of four in and four out. Four in and four out. Her lips were slightly parted so the air cooled the nausea from her mouth and down to her stomach. Four. Four. Four. Four.

'Everyone is allowed to eat God's food,' Símin mumbled. 'But sinners mustn't taint His altar.'

The words penetrated Arnaq's numbers. 'Water,' she gasped.

Símin reached behind him, grabbed a bottle of water and gave it to her. 'The Lord sanctifies it.'

Arnaq tried to shake her head, but she was too weak. 'It's just water.'

Símin got up. His expression was determined.

Arnaq looked up at the glowing light bulb. 'Stay for a while…'

'Me?' Símin glanced towards the door, then he looked back at Arnaq.

She took a sip of the water. 'Do you have something to do?'

He frowned. His eyebrows were just as white as his sparse hair. His eyes were so light blue that they almost disappeared in the white of his eyes.

'Women must be silent in church.'

'We're not in a church…We're in a fucking dungeon!' Arnaq exclaimed. She glared at him and tried to straighten up fully. 'Did you eat my friends? Tell me.'

'There's no other world than this one,' Símin said.

'I'm sorry…It's okay. You're right. It's just me…'

Símin pointed upwards and shook his head. 'The world up there has been abandoned by God and is full of demons.' He shuddered.

'Have you ever been there?'

'No,' he said, horrified. 'My dad says—'

'You have to help me,' she cut him off.

Símin looked up at the ceiling.

'Please let me go,' Arnaq said. 'Or I'll die here…And I can help you too.'

He shook his head.

'Where are we?' Arnaq wanted to know.

'I've never been anywhere other than here, under the City of the Dead Demons, and Dad's old house on the other side of the fjord,' Símin said.

Arnaq could hear from the hesitation in his voice that she had managed to sow a seed of doubt in his mind. 'There are many people up there…Many nice people who won't hit you.'

'No,' Símin said. 'They're sick and dangerous…All of them.'

'Your dad is sick and dangerous,' Arnaq said. She raised her voice. 'Hitting children is against the law…As is killing.'

'You're sick,' Símin shouted, and slapped Arnaq across the face with the palm of his hand. He tore at her blouse until it ripped, exposing her breasts.

'You're unclean,' Símin yelled at her. 'Unclean!'

'I'm sorry,' Arnaq sobbed, trying to cover herself up.

Símin clutched his groin. He stared at Arnaq's breasts. He rubbed his groin. With his other hand he grabbed her breast.

She tried to push his hand away, but she had almost no strength left. He was too strong.

He squeezed her breast. Squeezed it hard with his fingertips. He rubbed his penis through his trousers. Strangled moans erupted from deep down in his throat.

'Let me go,' Arnaq sobbed. 'Take your hands off me, you pervert!'

Símin jumped up with a yelp. A wet patch had appeared on the fabric covering his groin.

'You're a whore,' he screamed. His hands were trembling. He stared at her breasts. Rubbed himself again. 'You're unclean… Unclean.'

He spun around and ran to the door, pulling it shut behind him.

The light disappeared. It came back. Disappeared. Came back. Went away. Came back.

Arnaq slumped sideways onto the thin foam mattress. She whimpered and tried to gather the ruined blouse around her. Inside her head the numbers were already running.

36

The light had turned into darkness soon after Símin had disappeared. At first it had resuming flashing, as it usually did, before going out for good with no warning.

It had taken her several hours to let the light go. She had carried on counting although there was nothing to count. There was no record to beat. You couldn't count the darkness when it was there all the time.

After some time she had abandoned all hope that the light would ever come back. Everything was dark now.

She wondered if she had gone blind. If her brain had been so damaged by the light, starvation and lack of sleep that she had lost her sight. Perhaps the light was still flashing only she no longer sensed it.

Finally she had fallen asleep. She didn't know how long she had slept. Nor how many times she had dozed off and woken up again. She didn't even know whether it was day or night, or how long she had been a prisoner. When she checked her fingernails, it felt like a week. The eyebrows she would normally pluck had also grown long. They were so long that they no longer pricked her fingertips when she touched them.

While the light had been flashing she hadn't registered anything other than smells. The stench of her own urine. Her unwashed skin. Her hair getting increasingly matted and greasy with each passing day. Now she also grew aware of touch. She had no senses left but touch and smell.

She touched her nose. Felt her ears and eyes. Her lips. They were cracked. Her skin tasted salty. She nibbled the skin on her hand with her lips. Tasting the salty skin. She wondered how many days you could survive if you ate your own arm and nothing but that, or a leg. How many days' worth of calories were in a leg like hers?

The tears started rolling down her cheeks. The mutilated bodies kept dominating her thoughts. Lasse's blood spurting over her. Brain matter being forced out by the blow. Alma's empty gaze fading away.

She turned over onto her stomach and pushed herself up on all fours so that she could crawl towards the door.

The first thing she bumped into was the bucket. She grabbed it and pulled it with her towards the heavy iron door.

There was a hollow echo through the room when she started banging the bucket against the door.

'Hello?' she shouted without really shouting. There wasn't much fight left in her and her throat was sore. 'Hello? Help me...I'm going to...die in here.'

She swung the bucket against the door once more, but only the echo answered. Her body gave in and she collapsed on the floor. The concrete felt cold against her skin. She lost herself in the darkness. She lay still on the floor. She could smell urine.

A knocking sound brought her attention back to the door. No one had knocked on it before. Or had they? She couldn't remember.

The knocking resumed and she pushed herself into a sitting position.

She tried to speak, but her throat was raw and she coughed to clear it. 'Yes?'

She heard grating sounds from the bolt and the door as it was opened. A thin sliver of light penetrated, and she was forced to narrow her eyes.

She held up a hand and peered out between her fingers. It was Símin. She instinctively gathered the torn blouse in front of her.

He set down a tray of bread and water and handed her another blouse.

Arnaq snatched a slice of bread and stuffed it quickly into her mouth. It had been a long time since the last slice. Several days perhaps. While she chewed it, she considered spitting it out. Her hunger pains had almost gone away. Whenever she ate some bread, they would resume a few hours later. But there were two slices this time. She reached for the second slice and stuffed that into her mouth as well. She wasn't able to close her mouth properly, but she didn't care.

Símin waved the hand holding the blouse. 'Sorry.' He had squatted down on his haunches next to the tray.

She took the blouse carefully and hesitated for a few seconds while she looked into his ice-blue eyes. There was something familiar about them.

'Is this you playing the Good Samaritan now?' Arnaq mumbled, snatching the blouse. She quickly pulled it over her head and covered herself up.

Símin frowned.

She shook her head. 'Thank you.' Then she looked down at the empty plate. 'Thank you for all of it…I'm going to die in here.' Her stomach was already fighting the bread. First there would be several hours of pain and spasms in her stomach and intestines followed by a few good hours before her hunger would slowly begin to trouble her again and wouldn't disappear until many hours later.

'Símin?'

'Yes?'

'I had a backpack up in the house. A pink one. I think you took it.'

Símin nodded slowly.

'There was something inside it that I need.' She placed her hand on his thigh. 'Please would you fetch it?'

He looked down at her hand. The Adam's apple moved under the skin of his neck.

'I'm not allowed to touch it,' he said hoarsely. The words came from the back of his throat.

'I just want to show you something,' she said, trying to make her voice light. 'You'll like it.'

He glanced at the door. Then he nodded and got up from the floor.

•

Símin opened the door fully when he came back, letting more light into the cell.

Arnaq unzipped her backpack and checked it. It was clear that somebody had rifled through it, but nothing was missing. She took her back-up mobile from a closed side pocket at the bottom of her backpack and connected it to a small powerbank. In one of the backpack's external side pockets there was a freezer bag tied with a knot. It contained a SIM card from an Icelandic mobile company. It was wrapped in a yellow sticky note with the activation code.

Lars had given it to her, saying that on a good day the Icelandic reception was just a tad better than Greenland's TelePost.

She slotted the SIM card in place and entered the code. As with her other mobile, which had a Greenlandic SIM card, there was no 3G network. But there was a single telephone coverage bar. One out of four.

'Is that you?' Símin studied the small mobile with interest. It was an old Samsung. The background picture on glowing screen showed Arnaq and Alma outside their school in Denmark.

Arnaq looked briefly into his pale blue eyes. 'Símin, do you know where the other girl is?'

He shook his head and looked at the mobile. Carefully he touched the screen. It changed under his fingertip and he let out a gasp of surprise and looked at Arnaq.

'It's just like television,' she said, pressing her playlist. 'Listen.'

'We don't listen to music,' Símin said with a glance at the door.

'I'm sorry,' Arnaq said, switching the music off. 'Only it's so quiet here.' Her voice had grown thick. 'Let me try something else.'

She pressed her mother's number, but nothing happened. She tried it again and on her third attempt it rang. The connection was poor, but it did ring.

Her mother's voice could be heard softly.

'Help,' Arnaq whispered. Her throat contracted. 'I don't know where I am, but we haven't sailed anywhere.' The tears streamed down her cheeks and her upper body convulsed. 'I love you, Mum.' Else's voice was drowned out by white noise. Arnaq sobbed.

'What is it?' Símin said, taking the mobile from her.

'No...Símin.' She reached out her arm. Her gaze was desperate. Dissolving. 'It's mine.'

He knocked her hand aside and raised the mobile to his face. Else's voice spoke from the small mobile. She was shouting. She sounded agitated. Símin looked at the glowing screen. He could make out the picture of Arnaq and Alma. 'Demons,' he yelled, hurling the mobile onto the floor, where it shattered.

Arnaq collapsed in floods of tears. Her whole body was trembling. She felt Símin's fingers touch her cheek. Very carefully. He nudged her tears with the tips of his fingers.

The light disappeared for a second, but then returned along with a roar.

Both of them jumped in fear.

'The devil's spawn,' Bárdur thundered as his hand shot towards Símin, and he picked the young man up from the floor by the scruff of his neck as though he was nothing but a ragdoll. 'She's unclean.'

Símin winced under the blows raining down on his neck and back.

'Now get out of here,' Bárdur ordered him. He kicked Símin's side with his wooden clog boot.

'I'm sorry, I'm sorry.' Símin limped to the door.

Bárdur slapped Arnaq repeatedly across the face with the palm of his hand. She tried to crawl out of reach, but she wasn't strong enough to escape.

'You're a filthy whore,' Bárdur sneered at her. He raised his hand in preparation for yet another blow, then let it sink down slowly. 'Why did you give her one of Mona's blouses?' he called out towards the door.

'The other one got damaged.' Símin's voice was low and it was coming from the corridor.

'You idiot. Go to your room and say your prayers,' Bárdur shouted. 'I'll clear up here.'

FÆRINGEHAVN

37

'We've patrolled Færingehavn every day—twice—but there's absolutely nothing inside any of the buildings.' Rakel looked at Matthew. 'We've turned the place upside down and inside out. I don't get it. It's as if they've dropped off the face of the earth.'

Ottesen gestured towards some papers stapled together on the desk. 'You're welcome to read the report.'

Matthew nodded. 'So now what?'

'We carry on,' Rakel said. 'It's our number one priority. They must be found. We've also taken samples from several buildings for analysis; perhaps they'll give us something to go on.' She turned to Ottesen. 'We will find them.'

Ottesen looked out of his office window.

Matthew followed his gaze. There were scattered piles of snow outside, but it was mainly sleet that was raining down on them.

'I'm going to Ittoqqortoormiit,' Ottesen said. 'And I'll stop by the hospital in Reykjavik to have a chat with Nukannguaq.'

'So you'll be flying today, is that what you're saying?'

'Yes, in a couple of hours.' He trained his gaze on Matthew again. 'Rakel will lead the investigation while I'm gone.'

Rakel nodded and smiled at Matthew. 'Did you manage to read what I sent you earlier today?'

'The lab results from Jakob's murder? Yes, I ran through them on my mobile on my way here.'

'The Faroese guy didn't kill Jakob,' she went on. 'There was no DNA match between him and the evidence we found.'

'And that goes for vomit, hair and everything?'

'Yes, there's absolutely no evidence that Bárdur went to Jakob's house…We've nothing on that man.'

'Is he still here?'

'No…We couldn't keep him without any evidence.'

'And there was nothing in the car? I mean, in Apollo's car?'

'No, nothing.'

'Fuck it…It shouldn't be this hard. I know it was him who knocked me unconscious and abducted me. If I hadn't managed to escape, I guess I'd be dead now…Like Jakob…And Arnaq.'

'We don't know if Arnaq is dead,' Ottesen interjected. 'And, strictly speaking, all you know is that a very big guy knocked you unconscious and probably tried to abduct you.'

'I don't think Arnaq is dead, either,' Rakel added. 'But we've already talked about that.'

Matthew slumped in his seat. 'Are there any new developments in Ittoqqortoormiit, since you've decided to go there?'

'Yes and no,' Ottesen said. 'It's mostly because of Nukannguaq and some other stuff I've been hearing. I've decided to take a look for myself.'

'What are you looking for?'

'Nukannguaq keeps going on about these pills he claims that they took, and he has tested positive for several banned but familiar substances, but the bag of pills he insists was lying on the table wasn't there when our officer entered the house. He only found three dead bodies and Nukannguaq with his brains fried.' Ottesen sighed and rubbed his face. 'Nukannguaq says they stole the pills from someone they call the mask dancer…A Dane, as it happens.'

Matthew cleared his throat. 'I think that might be my father.'

'Your father?' Rakel exclaimed, staring at Matthew. 'I thought he was American?'

Ottesen exhaled heavily. 'Normally I would be just as surprised as Rakel, but in this case anything is possible.'

'Why do you think the pills belong to your father?' Rakel said.

'I received a letter in my father's handwriting,' Matthew said, closing his eyes for a moment. 'All it said was that I needed to come to Ittoqqortoormiit because he wants to tell me about a tupilak, and then that Briggs guy started talking to me about some pills and an experiment in which my father is supposed to have killed two other people.'

'Is there some way you can get hold of your father?' Rakel wanted to know. 'It might help us discover if the pills and the fatalities in Ittoqqortoormiit are as closely connected as they look.'

'We haven't been in touch for twenty-four years.' Matthew paused. 'Before that short note I didn't even know if he was still alive.'

'They could be connected,' Ottesen said. He had straightened up fully in his chair. 'If your father really is in Ittoqqortoormiit, then…' He hesitated. 'I didn't know about any pills being involved in the US military investigation into your father back in 1990—'

'No, and I'm sorry. I was about to tell you the day we discussed it, but then they rang…about Jakob…'

'Are you sure about the pills and your father?' Ottesen said.

'Yes. Briggs has been after me as well. We had only just got back from Færingehavn. He's very keen to get his hands on those pills.'

'As are we,' Rakel exclaimed, looking at Ottesen.

Ottesen mulled it over. 'Very well. I'd better take the pills more seriously…I might be able to find your father when I'm over there. If he really is in Ittoqqortoormiit, that is.'

'I don't know if he is there,' Matthew said. 'Like I said, that note is the only thing I've heard from him since I was four years old.'

'Quite,' Ottesen said. 'But I'll keep an eye out and I'll give you a call if I see him.'

Matthew nodded grimly. 'And then he gets locked up for good, doesn't he?'

'There's no way around that,' Ottesen said. 'Briggs made it very clear that the US military wants your father arrested.'

'I don't think he's there,' Matthew said. 'Or wouldn't your officer over there have just arrested him?'

'That depends on how well your father has settled in,' Rakel said with a grin.

'Rakel is right,' Ottesen said. 'Ittoqqortoormiit has a population of around four hundred, and they all look out for each other, one way or another.' He paused, and then said: 'However, I'll keep my eyes and ears peeled, and you carry on with the investigation here in Nuuk.'

'Agreed,' Rakel said, and got up. 'We need to find Arnaq...And Abelsen.'

'Yes, we do,' Ottesen said. He raised his palms to cover his nose and mouth and exhaled heavily. 'Please would you stay behind, Matthew? I want to have a word with you in private.'

38

Matthew watched Rakel as she left Ottesen's office. Then he turned his attention to Ottesen.

'I've started to have doubts about something,' Ottesen said. 'That's the real reason I asked you to come over.'

'Okay, what is it?'

'It's about Abelsen and Lyberth's murder.'

Matthew nodded pensively. It was less than two months since he had discovered the body of the dethroned national treasure in Tupaarnaq's empty flat. The old Inuit had been gutted from his groin to his chest and his intestines pulled out. He had been practically crucified on the floor.

'Abelsen killing Lyberth just doesn't sound right to me,' Ottesen began.

'What do you mean?' Matthew said with a frown.

'I don't see it,' Ottesen said. 'Lyberth was Abelsen's loyal ally for more than forty years. He would never kill him, and certainly not because of a little corruption scandal or an old child abuse story. We're drowning in such cases and seriously, does anyone care about them?'

'But didn't Abelsen confess?'

'Yes, in an outburst of rage when we found him in the house where you and Ulrik...well, you know. It just doesn't add up. Ulrik lost his mind and went ballistic when he learned that Abelsen was his real father and that Tupaarnaq was the big sister he had hated ever since he was a boy because she wiped out their family, but Abelsen— he would never lose his cool like that and kill in a blood rush.'

'So why did Abelsen admit to killing Lyberth?'

'Perhaps because he was under pressure and scared?'

'Scared? Who would he be scared of?'

'I'm getting to that.'

Matthew looked down. He smoothed a fold in his jumper. 'Are you saying Abelsen is innocent?'

'No, not when you look at the big picture,' Ottesen said. 'We know that Abelsen was in Tupaarnaq's flat on the day that Lyberth was killed, his mobile data proves that, but he wasn't alone and Lyberth wasn't murdered because of an old child abuse case.'

'So who did kill Lyberth?' Matthew said, twitching in his seat. 'Who was with him in Tupaarnaq's flat?'

'I don't know,' Ottesen said. 'But I intend to find out.' He hesitated. 'This whole business surrounding Lyberth's death and...It's as if the killing was also a warning to others with the same agenda as Lyberth.'

Matthew frowned. 'I don't follow?'

'I know,' Ottesen said. 'I've been keeping it to myself until now.'

'So Abelsen didn't kill Lyberth, but he was there? And there's someone behind him masterminding everything...and if you're right, then you and I went ahead and did precisely what they expected us to do?'

'Pretty much, but there's no point in brooding over that now; we need to move on. I've asked myself what Abelsen fears the most.'

Matthew closed his eyes and thought about it. What could make Abelsen sacrifice everything without any hope of ever getting it back?

What was Abelsen's most treasured project? He was known as the King of Greenland and although it was spoken in jest, it contained a strong element of truth.

'Independence,' Matthew exclaimed, and opened his eyes.

'Bingo,' Ottesen said.

Matthew got goosebumps.

'Total Greenlandic independence from Denmark would smash Abelsen's world for good,' Ottesen explained. 'There can be few CEOs or civil servants up here who don't realise the high cost of it. If Greenland were to become independent, anyone with knowledge, initiative or skill would be on the first plane out of here. It's something that's rarely mentioned when we debate independence from Denmark, but if Greenland loses the Danish block grant and NATO Arctic Command, and has to take over the administration of thirty government portfolios currently being run from Denmark as well, then it will go bankrupt before the ink on the independence treaty has dried. There will be no salvation and no rebuilding plan, because there'll be no money. After such a collapse, Greenland won't be able to generate even a fraction of the income needed to run the country as we do now. There'll be no wages for public-sector workers; everything will shut down. Town halls. Schools. Hospitals. Pretty much anyone with a halfway decent education will head for Denmark, Norway or Iceland before the door slams shut, and while every Greenlandic citizen can still exercise their rights and privileges as Danish nationals.'

'Yes, I've heard those arguments before and I think that you're right,' Matthew said. 'And Abelsen's deepest fear must be losing his kingdom, but who would back him to such an extent that Lyberth ends up getting killed?'

'That's what I want to talk to you about,' Ottesen said. 'I just wanted to give you the big picture first.'

'I still don't see how any of this clears Abelsen,' Matthew said.

'Surely it just gives him an even stronger motive—given that Lyberth wanted independence at any cost, while Abelsen wanted to avoid it, also at any cost? Lyberth was one of the strongest voices when it came to hating everything Danish, and from Abelsen's point of view, Lyberth must have been one of the most dangerous men in Greenland.'

Ottesen held up a USB stick. 'The most rabid of Lyberth's fellow Siumut Party members had this chucked into their postboxes yesterday.'

'What's on it?'

'I printed it out,' Ottesen said, sliding a slim stack of papers across the desk.

Matthew picked it up, glanced quickly at the top sheet and then looked up at Ottesen.

'Keep going.'

Matthew started flicking through the sheets. Every single one contained a picture of Lyberth lying on the floor in Tupaarnaq's flat. Matthew shut his eyes and pinched the bridge of his nose. Lyberth was alive in the first few pictures. He was nailed to the floor, but he was alive. His eyes were filled with terror. His jumper had been cut off. His eyes were screaming into the lens. The killer had stopped to take pictures as he cut open the stomach of the living man. There was blood everywhere. Any hope of survival was gone from Lyberth's eyes, and yet he still didn't die. Not until his intestines were cut free and pulled out. Across each picture the words '*First warning—who's next?*' were written in the kind of font you could add with a photo-shop app.

'Are you okay?'

Matthew shook his head. 'This…This is insane. Who the hell…' He had seen Lyberth's dead body on the floor in the flat himself, but this was much, much worse. 'Who sent it?'

'I've no idea,' Ottesen said. 'But I struggle to see Abelsen doing this. This was done by professionals, experienced killers…hitmen, possibly.'

'I can see where you're coming from now,' Matthew said, putting the sheets back on the desk. His hands were shaking. 'What about the USB stick? Can you trace anything?'

'Nope…These people know what they're doing. They know how quickly a human being dies from loss of blood and pain, and they know how you delete their IT footprints. We have nothing on them, but at least we now know that they exist, because Abelsen didn't do this. He doesn't have the contacts.'

A shiver went down Matthew's spine. 'So who do you think they are?'

'That's where I hit a wall, Matt. I just don't know that yet, but I was hoping that you could bear it in mind and keep your ears and eyes open. Now that you know as much as I do, perhaps you might think of something…But it stays between us, agreed?'

'Yes, of course.' Matthew's thoughts circled around Abelsen and the dead Lyberth. Who could execute something like that so cleanly? Who would think of it and get away with it? A business cartel? A political party? The Danish intelligence service? The state? The US military? No matter who it was, they were gambling with very high stakes, and Lyberth was unlikely to be the first or the last casualty.

Matthew took out his mobile to see if he could access anything which might help, but the battery had run down. 'I'll just charge it, if you don't mind.'

'Of course, go ahead…Anyway, it's time I went home to pack. Now, don't forget, this is strictly between the two of us, all right?'

'Else has tried to call me,' Matthew said, looking up at Ottesen. 'Twelve times…and that's her again now.' The mobile buzzed in his hand.

39

The red AS 350 helicopter flew low across the mountains south of Nuuk. The rock faces were speckled with white and grey. The snow came and went, and the sleet that had drifted across them had enclosed them in a thick layer of glossy ice.

Matthew looked down at the sea. Even the trip to the airport had been a challenge, as Rakel had struggled to clear the snow off the car for several minutes while the heating was on high inside it. Matthew had been very distracted. Arnaq had got through to Else's mobile, but the signal had been poor and Arnaq had only managed to say a few words. At the same time, he was trying to make sense of the killing of Lyberth, Abelsen's role in it all, and the prospect of Greenlandic independence.

'Phew, I'm glad it stopped raining,' Malik said. 'We would never have got off the ground in that sleet.'

Matthew looked at Malik. He was sitting opposite him with his camera resting on his thighs. Next to him was a small black bag of camera lenses.

'So why do you want to go to Færingehavn?' Rakel wanted to know.

'We need fresh footage,' Malik said. 'So I tagged along with Viktor when he got the call to fly. He was over at my place.'

'Good to have you here,' Matthew said, craning his neck in order to look out through the windscreen in front of the pilot. It wouldn't take them long to get to Færingehavn by air.

'Just watch it,' Rakel said, nodding at the camera. 'If we find something bad, don't even think of pointing that thing at it—do I make myself clear?'

'Sure, sure,' Malik said. 'Take it easy, sister sunshine.'

'Sometimes you're too much,' Rakel said with a smile.

'Having three of us might turn out to be to our advantage,' Matthew said.

'Four,' Malik interjected quickly. 'We've got Viktor as well.'

'I'm staying with my baby,' the pilot said. 'I'm not running around that dump.'

'Do the three of you think you could man up,' Rakel said in a reproachful voice. 'We're flying down there to look for Matthew's sister.' She looked at Matthew. 'I told you she was alive, didn't I?'

'Yes. But she was in a bad way. She could barely speak, Else said, and then it sounded as if someone smashed the mobile.'

'We'll find her.' Rakel placed her hand on Matthew's thigh and patted it a few times. 'We'll find her, Matt.'

'And Tupaarnaq,' Matthew added. 'I bet she's there as well.'

Rakel withdrew her hand. 'What was up with her?'

'No one could get hold of me or knew where I was, and then she suddenly left. She told Else that she was going hunting.'

'We can't be sure that she has gone to Færingehavn,' Rakel said.

Matthew shrugged. 'She seemed convinced that Arnaq and her friends were still there somewhere.'

'I'm guessing she nicked your boat,' Malik grinned.

'Five minutes,' Viktor called out from the cockpit, 'and we'll be there. Where do you want me to land?'

'Circle the town a few times,' Matthew said. 'If there's nothing to see, we need to land by the bunker point on the other side of the fjord.'

Malik hummed to himself while he changed the camera lens.

'Let's have a look at the town,' Viktor said, steering the helicopter to the left and flying across the shore.

The helicopter flew so close across the houses that they could see snow whirling up from the roofs.

'There's no sleet here,' Viktor said.

Malik got up and squeezed himself down next to Viktor. The camera clicked between his fingers, the lens zooming in and out. 'Fly low across the warehouses as well, would you?' Malik said.

'It'll cost you,' Viktor said.

'There's a truffle in it for you...Hey...' Malik glanced over his shoulder at them. 'That's your boat, isn't it, Matt?'

'What?' Matthew shifted in his seat and leaned across to the window on the opposite side. 'Yes, it is...That means Tupaarnaq is down there somewhere.' He pressed his face against the glass.

'Fly low across the ground,' Rakel said. 'Perhaps she's waiting for us.'

'Tupaarnaq?' Matthew said. 'She never waits for anyone.'

Rakel leaned back. 'You do know she's a killer, don't you?'

Matthew continued to focus on the boat.

'For real,' Rakel went on. 'She killed her family in cold blood.'

'No,' Matthew said. 'She stopped a man who had wrecked her life and who had murdered her sisters.'

'I'm not so sure...After all, she didn't appeal.'

'Well.' Matthew looked at Rakel. 'Perhaps it was better than going home.'

'But she doesn't have a home here in Greenland anymore.'

'My point exactly.'

'Mind you don't get your fingers burned,' Rakel said. 'Criminals know how to pull the wool over your eyes.'

'I believe Jakob,' Matthew said. 'He followed Tupaarnaq's trial and he said that she should have been acquitted.'

'There's no one on the boat,' Malik said. 'But the rubber dinghy is gone, and as you never sail without a rubber dinghy...she must be ashore somewhere.'

'There's Bárdur!' Rakel pointed towards the bunker point.

Matthew quickly turned his head and followed her gaze. 'We need to land,' he said to the pilot. 'Next to that guy over there...right now.'

40

Bárdur paced up and down the living room. He stared at all of them, but mostly at Rakel.

'Why don't we sit down?' Rakel said, looking firmly at Bárdur. 'So that we can have a chat.'

'About what?' the big man sneered.

In his mind Matthew tried to compare Bárdur's voice with that of the man who had attacked him in Nuuk, but his attacker hadn't said very much and Matthew had been terrified.

Rakel sat down on a seventies-style blue sofa. 'How very comfortable. Lovely house you have here.'

'Thank you.' Bárdur pulled out a chair by the dining table and sat down as well.

'Any chance of a cup of coffee?' Malik said.

'No.' Bárdur shifted on his chair. 'What do you want? I don't like visitors.'

'Oh, this isn't a social call,' Matthew said. 'You're the only person who lives out here where my sister and her friends disappeared.'

'I've already spoken to the police about it,' Bárdur said dismissively. 'I don't know why you've come back.'

'I need to take a slash,' Malik interjected. 'Can I use your loo?'

'No,' Bárdur said. He glowered at Malik. His eyebrows had sunk down over his eyes.

'You don't have a loo?' Malik went on in a quizzical voice.

'No,' Bárdur said. He closed his eyes. 'Yes…No…I want you to leave now.'

'Cool television.' Malik raised his camera and took a few pictures of the old-fashioned television set. 'Does it work?'

'Work?' Bárdur said, looking at them in turn.

'Yes, all the signals are digital today, and that old picture tube can't—'

'I don't use it,' Bárdur cut him off. 'It's just sitting there…It's nice.'

'It certainly is,' Malik said and aimed his camera at a picture of an old fisherman with a pipe and sou'wester instead. 'My old aunt had that exact same picture in her home.'

'Didn't all old people have that?' Rakel said.

Malik shrugged and lowered his camera.

'My sister and her friends saw you over in Færingehavn the day before they disappeared,' Matthew said. 'Together with a pale young man whose name might be Símin and who has just turned twenty-three?'

'No,' Bárdur said.

'No? You can't just say no. They saw you. Who was the pale guy?'

'I don't know,' Bárdur said.

'But you were there.'

'No.'

Matthew swore, and then said: 'There can't be any other red-bearded men your size running around out here now, can there?'

'Yes.'

'Who?' Matthew drummed his fingers on his leg impatiently.

Bárdur frowned. 'My brother.'

'Hey,' Rakel interrupted. 'You never said you had a brother?'

'Who is he?' Matthew wanted to know.

'My brother's name is Olí,' Bárdur said.

'Shit,' Rakel sighed. 'I'm tempted to haul you back to the police station again.'

'No,' Bárdur said. 'No…we're…no, we're not going to do that.'

'So where is Olí now?' Rakel asked him.

Matthew nodded.

'He looks like me,' Bárdur said, shaking his head dismissively. He was leaning forwards now and for the first time he looked straight at Matthew. 'I hardly ever see him. He keeps mostly to himself.'

'I thought you lived alone?' Matthew said.

Bárdur nodded. 'Yes, alone.'

'But where does your brother live?' Rakel said. 'If it's somewhere out here, surely you must know?'

'He's the devil himself,' Bárdur said. The expression in his eyes had grown more intense. 'He's everywhere…Inside and out.'

'And what about that pale guy you were with?' Rakel tried. 'Is his name Símin?'

'I didn't do it,' Bárdur said, leaning back again. 'You need to talk to Olí.'

'Seriously,' Rakel said. 'You really should have told us about Olí when we first interviewed you in Nuuk.'

'You don't talk about Olí,' Bárdur said.

'I think you'll find that's my decision,' Rakel said irritably.

Matthew caught Bárdur's eye again. 'Why did Olí attack me?'

'I didn't do it,' Bárdur said again, and looked away.

'I've had enough of you,' Rakel said angrily. 'We'll come back for you once we've searched Færingehavn.' She got up and zipped up her police jacket. 'Meanwhile I suggest you try to remember more about Olí and that pale boy…Argh.' She groaned with frustration.

Bárdur nodded reluctantly. He pressed his lips together so hard that they disappeared completely behind his beard.

Matthew studied the man's fleshy face. He was easily strong enough to gut Lyberth and nail him to the floor, but he seemed too stupid to be above Abelsen in the food chain. And besides, he hadn't killed Jakob; they'd had the result of the DNA tests. There was no match.

'We need to find that pale guy,' Matthew said wearily. He patted his thighs and got up. 'Let's fly across the fjord and take a look at Færingehavn.'

41

The snow whirled up around the red body of the helicopter. Despite there not being much snow on the ground, there was enough to create a brief white chaos under the downdraught from the rotors as the helicopter took off.

Matthew, Malik and Rakel watched it from the ground. They had agreed that Viktor might as well circle the area and carry out an aerial search while they checked the empty houses in Færingehavn.

They decided to start with the big grey house where they had found traces of blood. Malik's camera dangled around his neck and he had a backpack full of lenses.

Matthew looked at Rakel's back. The word 'POLICE' glowed in white letters across her dark blue jacket. Her kit was attached to the belt around her waist, visible right below the hem of the jacket.

Malik carefully raised his camera when they stepped up onto the worn wooden walkway that led up to the grey house. He aimed the lens at the woodwork below a window at the end of the right wing. It looked as if blood had run down the wall below the window.

'Is this the place?' he asked quietly.

'It's in there, yes,' Rakel said. 'But you won't be taking any pictures inside, understood?'

'Of course.' He raked a hand through his shoulder length black hair. 'This is seriously messed up, all of it…That business with Ulrik and everything was only a few months ago…'

Matthew looked down at the withered grass and the snow under his feet. He nudged a bit of dirty snow with the toe of his boot and avoided looking at Rakel. 'If Tupaarnaq was here, she would have come outside by now.'

'But the boat is here,' Malik said.

Matthew took out his cigarettes and lit two; he gave one to Malik. The wind was cold. It stung his cheeks. 'Somebody needs to flatten this shit hole.'

'I think it's flattening itself,' Rakel said. 'Let's search the houses… for the umpteenth time. There has to be something we keep missing.'

Matthew nodded grimly. Exhaled the smoke. It tormented him that Arnaq might be lying somewhere, praying to be found before it was too late, her hope of rescue slowly dying inside her. He rubbed his eyes. His fingers smelled of smoke.

The helicopter swooped close to them. Viktor shook his head to indicate that he had seen nothing new. Rakel, too, shook her head, but at that point the sharp nosed AS 350 was already on its way back out across the sea.

•

They searched the houses one by one and by the time they reached the laundry, which bordered the sea near the place where Matthew and Tupaarnaq had previously rowed ashore, the helicopter had finished its aerial search.

Matthew couldn't see the helicopter on the far side of the fjord, but he had seen it fly around the bunker point and heard its engine stop. He looked at his watch. It was just after five o'clock in the afternoon and it was slowly starting to get dark.

'There's a rifle in here.'

Matthew spun around and looked towards the laundry, where Malik was standing. 'What did you say?'

'Is there usually?' Malik went on.

'Why would there be a rifle in there?' Rakel rushed over to Malik.

'Eh, because there is!'

'Don't touch it,' Rakel ordered him as she stepped through the smashed door. 'Is that Tupaarnaq's, Matt?'

Matthew walked around Rakel and squatted down next to the rifle on the floor. 'Yes, it is. She bought it when she came back to Greenland.'

'Are you sure?'

'One hundred per cent.' He reached for the rifle.

Rakel shoved him aside. 'What you think you're doing? Our technicians need to examine it.'

He looked up at her. 'But we can't just leave it here and I want to know if it was fired.'

'Then let me do it,' she said, picking up the rifle. 'And yes, you're right. We can't leave it lying around. We don't know how many nutters are out here.' She removed the magazine and pulled back the bolt. 'One cartridge is missing from the magazine, but it could have been fired at any time.'

'Tupaarnaq never goes ashore without checking that the magazine is full,' Matthew said. 'She does it almost on autopilot. I've filled it for her myself before.'

Rakel surveyed the room. 'Apart from that, is there anything of interest here?'

'I don't think so.' Matthew rubbed his eyelids with two fingers. 'There's dust everywhere.'

'We'll find your sister,' Rakel said, placing her hand on Matthew's shoulder. 'Fuck it…We'll go back and talk to Bárdur again. I refuse to believe that moron doesn't know something.'

'I'm sure he was the guy who attacked me,' Matthew said. 'It can't be anyone else. He has to know where Arnaq is…and Tupaarnaq.'

'In that case we need to call Viktor and get him back over here so he can pick us up,' Malik said. 'What on earth is that twit doing on the other side?'

'Refuelling, I guess,' Rakel said. 'Perhaps it's complicated.'

'Ha,' Malik quipped. 'I bet he's looking for girls on his mobile inside that warm cabin of his.'

'But we haven't got a signal,' Matthew pointed out, waving his mobile in the air. He had done so regularly, but there was no coverage anywhere, not even one bar. 'How is it even possible that Arnaq could have made a call from here?'

'I've never found any networks in this precise place,' Malik said. 'But when we sail around the fjords closer to Nuuk, there are occasional spots with some coverage. Not very strong—you can't even open Instagram.'

'If she had a Danish SIM card, she might have got lucky and found a spot where she could get a short call through,' Rakel said, surveying the surrounding houses. 'But Malik is right; it's more common closer to Nuuk. This place is fairly dead.'

Malik let his backpack slide from his shoulder. He sat down on the dusty floor next to it. 'Does anyone want a rum truffle?'

'You actually brought some?' Rakel said, sitting down as well. She carefully placed the rifle on the floor and set down the magazine next to it.

Matthew brushed some wooden splinters away and sat down opposite the other two.

Malik nodded, smiled and produced a box of six big truffles. 'Or would you rather have some dried seal?'

'You brought that as well?'

He shook his head with a grin. 'No, but I would have packed

some whale blubber if I'd known that we would be sitting here freezing our backsides off…Matt loves whale blubber.'

'You do?' Rakel asked, looking at Matthew with raised eyebrows.

'No,' Matthew said, pulling a face. 'It's just Malik having a joke at my expense. He's forever trying to get me to eat it by telling me how the oil in the raw blubber warms you up.'

'It does!' Malik protested.

Rakel nodded. 'So can I have one, then?' She got her truffle and looked at Matthew. 'Has Malik ever told you that he's never shot anything himself?'

Matthew frowned. 'I thought he went hunting all the time?'

'Well,' Malik said. 'I go off with the guys…I'm cool with that. I just can't be bothered to shoot anything.'

'Go on, tell him about the seal,' Rakel said.

Malik swallowed a mouthful of truffle and wriggled on the floor. 'If we have to wait for that idiot Viktor for a long time, I'm going to make myself comfy on the old sofas in the community hall.'

'I'm with you,' Matthew said. 'So what about the seal?'

Malik looked around the old laundry. 'When I was eight years old, I was out with my dad one day emptying the nets…We lived up in Aasiaat. It was bloody freezing. And when we pulled the net up, there was a dead seal trapped in it. It was completely rigid. It had drowned and it was ice cold. But its eyes were staring at me, all black and shiny. My dad was over the moon at bringing home fresh seal, but I hated how it had stared at me…That it had drowned and everything. So as we walked home, I made up my mind that I would never kill an animal. It's not some vegetarian bollocks; I've just never felt like killing anything myself.'

'You wouldn't have lasted very long in Greenland a hundred years ago,' Rakel said.

'Never mind,' Malik said, stuffing the rest of his truffle into his mouth. 'You can always shoot a seal for us, if we end up stranded here for weeks.'

'You can certainly shoot a seal with that,' Matthew said, nodding at the rifle. 'But I'll take a raincheck as well. I nearly threw up the last time.'

'Why?' Rakel said.

'Eating raw liver...Tupaarnaq had just cut it out of the seal... Guts and blood all over the place. It tasted disgusting.'

'Of course it did—you need to prepare it properly,' Rakel said. 'You put the meat in clean water and you keep changing the water until it stops being muddy...And only the ribs are tasty...I'll cook some for you one day, and then you'll be converted.'

Matthew was lost in thought for a moment, then he popped the last bit of truffle into his mouth and looked up. 'Is there any way we can reach Viktor?'

'Not without a boat,' Malik said. 'It would take us days to hike down to the bottom of the fjord and then walk back along the other side to Polaroil, and I don't think we'd make it. We didn't bring any kit for a hike like that at this time of year.'

'How weird,' Matthew said. 'I mean, we can look right across to where he is.'

'That's Greenland for you,' Malik smiled. 'If you don't have a boat or plane, you're stuck where you are. And Mother Nature is just waiting to kill you.'

'You don't think anything has happened to Viktor, do you?' Rakel said suddenly.

Malik shook his head. 'No, and that's what so bloody irritating about him; once he reclines that seat, he can sleep for hours.'

42

Matthew held his breath. He was certain that the others had also heard the noise because they had fallen just as quiet as he had. It sounded as if someone was walking past the broken windows outside.

When it began to get dark they had moved from the old laundry to a square red building, which had once been some sort of canteen and community hall. It was where Færingehavn's former residents had watched movies, played pool, played the piano, listened to music and relaxed. Many of their things were still there, but in a terrible condition. The heavy pool table had collapsed and the piano had split open and barely looked like an instrument. But there were also a few old pieces of furniture which could still be used, and that was why they had sought shelter there when they gave up waiting for Viktor at the laundry.

Matthew was lying on a battered green sofa, Malik and Rakel on the other two. None of them had much battery left on their mobiles so they chatted in the darkness.

Until they heard the noise.

'Do you think that's Viktor?' Malik whispered.

Rakel hushed him. 'Not without the helicopter, you moron.'

The noise began again. It sounded like the crunching of someone walking on frozen grass.

'This is giving me the creeps,' Malik said.

Rakel slowly stood up.

Matthew heard her open one of the small bags on her belt and shortly afterwards a click as she removed the safety catch from her service pistol.

'Let's check it out,' she whispered.

'What?' Malik hissed. 'You're going outside?'

'Yes.' She hesitated for a moment. She stood still. 'To be honest, I was hoping this would happen when we flew down here.'

'You're nuts,' Malik said.

'Yeah, yeah,' Rakel whispered. 'Now, come over here and watch my back. And Matthew, pick up the rifle and load it.'

'Okay,' Matthew said softly, and got up. He struggled to keep his breathing steady as he slowly made his way to the sofa where Rakel had been lying.

Malik and Rakel crept towards the door to the hall and then onwards to the front door. Matthew picked up the rifle, inserted the magazine, slid the bolt back and then pushed it forward. For the first time he experienced a physical sensation of relief at holding a loaded weapon. He was still frightened and on edge, but the rifle gave him an unexpected feeling of control.

At that moment he heard a shot coming from the hall. Then Malik shouted. Something collapsed onto the floor. Something was shoved against the wall. Then there was silence.

Matthew raised the rifle. He stood with the butt pressed hard against his shoulder and the barrel pointing forward. He was breathing in short gasps. He jerked his upper body around so the barrel pointed in different directions.

'Rakel?' he called out, and jumped at the sound of his own voice.

There was crunching near the door to the hall.

'Stop,' Matthew croaked. His voice was close to failing him. The muscles in his throat contracted, preventing him from swallowing. He imagined Malik and Rakel lying wounded in the hall. 'I have a loaded gun…Who is it?'

There was more crunching in the dirt on the floor; Matthew aimed the rifle at the ceiling and fired.

The shot echoed in his ears and a brief silence followed. Then the noises from the hall resumed. It sounded as if someone was lifting a heavy object.

'I'll fire again,' Matthew said in a loud voice.

The sounds of scrambling continued, and moments later another shot was fired. Matthew heard the bullet hit the wall behind him. He threw himself onto the floor and lay very still. He listened to the night and the sounds from the hall. The rifle rested heavy against his shoulder.

Some minutes later the hall fell quiet. He heard someone walk across the frozen grass. The footsteps sounded far heavier this time. And clumsy.

Then there was silence.

Matthew rolled onto his back. The floor crunched underneath him when he turned onto his side and got to a standing position. The tears were running down his cheeks. He found the wedding ring in his pocket and slipped it back on his finger. Then he closed his eyes and inhaled deep into his lungs a couple of times. The air in the room tasted moist and dusty. Even now that the temperature was below freezing. He walked towards the hall. Slowly and taking short footsteps.

There was a cold draught coming from the front door. Matthew found his mobile and used it to light his way across the room and out through the broken door. There was blood on the floor, the walls and the concrete step outside the door, but it was nowhere near as disconcerting as in the grey house.

He switched off his mobile and stepped carefully outside. It was a starry night with a slim crescent moon. There were dragging trails in the grass and snow. The snow had been compressed and the grass broken in a track that led down to the sea.

Matthew followed the trail.

Down by the laundry he could see a faint light. It could be from a lamp or from an iPhone close to the window.

It took him a few minutes to walk down there. The light kept flickering in the darkness immediately outside the laundry.

He walked very carefully. Even so the frozen blades of grass sounded like branches snapping under his feet.

43

The laundry was just as empty as before. However, there was now a bit of blood on the floor and one of the tall cupboards in the drying room had been pulled out. Matthew had previously tried shifting them, but they hadn't budged. The row of slim cupboards took up the whole of the wall.

There was a faint track in the dirt across the rough concrete floor. Dragging tracks, just like outside.

Matthew crossed the room and grabbed the cupboard that had been pulled out with one hand, holding the rifle in the other. Behind the cupboard door there was an arrangement of rails, and it was clear that the cupboards could be moved along on them. There was a metal crossbar inside each cupboard so you could dry clothes the full depth of the cupboard.

The cupboard door didn't look like it could be moved, but it was open enough for him to climb inside. Once inside, it was spacious and at the back there was a ventilation shaft whose grate had been removed from the wall and set down below it.

The light he had been able to see from outside was coming from the hole where the grate had been fixed.

He held the rifle in front of him and inched towards the shaft while holding his breath, as much as that was possible.

A faint noise broke the silence. It sounded like footsteps coming closer. From a basement. Down the shaft.

Matthew retreated one step and kept the rifle firmly against his shoulder. He could hear someone start to climb up a ladder or some steps. The light flickered. A body must be blocking the source of the light. Matthew steadied his breathing. He aimed the rifle at the shaft.

A hand appeared on the bottom edge of the shaft; fingers scrambling to get a hold. A second hand appeared.

Matthew's fingers tightened around the weapon and his forefinger shook lightly over the trigger.

A head appeared and he pulled the trigger.

'What the hell do you think you're doing?' Rakel screamed, taking cover below the wall. 'It's me, you moron.'

Matthew let the rifle fall along his body. He was shocked.

'Right, I'm coming back up,' she called out. 'Hold your fire.'

'Sorry,' Matthew said through a short breath. He furrowed his brow and shook his head. He could see that she was on the verge of tears. 'I'm sorry...But what the hell are you doing down there?'

'It's Malik,' Rakel said in a thick voice. 'Come on down.'

Matthew engaged the safety catch on the side of the rifle, securing it, and went over to the shaft. 'What happened?'

'That big bastard got him.'

Matthew looked over the edge of the shaft and immediately saw Malik lying on the floor below. He struggled to keep his voice under control. 'Is he dead?'

Rakel shook her head. 'Not yet...'

'Is there anything we can do?' Matthew said as he climbed down the ladder, which was built into the wall.

'I've done what I could,' Rakel said. 'He received a heavy blow to the top of his back. I think he has cracked a rib and punctured a lung.' She looked up. Tears welled up in her eyes. 'There's nothing more we can do here.'

Matthew knelt down besides Malik. 'He seems totally out of it.'

She nodded. 'We have to get him to Nuuk or he won't make it.'

'What the hell is this place?' Matthew said, looking nervously down a long, grey concrete corridor. The only thing breaking up the corridor were the naked lightbulbs illuminating it. 'Are they here?'

'I don't know,' Rakel said.

He looked at her. One side of her face was red and swollen. One eye half-closed due to the swelling. 'Was it the same guy who hit you?'

'I don't know whether there was one man or two; it all happened so fast. I think they have my gun. I woke up down here next to Malik a moment ago.' She looked at Malik, who was lying very still on the concrete floor in the recovery position. She buried her face in her hands. 'We're all going to die.'

Matthew got up and hugged her. He could feel her pressing herself against his shoulder and body.

'I really want to go home,' she sobbed. 'My kids have no one but me.'

'I know.' Matthew kissed her hair lightly. 'We'll get out. I promise.' He could hear that she was crying. 'Did you see the man who attacked you?'

She shook her head. 'No, but he was tall.'

'If it's Bárdur, his boat must be up there somewhere or he couldn't be on this side of the fjord now.'

'Perhaps,' she said in a raw voice, moving away from Matthew. She dried her eyes. 'I don't know about that, but what I do know is that Arnaq and her friends are down here. We searched that town twenty times at least since they disappeared, and there's no trace of them above ground, but down here...I've never heard a word about this bunker.' She looked down the corridor. 'Because they also dragged Malik and me down here.'

Matthew stared down the corridor as well. 'We have to call for help now.'

'You can't call for help here…You know that just as well as I do.'

'I have to. I'll think of something…What will you do?'

She shook her head. 'Malik can't be left alone. Give me the rifle so I can defend us if they return before you come back.'

Matthew handed her the rifle. 'I'll go back up and see what I can find.'

She closed her eyes and breathed heavily a couple of times. 'We have to get out of here,' she said. 'We really do.' She looked at him and nodded grimly. 'I'll check if there's another exit close by. There has to be something other than that ladder.'

'Yes, do that. I'll climb up and check the shore.'

⁕

The darkness closed around him as he walked down towards the quay with the empty warehouses. He had been inside them many times now, including earlier today. The muscles in his arms were tense and he was sweating although the night was full of frost.

He took a deep drag on his cigarette and saw the tip light up in the darkness. He took another deep drag, but there wasn't the slightest calm to be found in the smoke, and there was no sign of a boat anywhere.

Arnaq and Tupaarnaq were being held somewhere in the corridors under the abandoned town, and given the state Malik was in, they couldn't afford to wait for help to arrive of its own accord. They had to summon help now, and so loudly that it could be heard across the fifty kilometres of uninhabited mountains between them and Nuuk.

He picked up a jerry can inside the door to the first warehouse. He knew that many old ten-litre jerry cans full of oil lay scattered around.

His hands were shaking as he splashed oil onto the wood of the old building. He tossed aside the jerry can and found an old cloth, which he dipped in oil and then ignited. Once the flames got a good hold of the cloth, he threw it at the oil-soaked wood. Soon flames were licking the high wall.

He set fire to the rest of the warehouses, one after the other, until all of the hundred-metre-long wooden quay was ablaze.

The quay itself went up like a massive wick. The flames reached thirty to forty metres up in the air, and the heat was so intense that he had to walk in a curve in order to return to the laundry.

The whole of Færingehavn was now lit with a violent, bright orange glow. Just before Matthew went back inside the laundry, he saw a building not far from the quay catch fire, ignited by the heat and the thousands of sparks in the air.

44

The heat from the burning quay was intense even as far away as the laundry. Everything was orange. The light flickered and the roar of the fire was so loud that Matthew could hear nothing else. The snow had melted in a big radius around the quay and the grass was burning in several places.

He looked at the laundry and placed his hand on the peeling boards. They felt warm. Two houses close to the quay had also caught fire and were now engulfed in flames.

Matthew entered the laundry. It was warmer inside than out, the heat had started to rise and there was an acrid smell. He hurried through the first room to the drying cupboards. Together he and Rakel had to get Malik out.

'It's me,' he called out. The blaze sounded just as loud behind the cupboards. 'We need to get Malik outside…I've set fire to everything.'

He looked down the shaft, but saw only an empty floor. There was no trace of Malik or Rakel. He climbed down to get a better look. There was nothing to see.

The light was still on. Above him he could hear the roar of the flames through the shaft. The walls were cold. He could feel that the long, underground corridor had been blasted out of the bedrock.

The air was dry. Stuffy, but without any moisture. Just dry and dusty.

Matthew kept a hand on the wall as he walked along the corridor. It was quiet. He regretted not bringing a rock or a club of some kind. If he encountered someone, he had nothing with which he could defend himself. He had expected Rakel and the rifle to be there, but now he was vulnerable.

The corridor split in two and he continued down the right-hand one. Shortly afterwards doors began to appear on both sides. Some were peeling wood, other were made from iron. Most were locked, but there were few places where he could get in.

There was one room that looked like a doctor's consulting room, and another that looked to be a bedroom. Sparsely furnished with a seventies couch, cupboards and a sink with a round mirror above it. There were some clothes in the room, and the bed was made up with clean linen. The room smelt as if somebody slept in there, but for now it was empty.

Further down the corridor there was an open door, which led to a smaller room with two iron doors on the same wall. Both doors were locked from the outside with bolts and sturdy handles.

Even before he reached the far side of the room, he spotted a pink backpack by one of the doors. There was something on top of the backpack—when he got closer, he could see that it was a smashed mobile.

He began to pull at the handle frantically and pushed the bolt aside. The door gave and rattled. The air behind reeked of urine and ammonium, and he was forced to cover his nose and mouth.

It was dark behind the door, but he could make out a figure lying on the floor near a wall. He jumped over an upended bucket and a tray of something that looked like ribs and knelt down beside the figure. He grabbed her shoulder and pressed his ear close to her mouth and nose to hear if she was breathing, but he couldn't hear anything. He pinched her ear. Twisted her earlobe.

She opened her eyes and started to cry when she saw him. There were no movements. Just her tears and some faint sounds from her throat.

'I'm here now,' Matthew said. 'I'm taking you home…Are you able to stand up?' He touched her cheek gently. 'Are you able to walk?'

She shook her head. Very faintly, but enough for him to see it.

He nodded. 'I just need to check next door, then I'll be back.'

Her eyes shone with fear.

'I'll be back,' he said. 'I promise…I think there might be someone there who can help us.'

Arnaq's eyes looked right through him. 'One, two, three, four, five, six, seven, eight…' she whispered to herself.

Matthew rushed outside and tried the next door. Even while he was pushing the bolt aside, he could hear life in there and as soon as he got the door open, he saw Tupaarnaq.

'I don't think I've ever been more pleased to see you,' she said. 'Do you know the way out? Are you alone? What happened?'

'I've no idea what this place is,' he said, looking into the room.

She pushed him back a little and closed the door behind her. 'There's nothing to see in there.'

He glanced at the cut to her temple. It was superficial. Mostly an elongated swelling.

'The bastard got me.' She touched the swelling gently, then looked about her. 'Are you alone?'

'Yes, I came with Rakel and Malik, but I think they've both been taken.' He could hear his voice break. 'Given the state Malik was in, dragging him around could kill him.'

'Shit,' Tupaarnaq said. 'There's just the two of us…And they've got my rifle.'

'Rakel had your rifle,' Matthew said. 'But she's gone.' He glanced up towards the ceiling. He should never have left Rakel and Malik alone.

Tupaarnaq looked at him. 'Do you know the way out?'

'Yes, but we need to take Arnaq.'

'You found her?'

'She's lying in the next room, but she's not strong enough to walk on her own…She's very weak.'

Tupaarnaq clenched her fists and ran to Arnaq in the adjacent cell.

Matthew hurried after her. 'It looks as if they've been starving her, but there's some meat in there, so…'

At the same moment they heard noises from the corridor. Footsteps and shouting.

Tupaarnaq grabbed Matthew.

Bárdur's voice echoed in the front room, and before Matthew and Tupaarnaq had reached the door, Bárdur and Símin had arrived.

Tupaarnaq picked up the metal bucket, but Bárdur floored her with a single punch before she managed to attack him.

The next moment Matthew was pushed over and his head smashed against the concrete floor before he had time to cushion the fall. He could feel the rough floor press against his skin while the blow and the pain made him black out.

THE
ESCAPE

45

'This can't go on.' Tom looked sharply at the thin man with the black hair. His face was just as pinched and tight as always. Demonic in so many ways, but no longer quite so frightening. Tom had managed to find a weakness in Abelsen: he lost control when he was high.

Abelsen rubbed his chin. 'So all you've been doing these last two days is hiding out, is that it?'

'Yes, what else was I supposed to do? Kill him?'

Abelsen smiled scornfully. 'Good luck with that.'

'Anyone can die.'

'Aha, you know my motto.'

'Jesus Christ...Come on, you need to see how they live.' Tom got up and glared at Abelsen. 'It can't carry on.'

'Live? What do you mean?'

'I mean that brute Bárdur.' Tom threw up his hands. 'This whole place is crazy. He rapes that woman you actually admit giving to him...she's chained to the wall! And what about the little girls? Solva and Kristina?'

The corners of Abelsen's mouth moved and he raised his eyebrows in an expression of indifference.

'Seriously, we have to put a stop this!' Tom raged. 'I mean, do you even know what's going on here?'

'Mankind,' Abelsen said, as he craned his neck and looked pensively at the ceiling, 'has grown so weak. Everything comes at a price, Tom. A hundred years ago progress always took priority over the individual. Building a bridge, a canal or creating a new industry cost human lives. People knew that, and they were willing to pay the price. It was what made Europe great. But look at us now!'

'What the hell does that have to do with Mona and the girls?'

'The girls are fine,' Abelsen said blithely, getting up. 'I often visit them myself.'

'You do what?'

'What did you imagine?' He extended his arms out to the sides like a crucified man. 'This is my experiment...My world.'

Tom slumped back in his chair. 'You're sick. It's much worse than I thought.'

'The blind are the ones who are sick,' Abelsen said. 'I'm the future.' He sat down again, very calmly. 'Tom, Bárdur knows perfectly well not to touch you. You're safe in this room.'

'My safety be damned,' Tom grunted angrily. 'What about Mona? She's chained up, for God's sake. He beats her and he rapes her...Have you seen her eyes?' Tom tightened his hands around the fabric of his brown trousers, creating taut folds down the legs. His nails dug into the fabric.

'I think it's best that you stay down here and focus on the experiment,' Abelsen said.

Tom looked at the Bunsen burner and the glass flasks. The many little boxes and plastic containers. The wooden moulds for the pills. He closed his eyes and exhaled slowly.

'Tom,' Abelsen continued, 'you and I have a deal, and you don't have to worry about anything other than keeping your end of it. That way your boy lives, and that's all there is to it.'

'But—' Tom protested and opened his eyes.

'Nothing down here will change,' Abelsen said. 'I thought you had realised that by now. Perhaps I've been too soft on you?'

'The whole thing is perverse.' Tom closed his eyes again and shook his head. His temples had started to throb. 'Do you ever air this place?'

'I thought I made myself perfectly clear when I told you about Bárdur the last time?'

Tom sat still and kept his eyes closed.

'Bárdur was born out here and he grew up in a very small and isolated community,' Abelsen said. 'And, as I told you, it was a deeply religious community, one built on corporal punishment, Bible school and, yes, at times also abuse. That was what life was like for most people out here, and it's very easy to judge other people's morality when you haven't been a part of it, for better or worse.'

'For better or worse,' Tom snapped back. 'There's nothing good about beatings and rape.'

'But if that's your whole world,' Abelsen said, 'then you know no other, and they haven't had a lot of schooling out here. In fact, I don't think there ever was a school...Just the Bible and God...And then Bárdur's world fell apart, his father disappeared without a trace. The fishing collapsed, everybody went away. Eventually only Bárdur was left. Always remember the context, Tom.'

'Context? What the...' Tom ground to a halt and stared at Abelsen in disbelief. 'You make him sound like a psychiatric patient we ought to pity, but nothing excuses this sick world and the rapes, nothing!'

Abelsen heaved a sigh and patted his thighs. 'I can see I'm not getting anywhere with you, Tom. I don't want to listen to you any longer. Shut up and make some more pills. I'll pick them up in a few hours. I'm going to have lunch with Bárdur. You won't forget that I also give your pills to his girls, will you?'

'You're even crazier than he is,' Tom exclaimed.

'I've brought you some boxes,' Abelsen went on. 'The kind of equipment I was able to get in Nuuk. It's from the university, so it should be the real McCoy, and you already have all the notes and your data from Thule, so you'll just have to make do with that. Now, get to work!'

Tom looked away. 'Make your own damned pills.'

'Very well, I'll arrange for you to travel to Denmark next week.'

'Eh?'

'I imagine you would like to attend Matthew's funeral.'

'You evil bastard,' Tom shouted, and jumped up. He grabbed Abelsen's throat and squeezed it, but felt at that same moment a pain shoot through his body so violently that he collapsed on the floor in spasms.

'Now, would you look at that.' Abelsen was holding a stun gun. He smiled at Tom, who was gasping for air. 'Matthew's fine, Tom. Only it sounded as if you wanted that to change, and I would like offer you the opportunity to see his coffin being lowered into the ground.'

Tom pressed a hand against his side where the electricity had entered. There was burning and stinging under his skin.

'Two hours, Tom. And I'll be back for some new pills.'

46

Tom's chest felt tight, as if his lungs were being dissolved by stomach acid. He knew that he could breathe, but it felt laboured. He was choking on his own bile.

It was just over an hour since Abelsen had picked up another portion of pills. This time Tom hadn't added any mind-altering substances. He didn't mind Abelsen overdosing and dying, but if he really did give the pills to the girls as well, then that would be unacceptable.

Tom wrung his hands. Then he got up and found the printed pictures of Matthew. He studied the boy closely, but it was impossible to work out the recipient of his son's smile. He caressed Matthew's pale skin and blond hair lovingly before folding up the sheets and slipping them into his back pocket. He also stuffed in a bag of pills and a small folding knife, which had arrived with the items for the experiment. Then he took out a thin file with the data from the Thule experiment, put it into a plastic bag and wedged it firmly in place under his shirt and the waistband of his trousers.

Out in the corridor, the light was off.

By now he had been around this section of the corridor so often that he no longer struggled to find his way in the dark. He knew exactly how far it was to the next corner, and how far to the abattoir and the rooms where Mona was being kept and the two girls were asleep. He could also make his way to the swimming pool blindfolded, but he had abandoned the idea of diving as his means of escape. The corridors above the water felt long and branched out, and if he didn't have enough air to swim the whole way in an underground channel, or if the underground channel narrowed, he would suffer a claustrophobic death and end up on the bottom of the pool with the other skeletons.

His hand trailed the rough concrete in the darkness as he followed the corridor around the first bend.

There was another corridor in the bunker, which he had also previously explored. It culminated in a wide iron gate, but the gate was impossible to open. It felt as if it was covered or bricked up from the outside, although it looked like it had once served as the main entrance to the bunker.

He slowed down. His hand carefully touched the door to the girls' bedroom. The hairs stood up on his arms. If he was lucky, they would be in there now. It was better if Mona was alone when he tried to talk to her. The girls were just as damaged as their father, but if he could convince their mother to escape, they might listen to her.

Tom looked up at the ceiling. The lights should have come on, but nothing happened.

He grabbed the handle to the living room door and opened it. It was the second time he'd been in there, but the first time he hadn't noticed very much except the chained woman and the girls on the floor. Now the living room was empty. The woman's armchair stood up against one wall and the chain lay slack across the floor like a dead snake extending its body into another room, through an open door right behind the chair.

In front of the chair was the rug the two girls had been sitting on. Slightly to his left were a coffee table and a sofa.

He looked at the crucifix on the wall to his left. It was large and hung right above an altar-like bookcase with two tall candles and a well-thumbed black Bible. Jesus hung on the crucifix. He looked tired. Worn out. Golden. Bloodstains had been painted onto his body, on his feet and hands and around his hairline. His mouth was open, his eyes staring impotently at the ceiling.

Tom continued to the armchair and picked up the chain. The iron was cold. It felt heavy in his hands. He straightened up and looked over his shoulder before he continued towards the door to the other room.

The door was open and he could see a double bed inside the room. On one side the chain continued under a duvet, while the other side of the bed was empty; the duvet hung over the edge of the bed. The air was sour and stuffy. Light from the living room reached the bedroom like artificial twilight. He took a cautious step through the doorway and cleared his throat.

The woman sat up in the bed with a jolt and stared at him. The chain clattered slightly as she pulled up her knees and folded her arms around them outside the duvet. Her eyes were simultaneously empty and filled with fear. She looked at Tom, then out through the open door.

'I'm here to help you,' Tom said as softly as he could. 'You can leave with me...now.'

She retreated even further.

He looked into her eyes. She wasn't as old as he had initially thought. No more than thirty. About the same age as Bárdur.

'Your name is Mona, right?' He extended a hand towards her.

She stared at his hand and then back at his face.

'How long have you been here?' Tom said. 'Don't be afraid, I'm here to help you.'

Mona said nothing. Her hair was messy, but not dirty. She just looked like someone who spent a lot of time in bed; she was pale and had rings under her eyes. There was no kind of colour in her face and her arms were skinny. Most of her body was hidden underneath the nightdress.

'You can leave with me,' Tom said, taking another step towards her. 'You want to leave, don't you?'

'I don't want to…' she said. Her voice was panicky and croaking. 'Don't touch me.'

Tom looked at her and held his breath for a moment. He felt a heavy weight spread across his chest.

'I'll bite,' she snarled. Her gaze had grown hard and crazed. 'Fornicator…You filthy fornicator.'

'But you need to get out,' Tom continued. 'This place.' He could feel the tears forcing their way out. 'This is a terrible, evil place.'

'I don't want you to fuck me,' Mona shouted. 'Fornicator! Go away!'

'What?' Tom said, waving his hands in the air to calm her down. 'I'm not going to…Please don't think…I…Sorry.'

'You all want to fuck,' Mona screamed. She released her grip on her legs and pulled the duvet over her head. 'Get out! Just get out.'

'Shhh…' Tom looked over his shoulder, but then returned his attention to the bed. Mona's lower legs had become exposed when she pulled the duvet over her head. She screamed under the duvet. She took a breath and then she screamed again.

Her legs were just as skinny as her arms. The ankle with the chain was covered in scars and red bruises after years of the iron ring being locked around it. Tom tried to grab her ankle in order remove the iron ring, but she started kicking out immediately.

'Demon,' Solva's voice cried out behind him. 'Dangerous man.'

Tom spun around.

'Dada,' Kristina shouted out into the air, staring deadpan at Tom. 'Dada!'

'Be quiet,' Tom hissed at the two girls in the doorway. 'I'm here to help you, God damn it. Don't you understand?'

He looked desperately back at Mona, who had poked out her head again.

Out in the living room the door to the corridor was opened, and Bárdur stormed inside with a roar.

Tom saw him stop when he reached the bedroom.

The big man's gaze flitted briefly from one to the other. 'This time I'll bloody well kill you,' he thundered. His lips were quivering and bits of saliva dribbled into his dense, red beard. His hands were shaking. 'To hell with Kjeld.'

'No,' Tom said, holding up his hands. 'I want to help you.'

Bárdur lunged at Tom, who at that moment ducked and punched Bárdur hard in the groin with his right fist; he continued the movement and made a half-turn, so his boot smashed into the side of Bárdur's right knee with full force.

The two little girls screamed. Tom looked at them. Their terrified expressions. Solva covered her eyes, but peeked out between her fingers.

'Dangerous man,' Kristina screamed. 'Punish him with the wrath of God, Dada.'

Tom stared at her pale, freckled face. She couldn't be much more than five years old. Her red hair was in pigtails and she wore an old-fashioned dress with green stripes. Red shoes.

He stared back at Mona. 'You need to get out of here!'

Mona gazed apathetically into the air. She looked straight through him. She seemed absent.

'I'm going to kill you,' Bárdur screamed at him again from the floor. He was trying to stand up and threw himself at Tom, who was knocked over, but rolled around and managed to get back up again. He couldn't fight the red giant lying down; he would get himself killed.

Bárdur went for Tom once more. He managed to grab Tom's

shoulder and drag him down onto the floor.

'Man must suffer death,' Bárdur shouted. His eyes were ablaze with rage and his saliva hit Tom's face. 'Let the whole church stone him, while I take great vengeance on him and chastise his sinful body in anger, so that he can know that I am the Lord when I rend him asunder.'

Tom punched Bárdur hard in the side and several times in the face, but it had no effect. Instead he felt Bárdur's hands lock themselves firmly around his throat, and he lashed out blindly. His right hand managed to grab some fabric and he heard one of the girls scream and kick his arm. He tightened his grip, then yanked the girl close to him.

She panicked and screamed hysterically and pounded him as hard as she could, but Tom kept hold of her and pulled her right between himself and Bárdur.

Bárdur slackened his grip and Tom seized the chance to wriggle free so that he could get up from the floor. He just had time to see Bárdur carefully set Solva down before he ran out of the bedroom door and through the living room.

'I'm going to kill you,' Bárdur roared behind him.

Tom ran as fast as he could. His own room, the doctor's surgery, the swimming pool or any other room in the bunker was no longer an option for him. He had to get out.

The light was on in all the corridors now. He followed one corridor around in a curve and reached a place where metal brackets cemented into the wall led to a large grate higher up. It was the first time he had seen them. He had been down this long corridor before, but it had been completely dark and he hadn't noticed the grate until now.

The grate shifted easily and a few minutes later he found himself in an empty industrial laundry. Several of the windows were broken, but the room looked otherwise functional.

He looked over his shoulder. There was no time to waste. It could only be a matter of minutes before Bárdur caught up with him.

As soon as he stepped outside the laundry, he saw a boat lying anchored near the shore. There were no rubber dinghies or small boats to be seen anywhere, so he simply carried on running, then jumped from the rocks into the sea and swam towards the boat.

The icy water knocked the air out of him immediately. He gasped a couple of times. The cold sank its teeth into his skin and stabbed at his muscles. Then he started to swim. He forced his arms through the water and fought back. The plastic bag under his shirt scratched his skin with every stroke he took in the cold water. He estimated that he would be able to reach the boat before he started cramping. This was what he had trained for: operating in the cold. His arms were working; his legs were kicking. His muscles felt better. Calmer. Slowly he drew nearer the boat.

He swung himself up on the small transom of the boat and crawled from there onto the aft deck. The wheelhouse looked empty and the rubber dinghy, which should have been on its stand near the stern, was gone. He looked towards the shore, but he still couldn't see anything. Perhaps he had hit Bárdur's leg more cleanly than he had thought.

The wheelhouse wasn't locked, but the engine needed a key to start it. With the small folding knife he managed to short-circuit the mechanism and start the engine. Everything seemed to be working and he had almost a full tank of fuel.

The engine engaged the moment he pushed the throttle forward. He glanced briefly back at the shore, but there was still nothing to see. He pushed the throttle a notch further. He would sail south, to Qeqertarsuatsiaat to begin with, and decide what to do next once he got there.

He carefully took out the sheets of paper with the pictures of Matthew and unfolded them. He put them on the area above the dashboard. They were soaked, but not dissolved. Water trickled over his face and he raked a hand through his hair.

He also took out the file with the Thule data to check that it hadn't been water-damaged. He placed the file next to Matthew and looked back at Færingehavn. The blood was roaring through his body and he pulled the throttle back again and sat down with his eyes closed. The scent of the sea entered the wheelhouse and he inhaled it greedily. Then suddenly the tears started to flow down his cheeks. His whole body trembled. The wet clothes stuck to his skin. They were the tears of the freedom he felt, tears of relief after thinking that death would find him in the darkness of the underground corridors. But they were also the tears of a new fear that had replaced his fear of death: his fear of losing Matthew.

47

It was dark when Tom steered the boat into the small harbour. The trip had taken him just under four hours, and it was coming up to eleven o'clock at night when he docked.

Most of the windows in the houses were dark, but the lights were still on in one or two. It was his first visit to Qeqertarsuatsiaat and it looked even smaller than he had imagined. Most of the houses were modest and made from wood, and he had seen no more than eighty buildings as he sailed towards it. There was still a little snow here and there, but not much.

Tom moored the boat and walked up the sloping, yellow wooden bridge, which took him ashore. He'd had the heating on in the wheelhouse all the way down from Færingehavn and his clothes had dried enough for them to no longer bother him. He had been hoping that he could buy some new clothes in Qeqertarsuatsiaat and hide out there for weeks or possibly longer, but the town was so small that there was unlikely to be a clothes shop or a hotel.

He closed his eyes and pinched the bridge of his nose. The hell that was Bárdur's world was churning around his mind so much so that he couldn't think straight. It must have been nearly a month since

Bradley and Reese were killed—possibly by Abelsen, but everything had been set up so that it was Tom who would go to prison for it. A US military tribunal would likely give him a harsh sentence.

A couple of dogs howled nearby. It sounded as if they were fighting, but they soon fell silent again. Very silent. There were no sounds. Even the sea was calm.

Tom kicked a pebble, which flew off and hit some empty fish crates. Surely someone in this town must have a telephone and a month's worth of newspapers.

'*Aluu!*'

Tom turned at the sound and saw two boys. One looked about nine, the other a few years older. 'Hello,' he said to them. 'Do either of you know a place here where I can stay the night?'

'*Paasinngilara,*' the older boy said. '*Qanoq ateqarpit?*'

'I've no idea what you're saying,' Tom said with a smile. 'Do you speak Danish? Or English?'

The older boy shook his head. '*Namik...*'

The younger one said something very quickly. The older one looked back at Tom and nodded. Then he pointed to a house with lights in the windows. '*Ikani.*'

'You want me to go over there?' Tom said.

'Yes, over there,' the older one repeated. Then he nudged the younger one; they turned away and ran down between some boats that had been pulled ashore.

Tom watched them before he started walking to the house they had indicated. It was blue, medium size, made from wood and had a black roof. The light coming from it glowed yellow in the darkness.

The man who opened the door was tall and about sixty years old. When Tom saw the man's eyes, a feeling of relief washed over him.

'Hello,' Tom said. 'Some boys suggested I tried your house...I think they only spoke Greenlandic.'

'I'm the only Dane here,' the man said, sticking out his hand. 'My name is Jakob. Do come in.'

'Thank you. My name is Tom. I've come...' He ground to a halt.

'I know.' Jakob showed Tom to a table in the living room, pulled out a pile of newspapers and skimmed the front pages. He placed two of them on the table and flicked through them before sliding the open newspapers towards Tom. 'Are you hungry?'

Tom nodded as he looked at the newspapers.

'You're a famous face these days, you might say,' Jakob said. 'But don't be alarmed, the boys you met just now don't read newspapers, and we don't have a lot of contact with the rest of the world down here in Qeqertarsuatsiaat.'

Tom closed his eyes and felt the hairs stand up on most of his body. He buried his face in his hands and deliberately slowed down his breathing. 'What are you going to do now?'

'I was a police officer once,' Jakob said. 'So I've seen many guilty people walk free while innocent people were punished. Right now I'm thinking that it's so unusual for the US military to leak details of an internal murder investigation that there must be a hidden agenda behind all of it. And the fact that a man the US military have reported dead has just turned up on my doorstep is enough to ring my alarm bells.' He looked Tom in the eye. 'Tell me your story and we'll see.'

Tom nodded and removed his hands from his face. Then he started his account. He told Jakob about the experiments, about the murders and about Abelsen forcing him to flee Thule. He told him about Bárdur's secret world under Færingehavn, the sadism, Mona, the girls and the swimming pool with the dead bodies. Jakob nodded repeatedly, but said nothing until Tom had finished talking.

'I believe you,' Jakob then said. 'I've experienced something similar.' He closed his eyes and rested his hands on his thighs. 'As soon as you told me about the film footage with the sadistic torture of the little girl, I knew that you had also been in Abelsen's clutches.'

Tom looked at Jakob with surprise. 'You know the girl?'

'I saw the same films in 1973.'

'And the girl?'

'I never found her,' Jakob said sadly. 'I'm sure that she died. My daughter…my stepdaughter, Paneeraq, was like the girl in the films, but I got her out.'

'That man is a monster. So what do we do now?'

'Can you fight him or is it hopeless?'

'I think it's hopeless,' Tom said. 'It looks like I've been set up. I'll either go to prison for life or I'll be executed.'

Jakob nodded grimly. 'I think you need to leave West Greenland for a while. What do you think?'

'I've no clothes or money,' Tom said. 'I think I've run out of options.'

'We'll help you get to East Greenland, but we need to leave now. It'll be daylight soon, people will wake up and they'll gather outside to see the man who came sailing under the cover of darkness.' He looked out of the windows down towards the small harbour. 'And if that's Abelsen's boat you've nicked, then he'll be here soon too, so the boat needs to go as well.'

'How will you get me to East Greenland from here?' Tom said.

'Across the ice,' Jakob said. 'I have everything you need.'

'You mean across the ice cap?'

'Yes. It's just under seven hundred kilometres to the town of Isortoq, and if you reach it, you can stay there for a couple of years. There are less than a hundred people living there and there are several empty houses.'

'So we're dogsledding across the ice?' Tom said, chewing his lower lip.

'No, you are…And it's no ordinary sledge.' Jakob slapped his thigh. 'We'll discuss the details as we head to the ice cap. I just need to have a word with my wife and Paneeraq. We also need to get you some clothes, pack provisions for you, and you'll need money.'

'So you're coming with me as far as the ice cap?'

'Yes, all three of us will be. Like I said, you're not the only one hiding from Abelsen…or the authorities, for that matter.'

'Thank you…Thank you so much, Jakob.' Tom ran a hand over his face. 'Is there a telephone here? I can't cross the ice without first making a short phone call to Denmark.'

'There's a telephone at the school,' Jakob said. 'We can use it, if there is a connection today, that is.'

'Can we get into the school now? I would like to call right away.'

'Yes, yes, the school is never locked. Paneeraq can walk you over there while I get everything ready here.'

48

Dawn was breaking when they docked a few kilometres from the ice cap at the bottom of the long fjord that reached inland south of Qeqertarsuatsiaat. On the last stretch the growlers in the water had increased in number and they had been forced to sail at a very low speed, weaving in and out between smaller and bigger chunks of ice. Many of the growlers were so big that they could flip the boat, if they suddenly upended in the sea.

Jakob's wife, Lisbeth, had sailed Abelsen's boat to begin with, but after half an hour they had stranded the boat and left Tom's clothing on the rocks, so that it looked as if he had been killed.

When they reached the hunting lodge about four hours later, they dragged their equipment ashore before Jakob sailed out to anchor his boat. He returned to the shore in a rubber dinghy.

Meanwhile, Tom, Lisbeth and Paneeraq had lugged all their boxes and clothes and provisions up to the hunting lodge where the three of them would be staying for a couple of weeks.

Tom looked along the coastline. The tide was out and there were many stranded growlers along the rocky shore. Foundered chunks of glacial ice of all sizes. Some of them were milky white, others crystal clear or turquoise. Some were the size of a truck, others so small that he could hold them in the palm of his hand. He closed his eyes and sniffed the air of the icy sea. There was no purer air in all the world than that on the ice cap and his senses quivered at the freedom he could feel.

'A thousand years ago the ice came down as far as here,' Jakob said. 'You can tell from the rock face. The paler imprints are where the ice reached.'

Tom nodded and looked at the slim, middle-aged man. On their way south and into the fjord Jakob had briefed him extensively about the surface of the ice, the many deep crevasses, the nuances of its surface, but more importantly what those nuances revealed: caves, crevasses and meltwater lakes, which might be covered by a thin layer of ice and snow, but could be hundreds of metres deep. To Tom the trek across the ice cap sounded like certain death, but Jakob knew several people who had made the trip and lived, and he himself had often spent several days out on the ice cap, but had never had a reason to cross it.

'Let me show you the equipment while the girls sort out breakfast,' Jakob said. 'I keep everything in the shed round the back.'

'I think I get the basic idea,' Tom said. 'But I would like you to go over it in detail.' He looked towards the glacier that lay across the sea like a thin wedge between two tall mountains at the bottom of the fjord. He inhaled so deeply that his chest expanded. The air slipped fresh and cool down his throat.

At the back of the hunting lodge Jakob pulled open the door to a narrow shed. 'I'll pass everything out to you,' he said, handing Tom a black metal sledge. 'It's lightweight metal,' he said. 'I built it myself.'

'And you've driven it?' Tom said, picking up the light sledge and looking at the narrow runners.

'For several hundred hours,' Jakob said with a wry smile, and passed him a heavy bag. 'This is the parachute. You need to be able to rig everything yourself. Once you're on the ice, you'll be on your own, because I can only sail you close to it. You'll have to manage without me from then on. That means getting onto the ice cap as well as moving across it.'

Tom looked quizzically at the equipment. 'So this sledge is less than half the weight of a wooden sledge, and rather than being pulled by dogs, it's pulled by a small parachute with a kite effect?'

'Yes, it's the same principle, more or less, and it saves you having to pack a ton of dog food.' Jakob handed Tom some long reins and ropes full of bights and splicing. 'These ones must be fastened around your waist and those two down there need to be attached to the front boom of the sledge here.'

Tom put on the harness and adjusted it. 'Am I attached to both the sledge and the parachute, then?'

'That's your choice, but if you wear the harness like that, you have a way of saving yourself should you end up in a crevasse or fall through the ice and into a meltwater lake. Just cut those two straps, which will separate the parachute from the sledge, which will then fall into the void while the parachute will pull you upwards.' He hesitated for a moment. 'You just need to remember to always wear the small backpack with provisions so you don't die of hunger instead. You can get water from the ice, so there's no need to lug that around.'

'I'm pretty good at withstanding the cold,' Tom said. 'But I will need to eat.' He hesitated, then furrowed his brow. 'If I lose the sledge, can I continue on foot?'

Jakob shrugged. 'That's a very good question, and honestly, I don't know. In theory, yes, but I've no idea how long it would take or how you would react. It's brutal on the ice. Some people go crazy from the cold and the light, and you won't survive that on your own.'

'I'm used to the cold and the light from Thule,' Tom said. 'And I've been imprisoned and subjected to light torture, so that won't break me.' He patted his pocket. There should be enough pills for a trip across the ice.

'The ice is lethal,' Jakob went on. 'But if I didn't believe in you and my equipment, I wouldn't let you go.'

'What about a tent?' Tom said.

'I have everything here,' Jakob said. 'And we'll give you whatever you need. Thermal trousers, a jacket, boots, goggles, a rifle, snow-shoes. Fortunately you and I are about the same size.'

Tom looked down at the boxes. The parachute, the sledge, the backpacks. 'I haven't got any money so I can't pay you for any of this. And it must be worth a fortune?'

'I'm rock collector,' Jakob said with a smile. 'Not far from here is something we call the red mountain. I spend a lot of time there. It's a place filled with rubies and pink sapphires.'

Tom looked at Jakob and raised his eyebrows.

'I'll give you a bag of those to take as well, so you can manage over there on the east coast,' Jakob said, surveying the equipment. Then he turned his gaze towards the sky. 'We need to get you going today. Come on, let's pack your provisions.'

49

FÆRINGEHAVN, WEST GREENLAND, 5 JUNE 1990

Jakob sat on a stone step in Færingehavn, eating his packed lunch while he looked around the abandoned town. He had been out here a few times as a police officer in the early seventies while the town was still a lively place. Now that everything was empty and dilapidated, it felt odd to sit here. Most windows were smashed and many doors had been forced. It was a waste of good housing, and a waste of a beautiful place, but that was Greenland for you. Its small towns were quietly depopulated without anyone paying much attention, as each generation discovered a much bigger world outside their home town.

He swallowed a bite of his sandwich and nudged an empty bottle on the ground with his foot. Föroya Bjór, beer from the Faroe Islands, except the bottle looked like just a regular Carlsberg.

On the day that Jakob had dropped Tom off close to the ice cap, he had waited at their agreed meeting place until twilight. For many days afterwards he had also sailed there and waited in his boat, but Tom didn't appear.

While they had gone through the equipment, Jakob had promised Tom that he would sail to Færingehavn in a few weeks' time to look for Mona and the girls. He had brought along three fishermen from Qeqertarsuatsiaat, since he had thought it unwise to search Færingehavn on his own once he had heard Tom's description of the underground world. They had been there for hours now and the fishermen were still looking, but they had found nothing; or at least nothing which suggested life or an underground bunker.

Since Tom's departure, Jakob had carried out some research from his home in Qeqertarsuatsiaat. He had looked for any information indicating a secret army facility in any books and magazines he could find at the town's small library, but neither the library nor the old friends he rang in Denmark had anything to offer. There was no evidence of an American bunker under Færingehavn. Nothing at all.

He packed his backpack, got up from the step and looked around the buildings closest to him. He could see a couple of the fishermen smoking cigarettes a few houses further down.

A long cloud covered the sun. Jakob gazed at the sky and then looked again towards the laundry from where Tom believed he had emerged.

It was very dirty inside. Most of the windows were still intact, but not all of them. The industrial washing machines were dusty, but they looked as if they might still work. At the back of the room there was a long row of tall drying cupboards. Jakob had tried them one by one, but had been unable to move any of them. There were no locks to be seen, and no way of opening them. It was just like when he had first tried them a few hours earlier, before he did a round of the empty town.

Tom had insisted that this was how he had escaped from the underground world, but not even the dust on the floor offered any evidence that people came here regularly.

Jakob rubbed his eyes with a flat hand, pinched his nose and breathed deeply.

'Did I make a mistake?' he whispered to himself. Perhaps Tom really was as crazy as the newspapers claimed. That day out by the ice cap, just before Tom had assembled the sledge and started walking up towards the edge of the ice, Jakob had seen him swallow some small white pills.

Jakob shook his head at himself and walked back to the quay where their rubber dinghy was moored.

The last of the fishermen was sitting near the dinghy.

'If you row me out to the boat first, you can get the others afterwards,' Jakob said.

The fisherman nodded and Jakob climbed into the small rubber dinghy. As they sailed, he pondered Tom's innocence and wondered how to tell fact from fiction. If Tom was guilty, his association with Abelsen must be a cover for something, because there was no doubt that Tom knew Abelsen. Then again, no one in their right mind would flee across the ice cap alone unless they had no other choice. Especially not when they had already been declared dead in the newspapers. But whatever the truth was was, Jakob's own investigation had reached a dead end. If he contacted the police, it wouldn't take them long to uncover his real identity, and he couldn't risk anyone looking into his own and Lisbeth's pasts; the fact that he and Lisbeth were alive would immediately link them to the murders of the men Lisbeth had killed in 1973.

The waves sloshed against the sides of the rubber dinghy. It felt as if the sea was waking up, but it could also just be the tide with the evening wind from the mainland. Jakob couldn't remember how the sea reacted to those two conditions in this particular fjord between Nuuk and Qeqertarsuatsiaat.

To get back they had to sail past the bunker point on the opposite side of the fjord. The last inhabitant of this place lived over there, as far as Jakob could recall. He might know if there was any truth in Tom's talk about an underworld in an abandoned American bunker.

THE POOL OF
THE DEAD

50

The back of Matthew's head was throbbing. He turned his head and touched his neck carefully. His mouth felt simultaneously sticky and dry, and his saliva tasted metallic.

'Shit,' he mumbled to himself. The pain in his neck hadn't been this bad since the weeks following the car crash.

The room was dark, but not far from him a strip of light slipped through the crack between the door and the door frame.

He reached for one of the water bottles lying on the floor. The liquid smelled like water, but he sipped it cautiously before taking bigger gulps and putting the cap back on.

He was in the cell where he had found Arnaq and where he had been beaten up. Now there was only him in the darkness and the stench. The water trembled in the bottle in his hand. He put it down and found his cigarettes. Everything was shaking. He was shivering as if he had a fever. The first drag made him so nauseous that he flicked the cigarette away.

He clutched his head with both hands and slowly rotated his head from side to side. He drank some more water and then got up. He discovered that the door wasn't bolted. They probably hadn't expected him to get up again.

In his mind he could still see Arnaq's shining eyes. Her panic as he had left the room. She'd had only had a few minutes of feeling safe and rescued.

He pushed open the door to the cell where Tupaarnaq had been kept, but it was empty.

Matthew went out into the corridor and looked in the direction he had come from. All the naked lightbulbs glowed brightly, except for one which had been smashed, but he remembered that it had been damaged when he first arrived. The corridor in the opposite direction ended in darkness. That was the way he would be going. The other way would only lead him out and up into the burning town. His fingers closed around the wedding ring.

After twenty metres and a couple of locked doors he reached an open door, which led to a room with a white tiled floor, unlike the concrete in the other rooms he had seen. It was dark in the room and there was an acrid smell. He pushed the door open fully and discovered that the tiles continued up onto the walls. There were a couple of steel tables in the middle of the room, and along the back wall there was a long kitchen table and shelves.

A figure was lying on one of the steel tables. Matthew froze. He held his breath and narrowed his eyes. The body lay completely still in the darkness. The hair. The jacket.

'Malik,' Matthew exclaimed and rushed inside the room. He touched his friend's face. Malik's skin was warm and soft.

A noise in the darkness made him turn towards the door. It sounded like a person kicking something. Matthew reached for a long, broad knife on the kitchen table and then looked at Malik, who hadn't stirred.

The noise resumed; a knocking sound that reached the kitchen from the corridor.

Matthew closed his eyes and pressed his left hand against his chest. He forced himself to breathe slowly. The fingers of his right hand gripped the knife.

He walked past Malik and up to the door, and just as he entered the corridor there was a new noise. This one sounded like a strangled shout, and it seemed to come from a nearby room whose door was ajar.

Matthew quickly looked about him and then retreated a few steps back into the kitchen.

'We'll deal with that later,' he heard from the corridor.

Matthew rushed back to the long kitchen table and threw himself onto the floor. He could just about squeeze himself in between the bottom shelf and the tiled floor.

He twitched when the light in the room was turned on. He struggled to breathe fully as his chest was pressed hard against the floor. He tensed his muscles in an attempt to gain control and breathed slowly although his body demanded more oxygen. His right hand was still clutching the knife.

There was no doubt that one of the voices belonged to Abelsen. Matthew had only met Abelsen once before, when Ulrik had tied Abelsen to a chair in Jakob's house. Abelsen's voice was very close to him, but now the tables had been turned. This time Matthew was the captive, while Abelsen was walking free.

Matthew couldn't see anything other than their shoes. A pair of black hiking boots and a pair of old, worn clog boots, several sizes bigger than the hiking boots.

'Seriously,' Abelsen said. 'I've had just about enough of this slaughterhouse.'

'I take good care of the dead, Kjeld.' The other man was wheezing as though he was carrying something heavy.

Matthew recognised Bárdur's voice, and heard him groan as he let go of something. The object sounded heavy and moments later water started dripping onto the floor not far from Matthew's hiding place.

'It's fine,' Abelsen continued wearily. 'Only I don't want to hear about it or see it, understand?'

Bárdur grunted something which Matthew failed to catch.

'That's your business,' Abelsen said. 'And you still chuck the dead girls into the pool?'

Bárdur muttered something about unclean creatures, but Matthew couldn't hear all of it.

'Bárdur,' Abelsen said sharply. 'When I tell you who lives and who dies, then that's how it is, do you understand? Or I'm clearing out this bunker.'

'I can't control Kristina and Solva,' Bárdur said. 'They only listen to themselves these days.'

'Nonsense,' Abelsen said. 'They're your daughters. Shorten their leash. They must be as obedient as Símin.'

Bárdur muttered a grumpy reply.

Matthew caught only the words 'the pilot' and 'the pool'.

'I don't give a toss what you do with the bodies,' Abelsen said. 'As long as those I need are kept alive. And make sure your two crazy daughters respect that. Keep your hands off my people.'

'From a woman came the origins of sin, and because of her we all have to die,' Bárdur chanted loudly.

'Yeah, yeah,' Abelsen said. 'Where are the girls?'

'Yours or mine?' Bárdur mumbled.

'Mine,' Abelsen snapped. 'Listen, you moron, if Arnaq dies before we catch Tom, I'll hold you responsible and you'll be punished for it—I'll make sure of it. As long as Tom is at large, we need her and Matthew alive. Is that clear?'

'I don't know about Arnaq,' Bárdur muttered. 'She…isn't doing too well.'

'No, because you idiots practically starved her to death, didn't you?'

'We gave her some meat,' Bárdur said in a wounded tone.

'Idiot,' Abelsen said again, and heaved a sigh. 'The Colonel has learned that Tom is in Ittoqqortoormiit. You want to find him too, don't you? You remember what he did to Mona? Vengeance is yours and also the Lord's right, my friend.'

'He must be judged and chastised in anger and wrath,' Bárdur said, sounding more cheerful. 'It is the wish and the word of the Lord.'

'Exactly,' Abelsen said. 'We need to find Tom before anyone starts poking their nose into this mess.'

Matthew held his breath for a moment. His cheek was squashed against the tiled floor and the cold numbed his skin. So Abelsen knew where Tom was. The floor pressed against his chest. Was there anyone not looking for his father? And why the hell was all this happening now? They'd had twenty-four years to find him if it was really that important. Why now?

'I can smell smoke,' Abelsen said. 'I told you so just now, didn't I? Something is burning.'

'I haven't done anything,' Bárdur said.

'This is bad for us,' Abelsen said. 'We don't need any more busy-bodies out here; honestly, it's like Copenhagen Central Station.'

Their feet moved back towards the door.

'Do you want me to get rid of your girls now?' Bárdur mumbled.

'No, God damn it,' Abelsen said harshly. 'I've just told you! The Colonel will bloody kill us...We need Arnaq...And I'll see to my own daughter myself if she doesn't pack her black rags and get her bald head out of my sight soon.'

'And the police lady?'

'The police what?' Abelsen's boots stopped. 'Listen, you moron. Just forget about her for now. We need to find out why we can smell smoke and we'll deal with everything else later.' He hesitated. 'All right, you can have her.'

'So she's mine? The police lady?'

'Yes,' Abelsen said with a weary sigh. 'If that's what you want, then yes, from now on she's yours...Keep her...After all, you've already chained her up, haven't you?'

Bárdur grunted happily.

'But right now let's get out of here,' Abelsen said. 'We need to find Tom...Get the boat ready and I'll be there in five minutes.'

51

Matthew stayed under the kitchen table until everything was quiet, then he crawled out on his stomach and spent a moment staring up at the ceiling. The men had turned off the light as they left, but his eyes had quickly adjusted to the darkness.

He took a deep breath and stood up. As Abelsen had pointed out, it was starting to smell like smoke in even the furthest corners of the bunker, so the fire must still be raging above ground.

Viktor lay soaking wet on a table close to him. That was the reason Abelsen and Bárdur had come to the kitchen. Bárdur dumped his victims in the kitchen, but he seemed unable to control his daughters, who had thrown Viktor into the pool where only girls could be thrown.

The knocking from earlier resumed and Matthew looked towards the door, then back at Viktor. There was no doubt that he was dead. Only his aviator jacket gave away his identity. His face had been smashed to a pulp. Matthew dipped his fingertips in the water around Viktor's body on the steel table. It tasted salty. He touched Viktor's arm gently and looked at his ruined face.

The knocking came back and Matthew hurried out into the corridor. He had heard Bárdur and Abelsen leave, so it couldn't be them making the noise.

He slowly pushed the door, which was half open, and found a living room behind it. It looked old-fashioned. The furniture was similar to that in Bárdur's house on the other side of the fjord, but this room was larger and smelled much more lived in.

The first thing to catch his eye was an altar and a large wooden crucifix with a crucified Jesus. He hadn't expected this. There were also two large silver candlesticks, each with a tall white candle, both lit. Jesus's eyes were sunk into his head and his mouth gaped emptily.

Jesus's golden skin and blood drops gleamed in the flickering candlelight.

In the middle of the room was a shabby armchair with a roll of gaffer tape on the seat cushion. Behind the armchair a narrow door was ajar.

Matthew took a deep breath and braced himself. There was light behind the door and he saw the two women on the bed as soon as he went in. One was staring at the floor, while the other was lying down and looking right at him. It was Rakel. She had gaffer tape over her mouth and her legs and arms were also taped together. An iron ring attached to a long chain was fixed around one of her ankles.

Her black eyes stared beseechingly at him, but at the same time she kept nodding towards the old woman sitting slumped on the edge of the bed.

Matthew's instinctive reaction was to free Rakel, but the sight of the old woman's hands stopped him. She was holding a live hand grenade in each, and next to her was a slim green metal box containing more grenades. The pins were lying on the floor by her feet. Her legs were skinny. One ankle was in very bad shape.

'Please,' Matthew said, taking a careful step forward. 'Allow me to help you with those?' His whole body trembled with fear. 'You're holding onto them very tightly, aren't you?'

She looked up. Her hair hung limply down either side of her face. Once it had probably been blonde, but now it was white. Matthew breathed slowly. She wasn't as old as he had first assumed, but she was apathetic and her eyes distant. He looked at her ankle again. Then he looked at Rakel in the bed. 'Please,' he repeated. 'Allow me to pick up the pins?'

'No,' she said in a flat voice, and dropped both grenades.

Matthew spun around and threw himself into the living room, where he had only just hit the floor when the explosion ripped everything behind him to shreds.

The shock wave rolled through the door and slammed him into the armchair. The door itself was blown off its hinges, and tongues of flames licked his neck and hands, which he held up to shield his face.

The tremors from the explosion made the plaster scatter from the ceiling and Matthew watched as the large Jesus figure crashed to the floor, where it shattered. The flames reached the living room from the bedroom and he could feel heat, but his hearing was almost gone. He touched his ears. One was bleeding; both of them were howling. He pushed himself onto his knees. His left little finger stuck out at awkward angle. He was aware that it was hurting, but found it difficult to distinguish between the different types of pain he was experiencing. The hairs on the back of his hands had been burned off, as had some of the hairs at the back of his head. The tears were rolling down his cheeks. 'I'm sorry!' he sobbed.

Jesus's head had been knocked off and was now lying close to the armchair. Matthew stared into the empty eye sockets and the open mouth.

'I'm sorry,' he whispered.

Inside the bedroom the fire was dying out, but there was still smoke everywhere and his throat and lungs were stinging. He looked at his crooked little finger, grabbed it firmly and pushed it in place. The pain sent a spasm through his body.

'No,' he screamed, bashing his undamaged hand against the floor. 'No, no, no!'

He got to his feet and found the knife and the tape on the floor. He coughed. His cough got worse every time he tried to move. He cut off a piece of tape and wrapped it around his broken finger and the finger next to it so the healthy finger could support the broken one. Pain shot up through his arm, but it was preferable to his finger being unsupported when he moved. The back of his neck where his hair had been scorched was sore. His eyes were stinging from smoke and tears.

He turned his face to the narrow doorway into the bedroom. His right eyelid felt droopy. As if it was dead. His mouth tasted of metal, smoke and rot, as if everything inside him had putrefied in a foul stench. He wanted to go back inside the bedroom, but he could barely lift his feet when he looked at doorway and the black patches from the explosion on the door frame, the floor, the walls and the ceiling.

Matthew raised his left hand up to his mouth. He bit his forefinger. Tiny bites. Repeatedly.

The bed had been upended completely. Everything else had been flung against the walls, which were pockmarked and spattered with blood and bits of human flesh. His knees buckled and it was only the sooty door frame that stopped him from collapsing completely. His mouth was open and he gasped for air in trembling breaths.

His fingers were locked around the knife in his right hand.

He turned and ran out through the living room.

He continued moving without looking around him. He ran down the corridor, his legs working without his brain joining in. He followed the puddles of water that had dripped from Viktor's clothing when Bárdur had dragged him to the kitchen. He followed the water trail past the cells. A little further on, the trail disappeared behind a damaged door.

The light was on in the room, which looked like a changing room with linoleum flooring.

The floor was stained with blood in several places and the stains reached both the door leading to the corridor and the double glass doors at the far side of the room.

Behind the glass he could see water shimmer in a pool. He opened the doors and immediately spotted Arnaq and Tupaarnaq, who were both lying on the floor with their hands tied behind their backs. Tupaarnaq's legs were also taped together, and there was tape covering her mouth.

'Are you okay?' he exclaimed, grabbing Tupaarnaq's shoulder.

She nodded and shouted something behind the tape.

He knelt down and carefully removed the tape covering her mouth.

'Get Arnaq out!' she wheezed.

'Now?'

Tupaarnaq nodded. 'We have to get out…now…I just need to catch my breath…The pool is full of dead bodies…We have to get out. Now.'

Matthew coughed. His lungs protested.

'They could come back any minute.'

'I think Abelsen and Bárdur have gone above ground.'

'They're not our only problem,' she said. 'Get Arnaq out now. I'll be all right in a minute.'

'Okay,' Matthew said, and cut Tupaarnaq's hands and legs free.

'You're not allowed near the pool of the dead, demon.'

Matthew spun around and looked towards the door. Two redheaded women were staring stiffly at them. One of them cackled. They were both skinny and pale. They were in their late twenties.

'This place is just for the dead,' the taller of them declared.

'The pool of the dead?' Matthew said, looking at the water.

'Yes,' the taller one said, her voice distorted as if she was mimicking someone. 'Girls go in the pool and boys in the stomach.'

They both chuckled, especially the smaller one.

Matthew frowned and got up.

'You're a demon from above,' the shorter one said. She shook her head as if frightened by her own words.

'Demons must die,' the taller one said.

Tupaarnaq got up and positioned herself next to Matthew.

'I've had enough of your bullshit,' she snarled, looking about her. Then she pushed Matthew into the two redheaded women, while she herself stepped back to pick up a mop. As he fell, Matthew brought down one of the two skinny women with him, while Tupaarnaq floored the other with a blow from the mop. She kicked both the women in their sides and legs as hard as she could.

The two women screamed hysterically.

'God will vanquish you and throw you into a pit of fire,' the taller one hissed. Her lips quivered from rage, but it also looked as if she was smiling insanely. As if she really was expecting God to crush Matthew and Tupaarnaq like bugs at this very moment.

'Get in the water,' Tupaarnaq shouted, hitting them with the mop and shoving them towards the water. She hit them hard, aiming for their faces. 'Go join the dead.'

The taller one reached for the mop, but Tupaarnaq was quick and shoved her in the chest so hard that the woman nearly stumbled into the pool.

Matthew managed to drag Arnaq out of the room and Tupaarnaq reversed out behind them. She closed the door and in the same movement slipped the mop through the two big handles, trapping the women.

The red-haired women hammered furiously on the glass. Their teeth were bared and their eyes shone with hatred. The shorter of them grinned and shook her head while she screamed and shouted about God's wrath.

Matthew stared into their shiny turquoise eyes.

'Come on!' Tupaarnaq hit his shoulder. 'Let's get Arnaq upstairs. What about the others?'

'Malik and Viktor are lying in the kitchen,' Matthew said, turning to Tupaarnaq. 'Viktor is dead.' He closed his eyes and shook his head. 'Rakel...' The saliva thickened in his throat and he was unable to speak.

'The explosion?'

He nodded.

She pressed her lips together and carefully traced her fingertips along the scorched hair on the back of his head. Then she looked at his fingers, which were taped up. 'I felt it. And I heard it.' She hesitated. 'Was it Rakel?'

'It...' His upper body convulsed. He exhaled a couple of times. 'There's nothing...left...she...' He shook his head again. 'Her children...'

Tupaarnaq heaved a sigh. Then she squeezed his arm. 'Come on, let's get your sister and Malik out of here.'

•

The rumble of the burning town was still so loud that it drowned out all other sounds when Matthew and Tupaarnaq got Arnaq up into the laundry. Although Arnaq was very weak, she was able to stay conscious long enough for them to support her up the narrow steps.

'There's someone outside,' Tupaarnaq said in a low voice, and fell to her knees.

Matthew ducked as instinctively as Tupaarnaq. He looked towards the broken windows. The noise and the smoke outside were intense.

Tupaarnaq reached for a long piece of wood and held it close to her, ready to attack.

'Wait,' Matthew said, and still crouching he made his way to one of the windows that overlooked the plain. 'I can see a blue Lynx helicopter...It must be from NATO Arctic Command.' He went outside and saw soldiers and police officers standing near the old office block in the centre of the abandoned town. 'Hey,' he shouted, waving his arms. 'Over here!'

DEATH AND
THE BOY

52

The crucifix swung back and forth like a pendulum in front of his face. He held the chain in an outstretched arm and followed the crucifix's monotonous journey. It had been his mother's. She had given it to him when they had left. He didn't know why, because she had been wearing it for as long as he could remember.

She had given it to him soon after they had chained the new woman to the bed. His father had looked at his mother and said: 'You're free to move, woman. Get up, take your bed and walk.' She had stayed where she was. She hadn't even looked up. Yet Símin had felt her eyes rest on him and then she gave him the crucifix.

Símin studied the granite ceiling in the abandoned cave. It was a big, cold room. Carved into the bedrock a long time ago. Kjeld said people had stored gunpowder in it in the old days. Símin's hand with the crucifix fell to the ground. Kjeld had given his mother a green metal box when they left. Perhaps that was why she had given him the crucifix. Then suddenly there was smoke and everything had changed. Símin had to leave now, his father had said. They didn't have time to find Kristina and Solva. Victims of the last few days, his father had called them. Símin didn't know about the victims of the last days from the Bible, but his father had said that those who are afraid to leave their children in the hands of God deny the power of God. God is testing us, my son, and who are we to doubt his ways?

His father would marry the new one. Símin knew that much. Kjeld would make sure of it.

His mother was free.

A smile spread across the pale, skinny man's face. Arnaq was his. His father had said so. Kjeld had said they could have her. He stuck his hand into his bag and found Arnaq's torn blouse. It smelt of her. He could feel her breasts through the smell. They were soft. They were warm. He began to pant. His penis hardened in his trousers and he pressed his hand against it, squeezing it hard. Arnaq was his. And his alone. When they came home, he would touch her again; he would bite her breasts, swallow them. His fingers clasped his penis so hard that it hurt. But first he needed to stay in the cave for a week. Kjeld had said so. He couldn't come with them, Kjeld had said, and neither could he stay at home in the corridors, his father had said, and so he had ended up in the cave with water, food and blankets. Stay here, Kjeld had said. Don't go outside. There are demons outside, his father had said. They're all demons. His father's eyes had been frenzied. The demons have set fire to our home, but Kjeld will catch the demons. We'll kill them in revenge and in great and violent wrath. You wait here.

He had his father's old, black Bible with him. His mother's crucifix. He rubbed his penis and pressed Arnaq's blouse against his nose and mouth.

'God created the harlot,' he moaned, glancing at the Bible. 'The virgin shall become fruitful.'

There was a noise of something rummaging around outside the iron gate that led to the cave. Símin stopped rubbing his groin and his hand with the blouse sank towards the ground.

He pressed himself against the raw rock wall and curled up on the ground when the noise returned, louder this time. There was someone at the gate. Someone alive. He stared at the Bible and his pale hand. He threw aside Arnaq's blouse and grabbed his mother's crucifix instead.

'Though I walk through the valley of the shadow of death, I will fear no evil,' he whispered to himself, gripping the iron crucifix so hard that it cut into his skin. 'For You are with me; Your rod and Your staff, they comfort me.'

Now he could see the man who had entered. The man walked around in the light which came in with the open gate. The man was dirty. His clothes were threadbare and shabby. His face and hair were also filthy.

The crucifix cut through the skin of Símin's hand and into his flesh. He closed his eyes and moaned from pleasure. He squeezed it again. Once more the crucifix bit into the palm of his hand. 'The Lord is my shepherd,' he groaned very softly. Blood trickled down the palm of his hand. 'My all in all; he has paid the wages of sin for me.'

'*Aluu?*' the man said in Greenlandic.

Símin looked up abruptly. He stopped squeezing the crucifix. 'Don't look at me,' he whispered slowly.

The man stepped deeper into the darkness and spoke to him. He sounded like a demon. His words were strange and lisping to Símin's ears. Símin's eyes widened. Maybe the man's tongue was forked? A lisping, filthy demon?

The man carried on talking as he came towards him.

'Don't look at me,' Símin said again, louder this time. He covered his mouth with his bloodstained hand.

'Ah, you're Danish,' the demon said. 'Didn't think there were any homeless Danes.'

'Don't look at me,' Símin said angrily, and stood up.

'Are you high?' the demon said. Its face contorted with laughter;

its teeth were brown stumps.

Símin took a step forwards and floored the man with a single blow. The man howled and squealed in his lisping, shrill demon language.

Símin looked about him. Soon the whole cave would be filled with demons, given the way this one was screaming. He straddled the small man and sat on his chest. He grabbed the man's head with his big hands, his fingers enclosing the skull. Except for his thumbs, which pushed their way into the man's eyes. The man shrieked horribly in pain and kicked out his legs, but they couldn't reach him, and Símin had a knee pressed against each of the man's upper arms.

'Don't...Look...At...Me...Demon!' Símin screamed. His thumbs kept digging into the man's eyes until they could go no further.

53

The many beautiful national costumes sparkled in an abundance of colours. Every woman wore red and sealskin, while the broad pearl collars from their necks to their chests were unique to each of them.

The white coffin was carried by six police officers. Paneeraq walked in front of the coffin, holding a tall, white crucifix.

Matthew looked at the mourners. Most men in the funeral procession wore a white anorak and black trousers, but many were wearing their everyday clothes, as he was.

They had to walk closely together on the sloping gravel path leading away from the church. Much more closely than Matthew would have liked. Many people had come to say goodbye to Jakob, which had surprised Matthew, given that Jakob had fled Nuuk over forty years ago. Even so, the church had been packed to the rafters.

Before the funeral service started many of the women, including Paneeraq and Else, had walked past Jakob's coffin to give it a single kiss.

Matthew had sat next to Arnaq and Else inside the church. They had picked up Arnaq from the hospital. Physically she had recovered well after being given saline and food.

Things had moved fast after they had been flown back from Færingehavn to Nuuk by helicopter, and when the dust finally began to settle, Matthew had taken twenty-four hours to himself. Tupaarnaq had been staying with Paneeraq in Jakob's house and Arnaq had been at the hospital. As had Malik.

Matthew looked at the angular white church, which sat on a rock in the middle of Nuuk. Right below the path leading to the church was the pub, Mutten, and next to that the office where Briggs worked. Across the street lay the large, rust-brown TelePost building, along with a café and the blue community hall.

A man shouted out something in Greenlandic down by the pub, but it wasn't aimed at the mourners.

The glossy varnish of the coffin gleamed in the sharp rays of the noontime sun. Jakob's funeral had been held up while they waited for forensic pathologists to arrive from Denmark, but now the time had come.

Tears had rolled down Matthew's cheeks during most of the service, especially during the hymns. The next funeral would be Rakel's, and Matthew could already imagine her children standing by their mother's coffin.

Someone grabbed Matthew's arm.

'We need a more detailed feature,' his editor said.

Matthew nodded slowly.

'And I've been thinking…Well, you know me, Matthew. I've been thinking that you're the best man for the job, so I've been putting it on hold because I couldn't contact you yesterday.'

'No, I…' Matthew hesitated. 'I needed some time out.'

His editor nodded. 'I don't blame you. You see, we've written about Rakel and all that, but we would like a big article about the underground bunker you discovered.'

Matthew's gaze slipped from the six pallbearers and the coffin in front of them and down onto the narrow path. A hearse was waiting to take the coffin to the cemetery in Nuussuaq, where it would be buried in what little earth was out there. 'That crucifix Paneeraq is carrying,' Matthew said. 'Is that to be placed on his grave?'

'Eh?' His editor looked perplexed, first at the coffin and then at the crucifix moving slowly down in front of them. 'Yes, the crucifix… Yes, it's a local custom.'

Matthew turned his attention back to his editor. 'I would like to take a look at it.'

His editor looked back, nonplussed. 'The crucifix?'

'The article and everything down in Færingehavn.'

'Oh, good…I'm really pleased to hear that. That's the way to go…You'll also write about Solva and Kristina, won't you? The two crazy women they dragged out of the tunnels. Have you seen them?'

Matthew raised both eyebrows. 'Yes, I've seen them, but first I need to speak to Ottesen when he gets back. Abelsen, Bárdur and his son managed to get away, as far as I know, and I'm not sure what we're allowed to write about an ongoing investigation.'

'Okay,' his editor said, and then he added: 'Except I don't think the son got very far.'

'So I saw,' Matthew said. 'On your homepage.'

'Yes, we managed to upload that story quickly,' his editor said, looking pleased. 'It's not every day a vagrant is found staggering around and screaming his head off in an old industrial area after his eyes have been punched out of his head by some pale guy with white hair ranting about demons.'

'That would be Símin,' Matthew said.

'Símin? Is his name Símin? The police said they couldn't confirm it yet.'

Matthew shook his head. 'Then forget I said it.'

'Hang on.' His editor turned to one side. 'I just want to grab Bjørn…We need to get an official quote from him.'

Matthew saw his boss make his way diagonally backwards in the procession until he reached the chief of police.

Most of the mourners had halted now. The coffin was being slid into the hearse, and Paneeraq placed the crucifix alongside it.

'Hello…'

Matthew recognised the deep voice immediately. 'Hello, Briggs.'

'A funeral always gets you thinking, doesn't it?' the tall, broad man mused. 'Especially a killing like this one; so pointless, don't you think?'

'Yes,' Matthew said slowly. 'I'm guessing Jakob was killed because of his past, but it makes no sense to kill an eighty-three-year-old man, whatever the reason.'

'True,' Briggs said, his eyes now on the hearse. 'One should never go digging up the past.'

'That…' Matthew shook his head. He didn't have the energy to explain to Briggs what he meant.

'Have you heard anything from Tom since we last spoke?' Briggs said. 'We would very much like to talk to him and, after all, I did promise him a long time ago that I would help you, should you turn up one day and need something.'

'I haven't heard a word,' Matthew said quickly. 'He seems to have drawn in his horns again.'

'Really, are you sure? Never mind, he'll turn up, you'll see.' Briggs patted Matthew's shoulder lightly. 'He was a good guy, your father, before it all went wrong. My best friend back in Portland at the dawn of time.'

Matthew nodded grimly. He was going to Ittoqqortoormiit to warn his father about Abelsen and Bárdur, but there was no need to share that information with Briggs. It was clear that Briggs and the US military were also very keen to get their hands on Tom, but Matthew would like to meet the man first. Given the messages he was hearing from all sides, his father could easily end up serving a very long prison sentence in the US.

54

'Would you like a lift to the cemetery?' Paneeraq asked Matthew. 'I'm going in the car with Karlo's cousin and there's room for more.'

'No, thank you.' Matthew cleared his throat and looked at the hearse as it slowly pulled away from the square and turned down the road to the junction between Brugseni and the Hotel Hans Egede. 'I've promised to take Arnaq home straight after the funeral so she doesn't spend too much time outside. But I'll join you shortly. I have Malik's car parked outside my flat.'

Behind them the flag flying by the church had gone from half-mast to flapping at the top of the tall pole.

His editor came up from behind and said to Matthew in passing: 'See you at the office tomorrow, right?'

'Yes, I'll be there,' Matthew said. Out of the corner of his eye he could see Briggs offering his condolences to Paneeraq. In a few days they would be back here again when it was Rakel's turn. Would they be offering their condolences to her children? How do you offer your condolences to a child? I'm sorry for taking your mum to meet a couple of crazed idiots who blew her to smithereens, so there's nothing even to put in a coffin or to say goodbye to?

Matthew's temples were pounding and the throbbing continued

right into the broken finger hidden behind the blue plastic brace. Viktor's funeral would be taking place here too, but he hadn't known him very well. It was Rakel who hurt. Her death had ripped open old wounds which had only just started to heal.

'Matt?' Arnaq called out to him. 'Time to go?'

'Yes, let's get you home.'

Her face had grown very gaunt during the week she had been held captive. Her eyes had changed as well. He offered her his arm so that she could lean on it.

'I can walk on my own,' she said, looking around the many mourners still gathered at the far end of the church car park. 'Where's Tupaarnaq?'

'She's at Jakob's…at his house, I mean. I don't think she likes funerals or people.'

Arnaq looked down at the tarmac. 'Neither do I now, but she's hardcore…'

They crossed the road. Matthew's own flat was only a short walk from where they were, but they were going up the steps behind the community hall to Else's flat in the low housing blocks at the top of Radiofjeldet.

They had only just reached the wide pavement on the other side when a tall, slim man in a grey hoodie shoved Matthew hard in the chest.

'Hey,' Matthew cried out. 'What do you think you're doing?'

'Are you an idiot or something?' Arnaq added. 'Watch where you're going.'

Matthew raised a hand to silence her. The man's face was half-concealed by the hood, but the pale skin and the turquoise eyes made Matthew's blood run cold.

The man reached out for Arnaq's arm, and when she saw his face she started to scream.

He pulled out a knife, pressed it against her throat and started dragging her with him towards the community hall.

'She's mine,' he said in a furious, snarling voice. 'Mine! Kjeld said so...This place is filthy. You'll ruin her.'

He kept on moving backwards.

'Símin!' Matthew ran up to them. 'It's not love when you force someone to be with you; they have to be free to choose.'

'Demon,' Símin sneered. The knife was pressed so hard against Arnaq's throat that Matthew could see a trickle of blood run down her skin. 'All of you people here must be struck down and sacrificed to God,' Símin ranted.

Arnaq stumbled and Símin had to steady her. The tears were streaming down her cheeks.

'Have no fear,' Símin whispered close to her ear. 'For I am with you...I will support you with the strength of my God.'

Several of the mourners were starting to cross the road and a car pulled up close by. Matthew gestured for them to keep their distance. None of them had any idea of the kind of person Símin was and how far his thinking was from theirs.

Someone started to shout.

Símin stared desperately around at the clusters of onlookers, which grew larger and larger and came closer and closer. 'God has determined that if you live the way you do, then you deserve to die,' he railed at them. His voice had changed. The sneering had gone. 'Was this what you wanted to save me for,' he said to Arnaq. 'Hordes of demons in human clothing?'

'It's...' She struggled to speak and had to swallow a couple of times. 'It hurts, Símin...Let me go.'

Símin trembled. His mouth was open. His eyes flickered. 'Is this your world?'

'Let me go,' she pleaded. 'Símin, please let me go.'

He tightened his grip on her and pressed her body against his. His breathing grew heavy in her ear.

'Let her go now,' Matthew said. He tried to catch Símin's eyes inside the hood, but they kept flitting. 'We can help you...You can be free.'

'She belongs to me,' Símin said. His tone was contemptuous once more.

At that moment Briggs stepped in front of Matthew.

Matthew reached out his arm to stop him, but Briggs was faster and had already reached Símin and Arnaq. For a brief moment Símin's eyes grew calm and a smile began to spread across his face. Then Briggs knocked him unconscious with a single punch to his face.

Arnaq freed herself and ran to Matthew, who hugged her and held her tight. Else arrived, sobbing, and embraced them both.

Briggs picked up the unconscious Símin almost effortlessly and threw him over his shoulder. 'I'll take this guy to casualty, and I'll stay there until the police arrive.'

Matthew nodded. He pressed his lips together, but then smiled briefly. 'Thank you.'

THE FURTHEST
TOWN

55

'Are you asleep?'

Matthew shook his head. The left side of his face was resting against one of the windows in the small helicopter. 'No, I'm just watching the view. It's mind-blowing.'

The approach to Ittoqqortoormiit was so different from Nuuk that Matthew experienced a moment of serenity. After Rakel's death and Símin's attack his head had been one big mess, and the fact that he had been forced to travel to Ittoqqortoormiit as early as the day after Jakob's funeral hadn't helped. There were only flights to the isolated town on Tuesdays and Thursdays, and he didn't want to wait until Tuesday in case Abelsen had made good on his threat to find Tom and had already have travelled there himself.

The helicopter flew over the small town. Everything around them was covered by a thick layer of snow, and along the rocky coast broad ribbons of ice reached the sea. There were ice floes several metres wide in the stretches of open water, and it was clear that not only the fjords and the bays but the entire sea was in the process of freezing over.

'How far north is this place compared to Nuuk?' Matthew shouted over his shoulder. The rotors made a racket in the small cabin.

'I've no idea,' Tupaarnaq said. 'A fair bit, I would think.'

'We're level with Ilulissat on the west coast,' the pilot shouted back. 'But the landscape here is harsher.'

Matthew looked down at the scattered, brightly coloured houses half-buried in snow less than fifty metres below the helicopter.

'And winter has also come early this year,' the pilot added.

'I had expected it to be dark all day over here by now,' Matthew shouted.

'No,' the pilot shouted back. 'But it won't be long; in twenty days it'll be dark twenty-four seven.'

'Do you know where house number eighty-seven is?'

The pilot shook his head.

'Can you see the church?' the co-pilot shouted.

Matthew looked down at the town and identified what he thought must be the church. 'Yes.'

'Count three houses up the slope and then one to the right. It's the blue one.'

'Hah, this dump doesn't have as many as three houses,' Tupaarnaq quipped dismissively.

•

Just under half an hour later they were outside number eighty-seven. It was a small house, but not the smallest one in town, and it was blue, as the co-pilot had said. There were no lights in any of the windows, but fortunately the daylight hadn't faded completely yet.

Tupaarnaq let her backpack slide down onto the snow, but kept the bag with her rifle slung over her shoulder. 'Someone has forced the door.'

Matthew frowned and took a closer look at it. She was right. It was slightly ajar and the handle looked damaged. He nudged the door. Behind it was a small hall with just enough room for the two of them.

'Do you think this is where your father lives?' Tupaarnaq said, picking up her backpack. She tossed it into the hall and continued to the next door that was facing them. Snow scattered from her boots and trousers as she moved.

Matthew followed, dumping his own backpack next to hers. 'Should we take off our boots?'

She shook her head as she opened the door. 'No, the place feels empty.'

Matthew began to feel distinctly uneasy. 'Don't you think we would have heard if Abelsen had managed to find Tom? I mean, only four hundred people live here, surely some of them would know if he had?'

'I think you can get away with pretty much anything here.'

The living room was simply furnished. There was an ancient sofa along one wall. There were also a couple of armchairs, a bookcase and a coffee table, which left room for little more. There was a duvet on the sofa and it looked as if someone slept there regularly.

At one end of the sofa was an old tiled stove. Matthew carefully placed his right hand on one of the tiles. It felt even colder than the room. He looked around him again. There were some magazines on the coffee table and several books in the bookcase. Someone had left a jumper on a sofa cushion.

He walked over to the sofa and picked up the jumper. It was a thick sweater knitted from coarse yarn and yet it felt soft. He pressed the sweater to his face and inhaled through his nose, dragging the air into every corner of his lungs through the fibres. It was so long ago since he had last seen his father. He had no idea if the sweater smelled of Tom, but it smelled of a human being; of a man.

Matthew sat down on the sofa and slumped. One hand held the sweater while the other slowly trailed the duvet. A part of him wanted to cry, but there was also a feeling of anger.

'What's keeping you?' Tupaarnaq demanded; she was looking into the room adjacent to the living room from the doorway. 'You need to come in here.'

'Okay,' Matthew said. His gaze was distant. 'I just have to—'

'Hurry up,' she said, disappearing into the neighbouring room. 'There's a small lab in here.'

'A what?' Matthew frowned. Briggs's stories about the Thule experiment and the pills suddenly felt very real.

'But I don't get why anyone would force the door,' she went on. 'Because I don't think that anything has been taken…Everything looks just as it should be…As far as I can see.'

'Wow.' Matthew stopped in the doorway. 'I wasn't expecting that.'

'No, me neither.'

He stared into the room in amazement. It was smaller than the living room, but much more was crammed into it. At the centre were two dining tables. On one were several tall piles of papers, a handful of books, boxes, plastic tubs and some glass flasks, while on the other there was a chaos of papers, mixed with slim files, ballpoint pens and an old computer with a clumsy tower and a small monitor.

'It certainly doesn't look as if someone searched this room,' Matthew said.

'No, besides, you can't sell stolen goods in Greenland. Everyone will know where they came from.'

Matthew walked up to the table with the boxes and the tubs. There were many different types of chemicals, several without labels.

'Why don't we look through it all?' Tupaarnaq suggested.

He nodded. 'Yes, let's see what we can find.' He glanced out of the only window in the room. The light outside was pink. 'We also need to do a tour of the town and find out if anyone knows anything about my father,' he said. 'And ask if Abelsen and Bárdur were here the other day.'

'Yes.' Tupaarnaq had already begun to search. 'What are we looking for?'

'Good question,' he said, examining the papers next to the computer.

'Okay…' She stopped her search and turned to him. 'I'll just check the rest of the house.'

He looked up at her with a frown.

'Somebody forced the door,' she said. 'And if Tom is lying dead somewhere, us trampling all over a crime scene isn't a very bright idea.'

The hairs stood up in Matthew's arms. 'No,' he said in a low, croaking voice. He knew there had to be a first floor of some kind because there was a narrow staircase in the hall.

'You carry on down here,' Tupaarnaq said. 'I'm guessing there's only room for one upstairs anyway.'

Matthew nodded slowly and resumed examining the piles of paper. Most of them were handwritten notes and data collected from different experiments; others looked more like chemical formulas and hand-drawn models of molecules, but there were also several printed sheets which looked like articles or possibly even a thesis.

The light was fast losing strength outside and the small window didn't help much. He flicked the switch near the door and the ceiling light came on. Then he turned on the computer. Nothing happened and he couldn't see if it was even connected to a power source as it was pushed right up against the wall.

'Hey, take a look at this.'

Matthew turned to Tupaarnaq, who had come back downstairs. She held out a small metal box and a faded buff file in front of her. 'Your father's not here, but I found this box upstairs and these papers in the bin.'

'What is it?'

'There's a pistol and two dog tags in the box…'

'Oh, shit.' Matthew closed his eyes.

'Are you okay?' She set down the box on the table in front of him and placed the file next to it. 'I didn't think you could get any paler than you already were.'

He gulped. 'What do the dog tags say?'

'Christian John Bradley and Mark Reese...Blood type A+ and O.'

Matthew cleared his throat, took a deep breath and exhaled. Then he removed the lid and looked inside the box.

'Don't touch the pistol,' she said quickly. 'Everything must be tested by forensics.'

'All this stuff...' Matthew sat down on the chair by the table with the computer. 'I'm starting to think that my father really did kill those two men, that...' He shook his head. 'But then why keep the evidence?'

'I don't know,' Tupaarnaq said. 'As a trophy? Out of guilt? It's been known.'

Matthew sighed. 'I'm not sure I can take much more of this.'

'We'll try to see the bigger picture when we're done here.'

'Yes, and Ottesen needs this evidence as soon as possible,' Matthew said, picking at one of the hinges on the box. The lid slammed shut with a bang that made him jump.

'Idiot...What about the papers from the bin?'

'No idea, did you read them?' He looked at the buff file. On the cover the words US NAVY and CONFIDENTIAL had been stamped in purple a long time ago; a little further down the word TUPILAK was stamped in red.

'Only briefly,' she said. 'It looks like data, but most of it is medical jargon.' She opened the file and spread out the pages. 'Apart from the fact that the doses are rather alarming, it doesn't mean all that much to me.'

Matthew skimmed the sheets. There appeared to be two types of documents. One was a comprehensive list of purchases and requisitions, while the other looked like data. A number of readings taken over a longer period had been entered into a table.

'Briggs seems to have signed off on a lot of these,' Matthew said in a low voice. 'Now, he told me that he had left the experiment, but of course I don't know when. These papers go as far as the middle of March 1990.' He looked up at Tupaarnaq. 'I need to find out when the murders happened…The postcard I got from my father was sent from Nuuk in August 1990.'

'Remind me what he wrote, will you?'

'That he couldn't follow us to Denmark as quickly as planned.'

She nodded. 'Does the other information mean anything to you?'

Matthew skimmed the various readings. 'Vitamin B12, BP 157/97, 163/101, 172/105, ECG.' He looked up at her. 'I haven't got the slightest idea what homocysteine is, but the numbers are rising alarmingly, and if a hundred is the norm, then the guinea pigs would have been pretty out of it at the end…Or whatever happens to you when you're given too much homocysteine.'

Tupaarnaq had found her mobile and was staring at the screen while she nodded. 'Mobile coverage here is patchy.'

'Yes,' Matthew said. 'So I've heard.'

'I certainly can't access the internet right now,' she said, letting her hand drop down. 'So what do we do?'

'Raid the fridge?'

'I was rather thinking that we need to find out if Abelsen and Bárdur are in town.'

'What if they are?' Matthew said. 'I mean, there's no way we can leave this place, is there?'

'Then I'll sit here and wait for them,' Tupaarnaq said, patting her rifle bag.

56

The living room smelled of cup noodles. There hadn't been much else in the kitchen so they had ended up with boiling water and a handful of colourful plastic beakers filled with chicken-flavoured dried noodles.

Matthew had just stuck his spoon into his second cup when the front door was pushed open and they heard boots.

They both looked up, but neither of them could see the door from where they were sitting.

Tupaarnaq rose quickly and disappeared into the adjacent room, while Matthew merely set his food on the coffee table and stood up.

'Tom?' someone called out from the hall.

'Hello,' Matthew answered tentatively, glancing towards the door to the lab where the muzzle of Tupaarnaq's rifle was sticking out. It was aimed at the door to the hall.

A short Greenlandic man appeared in the doorway. He was wearing a sturdy jacket and he brushed snow from his hair.

Matthew closed his eyes briefly and heaved a sigh of relief.

'You're not Tom,' the stranger said.

'My name is Matthew.'

The short man narrowed his eyes and came closer. 'You're

Matthew? Tom's Matthew?'

'Yes...' Matthew wanted to say something more, but the words refused to form a sentence.

'I'm Sakkak,' the Inuit said shyly, extending his hand. 'I saw that the light was on and I wanted to see if Tom was back.' He turned to the other door. 'You can put your rifle away. I'm Tom's friend.' He frowned. 'But you wouldn't know that, of course.'

'Where is my father?'

'I believe he has driven up along the coast.'

'Driven?'

'Yes, on his sledge.' Sakkak smiled. 'He has this monstrosity that uses wind rather than dogs. Not my kind of thing, but Tom is very proud of his kite sledge.'

Tupaarnaq entered the living room. She had put down the rifle.

'I think he gave up waiting for you,' Sakkak added, looking at Matthew. 'He wanted to go as far as Daneborg, which is several weeks travel north of here, and after all, he's on his own...We'll have to see.'

'I haven't seen the man for twenty-four years,' Matthew said in a wounded voice. Anger had bubbled up inside him at Sakkak's words about Tom having given up waiting. It was only two weeks, that was all, since he had received Tom's note, and where had Tom been when Arnaq's life was in danger?

'Would you like some coffee?' Tupaarnaq interjected.

Sakkak looked at her with a smile. 'I never say no to coffee.'

She nodded and carried her own and Matthew's noodles out into the kitchen.

Sakkak turned to Matthew again. 'I've known your father for many years. We met at the Thule base where I took part in an experiment involving some pills.' He nodded his head in the direction of the lab. 'Tom is obsessed with all that chemical mumbo jumbo.'

Matthew smiled without quite smiling.

'Why has he gone to Daneborg?' he asked Sakkak. 'I don't understand. Only soldiers live there, don't they?'

'Yes, pretty much. It's the main camp for the Sirius Patrol.'
Sakkak unzipped his thick jacket so he could reach his inside pocket.
'I moved to the east coast with my son seven years ago, when my
wife died, and I found that Tom was already here.' His eyes lit up. 'I
recognised him immediately. The two of you look so alike.'

'Here you are.' Tupaarnaq placed a steaming cup of coffee on the
table in front of Sakkak, who was still looking for something in his
jacket.

'Thank you,' he said, finally getting hold of a mobile phone.
'If you want to see your father, I have some videos I shot last year.
My son, Nukannguaq, recorded them while we were dancing.' He
smiled sadly at Matthew and took a sip of his coffee. 'I taught Tom
mask dancing and qilaat playing.'

Matthew reached across the coffee table and took the mobile. On
the screen was a video of two men performing a mask dance while a
young Inuit played a round, slim drum.

It was the first time in twenty-four years that he had seen his
father, and he didn't recognise him. He just saw a tall, slim man
whose face was painted red and black like a proper Inuit mask
dancer. His blond hair shone through the dark paint, but his face
was made up and distorted beyond all recognition. A black and red
face with the cheeks puffed out. The two mask dancers moved to the
monotonous and viscous sound of wood against wood from the qilaat
drum as if in a trance.

When the video stopped, Matthew kept staring at the screen.
Tupaarnaq patted his thigh gently.

'I don't recognise anything about him,' Matthew then said,
handing back the mobile. 'But the guy playing the drums, I saw some
pictures of him the week before last.'

'Yes.' Sakkak nodded grimly. 'That's Miki who is playing the qilaat. He's dead.'

'Oh, yes, the murders,' Matthew said in a quiet voice. 'I'm sorry. I'm a reporter and I covered the story, but I haven't been able to make head or tail of it yet…It's all right if you don't want to talk about it.'

'I know that you write for *Sermitsiaq*,' Sakkak said. 'Your father is always very proud when he shows me your articles, and I read what you wrote about Nukannguaq.'

'It all seems quite far-fetched,' Matthew said, picking at the scatter cushion under his arm. Tupaarnaq sat down next to him with her legs pulled up underneath her.

'Tom was helping me create a life for our young people,' Sakkak explained. 'Given how things are going, they need special skills if they're to have a future in this area. Our numbers decline with every year, and the council and the government in Nuuk don't care; they prefer to choke us slowly…It was exactly the same in the village I was from, Moriusaq. We had to leave it in the end, and now the same thing is happening here.'

'It's like that all over the world,' Matthew said. 'People leave their villages for a better life, and I can't imagine that being as cut off from everything as you are up here helps.'

'That's true, but then it's up to us to create a better life and more opportunities,' Sakkak said, and took another sip of his coffee. 'The young must get stronger so they can make the most of those opportunities. That was why we decided to make Salik, Miki, Konrad and Nukannguaq more resistant to very low temperatures…To further their opportunities. After all, we have a nine-month-long winter here, so if they could withstand the cold better, that would make it easier for them to hunt in the winter. And Tom also thinks we don't make the most of our opportunities for winter tourism.'

Matthew had straightened up on the sofa. 'What did you do to make them stronger?'

Sakkak exhaled slowly with his mouth almost closed so that his cheeks grew round like those of a mask dancer. 'Only fifty years ago a hunter could easily catch five times as much up here as they could down in Tasiilaq, but those days are gone. Hunting has become more difficult and we have no other source of income.'

'So what did you do?' Tupaarnaq asked.

'Tom doesn't feel the cold,' Sakkak said, fiddling with the coffee cup on the table. 'When we went hunting together, he was never affected by the cold, or anything else, for that matter. I wanted my Nukannguaq to have the same ability so I asked Tom if it was because of the experiment in Thule where I would always get cold before he did, and he told me about the pills.' Sakkak looked emptily into the air. 'He also told me how they had tricked me during the experiment, and that our young people would benefit from the pills just as much as he had.'

'So it was my father's pills they had swallowed the day when...'

'Yes. They were only supposed to take one a day...but the young men...' He shook his head. 'The place looked like an abattoir.'

'Did you remove the pills?' Tupaarnaq wanted to know.

'No,' Sakkak said quickly. 'I saw no pills in there.'

'Would it be possible for us to see the house?'

'Yes, we can do that tomorrow.' Sakkak picked at the seam of his trousers with a thumbnail, making a faint clicking sound. 'It's not a problem, no. And we've just had a visit from a police officer from Nuuk...He travelled on to Reykjavik to talk to Nukannguaq.' He looked up. 'I was also in Reykjavik for five days after the shooting, but I travelled home once my boy was stable. Hotels and plane tickets cost a lot of money.'

'It's insanely expensive up here,' Matthew agreed. 'Did you tell the police officer about your little experiment?'

Sakkak shook his head. 'Nukannguaq is innocent,' he said firmly. 'I know my son. It was Konrad who talked the others into it, and if anyone broke in here to get more of Tom's pills, then it would have been Konrad.'

'You think they forced the door?'

Sakkak shifted in the chair. 'Nukannguaq keeps muttering about pills and demons and God knows what else that made them want to kill themselves.'

'I thought two of them were shot in the chest?' Tupaarnaq interjected.

'Yes,' Sakkak said, staring down at the table. 'And that's why Nukannguaq is still in custody.' He cleared his throat a few times. 'Two of the four men were brothers. Salik and Miki.'

'Brothers?' Matthew said. 'Does Nuuk Police know that?'

'Yes, yes, they know,' Sakkak said.

'What do you think happened?' Tupaarnaq asked him.

'I don't know,' he said. He hesitated and then added: 'It was to do with their little sister and Konrad, but it's not something people talk about.'

'Whose little sister?' Tupaarnaq said quickly.

'Salik's and Miki's.'

'How old is she?'

'Seventeen, I believe. Yes, Sika must be seventeen now.'

'And the police know this as well?' Matthew said. 'I mean, the officer from Nuuk who came here.'

'Yes,' Sakkak said. 'I believe he spoke to her a couple of times.' He looked up. 'It's definitely Konrad. If something bad has happened, it would have been Konrad who did it.'

Matthew furrowed his brow. 'But Nukannguaq shot himself, didn't he?'

Sakkak nodded slowly.

The room fell quiet. Outside darkness had descended upon the town.

Tupaarnaq got up. 'Apart from Tom, does anyone use this house?'

Sakkak shook his head. 'No. Normally it's just Tom. Why?'

'We need a place to sleep,' she said, glancing at the duvet on the sofa. 'I'll see if I can find some clean bedlinen. There are more duvets upstairs.'

'I'll be all right on the sofa,' Matthew said.

'Yes,' was all she said as she left the room.

Sakkak slapped his thighs. 'Time for me to be getting home.'

Matthew pushed the scatter cushion aside and turned his attention to Sakkak, who had stood up. 'Before you go, have any strangers been here asking for Tom?'

'That police officer wanted to talk to Tom, but Tom had set off before he got here, so I don't think he found him. And then two men arrived yesterday who also wanted to talk to Tom.'

'Someone came here on a Wednesday?'

'Yes, by sledge. Just like the Sirius Patrol in February.' He frowned and then said: 'There was something military about them, but they weren't from Sirius because we know them. These two men were dressed in white Arctic clothing from top to toe.'

'Was it a slim man with black hair, about sixty, and a big, ruddy-faced man about fifty?'

Sakkak shrugged and tilted his head slightly. 'They could have been about fifty, and one of them might have had red hair. It was hard to see because they were wearing thick fur collars on their jackets and trapper hats.'

'Was one of them called Abelsen?'

'I don't know their names, but there was something about one of them that seemed familiar, or so I thought.'

Matthew got goosebumps all over his arms. 'Where are they now?'

'I think they drove on.'

'They followed Tom?'

'I don't know. They didn't say very much.'

Tupaarnaq returned to the living room. 'Right, that's the bedding sorted out,' she said, and threw a set of clean bedlinen at Matthew.

57

Matthew turned over on the sofa. The duvet wasn't very thick, but it didn't matter because after a few failed attempts they had managed to light a fire in the stove. It wasn't sealed properly, so there was a faint smell of smoke in the living room, but it was preferable to being cold.

He had spent most of the evening sending text messages to Ottesen about his discoveries in Ittoqqortoormiit so far, and was now scrolling through them to see if he had remembered to include everything.

I don't know how far you got when you were here, but I think I've found the murder weapon from Thule. It's a pistol that was in my father's house. We will bring it to Nuuk—haven't touched it. My father is in big trouble. Have you found him? I've heard more about what happened that night in Ittoqqortoormiit. I've spoken to Nukannguaq's father, Sakkak, as I gather have you. The four young men smoked cannabis and took some pills similar to those from the US military experiment in Thule in 1990. They contain substances which seemed to trigger severe psychoses and delusions, if you take too many. Sakkak hinted that Konrad raped Salik and Miki's younger sister, whose name is Sika, but I believe you already know that? He's also the opinion that it must have been Konrad who shot them—if they were killed. Perhaps he's right. Nukannguaq was off his face and he may not have experienced any of it as real until Konrad started shooting and finally shot himself. And then there was that business about the demon knocking on the window. Perhaps Nukannguaq panicked and shot himself?

Matthew was distracted from his texting when something was thrown down the steps.

Shortly afterwards Tupaarnaq appeared with a mattress and some bedding draped over one arm. She was wearing trackpants and a black tank top.

'There's ice on the inside of the wall upstairs,' she said, chucking her duvet and pillow on the floor. 'No wonder your father sleeps on the sofa...I'm moving down here to the stove.'

'Would you like the sofa?'

'No need, I bought the mattress.' She pushed the mattress in place near the stove and sat down on it with her duvet wrapped around her waist and legs. 'What are you doing?'

'I was just updating Ottesen.'

'You're such a snitch.'

'I haven't told him everything.'

'Sure you haven't.' She threw back her head and looked up at the ceiling. 'I'm just teasing you; it's okay. We need to find your father.'

Her skin gleamed golden in the faint glow from the stove door. Mostly around those parts of her face which weren't tattooed. The tattoos on her collarbones, shoulders and arms seemed almost alive in the flickering light. The many leaves, stems and vines looked like slowly moving, languid snakes.

She looked at him and pulled the duvet up around her shoulders. 'Do you think your father is here?'

Matthew raised his eyebrows and stopped staring at her skin. 'It makes no sense for him to head to Daneborg now, given that he has been hiding from the US military for twenty-four years.'

'He might be desperate,' she said. 'Besides, Daneborg is Danish territory, not American.'

Matthew nodded. 'I don't think that Abelsen and Bárdur were the men who came here looking for him. Why would they take a dog sledge across the ice cap rather than fly? It sounds more like the Sirius Patrol, even though Sakkak didn't recognise them.'

'What would Sirius want with your father?'

'Probably the same thing he wants from them.' Matthew raised a hand to his face and pressed his eyelids while he exhaled heavily. 'I think it's all connected to the 1990 experiment.'

'The one described in the files in your father's study?' Tupaarnaq said. 'Tupilak?'

'Yes. It looks like the experiment was never cancelled completely, and now that it has resurfaced, it appears to have rattled someone's cage.'

'Do you know the original meaning of tupilak?'

'It's to do with spirits, am I right?'

'It's your ancestor's spirit, which you summon by carving a small demonic figure, and then you can ask the spirit to go after your enemy. It can backfire, though. If your tupilak meets an even stronger spirit, it can be turned and come back to destroy you. It looks like some of the people involved in the experiment have realised that it's coming back to bite them.'

Matthew rolled over onto his back. 'Do you believe in that spirit business?'

'No,' she said. 'I don't really believe in anything.'

He looked around the edges of the ceiling. It had been wall-papered a long time ago, but it was starting to come off. In one place he could see that a whole length was loose. 'I want to believe in souls and spirits.'

'Because of the people you have lost?'

'Yes.' He could feel the cold spread like a shiver through his body and he tightened the duvet around him.

'It was a traffic accident, wasn't it?'

Matthew coughed. In just a few seconds the chill in his body had turned to heat, and the skin on his forehead and chest started to feel clammy.

'It was a red car. With four Romanian men. They overtook when they shouldn't have and forced us off the road. The driver survived, but Tine and Emily died.' Matthew gulped. Pushed the duvet off his upper body. 'The car rolled across the ground. I was conscious the whole time. Tine died. I touched her belly. They were trapped. She was bleeding.'

'Have you ever thought of tracking him down?'

'Who?'

'The man who killed your wife and daughter?'

Matthew carefully wiped the lower rim of his eyes with a forefinger. 'Sometimes…Not really. I don't see why I would. I don't want to see him. I wouldn't know what to do with him.'

'Kill him.'

The room fell silent. The fire crackled in the stove.

'Is the pain still raw?' Tupaarnaq then said.

Matthew touched his empty ring finger. 'I carry my wedding ring in my pocket nearly all the time.'

'Why?'

'Oh, you know what it's like,' he said in a trembling voice. 'And your pain is worse than mine, I think.'

'But I want to be rid of mine,' she said. 'And I want to find Abelsen and kill him.'

'Because you think it's his fault that your family died?'

'Because I know that he signed my mother's death warrant and that of my sisters when he raped my mother,' she said angrily. 'Even his rapist son ended up dead. There's just me and Abelsen left, and he must die.'

'He needs to go to prison,' Matthew said, straightening up in order to see her. 'If you kill him, you'll be locked up for the rest of your life…What's the point of that?'

'There's not much else I need to do apart from watch him die.'

'When I was in the bunker, I hid under a table and I overheard Abelsen and Bárdur talking.'

Matthew sank back onto the sofa and stared up at the wallpaper on the ceiling. His pulse had risen and he was breathing more rapidly.

'And?'

'He…' He ground to a halt. 'Abelsen. He said…He called you his daughter.'

There was silence for a moment. Then she got up and let the duvet fall to the floor. She didn't even look at Matthew. She just walked out of the room. Her back was straight and her fists tightly clenched. The muscles stood out sharply under her tattooed skin.

'I'm sorry,' Matthew called out after her, and sat up fully. 'I had to tell you at some point.' He waited. Listened to her moving about upstairs. 'We don't even know if it's true.' He buried his face in his hands. Abelsen had had absolutely no reason to lie when he was alone in the kitchen with Bárdur, the dead Viktor and the unconscious Malik.

Matthew got up and found his trousers. He had only told her in order to get her to drop the idea of killing Abelsen, but now he was afraid that it had had the opposite effect. He hadn't thought it through. The man everyone believed to be her and Ulrik's father had killed their mother and their two little sisters because he found out that he wasn't Ulrik's father, that the boy's real father was Abelsen. What if he had learned at the same time that he wasn't Tupaarnaq's father either? She had been imprisoned for twelve years for killing all of them, but she knew that she had only killed her father, who, in her eyes, deserved to die for so many reasons. What if she now felt that she had indirectly caused the deaths of the others by being yet another catalyst for her father's rage?

Tupaarnaq dropped something upstairs.

Shortly afterwards she came back down. She was wearing her outdoor clothes. The rifle hung over her right shoulder. Her gaze was fixed on the floor and she didn't look up for one second. She just disappeared out of the door and into the dark, Arctic night.

58

The wind had increased dramatically during the night. Around two a.m. it had grown so strong that Matthew could feel it inside the house whenever a gust of wind blew down the cliff at the foot of which the small town was situated. Apart from a few Danish soldiers in Mestersvig, the next town was over six hundred kilometres away, and the only means of getting there was by helicopter or dog sledge.

Outside the small windows everything was black and the snow was whirling around in sweeping blankets of piercing ice crystals.

He had slept only in snatches. Without a steady rhythm. Instead he had spent some of the night reading through his father's papers, but they still made little sense to him. The only thing that seemed clear was that the Thule experiment must have been extremely hard on everyone, physically and mentally, judging from the readings. And though he didn't know precisely how the pills affected the body, it didn't come as a total surprise to him that the experiment had ended in disaster when one of the participants ran amok. What did seem completely insane—apart from them having exceeded all safe dosages—was that Tom had then attempted to recreate the experiment many years later in Ittoqqortoormiit. Even if it was a lesser version, and even though the town desperately needed a boost, it seemed indefensible.

Dawn broke around nine o'clock. Matthew pushed the duvet aside and got up. The clouds had been blown away and everything was bathed in a pink glow. The snow had rearranged itself around the houses, and in a few places people had gone outside to clear snow from their doors.

Matthew went to the kitchen and poured himself a glass of ice-cold water from the tap. He also found a packet of crackers in a small wooden cupboard. He sat down on the sofa and opened the metal box that contained the pistol. It was shiny and it looked heavy. It was a powerful hand weapon. 9 mm. He was tempted to pick up the pistol purely to gauge if it could tell him anything, but he decided against it, and when at the same moment he heard a snow scooter pull up outside the house, he closed the box and pushed it to the centre of the table.

Before he had time to get to his feet, the front door had already been pushed open and moments later Tupaarnaq appeared in the doorway to the living room. Her clothes were covered in snow, and her scarf and cap were iced over. The skin on her face blossomed pink at the sudden encounter with the heating in the living room. The rifle hung over her right shoulder and in her right hand she held three dead Arctic hares by the ears.

She let the hares fall to the floor. 'I'll gut them later.'

'I'm sorry—'

'Shut up,' she cut him off. 'We were meeting Sakkak at eleven, weren't we?'

'Yes.'

'I'm going to take a shower.' Her gaze seemed locked to the floor. 'Keep away.'

59

The sun hung low on the horizon when they met Sakkak outside number seventy-three.

The short, compact Inuit smiled happily at them as they approached him. He glanced at the rifle hanging over Tupaarnaq's shoulder. 'We're not going hunting.'

'I'm always hunting,' she said in a flat voice without making eye contact.

'Shall we take a look inside?' Matthew said quickly.

Sakkak nodded grimly and pushed open the door.

Even from the outside it smelled mouldy, and it only got worse once they stepped inside. The air reeked of stale beer and smoke, and there was a cold dampness everywhere.

'Shouldn't it have been cordoned off?' Matthew asked as he entered the living room.

'Well,' Sakkak said quietly. 'I think it was a free-for-all while I was in Reykjavik. Everyone wanted to take a good look at where it had happened.'

'So lots of people have been tramping about in here?' Tupaarnaq concluded.

'Yes, pretty much the whole town.' Sakkak pointed across the coffee table. 'That's where it happened.'

Matthew looked at the carpet by the coffee table. There was a lot of dried blood. He closed his eyes, and for a short moment his nose remembered the smell in the corridors under Færingehavn. The police had found the bodies of Andreas and Lasse in a big freezer in the abattoir close to Bárdur's quarters. Matthew was still tormented by the fact that he hadn't brought the four young people back from Færingehavn when he first went to see them. But how could anyone possibly have known that a crazy family lived under the town? The police had found Alma's body at the bottom of the pool. There were many other dead bodies in the water and it had taken Arctic Command divers a whole day to recover their remains as sensitively as possible. Most of the dead were reduced to bones, while Alma was still in one piece. The youngest skeletons were those of newborn babies. There were many of those. All had had their necks wrung.

'Nukannguaq was sitting over there,' Sakkak said.

Matthew forced the disturbing thoughts out of his mind and looked at Sakkak, who was pointing to a frayed, stained armchair. There was blood spatter on the wall behind the chair, right above its back.

'And Salik and Miki were sitting over there,' Sakkak went on, pointing to the sofa on the other side of the coffee table, which was still littered with empty bottles and overflowing ashtrays. 'Konrad was lying on the floor.'

There was blood everywhere. On the sofa, in front of the sofa and on the carpet.

'And he had been shot through the mouth, just like Nukannguaq, is that right?'

Sakkak nodded without looking at either of them. He seemed exhausted.

Matthew positioned himself right next to the bloodstain on the carpet where Konrad had lain and pointed at the sofa. He found his mobile and swiped to the picture were Salik and Miki lay dead on the very same sofa. 'Konrad really did shoot them,' he whispered to himself and looked towards Tupaarnaq. 'But why, if he was the guy who had raped their sister? Surely you would expect them to have shot him, wouldn't you?'

Tupaarnaq shrugged. 'Don't forget that they were high as kites. Possibly psychotic. But, yes, I would have shot Konrad, if it had been me.'

Matthew chewed his lip. It was the exact same scenario as on the Thule base where his father was alleged to have killed two men in some kind of psychotic rush triggered by the experimental drug. Only something didn't add up. He looked towards Sakkak. 'The rifle was lying next to Nukannguaq when they were first discovered, correct?'

'Yes, he was the last person to shoot himself,' Sakkak said.

Again Matthew turned his gaze to the old armchair opposite the sofa. 'How well did Nukannguaq know their sister?'

'Everybody knows everybody here; there are so few young people.'

'Is it possible to talk to her?'

'She was gone when I came home from Iceland. I believe she went to visit her aunt in Tasiilaq right after that police officer had spoken to her.'

'Because I would like to...' Matthew was interrupted by a noise from the adjacent room.

Tupaarnaq let her rifle slip into her hands and eased the bolt forward to chamber a round.

'Is someone here?' Matthew asked with a frown.

Sakkak shook his head. 'No, there shouldn't be.'

Matthew looked at Tupaarnaq. It was the first time since last night that she had made eye contact with him.

She pointed to the door with her rifle.

Matthew nodded grimly. His chest tightened. He pushed open the door without blocking her line of fire and looked back at Tupaarnaq and Sakkak.

'Tom!' Sakkak cried out.

Matthew turned to the doorway. A tall, blond man was tied to a chair in the middle of the room. The man looked at them. His face was stained with dried blood.

'Are you okay?' Sakkak said. He had rushed past Matthew and was squatting next to his friend. He removed the strong tape from Tom's mouth and began untying the ropes with which Tom was restrained.

Matthew's hands were shaking and he started to hyperventilate.

Tupaarnaq placed a hand on Matthew's shoulder. 'So he does exist after all.'

'Yes.' Matthew's voice was so feeble that his reply escaped his lips only as a whisper. His shoulders twitched and for a moment he was a little boy, barely four years old, standing on the top step of the plane waving to his daddy. He nodded and was aware of Tupaarnaq walking past him. Towards Tom.

The first few months, Matthew had refused to believe that his father would never come to Denmark. The meaning of the word *never* still didn't exist for him, but he learned it eventually. It didn't happen suddenly, but over time. One day he finally understood that *never* really did exist, and he started to cry. He had cried silently for years. He had cried when he sat alone in the darkness, and whenever he saw films about fathers. Even at school, he had secretly cried at parents' evenings when his classmates turned up with their fathers. To begin with he had told everybody that his father was a spy at the American base in Greenland, and they had all believed him, but that stopped and turned into *never*. To nothing. Eventually he couldn't even remember his father's face, his smile, his smell or the sound of his voice.

Sakkak had finished untying the ropes and Tom sat rubbing

his wrists without saying anything. His eyes were locked firmly on Matthew.

Tupaarnaq watched Tom in silence, and then left the room with her rifle draped over one arm.

Tom chewed his lower lip tentatively. 'Matthew,' he whispered as the tears started rolling down his cheeks.

Matthew trembled at the sound of his name. And the memory of his father's face, his voice, the nuances, the depth, the warmth came flooding back. He wanted to clasp Tom's face with both hands. He wanted to press himself against his chest. Feel his adult heart beat strongly in there. But he stopped himself. He tried saying the word *dad*, but he couldn't.

'Who did this to you?' Sakkak's voice cut through.

Tom shook his head. 'I don't know...I didn't see them.' He turned to Sakkak. 'I've been sitting here since yesterday morning.'

Tupaarnaq returned with a glass of water, which she handed to Tom.

He took the glass and drained it in a couple of big gulps. He then exhaled noisily and said, 'Thank you.' He tried to get up, but fell back onto the chair. 'The muscles in my legs have seized up.'

'Would you like me to get you some clean trousers?' Sakkak asked.

Tom looked down and nodded. The stains were not only blood. 'Yes, please...I guess I need to sit here and stretch my legs for a while before I try standing up again.'

Sakkak left the room to go back to Tom's house and it fell silent. Tom slowly extended his legs.

Matthew had sat down on the bed next to Tom's chair. Tupaarnaq was standing up, looking out of the window.

'Say something,' Tom said, looking at Matthew, who had yet to speak.

Matthew shook his head. Everything that was going on inside his head was too complex to say on the edge of a shabby bed in one of the world's most remote towns. He hugged himself and rubbed his arms.

'There's so much,' he began.

Tupaarnaq turned around and looked at them. 'Let me know when you're good to go. We shouldn't stay here any longer than we have to.'

'I won't need long,' Tom said.

'Back in Thule,' Matthew said. His gaze was fixed firmly on the floor, which was just as filthy as the rest of the house. 'Did you do it?'

Tom rubbed his face with both hands. He took a couple of deep breaths. 'How much do you know?'

'Pretty much everything,' Matthew said. 'Tupilak, the pills, the disturbing data, Sakkak, Briggs. I just want to know if you really are the man everyone wants to lock up for murder.'

'I doubt that you know as much as you think you do,' Tom said. 'We were in bad shape that night. It had spun out of control, all of it, and we probably went too far.'

'Probably? It looks like you were all on the verge of a mental breakdown and a stroke,' Matthew said.

'Those weren't exactly the words I was looking for,' Tom said. 'But you're not far wrong, either. Sakkak, who I see you've met, was performing a mask dance for us, but somehow the dance and the sounds affected the darkness inside us. Suddenly Bradley and Reese were at each other's throats. They went berserk, their emotions were heightened. Sakkak fled out of the door and then Abelsen appeared. I don't know where that bastard had been hiding. I screamed at him that those pills must never leave Thule, but that man doesn't give a toss about anyone but himself.' Tom rubbed his face again. 'I don't remember anything else. Only flashes…Bradley and Reese covered in blood. They lay still. I think they had been shot.'

'But who shot them?'

'I don't know,' Tom said in a weary tone. His eyes were wide and his lips pressed shut. 'I don't know who killed them,' he said. 'There's a black hole in my memory. Perhaps Abelsen did because I wanted to stop the experiment…Perhaps I did. I don't know. After all, I did have my pistol, there was a struggle…I was knocked out. There were three empty shells next to me when I woke up, and Bradley and Reese were…but…I didn't have my pistol anymore…I think.' He shook his head and squeezed his eyes shut. 'It's all a blur.'

'Doesn't Sakkak remember anything?'

Tom shook his head. 'Even less than me. Don't forget that he ran away shortly before Abelsen arrived.'

'We found a small box in your house,' Tupaarnaq said. 'It contains a pistol and Bradley's and Reese's dog tags.'

'That's impossible,' Tom said. 'At no point did I have their dog tags and I haven't touched my pistol since that night. It was Abelsen who forced me to flee and go AWOL, and I took nothing with me from the base. Nothing.' He stared down at the floor.

'I don't know what to make of it,' Matthew said with a sigh. 'We have a lot to talk about.' He looked towards the living room. 'Like the young men in there. It was Thule all over again, wasn't it?'

'No,' Tom said, shaking his head.

'Can it wait?' Tupaarnaq interrupted. She looked at Tom. 'Let's get you on your feet so we can go back to your house. This place gives me the creeps, and whoever tied you up will surely come back.'

60

As soon as they turned onto the path in the snow that led up to Tom's house, they could see that the front door was wide open. The blue wooden walls were draped with curtains of snow, held in place by the wind and the frost, and in the short time the door must have been open, a small mound of snow had been blown into the hall.

Matthew wiped ice off his eyebrows. The snow had got a tight grip on them in the less than sixty metres that separated the two houses. He dusted snow off his jacket and went inside.

Behind him Tupaarnaq had released her hold of Tom, who turned to face the wind and squinted at the prickling, flying snow.

'It's wonderful that it can snow this much,' he said. 'Without it snowing.'

'Sakkak?' Matthew called out.

Tom looked quizzically at his son, who rushed inside the house.

Tupaarnaq raised her rifle.

Matthew knelt down alongside Sakkak, who was lying flat on his stomach in the living room.

'What's happened?' Tom said. He bent down next to Matthew and put his hand on Sakkak's neck.

Matthew was about to say something, but was interrupted when a tall man appeared in the door to the small lab. He was dressed for the Arctic winter in white clothing from his boots to his trapper hat and fur collar. He stared at Tom, then he pointed his pistol at him. Matthew jumped up to shield his father the moment the man pulled the trigger. The bullet hit his right arm, which felt as if it had been ripped off.

Another man dressed just like the first appeared in the doorway.

Matthew cried out and gasped for air while he pressed his left hand against the wound to his arm. Tupaarnaq was standing right behind him with her rifle aimed at the man who had shot Matthew. The man continued to point his pistol at Tom.

Then the second man kicked a small, dark green plastic cylinder into the living room, and it exploded seconds later, filling the room with dense, grey smoke. Three shots were heard. Two from the pistol and one from Tupaarnaq's rifle.

'Out!' Tupaarnaq's voice shouted somewhere in the smoke.

Matthew looked around, but he couldn't see very far. He was coughing so violently that he had to spit on the floor.

'Get the hell out of here,' Tupaarnaq shouted again.

Matthew felt her shoving him. Both his arms were working, although one of them was injured. The smoke almost made him throw up and he could hear the others cough and splutter. He fought his way to the door and was soon back outside in the snow. Smoke was pouring out of the house and the roof. He looked at his arm and pulled off his jacket. It seemed to be a flesh wound only, but there was quite a lot of blood on his clothes. The bullet had gone straight through his clothes and his arm without doing any damage other than severing some blood vessels.

'Help me,' Tupaarnaq called out from the hall.

She was trying to drag Tom outside, and Matthew rushed to help her get his father out.

Tom wheezed and groaned. He growled deep in his throat, his

face contorted in pain and his forehead covered with beads of sweat.

A burning smell was coming from inside the house. A dazed Sakkak appeared in the doorway and Tupaarnaq quickly helped him out and down to Tom before she herself ran back inside the house.

Tom was getting increasingly breathless, and pulled off his jacket and jumper with a grunt. Underneath he wore a black bulletproof vest, fixed around his waist, and he loosened it in order to breathe more freely. There was a big, red bruise to his skin right above his rib cage. He was bleeding from one arm, as was Matthew.

Tupaarnaq reappeared and chucked her own and Matthew's backpacks into the snow.

'No, it can't be,' Tom said, staring emptily out into the air. His face was pale and his lips were trembling slightly.

Behind him the flames had started licking the windows of the small house.

Tom tried to stand up, but had to abandon his attempt and collapsed with a strangled yelp.

'It's too late,' Tupaarnaq said. 'They've torched the lab, everything in there is gone.'

'They're crap shots, though,' Sakkak said, looking at Tom's arm.

'Oh, he never misses,' Tom said. The snow had started to settle on his skin. 'Those three shots landed precisely where they were supposed to.'

'He?' Matthew said. 'You know who it was?'

'The shooter was Bradley. The other guy was Reese.'

61

Tupaarnaq grew smaller and smaller below the helicopter. Matthew sat with one hand held up against the window. She had only waved briefly as they took off and now she was nothing more than a dot standing alone outside the tiny airport at Constable Point.

Ottesen had requested a helicopter and a doctor from Iceland, which had arrived at Ittoqqortoormiit two hours later.

Meanwhile they had put pressure on the injuries and administered whatever pain relief they could find in the small town's health centre. There was no doctor at the centre this week, but the town's only nurse had assisted them.

The doctor from Iceland soon concluded that they might as well be flown to Nuuk, given that neither Tom's nor Matthew's injuries required specialist treatment in Reykjavik.

The helicopter from Iceland had then taken 'them from Ittoqqortoormiit to Constable Point, where they boarded an Air Greenland Bell 212.

Tupaarnaq, however, had said that she needed time on her own and that she would catch the next helicopter from Constable Point to Tasiilaq.

Matthew looked away from the window. Constable Point itself was now nothing but a tiny spot somewhere far below them. He took a sip of his cola and glanced furtively at Tom.

They were sitting in the same row, but with a vacant seat between them. Matthew's backpack lay on the floor. Tom had nothing.

'You're smiling,' Matthew said.

'Yes,' Tom said with a grin. 'I've seen my son for the first time in twenty-four years and I discovered that I'm not a killer after all.'

'Have you any idea why Bradley and Reese would turn up now?' Matthew asked. 'Briggs told me that the three of you were repatriated to the US back in 1990, so those coffins must have been empty?'

'Until a few hours ago I had no doubts at all that Bradley and Reese were dead,' Tom said. He pressed his eyelids with his fingers. 'And I'm sure the number of people who know that they're alive is very small.'

'But it doesn't make any sense, does it?'

'Yes, it does, as it happens, but it requires a long explanation, which is why I wrote to you and asked you to visit me.' He adjusted the sling supporting his arm. 'I had a lot of evidence in my house, but it was lost in the fire, so now you'll have to take my word for it.'

'Okay,' Matthew said, with a glance at his trouser pocket where his mobile lay. He would like to make notes, but it seemed impossible as long as his right arm was in a sling like Tom's and his broken finger was strapped to a clumsy brace. He took another sip of his cola and wedged the can in place between his thighs.

'You've read about the Chinese man who disappeared near Kangerlussuaq seven weeks ago, haven't you?' Tom began.

'Yes, we wrote about it, why?'

'Even when I read about him the first time, I had a hunch that there was more to it than the press was aware. After all, Kangerlussuaq isn't just a civilian airport, it's also a military one, and when I saw the pictures taken of the Chinese man as he headed off on his hike, I could see that he wasn't carrying standard photo equipment. There was no way he was a tourist, and I'm quite sure that he was there to survey the landscape and possibly the entire complex.'

'So you believe that the US military is involved in his disappearance?'

'A Chinese national walking around with surveyor's equipment in an area of Greenland with American military interests? I'm pretty sure he didn't just fall into a crevice or drown…at least not by accident. The situation up here is much more tense than people think. Danish Intelligence is very aware of the need to prevent Chinese acquisitions in Greenland, because neither the Danes nor the Americans want China to be able to influence the political situation up here. Several news agencies have picked up that the Danish prime minister has gained a cross-party agreement to reopen the Grønnedal naval base in south Greenland in order to block a bid from a Chinese mining company.' Tom coughed briefly into his left hand. 'The Danish Security Service distrusts big Chinese corporations because they're constructed in such a way that it's impossible to see how closely they're related to the Chinese government and thus the Chinese army.'

'I'll need to write all this down when we land,' Matthew said. 'And understand how it's connected to Tupilak. You wrote that you wanted to tell me about something called Tupilak, and in your house we found a file with data from the Thule experiment. That file was labelled Tupilak.'

'The Thule experiment and the pills were part of a large operation codenamed Tupilak. When the Chinese man disappeared, I began to suspect that perhaps Tupilak had been sucessful after all. I admit it was just an educated guess, but today we got the proof that my guess was right.'

'You mean Bradley and Reese?'

'Yes…Stupid bastards! The worst thing is that I can't even allow myself to be mad at them, because all they've done is carry out the plan for all four of us. That was what I wanted to tell you.' He hesitated for a moment. 'Only I hadn't factored in you going to Briggs, of all people, and telling him about me and Tupilak.'

'I had no way of knowing that Tupilak was a secret army operation,' Matthew said, staring at the floor of the cabin. 'And Briggs told heartwarming stories about your lifelong friendship.'

'Fair point,' Tom said. 'Besides, it turned out to be a blessing in disguise, because we've discovered that Bradley and Reese are alive.' He rubbed his face. 'Only I don't understand how? I mean, I saw them back then…There was blood everywhere.' He lowered his hand and looked at Matthew. 'I had blood all over my hands…I find it really hard to believe that they're not dead.'

'Do you think they came to kill you?'

'Yes, once they discovered the file.' He ground to a halt and looked at Matthew. 'They planted the box with the pistol and the dog tags.'

Matthew nodded slowly and glanced at his backpack. He had managed to bring the box, but the Tupilak file had been missing from his backpack when he had gone to take it out earlier. He had no doubt that Bradley and Reese had found it and possibly burned it along with the house. But they hadn't taken the box, even though it had been right next to the file. Fortunately he had already photographed the whole file with his mobile before it disappeared, sent the pictures to his fellow reporter, Leiff, and asked him to investigate what the data was all about. He looked back at his father. 'Why didn't they just tie you up in your own house?'

Tom raised his eyebrows. 'They ambushed me in Konrad's house. My guess is that they watched the town for several days before they struck.'

'Why were you in Konrad's house?'

'I've spent some time there recently,' Tom said, looking up at the ceiling of the cabin. 'Leaving the pills lying about so that four young lads could get hold of them isn't something I'm proud of. Bradley and Reese may not be dead, but Konrad, Salik and Miki are definitely gone forever.'

Matthew watched the ice cap glide past underneath them. The sun hung low, pink and orange over the horizon, and in less than half an hour everything would be dark. 'I don't think you can avoid Nuuk Police,' Matthew said at length.

'I don't think I can avoid anything.' Tom pressed his lips together, then said, 'How many people do you think will believe me when I tell them that Bradley and Reese aren't dead?'

'Briggs, possibly?'

'Briggs? Briggs was much higher up in this than I ever was. He's not going to take my side. If Tupilak has succeeded, then Briggs is one of the few people who has known about it all along.'

Matthew closed his eyes and rested his cheek against the cold glass. 'I've been such an idiot,' he said, bashing his head lightly against the window a couple of times. 'What exactly is Tupilak? What roles do Bradley and Reese play in all this?'

'Yes, what is their role? The original intention was to create elite military units similar to the Danish Sirius Patrol. The American version would be programmed to be extra resistant to the cold, among other things. Tupilak would be shadow units trained to operate from dog sledges and crisscross the ice. Briggs and I were to form one group, while Bradley and Reese would make up the other. Pairs, just like in Sirius. Our mission was to protect American interests in Greenland, with Danish acceptance…military as well as political.' Tom heaved a sigh and shifted in his seat. 'Again, exactly like Sirius, but ratcheted up a notch and underpinned by a hidden strategic defence agenda. However, if Tupilak still exists, which after today's events there's every reason to believe, then I dread to think how far its remit has been extended. I wanted out precisely because I realised that we were on our way to becoming state-sponsored assassins.'

'So you believe that Bradley and Reese killed the Chinese man?'

'For spying on a military complex, yes.'

'And what about Lyberth?'

'Lyberth?'

'He was murdered in a flat in Nuuk two months ago. Some people believe his death was a warning to those who are fighting hard for Greenlandic independence.'

'Okay, I see. Yes, it's possible that Tupilak killed him too. Greenland will never be just Greenland. This enormous island in the Arctic is either Danish or American, and as far as the US is concerned, it's better for Greenland to remain Danish than it is to deal with the political mayhem that would ensue if the US was forced to annex an independent Greenland for security reasons.'

THE THULE MAN

62

Matthew had been sitting staring into the air for almost an hour when the door to the side ward opened. He had chased Leiff by text to hear if his doctor friend had examined the Tupilak data, but Leiff had yet to reply.

'They told me I would find you here,' Ottesen said.

'Yes.' Matthew coughed and straightened up in the chair. 'Arnaq had a check-up today and I decided to come with her and look in on Malik at the same time.'

Ottesen looked at the sleeping young Inuit. 'At least he's stable.'

'They say he wakes up every now and then, but he's still heavily sedated.'

'It's a miracle he survived,' Ottesen said. 'What was it the doctors said? His lung was pierced by two ribs?'

Matthew looked at the thin tube running from the bandages on Malik's chest and into a container. 'No, I think his lung just collapsed, but he had broken three ribs.'

Ottesen grimaced and narrowed his eyes. 'Poor guy. That's hurts like hell.' He adjusted his jacket. 'Can I have a word with you?'

'Yes.'

'It's about your father. Is it okay to talk in here?'

'Sure.'

'We've questioned him,' Ottesen said, sitting down on a chair on the other side of the low hospital bed. 'And he has told us quite a lot, but not everything makes sense to me.'

'Which bits?' Matthew said, and coughed again. The back of the chair was flimsy and he could feel it give when he pressed his back against it.

'Most of it, to be honest,' Ottesen said. 'The good news is that he has given us plenty of information about the killings in Ittoqqortoormiit, but he'll pay a high price for that.'

'Because he didn't come forward straightaway?'

'Yes, and then there's the business with the pills...But it'll count in his favour that he travelled with you to Nuuk, knowing the consequences it would have for him.' Ottesen narrowed his eyes slightly. 'We've had the test results from the rifle. Only Konrad's and Nukannguaq's fingerprints are on it, so one of them shot the two brothers on the sofa.'

'Do you think Konrad did it?'

Ottesen nodded slowly. 'Your father claims that he saw Konrad and Nukannguaq shoot themselves, and if that's true, then the finger points to Konrad as he had the rifle before Nukannguaq. That also matches Nukannguaq's own account, but I can't be sure of what Tom really saw. It was during a snowstorm and the windows in the house are small and filthy.' He shook his head. 'I don't know right now. Has Tom told you about this as well?'

'No, only that he felt bad about the pills.'

'Yes, what a stupid idea that was, and now the pills have vanished into thin air. Tom says that he took them, but it could just as well have been Sakkak. Like I said the other day, they're as thick as thieves over there.'

'So you think Sakkak went into the house right after the shooting?'

'Yes, he did what he could to save his boy…but I'm guessing that he had doubts as to who killed who, too.'

'And then there's the girl,' Matthew said. 'I think Sakkak suspects Konrad of raping Salik's and Miki's sister.'

'I don't know how Sakkak can know anything about that,' Ottesen said, giving Matthew a puzzled look. 'She told me that she had only told the nurse at the health centre.' He snorted angrily. 'It's always the same in those small, closed communities; everyone knows everyone else's business, but everything is hidden from the outside world. I'll speak to Sakkak and the girl again, and I might ask your father about it as well.'

'Yes, that's just it…Has my father explained why he was even near the house where the shooting took place?'

'Yes, but I'm not happy about it,' Ottesen said. 'He said that he heard shots and went down there, but as I've already mentioned there was a violent snowstorm raging there that night, and I just don't think he could have heard a couple of rifle shots. Perhaps he discovered that the pills were gone and went to have a word with the young men.'

'When we were in Tom's house,' Matthew said, 'Sakkak told us that they had made the pills to make the young men more cold-resistant. They're pretty desperate in every way over there.'

'The road to hell is paved with good intentions,' Ottesen said. 'But to be fair, most of your theories have been proved right. Drugs, cannabis, the side effects of the pills, murder and suicide. If it hadn't been for Tom and the pills, it would have been just another Greenlandic murder case, admittedly one of the more violent.'

'Did my father also tell you about Tupilak and the US military experiment with the pills on the Thule base?'

'Yes, but it's not something that really helps us.' Ottesen got up and went over to one of the windows in the side ward. It had started snowing again. 'To be perfectly honest, it sounds like a desperate man's last-ditch attempt to save his own skin after he has been caught. We've no evidence to support his stories.'

'I feel the exact opposite,' Matthew said with a frown. He looked at Ottesen, who stared firmly out of the window. 'I saw the file and Bradley and Reese in Ittoqqortoormiit. Can't you do something to look into it?'

'Nuuk Police can't demand insight into a US military investigation, and all the Americans care about is putting their killer behind bars.' He looked back at Matthew. 'You yourself found the murder weapon and the dog tags over there.'

'I think they were part of a set-up. It makes no sense for the dog tags to be there. Why on earth would my father have taken them in the first place? They were planted in his house to incriminate him.'

'Loyalty is a beautiful thing, Matthew, but it doesn't beat cold hard facts.'

Matthew managed to free his phone from his trouser pocket with some difficulty, switched it on and found the photographs of the Tupilak file. 'What about this, then? Secret documents from Thule in 1990.'

Ottesen took the mobile and swiped through the pictures. 'I would like to look into it more closely, Matt,' he said. 'Do you have the originals?'

'No, sadly,' Matthew said. 'And I've no idea if Bradley and Reese took them or if they were lost in the fire.'

Ottesen shrugged and handed the mobile back to him. 'It'll take more than a few photos, and I saw nothing relating to the murders in those pictures…Sorry, Matt, your father will take the rap for this, and from where I'm standing, he's looking increasingly guilty.'

'But I saw Bradley and Reese myself! Surely that must count for something? My father didn't murder anyone!'

'Matthew, you and Tom saw two men who Tom claims are Bradley and Reese, while the US military insists that Bradley and

Reese were killed by Tom at the Thule base in 1990. They've been buried for more than twenty-four years.' Ottesen looked up at the ceiling and held his breath for a moment. 'The only thing that remains outstanding in this investigation is for Tom to be handed over to the US military, and that's all there is to it.'

Matthew rubbed his neck. 'Then what about my father's coffin? He was also buried in 1990, according to Briggs. But Tom is alive, so if there really were three coffins, at least one of them must have been empty.'

'I don't know, Matthew. Tom turning up alive has come as a bit of a shock to the Americans, it's fair to say, but no matter how we twist and turn it, I've no authority to demand insight into an internal matter at an American military base.'

'It still doesn't add up,' Matthew said wearily.

'I just want to conclude my investigation,' Ottesen went on. He sounded weary as well. 'We only buried Rakel yesterday and it was a really horrible day, so pardon me for speaking plainly, but all I want to do is hand over your father to the Americans and then find Abelsen and Bárdur. Rumour has it that they're hiding in Tasiilaq. Then I want to close down this insane investigation for good.'

Matthew stared at the floor and covered his face with his hand. 'Was it okay? Rakel's funeral.'

'Yes,' Ottesen said, and his voice trembled. 'She was laid to rest next to Jakob.'

'I'll drive out to the cemetery once Arnaq's appointment is over.'

'The church was packed again,' Ottesen said. 'I helped carry the coffin.'

There was silence. Out in the corridor they heard someone hurry past.

'Do you need to talk to a psychologist?' Ottesen asked him gently.

Matthew shook his head slowly without taking his hand away.

'I'll make you an appointment anyway,' Ottesen said, still in a soft voice, then his face lit up. 'We have a match to the DNA evidence we found in Jakob's house. The match is Símin.'

'What?' Matthew lowered his hand and looked at Ottesen. 'So why was there no match with Bárdur? I thought Símin was Bárdur's son?'

'That's just it, Matt. It turns out Bárdur isn't Símin's father at all, but I can't imagine that either of them knows.'

'Then who is it?' Matthew froze. 'My father was there in 1990, so if Símin is twenty-four, then—'

'There was no match to your father either,' Ottesen said with a smile. 'I've no idea who his father is and it doesn't matter now. I just thought you ought to know that Símin killed Jakob.'

'He must have travelled to Nuuk with Bárdur to kill Jakob, since Jakob was murdered around the time I was attacked.'

'Yes, I think you had a lucky escape that night,' Ottesen said, and smiled again. 'Símin isn't making much sense yet, but they appear to have killed Jakob because they believed that he murdered Bárdur's father back in 1973.'

Matthew looked at the floor in exasperation. 'This is all wrong.'

'Yes.' Ottesen checked the time. 'I had better get going. The plan is that your father will travel with Briggs to Thule tomorrow morning. A plane has been booked for them at nine-thirty. I can pick you and Arnaq up, if you want to come to the airport to say goodbye to Tom. I might have some other business at the airport myself, if we get it done in time.'

'Thank you,' Matthew said, 'but we'll make our own way there.'

'There was only one thing your father asked for in return for telling us everything.'

'What was it?'

'That we got the test results for the pistol before he leaves Nuuk.'

63

The snow had settled like a soft, protective blanket over the many graves on the long slope towards the sea. Matthew had visited the new cemetery before, but only to look at it. It was one of the most beautiful places in the Nuuk area. The nearest neighbours to the cemetery were the University of Greenland, some residential houses on the outskirts of Nuussuaq and then Mount Lille Malene. On the other side of the fjord, Mount Sermitsiaq rose from the sea like a snow sculpture.

Matthew studied the row of graves. They lay close. Each individual grave wasn't much wider than a coffin, and many of them were covered by a thick layer of artificial flowers in many different colours. Soon the snow would be so deep that the flowers would be hidden for months.

'I don't know if I dare,' Arnaq said.

'Meet our dad?' Matthew said, picking up a little virgin snow from Rakel's grave.

'Yes.'

'I agree it's weird.'

'I'm not sure...I mean, if he's going to jail for a hundred years, what's the point?'

Matthew looked at his sister. Her face was still gaunt after her imprisonment. 'Do you still see that psychologist?'

Arnaq sniffled briefly and sighed. 'Three times a week.'

'Does it help?'

'It's okay, I guess,' Arnaq said with a shrug. 'But she knows fuck-all about what it's like when your friends are killed and you're locked up by some psychos who starve you.'

'But Tom does,' Matthew said.

Arnaq looked down and nudged some snow. 'I guess he does.'

'I spoke to him on the plane from Ittoqqortoormiit and I think you were held in the same cell.'

She looked at him. 'What do you mean?'

'He was held in a cell under Færingehavn with the flickering light, the starvation and everything.'

'When?' Arnaq said in a hesitant voice, frowning.

'Back in April 1990, but those lunatics were already living there, except for Símin, who hadn't been born yet.'

'So Tom was a prisoner there, is that what you're saying?'

'Yes, but he managed to escape and sail to Qeqertarsuatsiaat. Then he travelled across the ice cap to a small town in East Greenland where he hid out for a few months before making his way back across the ice to Nuuk at the start of August that same year.'

'He should have stayed over there.'

'Perhaps, but then he wouldn't have met your mother.'

Arnaq nodded grimly and her gaze wandered across the low forest of white crosses. 'Were they your friends, the people who died?'

'Jakob and Rakel?'

She nodded. She sniffed hard again. The frost made their noses run.

'Yes,' Matthew said, looking at the two graves. 'Yes, they were. It was Jakob who helped our dad get from Qeqertarsuatsiaat across the ice cap and to safety back in 1990; Rakel helped save your life.'

'Shit.' Arnaq wiped away a tear. She held up a dismissive hand when Matthew stepped closer.

Matthew stopped and nodded softly. 'If you want to talk about what happened out there, just tell me.'

She turned around and nodded. She gazed across the sea. 'I would like to visit Símin one day.'

'Símin?' Matthew said with a frown. 'But he was—'

'I just want to see him. I don't think people understand what kind of person he is.'

Matthew took out his mobile and cigarettes and lit one. 'We'll talk about that later.'

Both his gunshot wound and the broken finger hurt whenever he searched for something in his pockets. He should still have his arm in the sling, but he couldn't be bothered with that any longer. When he put on fresh bandages in the evening, the wound would bleed anyway.

He took a deep drag on his cigarette and checked his mobile. He had sent nine text messages to Tupaarnaq after returning to Nuuk, but she hadn't responded to a single one of them.

'Let's have one.'

Matthew looked at Arnaq, who had stuck out her hand to him. 'You don't smoke, do you?'

'Yes, I do,' she said without missing a beat. 'And if it's okay for you to do it, then surely it's okay for me too?'

'That's it!' he exclaimed, and took another drag before extinguishing the cigarette. 'I'm quitting right now.'

'What?' Arnaq frowned. 'Are you serious?'

He nodded and looked about him for a bin. 'I only started a few years ago...and it was a dumb decision.'

Arnaq laughed and looked at Matthew. 'How was Tom able to live in Nuuk for so long if he was on the run?'

'Because nobody knew who he really was and everyone thought

he was dead. He lived with your mother for ten years until he discovered that a former US officer had moved to Nuuk from the Thule base, and then he had to leave immediately.' Matthew looked at Arnaq. 'The crimes our dad is charged with could very easily lead to the death penalty. Last year an officer in the US Army was sentenced to death for something similar by a military tribunal.'

'Shit...Why couldn't he just have stayed away! Why did he come over here?'

'Because those small villages in East Greenland had no contact with the outside world in those days and he was scared that something had happened to me.'

She looked at the snow around the toes of her boots. 'Do you think he has also been following my life...from a distance?'

'I know that he has.'

64

NUUK, WEST GREENLAND, 2 NOVEMBER 2014

Matthew ran a finger down the blue brace around his little finger while Tom greeted Arnaq. He could see Tom moving in to give her a hug, but she flinched and withdrew. Only a little, but enough for Tom to get the message.

'You've grown,' Tom said. His eyes kept trying to catch Arnaq's, but she wasn't letting him. His arm was still tied up in the sling, but it was a more modern version than the one he had been issued with in Ittoqqortoormiit.

'Arnaq is in her last year of school now,' Matthew said.

'I'm so happy to see you,' Tom said to her.

She nodded.

'Do you like your school in Nuuk?'

She shrugged. 'It's all right.'

'It has been a tough few weeks,' Matthew quickly interjected.

'Yes.' Tom turned his gaze down towards the brown tiled floor in the waiting area. 'But thank you for coming, Arnaq. I haven't seen you since you were two years old.'

'I'm aware of that,' she said.

Matthew looked at Tom. 'And it could be a long time before we next see you.'

'You can say that again,' Briggs quipped. He looked like a man who was excited and exhausted at the same time. 'We're talking desertion, misuse of army property and two killings.'

'But they're not dead,' Matthew protested. He shook his head in despair. 'We saw them in Ittoqqortoormiit. They were the ones who shot Tom and me.'

'They've been dead for more than twenty-four years,' said Briggs, dismissing him. 'It couldn't possibly be the same men.'

'But you also thought that Tom was dead,' Matthew argued. 'And yet here he is, so who was in his coffin back in 1990?'

Briggs stared stiffly at Matthew. 'I can hear that it hasn't taken your father very long to convince you of his fanciful stories. Matthew, Bradley and Reese died a very long time ago. Your father shot them.' He threw up his hands. 'You yourself carried the evidence back to Nuuk from his house!'

'I also saw some documents, where you—'

'Stop!' Tom stared hard at Matthew. 'I'll handle this.'

Matthew looked across to Arnaq.

'You're as crazy as he is,' Briggs said.

Tom turned to Briggs. 'Do I have time to go to the bathroom before we board?'

Briggs checked his watch and nodded.

Matthew's mobile buzzed in his pocket. It was a text message from Leiff who wrote that his friend at the hospital had finished studying the Tupilak file and had sent Matthew an email.

'Hello, sorry, it took a while.'

Matthew turned and saw Ottesen walking towards them.

'We have all the results now,' Ottesen went on, shaking Briggs's hand.

'Couldn't you just have emailed them to me?' Briggs said, sounding mildly irritated.

344

'Yes,' Ottesen said. 'But I had a few questions for you and I thought I might as well ask you in person before you take off because then I, too, can close my investigation.'

'Such as?'

'Let me start by confirming that it was Tom's pistol that Matthew found in Ittoqqortoormiit.'

'Surely there was never any doubt about that?'

'No, I guess not, but there was something else, which I think is significant: the last set of fingerprints doesn't belong to Tom, but to Kjeld Abelsen, and the same goes for the prints on the trigger.'

Briggs exhaled heavily and stared right into Ottesen's eyes. 'What are you saying?'

'And we found traces of Tom's blood on the barrel, which suggests that he was knocked unconscious with his own pistol...by Kjeld Abelsen.' Ottesen paused. 'Going on the ballistics evidence alone, there's much to indicate that Kjeld Abelsen knocked Tom out and shot the other two. That is if Tom's pistol really was the murder weapon.'

'Of course it was,' Briggs said quickly. 'Our examination of the crime scene proved that as early as 1990. Why couldn't you just have emailed me this information, that's what we agreed?'

'Yes, of course. And we will.' Ottesen flashed Briggs an amicable smile. 'I just wanted to give you the good news that it doesn't look like it's one of your own who committed the murders. You'll be hearing from us in due course as I'll need an explanation as to what Kjeld Abelsen was doing at the Thule base in March 1990, and why it now looks as if he got away with killing two US soldiers while he was there.'

Briggs lowered his gaze. 'We'll give the matter our consideration.'

'Once you're done with Tom,' Ottesen went on. 'We want him extradited.'

'Who says we'll ever be done with him?' Briggs said, looking up again.

'He faces some civilian criminal charges,' Ottesen said. 'They include the manufacture and possession of banned substances and, if he's unlucky, potentially a charge of manslaughter.'

'Yes, yes,' Briggs said, glancing towards the door to the lavatories.

'Your prints were also on Tom's pistol,' Ottesen said. 'Both on the handle and the trigger. Then again, you were an officer at the Thule base, weren't you?'

Briggs nodded slowly. 'Yes. Tom and I were buddies, if you know what that means?'

Ottesen raised his eyebrows.

'We often practised on the shooting range using each other's weapons,' Briggs explained. 'You can't go into battle with an unfamiliar weapon and so you need to know your buddy's weapon as well as you know your own.'

'Even somewhere as remote as Thule?' Matthew interjected.

'If you slack on discipline in one area,' Briggs said, 'the rot will spread.'

Matthew nodded and then turned to Ottesen. 'What about Bradley's and Reese's fingerprints? Were they also on the pistol?'

Ottesen shook his head.

'You really don't have a clue about buddies, do you?' Briggs said. 'We always trained in pairs. Tom and me were one, Bradley and Reese another.' Briggs furrowed his brow. 'Surely it doesn't matter if my prints are on the pistol. I was negotiating contracts with a Greenlandic civil servant when the shots were fired.'

'Was that civil servant Kjeld Abelsen?' Matthew said quickly.

Briggs expelled a short, contemptuous snort. 'Well, it couldn't have been if he was the shooter, could it?' He clapped his hands together. 'Tom has had enough time in the bathroom.' He stepped away from the others, went to the lavatory door and knocked hard.

Matthew, Arnaq and Ottesen followed Briggs, who knocked on the door again.

The door opened and Tom came out. 'Take it easy, Colonel. It's a bit tricky with just one arm,' he said.

'We'll be boarding soon,' Briggs said in a surly voice. 'Time to say goodbye.'

Tom nodded slowly and looked at Arnaq. 'You loved it when I carried you around so you could bash the lamps at your mother's.'

She looked at him without expression.

He smiled grimly. 'I'm sorry,' he then said, turning to Matthew. 'I know it has been too long. That you were far too young to remember me.'

'I remember you,' Matthew said, his voice shaking. 'We'll see you soon. Ottesen has just told us that the last person to use your pistol was Abelsen.'

Tom buried his face in his hands. He breathed heavily.

'Even if they keep insisting that Bradley and Reese are dead,' Matthew said, 'then you didn't shoot them.'

'You're jumping to conclusions,' Briggs snapped. 'Abelsen could have picked up the weapon after Tom had killed them.'

Matthew looked at Ottesen, who shrugged and said, 'You're right in theory, but you can't convict a man of murder if there are doubts as to who fired the kill shot.'

'Come on.' Briggs grabbed hold of Tom.

'Dad!'

Tom turned around and looked at Arnaq.

'Can I call you sometime?'

'Yes...always. Matthew has my number.'

'Let's go!' Briggs said.

Matthew watched them leave. 'This is so wrong,' he said to himself, and opened an email on his mobile. It was from Leiff's doctor friend. He had examined the pictures Matthew had taken of the Tupilak experiment in Thule in 1990.

The numbers are disturbing. The individuals who were experimented on must have been close to death; very high blood pressure, high homocysteine numbers. Even an argument could kill them. If this really is from a long-lasting experiment, I would regard it as medical murder.

Matthew closed the email and wrote a text message to Leiff:

About the pictures I sent you. Can you find a similar buff file in our old archives and then print the same words on the cover using the same colours? And then print out all the pictures and make them look like the real thing? I need it now, sorry. I'm coming over.

He stuffed the mobile back in his pocket and grabbed Ottesen. 'Stop them…They mustn't take off.'

'Why not?'

'Everything that happened in Thule; it was Briggs's doing…He might even be controlling Abelsen.'

'But we've already discussed that,' Ottesen said. 'Are you saying now that you've finally found some evidence?'

'While I was in the bunker, I overheard Abelsen say that the colonel had told him that Tom was in Ittoqqortoormiit. A few days earlier I had mentioned to Briggs that my father was in Ittoqqortoormiit…and Abelsen seemed scared of this colonel.' Matthew shook his head. 'Briggs is the colonel, and ever since I told him about the letter from my father, he won't leave me alone…Can I borrow your car?'

'Just because they both use the term *colonel* doesn't mean there's a connection.' Ottesen looked towards Tom and Briggs, who were making their way to the gate. Briggs was holding tight to Tom's arm.

'Briggs also told me that Bradley and Reese were shot with Tom's pistol,' Matthew continued. 'But how could he know that if both the pistol and Tom were gone before the bodies of Bradley and

Reese were even discovered? The investigation he's talking about never happened! In order to prove that Tom's pistol was the murder weapon, surely they would need to have had it?'

'But you don't even believe that they were shot?'

'No, but Briggs insists that they were,' Matthew said. 'But how could he know anything about a murder weapon that went missing before the dead bodies were found? And why are the Americans insisting that there were three coffins? There shouldn't have been more than two, but no one seems to care about that. They're full of crap!'

Ottesen nodded grimly and looked at the queue at the gate again.

Matthew scratched his wounded arm carefully. 'The man who shot me was either Bradley or Reese even though, according to the US military, they were killed in Thule in 1990,'

'You only have your father's word for that last bit, don't you?'

'I also have some documents from the army operation that they were part of. Briggs's name is on most of them.'

'I thought they were lost in the fire?'

'Briggs is the man behind Abelsen...The man behind the killing of Lyberth. Give me a break...He's going to kill my father!'

Ottesen handed him his car keys. 'I can hold the plane. You have one hour.'

'Get them inside,' Matthew shouted as he ran towards the airport exit. 'And throw Briggs in a room of his own.'

Ottesen shook his head.

Matthew continued out the door, towards Ottesen's car.

65

Two reporters from KNR and a couple from Nuuk TV were hanging around when Matthew returned to the airport just under an hour later. There were also a few police officers. Matthew recognised all of them, and he had no doubt that it was a combination of the police presence at the airport and the delayed plane that had attracted reporters from the other two news agencies in town. The weather often delayed planes in Greenland, but it was rare for there to be police at the airport at the same time.

Matthew placed his hand on the arm of a police officer. 'Hello, Frederik,' he whispered close to the young officer's ear. 'Don't let them go near Ottesen's car.'

'Okay.' Frederik looked towards the car and nodded. A man was sitting in the passenger seat. He had black hair and had his back to the airport terminal.

Matthew smiled to the female journalist he knew from KNR. Then he continued inside the small waiting area.

Ottesen was sitting on one of several moulded grey seats overlooking the road. Briggs was next to him. Matthew stamped his feet to get the snow off his boots and smiled to himself, knowing that they had probably seen him arrive by car with someone in the passenger seat.

Tom was waiting at a table in the cafeteria along with Arnaq and a police officer Matthew didn't know very well.

Matthew waved to them and then rushed over to Briggs and Ottesen. An older officer was sitting opposite them and Matthew took a seat alongside him and placed a shopping bag from Brugseni on his lap.

'I've got Abelsen in the car,' he said, patting the bag lightly. 'And I found this at Tom's place.'

Briggs shot up and rushed over to the windows. He peered through the windowpane, then took out his mobile.

'That can wait,' Ottesen said sharply.

'I can call whoever I want whenever I want,' Briggs retorted angrily.

'And we can continue this conversation down at the station,' Ottesen said, looking at Briggs.

Briggs shook his head and sat down.

'Why don't you put that back in your pocket,' Ottesen said, pointing to Briggs's mobile.

Matthew was aware that Briggs was staring at the shopping bag on his lap. On top of the bag there was now a buff file with the words US NAVY and CONFIDENTIAL stamped in purple on the cover, and TUPILAK in red.

Matthew opened the file and selected a couple of pages. 'Your signature is on an awful lot of these, Briggs. Except you told me that you had pulled out of the experiment, didn't you?'

Briggs stared stiffly at the windows.

'You certainly never mentioned that you were still involved,' Matthew went on. 'And strictly speaking, it was your experiment, wasn't it, Colonel Briggs? That's what they call you, Abelsen and Tom. *The Colonel.* Is that your actual rank now? That HR job was just a front. You never left the army, although Tom and the others thought you did…You were in the background the whole time, ratcheting it up more and more, isn't that right?'

Briggs shook his head. 'Why would I do that?'

'Tupilak,' Matthew said, searching through the papers in the file. 'The experiment was just a small part of something much bigger. Ultimately it was about US security policy and power in the Arctic. And then there was the financial aspect, which Abelsen got so enamoured with. I'm guessing that you kept him sweet by letting him think that he could one day become filthy rich from the drug that Tom and the others were developing?'

'I've no idea what you're talking about.'

'You don't? Well, that's not what Abelsen says, but that's probably a job for the police. Abelsen was undoubtedly a stooge for you, given his position in the Greenlandic government administration, but you should have killed him this summer when his house of cards collapsed.'

Briggs glanced furtively at the car and shook his head. 'What a load of nonsense. Which decade do you think you're living in?'

'I'm going to give this to the police,' Matthew said, flicking through a few sheets in the file. He looked up at Briggs. 'You ordered a hell of a lot of drugs back in 1990.'

'Nothing unusual about that. It was all part of my work.'

'Yes, but it would be fun to check with them up in Thule if their lists match yours. There are a lot of banned substances here…looking at it from a civilian point of view.'

Briggs glowered at him with contempt. 'You're bluffing.'

'And these readings!' Matthew heaved a sigh and frowned. 'The blood pressure is rising steadily. 157/97. 163/101. 172/105. ECG. Homocysteine figures shooting up well over 200.' He looked straight at Briggs. 'I've spoken to a couple of doctors and they say that this looks like medical murder.'

'Medical murder?' Briggs snorted and rolled his eyes. 'You've no idea what it takes to keep the world in one piece while the rest of you sleepwalk. Fucking hell.' He glared at Ottesen. 'Tell me we don't have to sit here listening to some upstart? A failed journalist who couldn't even hack it in Denmark.'

'We'll let the man finish,' Ottesen said patiently. 'I'm becoming increasingly interested…purely from a civilian perspective, of course.'

Briggs's shoulders slumped and he muttered something unintelligible. His face was growing paler.

Matthew closed the file. 'When you gave Tom's pistol to Abelsen so that his prints would be on it, you forgot to make sure that he actually fired the pistol, rather than just put it in a box.'

'What the hell are you on about now?' Briggs exclaimed, narrowing his eyes.

'Yours are the only prints on the trigger, so my question is: did you kill Bradley and Reese?'

'What?' Briggs shouted, and leapt up from his seat. 'That's enough of this farce!' He turned to Ottesen, who had also stood up. 'He's a bloody journalist, that's all. Ignore him. You told me yourself that Abelsen's prints were on top?'

'He lied,' Matthew said quickly.

'Not that it matters anyway,' Briggs went on. 'They…They…'

'They were never shot?' Matthew ventured. 'Is that what you're trying to say?'

Briggs shook his head with a groan and Matthew sized up the tall man with the short blond hair. 'Why don't we take a DNA sample from Briggs as well? He looks like Símin, doesn't he? Perhaps he killed Jakob?'

'Are you out of your fucking mind?' Briggs screamed furiously, and took a step towards Matthew.

Ottesen loosened the top of a small pouch in his belt. 'I think it might be better if we continue this conversation at the station after all.'

Briggs nodded wearily and looked at the floor. 'Yes, we might as well get to the bottom of that idiot's conspiracy theories.'

The moment Ottesen took Briggs's arm, Briggs's fingers pinched the soft tissue between Ottesen's neck and shoulder. He squeezed so hard that Ottesen collapsed on the floor immediately. Briggs bent over his victim and snatched the service pistol from his belt.

'This is where we go our separate ways,' he sneered. 'I've had enough of this shithole and all you bumbling idiots.'

He pulled Ottesen up from the floor and grabbed him by the throat, while pointing the pistol around the waiting area.

Matthew and the other police officer both raised their hands. Tom and Arnaq had thrown themselves onto the floor.

Briggs retreated through a staff exit near check in. He kept his hand firmly locked around Ottesen's throat.

66

'Is that yours?' Briggs demanded, pointing to a dark blue SUV with POLICE in white on its side.

'Yes,' Ottesen squawked. He was struggling to breathe because of Briggs's grip on his throat.

Briggs nodded, then hit Ottesen hard right where his skull met his neck vertebrae.

Ottesen's legs buckled; Briggs released his hold on him and let him fall onto the compacted snow on the tarmac.

'What the hell are you doing?' Frederik shouted.

The KNR reporters had sought cover behind a car, while the cameraman from Nuuk TV turned his tripod so his camera was pointing at Briggs and Ottesen.

Briggs aimed Ottesen's pistol at Frederik, but then fired a shot into the air before pointing the muzzle back at Frederik and the cameraman.

Frederik grabbed the cameraman's shoulder and dragged him to safety behind a car.

Briggs turned and pointed the pistol at the side window on the passenger side of Ottesen's car. 'Get out, Abelsen!' he roared.

Nothing happened. A moment later he tore open the door

himself. He stared at the old Inuit. 'What the…you're Leiff from the newspaper!' Briggs turned to walk away, then had second thoughts, spun around and shot Leiff in the thigh.

Leiff screamed in pain and clutched his leg while pushing himself out of the car. He tried to put weight on his leg, but collapsed onto the snow, which turned red from his blood.

Briggs continued to aim the pistol at him, but then let it fall to his side and turned his attention back to Ottesen, who was trying to get up.

He waved his pistol at Ottesen. 'Keys! Now!'

'Matt has them,' Ottesen croaked, clutching his neck.

'I've just about had enough of this,' Briggs said, and pressed the pistol against Ottesen's forehead while he shouted for Matthew.

Ottesen looked at Leiff, who had managed to get himself into a sitting position up against the SUV. Leiff was pressing both hands against the gunshot wound to his thigh. His trousers were soaked in blood.

'Robert!'

Everyone turned to the airport terminal, from where Tom had emerged.

'No,' Ottesen called out. 'Go back, Tom.'

Tom began walking towards them. He was holding up his hands.

Briggs pointed the pistol at Tom instead, while brutally pushing Ottesen aside.

Ottesen retreated a short distance and looked towards the double doors leading to the airport terminal. Arnaq and Matthew had come outside, as had many other people. 'Keep the public back,' he called out to Frederik and another officer. 'I'll look after Leiff.'

Tom continued moving until he was so close to Briggs that the muzzle of the pistol touched his coat.

The two men stared at one another. Briggs was clutching the pistol so hard that his arm was shaking.

'You owe me a life, Robert.'

Briggs shook his head. 'You know better than that, Tom.'

'Twenty-four years,' Tom said. 'That was the price I paid when my brother threw me under the bus.'

'We both knew the terms from the start,' Briggs said. 'Nothing's bigger than Tupilak.'

'My children,' Tom shouted, staring Briggs in the eye. 'You cost me my children.'

'Matthew,' Briggs hissed without taking his eyes off Tom. 'I want the keys to Ottesen's car, now!'

'No,' Tom called out. 'Matthew, stay where you are.'

Briggs moved the gun to Tom's forehead. 'The keys, now!'

'Is that what you've been reduced to?' Tom said with forced calm. 'Are you willing to shoot me for pills and money?'

'Pills and money?' Briggs exclaimed. He shook his head. 'Are you kidding? The pills were just to distract Abelsen. This is about power in Greenland, you know that!'

To the right of the two men, Ottesen had managed to get Leiff standing and was helping him around the other side of the SUV.

'A lot has changed since 1990,' Tom said, catching Briggs's eye. 'I believe the Soviet Union has collapsed.'

'Yes,' Briggs said. 'But if you think that was good news for us, then think again. The balance of power in the Arctic has never been more unstable than it is now. Trust me. The day the Danish army leaves, we'll take over Greenland. The US can't risk or accept Greenland being exposed to other nations; we'll seize power in the country from day one, if Denmark goes and Greenland gets independence.'

'Thank you, I do remember what Tupilak was all about,' Tom said.

'You do? Doesn't seem like it. Look about you. There are too many voices clamouring for independence today. They just don't get it, do they? This island can't lie unprotected, and the US won't accept any other troops here than its own and Denmark's. China is knocking at the gate. They very nearly bought the Grønnedal naval base.'

'Ah, so it was you who killed the Chinese man,' Tom interjected. He had noticed that Briggs was slackening his grip on the pistol.

'You've grown older, but not wiser,' Briggs said, shaking his head. 'The Chinese military keeps trying to get a foot in the door, but so far we've managed to stop all Chinese acquisitions.'

'And the politicians?'

'The politicians?'

'Those who call for independence.'

'What about them?' Briggs said wearily. He looked towards the group of people standing some distance from them. 'Lyberth and a few like him have gone too far in their demand for independence and they've heard rumours of Tupilak, but they've no idea who they're dealing with. They live in a bubble with no understanding of consequences. They just don't get that independence isn't an option. We would never permit it. Denmark shouldn't permit it, especially as the world is now, with unstable military powers such as Russia and China hungry for the Arctic.'

'You're not telling me anything new,' Tom said, holding his breath for a moment. 'I already know this. And that's not what pushed you over the edge. That was your job, after all.' He hesitated for a moment. He looked at Briggs's fingers around the handle of the pistol. 'You went for the money,' he exclaimed. 'You bastard! You spotted an opportunity and you went for the money.'

'Do I look like a rich man?' Briggs said.

'Well, we'll soon find out, won't we?' Tom went on. 'You've been playing both sides for years, haven't you? Tupilak provided you with information as well as protection. Abelsen was your eyes and ears behind the closed doors of the Greenlandic government, and you supplied pills from the base, because Bradley and Reese running around the ice cap must mean that Tupilak succeeded.' Tom frowned. 'You moved the whole operation to Færingehavn after my disappearance. Bradley, Reese and the whole caboodle? Did you go with them?'

'You're just guessing now,' Briggs said, letting the hand with the pistol drop. 'You're not even a threat anymore.'

'Were you involved when Abelsen threatened to kill Matthew in the bunker in 1990?' Tom asked, pressing his lips into two thin white lines. 'Answer me! Were you?'

Briggs closed his eyes and exhaled heavily.

'You had just given me your word that you would protect him,' Tom said. He flung out his arms in anger and glowered at Briggs. 'For God's sake!' He pulled up his left sleeve and shoved his wrist with the scar right up in Briggs's face. 'Do you remember this?'

Briggs flinched and instinctively closed his eyes.

At that moment Tom reached out his other hand and snatched the pistol from Briggs, while at the same time pushing him hard in the face and taking a step back.

Frederik and the other officer moved in. Both of them were training their weapons on Briggs.

Tom looked into Briggs's eyes. There was so much more going on behind the grey blue than he could read.

Briggs nodded briefly and looked at the officers' outstretched arms with the pistols. 'If I remember? For fuck's sake, Tom! I saved your life!' He closed his eyes again and shook his head slowly. 'When you said you wanted out, when you threatened to go to the papers because you had realised what sort of missions our unit would be carrying out, you should have been killed. That day with the mask dancer, the plan was that Bradley and Reese would officially die so they could disappear completely into Tupilak, but then JJ suggested a last-minute change. You would die for real and take the fall for the two fake deaths.' Briggs jabbed his finger angrily at Tom. 'You were supposed to get killed, you bloody fool, and I was meant to kill you because it was my job to stop you from exposing the whole operation. You just didn't get it, did you? You never realised that the cold-resistance drug was only a small part of the mission, while the elite units were the end goal that justified all means.'

'How the hell could you accept that we were going to be hired killers?' Tom said angrily. 'That's not how the world works.'

'That's exactly how it works,' Briggs said, staring hard at Tom. 'And it has got nothing to do with being hired killers. It's all about the balance of power. At times I really wonder if you've ever understood what it truly means to defend America's interests.'

'No,' Tom said in a controlled voice. 'If it's in America's interest to kill civilians who speak out, then no! I don't get that. And now you're telling me that JJ wanted me dead? Jesus Christ. Can't you see that's insane?'

'And I fixed it,' Briggs said with a shrug. 'By killing you all on paper I gave you a life, I sent you away with Abelsen without anyone but the three of us knowing about it. Everyone thought you were dead and in one of the three coffins, but all they contained were reindeer. I gave Bradley and Reese some extra pills that day, which explains why they went berserk.'

Tom tightened his grip on the pistol without raising it. His fingers just locked around the steel more tightly. 'You've known all along... You knew about Færingehavn.'

Briggs's shoulders drooped. His gaze became resigned. 'I had no idea that Abelsen was a full-blown psycho with his own little underworld, and when I realised the extent of it, it was too late. There's no way back when you've done the things I've done. I could either let you live in secret or have you killed. I chose the former because I had already buried you once and JJ was unlikely to let me live, if he discovered the truth.'

'You're an officer, for fuck's sake! Who would JJ get to kill you?'

Briggs gave Tom a tired look. 'You still don't get it. None of us is bigger than Tupilak.'

'Except JJ.'

'That includes JJ.'

Tom narrowed his eyes and scanned the sloping, snow-covered mountain opposite the airport. 'How much time do we have?'

'Until I raise my arms in the air.'

'We can help you.'

Briggs clenched his jaw and shook his head slowly. 'We're finished.'

Tom looked up at the mountain again. 'Get down!' he screamed and threw himself on the ground; at that moment the first shot was fired. Tom was knocked over. There was another shot and this time his leg was flung backwards as his trousers were ripped open in a spray of blood that dripped scarlet onto the snow. Another two shots followed, one brushing Tom's head.

Frederik shouted to everyone to seek cover, and police officers grabbed Tom and dragged him behind Ottesen's car.

'Fire towards the mountain,' Ottesen shouted. 'Let's get a helicopter in the air.'

From his shelter Matthew could see Frederik tending to Tom's injuries, while Ottesen barked orders into his mobile.

Between them, out in the open, Briggs lay limp on the snow. The back of his head was a bloody crater.

Matthew could feel Arnaq very close to him. Her mouth was open and she rocked her upper body back and forth. Her lips mumbled.

'...twelve, thirteen, fourteen, fifteen, sixteen, seventeen, eighteen, nineteen...'

'It's okay,' Matthew said gently, pulling her close. She buried her face in his jacket and shook so much that both of them wobbled. His own fear disappeared. He closed his eyes and felt a sense of calm spread through him.

Soon afterwards a red helicopter flew low over the airport terminal towards the mountain, where it followed its sloping rise before turning around in a short curve and flying back across the mountain to the airport.

Several ambulances had arrived and paramedics had rushed up to Briggs, Tom and Leiff.

'Would you like to see Tom?' Matthew said.

Arnaq nodded. 'Is it okay now, do you think?'

Matthew shrugged. 'I'm guessing the shooters must be gone by now.'

'I was talking about Dad,' she said.

Matthew smiled. 'Yes…Come with me.' He got to his knees and peered towards the mountain. Then he stood up fully and offered Arnaq his hand. 'It's safe.'

'Shit,' she said, grabbing his hand. 'Was he shot? Dad?'

'Yes, he…He…' The words stuck in his throat. 'Come on.'

They hurried across the small area between the terminal and the car park. Matthew kept Arnaq on his left, away from the mountain.

The flashing blue lights on the ambulances were going. Briggs lay covered on a stretcher, while sections of Tom's trousers and jacket had been cut off. He had been shot in the shoulder and the shin. The shot hitting his head had merely grazed it.

Tom grabbed Matthew's arm and pushed away the oxygen mask that covered his mouth and nose. 'We need to talk,' he said. 'But not… right here…this could affect the whole world.' His face contorted in pain. 'And we need to track down Kjeld Abelsen…It's crucial now that Robert is dead.'

'Okay,' Matthew nodded.

Tom looked towards Ottesen. 'We need to talk to him as well… him and Abelsen.'

The stretcher was lifted into the ambulance. Arnaq reached for the stretcher, but then withdrew her hand.

Ottesen came up to Matthew. 'The murder charges against your father will be dropped now. Nothing else makes sense.'

'If there even were any murders.'

'Yes, that's just it. You're claiming that the victims are alive.'

'I know they are,' Matthew said. 'Who do you think shot Briggs and Tom just now?'

'I don't know,' Ottesen said. 'The shooter has vanished into thin air...Or into the snow.'

'Precisely. It was what my father's experiment and Tupilak were really about right from the start: to create elite units that appear out of nowhere, strike, and then disappear without a trace in the ice and snow.'

'Whatever happens, your father won't be charged with those killings—if they did take place—because both Briggs and Abelsen are in front of him in the queue of suspects.' Ottesen rubbed his eyes. 'What did Tom say about Abelsen?'

'He said that we need to find Abelsen so that you and he can question Abelsen together, and then he said that he knows something which could affect the whole world.'

'I'm starting to think he might be right,' Ottesen said. 'Abelsen is alleged to be hiding out in Tasiilaq. I'll send some officers over there. Perhaps we could get some flown up from Denmark as well.'

'I think Tupaarnaq has gone to Tasiilaq too,' Matthew said. He turned his gaze to the hardened snow under their boots. 'She has talked quite a lot about killing Abelsen.'

'Please tell me she's not that stupid?' Ottesen exclaimed. He looked away from Matthew and up at the mountain. 'Has it ever crossed your mind that Tupaarnaq might not be who we think she is?'

Matthew frowned at Ottesen, who was still peering in the direction from which the shots had been fired. 'What do you mean?'

'It's just an idea, Matt.' He turned back to Matthew. 'I'm starting to wonder if she really was in prison for quite as long as we think. Who paid for her tattoos, and who made sure that she could get enough leave to have them done? It must have taken a long time.' He hesitated and rubbed his eye. 'Worst case scenario, Matt, and I really mean worst case: she could have killed Lyberth, and Abelsen might be one of the few, or possibly the only person, who knows it, because he was there.'

'I haven't got the energy to discuss that now,' Matthew said. His stomach muscles contracted.

'I did say that it was just an idea,' Ottesen said.

Matthew looked at the ambulance. The doors had been closed and it was about to leave.

'Would you like a lift into town?' Ottesen said.

'Yes,' Matthew said absentmindedly. He was troubled. It had been Tupaarnaq who had found the box with the pistol and the file from the experiment, and she had insisted on searching alone. And down in the bunker under Færingehavn she had pushed him away as he tried to enter the cell where she had been kept. Lyberth had been nailed to her floor and she had turned up in Matthew's flat only hours after the murder with blood on her clothes and on her hands. If Abelsen hadn't confessed to everything, she would have gone straight back to prison.

TUPAARNAQ

67

Tupaarnaq sat very still in the snow. It wasn't very deep yet, so she looked like just another dark lump of rock in the white landscape. There was a game track not far from her where the snow had been compressed and was slippery to walk on. She sat still. She had sat there for several hours already today, as she sat there every day. She watched the town with her rifle resting across her lap.

Most roofs in Tasiilaq were covered by snow. Not the colourful wooden walls, but the roofs. There were no icebergs in the sea now, and at the heart of the bay the water was starting to freeze over.

She could see pretty much the whole town from her location. It was dark or twilight most of the day, but there were some hours where the light dominated and then she would be on her spot by the path.

Tupaarnaq moved her upper body slowly from side to side and arched her back. She rotated her neck. Pressed her shoulders backwards and exhaled heavily.

She took a deep breath and looked down the path. She had seen the three men even as they made their way to the mountains at the outskirts of the town. They were slowly approaching the spot where she was sitting.

She got up in a calm, gliding movement while she pressed her lips together and tilted her head slightly. They hadn't noticed her until now. She could tell from their movements that they were discussing something, but she couldn't hear what they were saying. One of them flung out his arms. It was the man in the middle. His body language indicated anxiety.

She lifted the rifle to her shoulder. Eased a cartridge into the breech and aimed at them. The three men began to get uneasy. The man in the middle pushed one of the others in front of him, while the third raised his hands in a placatory gesture and shouted at her.

She fired a second later, knocking over the man who had been waving. He clutched his leg and wailed. Her second shot took out the man on the other side. He rolled around screaming in the snow, cursing into the air while clutching his thigh. The snow was red where he had fallen.

The last man carried his rifle on his back and he pulled it around in front of him. He loaded it and shouted something to the two men who were howling in the snow.

Tupaarnaq let the man raise the rifle to his shoulder. She even let him press his cheek against the butt and look through the telescopic sight so that he could see her. It wasn't until she saw the slight jolt of his head as he recognised her that she fired her rifle again.

Her shot ripped open the back of his hand and he dropped the rifle before he had time to recover from the shock and shoot back.

She aimed at his knee and fired again.

One of the other men had stopped whimpering and was reaching for his rifle, but before he could lift it, a bullet brushed his arm. He screamed again and dropped the rifle.

Tupaarnaq inhaled deeply into her lungs, filling them with the pure, frosty air. She closed her eyes briefly and exhaled. Then she walked towards the three injured men, shaking her head. The corners of her mouth were pulled down in anger and disgust.

'Shut up,' she ordered them. 'If you keep squealing like little girls, I'll bloody kill all three of you.'

'You're finished,' said the man whose leg and arm she had wounded. 'We should have killed you twelve years ago when we found you with the bodies.'

She raised her rifle and aimed at his head. 'Do you think you can shut up or do you want me to do it for you?'

He shook his head. He glared furiously at her with bloodshot eyes. The snow under his legs was squashed and stained with blood.

She turned her attention to Abelsen. 'Is it true?'

'Is what true, you crazy bitch?'

'You know what I'm talking about, you pig.' She tightened her grip on her rifle. 'Am I another one of your rape children?'

'What?' exclaimed the man she had shot twice. 'What's she talking about? Surely my brother was—'

'Shut your mouth,' Tupaarnaq sneered, and fired into the snow right next to him. 'You're too stupid to understand, so just keep your mouth shut, all right?'

He looked down at the red snow underneath him and she turned her rifle on Abelsen again. 'Bloody answer me!'

'It wasn't rape,' Abelsen sneered. 'She loved it, your mother. She was a slag, just like all the others. They were paid for it and your father got plenty of money to keep you, that's all there was to it.'

Her arms slipped down.

Abelsen grinned. 'That was why he fucked you. You weren't his. He didn't give a toss about his daughters. It was when he discovered that his only son wasn't his that he went mental.'

Tupaarnaq's muscles tensed under her clothing, contracting and then relaxing once more. Her breathing was controlled and slow. She stared into Abelsen's black eyes. Then she raised the rifle again. The muzzle was less than half a metre from Abelsen's face.

'You won't get away with this,' said one of the men in the snow in a strangled voice.

She kicked the man's gunshot wound and he curled up in pain. 'If I ever hear even the slightest hint that the two of you have breathed a word of this to anyone, you're dead. Even if it takes years, because I'll have to go to prison first, you will die. They'll let me out one day and you know it. And then I'll come looking for you. You won't be able to hide, because I'm everywhere. I'll be waiting in the darkness one day when you think that the danger has passed and I'll kill you. Not like this, with a gun. No, I'll gut you and I'll cut out your intestines while you scream and squirm.' Once more she aimed her rifle at Abelsen. 'You know I've done it before, and I promise that I'll be happy to do it again, just for you.'

'You're insane,' Abelsen screamed.

'I'll smear these idiots with your guts,' she vowed, and shot Abelsen in the shoulder.

He screamed hysterically and clutched his shoulder with his undamaged hand. He gritted his teeth and growled from deep down in his throat. 'You daughter of a whore. You can't kill your own father…This time you'll get life.'

'The pig that was once my father sentenced me to life a long time ago,' Tupaarnaq sneered. She gripped the rifle and pointed it at Abelsen's head. 'You have one minute left to live.'

Her forefinger rested firmly on the trigger. Abelsen stared into her eyes, terrified and furious at the same time. His mouth was open in a scornful grimace. His veins pumped hard under the skin across his forehead and throat. His chest heaved and sank.

'Fuck,' she said, and fired two shots.

The two men in the snow cried out. She heard no words. The shots lingered above them in the crisp air. Blood spread in the snow on both sides of Abelsen's head.

'Fuck you,' she muttered under her breath.

Then the scream came. Delayed by the shock. His eyes flitted madly from side to side. He raised his left hand to his ear. Then he screamed again. She could see that he couldn't hear anything; his eardrums had burst. She had shot off his ears. He rolled around the snow, trying to numb the pain by pressing snow against the bloody and fraying remains of his ears.

'Pig,' Tupaarnaq hissed. She kicked him hard in the ribs, then grabbed him and rolled him onto his back. She kicked him again. Then she rifled through his jacket pockets and got hold of a mobile and a leather wallet.

She stuffed both into her own pocket and looked at the two other men. 'If you breathe a word about me to anyone, you're both dead.'

68

Matthew pushed off his duvet. He had the heating on too high, but he couldn't be bothered to get up and turn it down. He pulled his laptop back and placed it between his legs so he could continue writing. He had started compiling material for a major article about Tupilak, but he was already wondering whether one article would be enough. It all seemed so far-reaching, and there were so many offshoots that writing even a broad summary was proving to be a major challenge. His editor wasn't sure just how many details they could publish, either. Some people will kill to keep this secret, he'd said.

Wind lashed the bedroom window. It was late in the evening and the daylight had disappeared long ago. During the day a storm had gathered over Nuuk and now it was playing with the snow outside, making it look like a snowstorm.

Matthew turned his attention back to his laptop and started typing. *Tupilak—an elite Arctic unit with a licence to kill.* He shook his head at himself and deleted the line. He had spent most of the day at the hospital writing down everything his father could remember, and although that was a lot, it was only one man's word, and supporting evidence was needed before it could be used or even made sense of.

Abelsen was also in hospital, but it hadn't been possible to interview him yet. He had gunshot wounds to his knee, hand and shoulder, and both his ears had been shot off. He insisted vehemently that Tupaarnaq had shot him, but the men who had been with him were adamant that they had been unable to see the shooter. Personally, Matthew didn't care. Abelsen had been caught and was now under constant guard. Briggs was dead. Símin and his half-sisters were locked up and it could only be a matter of days before they found Bárdur, who no longer had Abelsen to protect him. Matthew watched the howling storm outside his window. Bradley and Reese, however, were still out there—if they really were the ones who had secretly crisscrossed the ice and snow in order to liquidate people.

His mobile buzzed on the table. Matthew reached for it. It was a text message from Tupaarnaq. He had texted her several times every day, but hadn't heard from her since Constable Point. The last time he had texted her was a couple of hours earlier at the hospital. *Did you shoot Abelsen?* he had asked, and now he had her reply: *I was the one who let him live. I'm coming over.*

'Coming here?' Matthew exclaimed, looking down himself. 'Shit.'

He had only just put his laptop on the bedside table when there was a knock on the door.

He sniffed his armpits and looked out of the open bedroom door; the room itself didn't smell too good either.

'The door was open,' she shouted from the hallway. 'Why don't you lock it?'

'I, eh…I…' Matthew looked around, jumped out of bed, snatched the duvet and wrapped it around himself.

'What are you doing?' She looked at him and shook her head. The heating was turning her skin red. She had already kicked off her boots and left her jacket in the hallway.

'I was in bed,' Matthew said, pointing at his trousers on the floor.

'Okay.' She looked towards his wardrobe. 'My clothes are wet, the weather is insane and I'm cold.'

'I thought you were never cold.'

'Oh, do shut up,' she said, closing the bedroom door behind her. The only thing lighting the room was the flickering street lamp, which was swaying in the storm.

He could see her silhouette in the twilight by the door. She pulled all her jumpers over her head in one go and dropped them. Then she unbuttoned her trousers and let them slide down onto the floor and calmly kicked them off.

'I'll have that,' she said, snatching the duvet from him.

He watched her as she climbed into his bed and covered herself with the duvet.

There was silence for a moment.

'I'll go sleep on the sofa, shall I?'

'Are you always this dim?'

'What do you mean?'

'Just join me.'

'Under the duvet?'

She moved in the dim light. Squatted onto her haunches and pulled him down to her. He felt her skin press against his. His hands grabbed her and moved slowly, tentatively across the tattooed plants. Her breath crept into his ear. It was warm and alive. He explored her with his lips. Kissing her neck and breasts. Biting her. Carefully. She moaned. She pulled off his jumper, pushed down his underpants. He embraced her back while she pushed him down and straddled him. His hands explored her back. It was smooth, as though she were made from glass. His breathing was deep and trembling. He let his fingers trace the skin over her hips and across her stomach, until he closed his hands firmly around her breasts. With a finger she explored the gunshot wound on his arm. Caressing it. Then she leaned forward and swallowed him up.

•

Matthew was lying very still on his back when his mobile rang. Tupaarnaq had gone to shower, but it was now some time since the water had stopped running.

He reached for his mobile and saw that Ottesen was calling him.

'Yes?'

'Hello, Matt. Are you free to talk?'

'Yes,' Matthew got out of bed and went to the living room, closing the door behind him.

'It's about Abelsen.'

'Go on,' Matthew said, and looked down at the street. The storm was still hurling the snow about outside.

'He was shot an hour and a half ago.'

'What?' Matthew exclaimed. 'I thought there was a guard by the door?'

'Yes, but he was getting coffee. He was only gone a few minutes.'

'Who shot him?'

'We don't know. He was killed with a single shot to the head, and the window lock had also been shot to pieces.'

'What about Tom?'

'He's fine, but we're posting two men outside his ward now.'

'Okay…Thank you.'

Matthew hung up and raked a hand through his hair while he peered through the balcony door and down at the big glass jar filled with cigarette butts. He clenched his fists. His mobile lit up in his hand.

You were real.

That was all it said.

Matthew ran back to the bedroom and from there into the bathroom. He already knew what he would find, and every single step felt like wading through treacle. He just had to see for himself that she was gone.